The Isle of the Demons

The Isle of the Demons

THE MID-WORLD OF THE TRUCE

BOOK FIVE

STEVE DOUGLAS

ISBN: 978-1-7778868-4-4

The Isle of the Demons is a work of fiction. The names, characters, businesses, places, events, locales, and incidents are either products of my imagination or used in a fictitious manner. Any resemblance to actual persons, living or dead, or actual events are coincidental.

Illustration and cover design by Thea Magerand
Typesetting by C'est Beau Designs

For everyone who gets up each day and tries
to make the world a better place both for themselves
and for those around them.

Contents

ONE SIDE OF

The Game of

THE MAN AT ARMS

THE MID-WORLD SPY

THE ILLUSION

THE APPRENTICE

THE CHARMED KNIGHT

THE PRINCESS

THE TALISMAN

THE WEB OF FATE

THE GREY COUNCILLOR

T... MAG...

THE ARMED HOST

THE GREAT SPELL

THE WIZARD

THE MASTER

the Masters

THE APPRENTICE

THE CHARMED KNIGHT

THE ILLUSION

THE MID-WORLD SPY

THE MAN AT ARMS

...E ...CIAN

THE CAPTAIN

THE SENDING

THE MID-WORLD WEAPON

THE ARCHERS

THE MID-WORLD POWER

THE ANCIENT SECRET

THE SORCERER

THE FORTRESS

Chapter One

Vipers in the Nest

THE SOUTH WIND SWEPT through the night over a darkened ocean, barely stirring the sand, but as it reached the bluff, scythe grasses rustled together like a forest of tiny spears. At the peak of the cliff, two men lay still in the darkness, each wondering if sand fleas could pass through their outer cloaks and the tightly woven clothes underneath. Clouds surged overhead, though the cloud cover was ragged, and streams of moonlight made the night landscape bright. The shoreline beneath them curved only slightly, so it was possible to see for leagues before the beach curled away from them and vanished. The distant signal fire that the two men looked for was still unlit, had not been lit the night before, and might never be lit again.

Galad stirred and rolled over onto a patch of scythe grasses, muttering, "When we return, the Sword will be moaning for me like the ghost of some demented hobgoblin."

"Your Sword is strange enough," whispered Kalanin, "though when *you* start moaning for the Sword, then we have a real problem." Galad laughed quietly, then still lying on his back, sang softly into the overcast night sky:

Not for me the strange unnatural vices,
Not racks nor brands nor torturous devices,
Not Catamices, nor Succubices,
Or even — Ancient Ghouls in slices,
But a chilled white wine in a warm dark inn entices.

Galad lay still, almost seeming to sleep, so Kalanin alone stared over the bluffs, watching for signs of the spies and assassins who had slipped into the League like an invisible, unforeseen plague. After the Mid-World Powers — aided by the Wizards — had cast the Demon Princes from Alantéa, the Powers had released hordes of servants of the Maker from their own realms, and from the townships and villages of Alantéa. Thousands of refugees had surged over League boundaries, welcomed by the Wizards and their war weary peoples. Yet along with genuine refugees, several of the Powers who hated the Wizards' League had hidden many scores of cunning night stalkers, spies, and assassins.

Night watchmen of the League had been killed by the bowshots of carefully concealed assassins, while lone guards were murdered silently by daggers in the middle of their watches.

The Wizards, already preoccupied, were further distracted by probes and Sendings crafted by the Powers. And all the intruding spies had been given charms that alerted them to sorcery, so that even the presence of the Tarnished Sword made them wary, driving them further into the shadows.

The cloud cover shifted again, and moonbeams brought a bright, shifting light to the long beaches below. Had footprints made new marks in the sand, or was the shoreline being altered by wind and water? Galad stirred, moving again to Kalanin's side, staring down over the bluff, but then night and the dark shadows of clouds once more slid over their view of the beach.

A time of dullness and sluggishness had passed before the League realized that there were scorpions underfoot. Rafir had been struck first; cunning snares of wire had severely damaged his left shoulder. The wily Rostov was struck down next, poisoned darts nearly killing him before Julian's healing powers began his slow recovery.

After those events, Kalanin, Julian and Galad began to understand the challenge to the League's security. Planning and intelligence were evident in their opponents' opening moves: Rafir, the utterly undetectable, and Rostov, the cunning organizer of the night watch — these two were the greatest threats to the nest of spies that had gathered around Sea's Edge.

Kalanin leaned forward, becoming more alert as he peered into the darkness. Were there movements down the far bluff? A stone rolling down the hillside? But there were shuffling sounds, and then a splashing sound from deep water, as though saltwater longboats lay hidden in deep swells offshore, waiting for a full curtain of darkness before surging to the beaches. Then came silence, and only the slightest dimming of moonglow.

Both Rostov and Rafir now healed in places of safety, while others sought to stem the plague: Harmadast and the Eye of Merlin searched for agents lurking near the shattered fortress of Stone Mountain; Julian and Sebastian moved among the camps that ringed Gravengate; just as he and Galad stalked the assassins of Sea's Edge in a darkness broken periodically by shafts of moonlight.

But the time was passing slow and heavy, with sleep tugging at their minds, telling them that all was well, like some lying priest promising life eternal without any mention of death and the Long Sleep. Kalanin shook his head, waving sleep away while letting his mind drift from their long night watch, passing into an almost waking dream, the memory of his greatest moment, a time to be recalled as though it was always new and fresh:

Many hundreds of hands had cleared the abandoned wheat fields that lay to the northwest of Sea's Edge, and there a broad, low platform had been set in the middle of the fields' lush grasses. Windbreaks of trees separated field from field. Breezes were rustling through the trees' uppermost branches, while above them the skies were sunlit and blue.

He and Géla had gathered beside their platform, watching as Galad and Julian sent runners and messengers scurrying about their tasks. It was early in the day, and yet already it seemed that the two watches called out by Rostov would not be enough to control the number of people gathering for the ceremony.

Wildflowers were cast on the fields about the platform: pink and azure, white and scarlet, bouquets of yellow and dark purple. And yet neither in beauty nor in color could they compare with Géla who stood serene and joyful, clad in the rainbow-hued garments fashioned long ago by the Mistress of Illusions. Within her, already Géla carried their first child, a daughter he knew and loved from visions shown to him in the Gangean Range.

As the noon ceremony neared, thousands more flocked to the fields, casting flowers over the sentinels at the outskirts, some climbing trees for better views of the platform. Snatches of Maker hymns and tavern songs drifted back and forth over the long fields. Harlond and Rostov spoke together in low voices, and more guardsmen were pressed into service; while Julian and Galad seemed unconcerned, filled with a joy and laughter that could scarcely be contained. On the platform's railing, Sebastian perched, with Rafir curled beside him on the top of a broad post, and their faces were filled with delight.

Noon approached, with sounds of celebration building around them. Peoples of the League who had suffered war and devastation followed by complete defeat, now mingled with long suppressed Servants of the Maker in Alantéa. A feeling of triumph built within many people, while others felt a release from torment, a reprieve from death.

Then, moments before the hour, a speck seemed to emerge from distant skies. Circling in a great arc with thousands of eyes watching its slow, majestic drift downward, came the newly healed Eye of Merlin. When the Eye landed upon the platform, the eagle gave a great cry of triumph and defiance that echoed and re-echoed over the sunlit meadows.

And after, as though summoned by their herald's cry, the Wizards emerged: from three sides of the platform, huge, arched Portals shimmered into being. Merlin emerged from the center Portal, with Balardi coming from his right and Thorian from his left. The Wizards were garbed in white, glowing with blue and gold radiances. Power and confidence seemed to emanate from the three Wizards, as though they, the greatest of the Mortal Magic Wielders, would never again be challenged.

Then he and Géla were wed, pledging themselves anew to the Maker as they stood in the broad clear sunlight, surrounded by thousands of cheering onlookers, while all the leaders of the League stood beside them, radiating pleasure. It was a day to cherish, one to relive whenever misery or grief crowded in upon them.

"And no doubt it was the ceremony, the open display that aroused the jealousy of the Gods," Galad murmured softly beside him.

"What's that?"

"Oh, it's not hard to read your features," Galad continued in a whisper. "It's not moonbeams that make you moony eyed, but thoughts of you and your lady standing beside the Wizards in the middle of thousands of admirers. It was a brilliant time that still stirs me when I think of it. Yet that display — one that the Wizards avoided for so many scores of years — may well have brought down the vengeance of the Gods upon us."

"The Gods, the Powers of the Mid-World," Kalanin said softly, shaking his head, "so wise, so mighty, and so blind. Only after months of struggle did they understand that a Demon Prince in disguise tried to destroy the

League. Then they watched on as we battled Sorcerers and Marids until finally, the Mid-World of the Truce had to be called down against an alliance of Demon Princes, Marids, and Sorcerers. After all that, the Gods should have become our allies, protecting our League. Instead, we have confusion, stupidity, with midnight skulking and death in the darkness."

Galad laughed a soft, dark laugh. "You assume that the Gods are rational and not crazy. There are so many of them, with long histories of rivalry and infighting among themselves, so how can we ever assume that they will act together, wisely? Also, don't you think that they feel fear when they view the newly risen, distant Isle of the Demons?"

"Even I am dreaming of the Isle," Kalanin said softly, "and though it's not a complete, unending nightmare, the Isle is a strange and fearsome pla—" He broke off, watching as a distant firelight seemed to glow, then flare, then burst into fragments as though kicked apart by heavy boots.

"Not a happy place to be," Galad finished, rising slowly. "But now it's time for Captain Hangnail and Ranger Lad to do a little midnight skulking. Let's be gone."

Fully hidden by banks of dark clouds, they scurried down a stream channel that led to the broad beaches and turned to the east. For the first five hundred paces, they raced at three-quarters speed, hugging the cliffside, staying far from the crashing waves and white foam lines that swept up over damp beaches. Each of them held the base of his leather scabbard to keep the blade's flat edge from slapping against his side. Darkness aided them, with surf sounds blotting out the push of their leather boots against dry sands. No firelight could be seen, nor were there signs of longboats or landing craft sliding shoreward over the ocean's churning surface.

A dim moonlight glowed feebly, and they slowed, halting as the light grew stronger. Hunched down upon the sands, cloaked from head to toe, they hoped that onlookers would see nothing more than moon shadows passing over lumpy, dark stone. From a distance came the first sounds of muted, hushed voices. They lay still, catching their breaths, waiting until shadows again swept over the long beaches. Then they moved forward, hunched, scurrying like crabs catching the scent of dead things along the beach.

·)(·

Tiny lights could be seen now, fading coals glowing briefly from the quickly extinguished fire. Sounds of the voices in front of them seemed to carry farther, or they were being raised in anger. As they crept closer, each coal from the fragmented fire could now be seen clearly, glowing then fading with small trails of smoke leaning away from the steady pressure of the South Wind. One voice was rising louder, lifting above the others,

"Do you truly believe that our Masters, the Great Dark Gods, will leave your festering Isles of the Sorcerers in peace?" The speaker stood hunched, shorter than those around him, yet he spoke with an Elder's authority. "There will be war in Alantéa and its surrounding Isles, with all those outside of the Truce cast down — and you will be among them. Wizards and Sorcerers who do not serve the Gods will be forced from Alantéa, either to drown at sea or flee to the Far Lands to live as witless Shamans among the slowly evolving, only partially human creatures that dwell there. War is coming."

"Old fool, why are you nattering at me? Are you commissioned to open this war? If so, begin —" The second speaker was taller, heavily weaponed and stood before the Elder as though a fearless Captain confronted a renegade Priest.

"And if," their Captain continued smoothly, "if your task is like ours, to disrupt and poison this alliance of Wizards and worshippers of this failed, so-called Maker, then stand aside."

"None of your disruptions have worked, you fools," said the hunched man, "and what should we have expected from your dimwitted masters, the Sorcerers of the Isles?" Then his hand drifted to the long knife at his side. "Two of your strikes have miscarried, and now the night guards search for us ceaselessly."

Their Captain turned to the group that stood just behind him murmuring, "No weapons, not yet." His party seemed less than a score, while those surrounding the Elder were more than thirty. To the Elder, he said reasonably, "We were bound to find resistance at some point; we expected a reaction. Alcman and Houma and their dead brethren carved bolt holes throughout League lands that they once ruled and made these known to old allies on the Isles of the Sorcerers. We will share the locations of these hiding places with you. Continue with your skulking and sneaking. As for us, we will kill and kill again."

"No," spat the Elder, and he drew his blade. More than two score other weapons whispered against leather scabbards, but the sounds were eclipsed by the crash of a great wave that came surging shoreward, spreading foam over the feet of those closest to the ocean.

A moment of hesitation hung in the air as the great wave receded, and then the Elder stiffened and died. As he pitched face first into the sand, only the slightest bit of metal could be seen extending from the Elder's back.

"Put aside your weapons." A third man spoke, one who stood just behind the Elder's body. "Unless you wish your own hearts' strings carved. This one," he nudged the fallen Elder contemptuously with his boot, "was overly rash, and took too much upon himself. Yet you of the Isles are also foolhardy. Will you not restrain yourselves?" The Captain standing before him spoke calm reasonable words to his followers; swords were sheathed and some even sat warily on the soft sands, hunching against the cool pressure of the South Wind.

· 𝄪 ·

In the darkness, Kalanin shook his head grimly. *That's a pity —they were at the edge of bloodletting and most of our night's work would have been done, with us as bystanders. Yet these night stalkers killed so casually.* Snuffling, gasping sounds tugged at his thoughts: turning seawards, he watched as longfurred creatures crested the foam lines and raced, panting, toward them over wet sands — a pack of dogs, trained as killing machines.

Kalanin and Galad rose, drawing weapons in one motion. Attack-dogs came hurtling through the night. They met steel and died — soundlessly, for their vocal cords had been severed long ago to preserve their stealth.

But nearby night stalkers were roused, speeding toward Kalanin and Galad with drawn swords.

"Shield-breaker!" Kalanin called out, then he and Galad leaped at their assailants, swords weaving patterns of instant death. Some intruders melted into the shadows, but their Captain called out, "Wait! Here are the two we sought most, alone and unarmored!" For his words, Kalanin cut him down, but others circled, ringing the two. More dogs emerged, leaping, and dying soundlessly in the night. Hurled daggers were slapped away by the flats of swords. Again, Kalanin and Galad smashed at their assailants: more died, spurting dark blood onto shadowed sands.

Clear of the circle, Galad put a horn to his lips, sounding the alarm for the night watch. After a moment's hesitation, the distant, almost feeble answering call sounded tentatively; those circling the two laughed. But Kalanin and Galad backed away as crossbows were being drawn, arrows notched.

"Had we armor..." muttered Galad.

"Most of these would die," finished Kalanin. As one, they sheathed swords and sprinted for the surf. They dove, with crossbolts lashing the water around them. They swam deeper and further underwater, seeking to put a wall of water between themselves and a flurry of arrows. In the distance, torches could be seen, moving hesitantly along the beaches as the night watch sought to reclaim the night.

But there were Vipers in the Nest, two sets of them: one sent by jealous Dark Gods, the other by hate-filled Sorcerers.

Chapter Two

The Assassins

AFIR RACED THROUGH THE scattered rubble that lay on the western side of the ruined Plain of Gravengate. All that was left of the great fortress was shattered stonework, slabs of masonry and huge, broken beams. Each day though, the ruins grew gradually less, as stone cutters and rock haulers hauled the rubble away, while others worked to rebuild the fortress.

The fox sped around a splintered, jagged beam and felt the twinge in his shoulder that marked the beginning of fatigue: his whole side would ache later, but that was a small price to pay for running free and wild through the soft breezes of early morning.

After another hundred paces, the fox slowed, sniffing at the ground. Here at the west and north of Gravengate, pits had been dug, with a foundation of poured stone still settling and hardening. It was to be a shrine, Rafir decided, for this was the place where Kalanin had struck down the Ruined Angel, a being who had proved almost as deadly in death as it had in life.

Stonework everywhere, thought the fox as he looked over the Plain, *and they know it won't stop Demon Princes or Marids or Sorcerers. All this building is really an act of faith, part of some strange human ritual.* Rafir looked away, drawing a deep breath. Pain was rippling through his shoulder, and the fox began to limp back toward the recently built watch tower that lay to the south of the Plain.

Builders thought that the watch tower had been planned by Balardi and built for the Wizard's stargazing. Only a few shared Rafir's secret understanding: the tower's design came from Julian's night visions and was intended to extend his dream link with his parents. Panting, tongue extended, the fox stared up to the tower's peak where Julian the Apprentice still slept.

· ✳ ·

"War at the seas surrounding the Isles of the Sorcerers is of little importance," Julian's father was saying. *"The Gods may seek to dislodge the Sorcerers from their havens, but it seems likely to be a sideshow, with little relevance to your critical struggle with the Demon Princes."*

"Julian knows this," his mother added gently, *"and that his destiny lies within the enchanted Isle of the Demons, a subject on which we have counseled him many times."*

"Even if you repeated yourselves scores of times — which you have never done," Julian said smiling, *"I would listen to you another hundred times, just to be with you and to hear your voices."*

"Yet it is time to wake now, Julian," his mother said softly, almost sadly. *"It is morning. The fox limps. And your time of searching for spies is coming to an end. The future is likely to be violent, and when you look back on these days, they may seem almost a time of peace."*

With these last words, the images of his parents grew thin as smoke then vanished. Julian woke to find himself once again in one of the topmost sleeping chambers of the watch tower, refreshed yet wary.

Sebastian was perched at a window that faced north, watching as Rafir neared the tower: the fox was using only three legs now, holding a stiff left paw half frozen as he limped gingerly over ragged earth and chipped stone.

"Don't feel too badly for him," Sebastian said with a slight smile. "He made good progress earlier, and now he's just looking for sympathy." In a little side alcove, Julian washed the sleep from his eyes with water from a basin, then stepped quickly down the tower stairs and went out into the sunlight to tend to Rafir.

"Those who think magic is an 'anything box' should watch you limp," Julian said as he rubbed a mixture of Bindweed and Serpine into the fox's shoulder. The South Wind was blowing in from the ocean, ruffling the tiny forest of red fur that covered Rafir. Furry hills and valleys rose and fell as the fox panted, resting with his eyes closed after his exertions. From the upper window ledge, Sebastian's wings caught a steady stream of wind, and the Familiar seemed to float down, coming neatly to rest on Julian's shoulder.

"You should have seen them, Julian," Sebastian said with a touch of malice. "At daybreak nearly two score of Gravengate's footmen were out, clearing a path for Rafir, whipping the ground with flails made of ropes and sticks, dragging mats over imaginary traps — just so one small fox could play 'wild thing'." Julian smiled and continued to rub the ointment into Rafir's slowly healing shoulder.

"Twice that number would have volunteered," the fox finally responded, eyes still closed, "because we're the cleverest little heroes in Alantéa. But Julian, in addition to all the clearing work, there were outriders keeping pace with me again this morning — I may be hurt, but I'm not blind. Are all these precautions necessary?"

"The night stalkers have retreated," Julian said quietly, "though they haven't vanished. They're like wolves backing from firelight, waiting for the flames to die down. I would even guess that one or two of the outriders...."

Julian hesitated, his treatment of the injury halting as both he and Sebastian gazed south.

"The wind's changing," Rafir commented, eyes darting wide open. "It's more from the east now, and there's a touch of burning in the air. I can sense that — but more is happening, isn't it?"

"Warfare to the south and east," murmured Sebastian, "echoes of strong magic, with ships burning in the ocean far from Alantéa."

Julian lowered his voice. "There's warfare on the shores of the Isles of the Sorcerers, but there's something else moving, heavily shielded, and it holds little love for those of us defending Gravengate." He drew a deep breath, then finished his treatment of the fox's injured shoulder. "Let's go about the day's business: we need to scatter shadows and push the lurkers farther from Gravengate and back into the darkness."

"Before we start," Rafir said, "tell me again why the Gods aren't more helpful. Basically, they survived because the Wizards led an alliance of Elves, Tanu, and Sidhe warriors against their foes. So now the Gods should be our allies — they should be the ones chasing all these lurkers back into the shadows."

Julian laughed a long, dark laugh. "Well put," he said, again keeping his voice low. "But during the struggle with Demon Princes, Marids, Sorcerers and Guardians, some of the Gods were destroyed. Now they are retreating into their own kingdoms because they fear death. None of the Gods wishes to die."

Julian stared into the distance for a moment before continuing. "Also, the struggle rekindled the Gods' hatred of humans with power, and so we find ourselves in a strangely confused conflict. From the north, Dark Gods like Moloch, and Ahriman slip bands of raiders through our borders, while from the south, war parties attack our shores from the Isle of the Sorcerers.

"These two forces can't work together, because simultaneously Emissaries of the Gods are carrying warfare to the Isles of the Sorcerers, with a goal of eventually forcing both Sorcerers and Wizards far from Alantéa. Meanwhile, the Isle of the Demons is left in peace to plot its next moves in its war with the Mid-World, while Alcman and Houma linger in the shadows, looking for some way to destroy the League."

"What a mess," Sebastian muttered, while Julian gingerly lifted Rafir onto his right shoulder, a place usually reserved for Sebastian, but now the little Familiar slipped down and alternately flew or scampered at Julian's side as the Apprentice ranged through the ruined Plain of Gravengate.

·)(·

Bright sunlight spilled over the Plain, broad fields where vineyards had once flourished alongside orchards and lush gardens. Now, struggling crab grasses were mingled with desert plantain, as the land fought to heal itself from the aftermath of dark sorceries, slash burning, and the movements of thousands of mailed feet. Every gust of wind blew clouds of dust into the air so that most of the stone workers and craftsmen who labored on the fortress walls had to protect their lower faces with scarves or cloth masks.

Only the most basic work was being done to the outer walls, for none of the inner defenses or passageways could be constructed until those devices could be hidden from unfriendly eyes. As Julian passed among the stone masons, he again searched their dusty, sweat streaked faces for any suggestion of treachery or wariness — even a quick shifting of the eyes. He found nothing, nor were there hints among the tent camps that intruders lurked within the borders of the League. And yet as Julian made his rounds, the Sight within him brought images to his mind: small, dark things were racing far from lamp light with the scurrying motions of spiders.

At midday, staff controlled by the Captains of the Guard brought food for Julian and his small companions. Months after their struggles with the Sorcerers and the Marids, Julian was still treated reverentially, almost as a demigod. No amount of humor or polite banter seemed able to change his own status, but Sebastian and Rafir were making progress — they had begun to bicker whenever those who were overly respectful came near.

When demigods quarrel, Julian thought wryly, *then they grow closer to mankind.*

The long bright afternoon slipped by as so many had in recent weeks: the clank of stone and metal, the swirl of dust in the air as masses of food and water caravans passed amid the camps, the slow healing of the fox, and the uneasiness of the guards as night drew near.

·))(·

At sunset they stood once more near the base of the South Watch Tower, faces turned west where a swollen red sun seemed to hover like an open furnace over the ruined land. They stood still and silent for a moment, with the winds of early evening tugging at Julian's cloak. Dusk was coming, and Sebastian felt fear — something more than darkness surrounded by danger. Spies and night stalkers raised all the old fears, yet now stronger, and stranger forces were beginning to stir; and the air above the long shadows on the plain seemed to tremble with tension.

Sebastian searched Julian's face for some note of reassurance, but open disquiet showed itself as the wind tugged at a lock of dark hair that lay across the forehead of the Apprentice. Throughout the Plain, figures hesitated, while a few of those most fearful of magic were moving swiftly toward shelter.

"Something's wrong," Julian muttered. "We felt it earlier, and now it's getting stronger. Where's Balardi?" Neither Sebastian nor Rafir responded: the Wizard was always coming and going, keeping no fixed dwelling, with his mind seeming to be far from Gravengate.

Whispers reached toward him, almost inaudible, as though carried by some trick of the wind. The Gift within Julian reached out and found only a dark quiet touched by menace. In the distance, the skyline was darkening as a sunset that was red as lava faded into black.

Sebastian could hear distant sounds now as whispers rose to murmuring noises, echoes rising from some distant gap in the Earth's surface. His wings flared in disquiet while the fox stared up into the tense faces of Julian and Sebastian.

"If we were alone," Julian said quietly, "we would take shelter behind strong walls, but now, without Balardi, we are the only force of magic at Gravengate. Watch carefully and protect yourselves." Sebastian slipped from Julian's shoulder to the ground, while Rafir vanished.

The three moved from the tower's base, investigating the night, while all around them the air grew thin, as though *things* were consuming its essence. From the corner of Sebastian's eyes, the images of dusk seemed to shudder and twist at the edge of transformation.

As Julian moved forward into the oncoming night, spell-words passed from his lips and sorcerous shields shifted into place. The South Wind blew harder, whipping at his cloak, and standards rippled and flapped through the camp; but at the edge of their hearing, small breaking sounds could be sensed, like echoes from a dark forest, where frozen leaves were fluttering to the ground then shattering.

Julian's voice deepened and more power surged to the Apprentice. At the edge of his own senses, Sebastian could feel a distant motion of coiled power, as the massive serpent form of their ally, Kath, moved into position.

Rafir circled to the left, watching as Julian strode forward, staff clenched in both hands. Even the fox could now hear the low moaning sounds building in the air, like dead voices calling for help from a place of darkness. The fox remained invisible, but as the fur of the fox bristled in alarm, he bared his own slight fangs and limped forward into the shadows.

Julian's feet moved more swiftly and now the counter spells from his mouth became louder and more harsh. In response, the creaking and groaning sounds rose over the noises of the wind, and at the edge of Julian's senses came further hints of malice as though greater and darker forces were moved to mockery, even laughter.

But as the head of Kath slipped onto the ruined Plain of Gravengate, light was beginning to blossom from the Plain's center, a calm radiating from the eye of a storm.

"Balardi..." Sebastian whispered.

"The Master of Gravengate returns," Julian said, moving swiftly toward the light waves that swept outward from the Plain's center. "A Wizard will know something about this strange magic, much more than I do." All throughout the Plain, unnatural forces were receding, and as the strength of magic lessened, the great head of Kath slipped back into the darkness.

Captains and tier-leaders were emerging from tent camps, walking quickly toward the Wizard, their red torches mingling with the white light radiating from Balardi. Light waves reached the rim of the plain and began rippling back, leaving a stillness, an uneasy questioning in their wake. Julian slowed, letting the guard reach Balardi before he did. As he paused, he stared skyward, discovering that the Wizard's light spell extended only a few score feet up, and where it ended the night sky was filled with stars.

"Spell-guards and Talismans are all very well," the Wizard was saying. "Yet those who are able should remove themselves from the center of

Gravengate, for the place where the fortress once stood is the focus of many energies. Beyond the rim, on the outskirts of the plain is best."

Voices murmured, almost arguing with the old Wizard. "No, it's not Marids," Balardi continued, struggling to keep the impatience from his voice. "If only it were — at least now we have weapons that can deal with the power of those beings." From a distance, horns were blowing from the camps, rousing the second watch: an afterthought, with the crisis, seemingly passed. The Wizard spent a few more minutes advising his captains and camp leaders until they departed, leaving somewhat more slowly than they had arrived.

"In another century or so I might learn patience," Balardi murmured to Julian. "Merlin's tolerance is the stuff of legend, while Thorian is a complete stoic; his intellect seems to retreat into some secret place while he hears out tier-leaders and suchlike." The bright light radiating from Balardi was fading, yet strangely, at the Wizard's side, a pouch seemed to glow, several colored lights escaping unbidden from its fabric.

"Yes, there's part of the answer to your questions," Balardi said, noting that eyes had shifted from his features to the glow at his side. "Come, Julian, be a pupil at my side once again — although your first master, Merlin, has more wisdom in matters of magic than I do." Balardi led them back toward the South Tower, the only completed structure amid the ruins. Night was filling the Plain, but in the tent camps, watch fires were being built higher. Captains and tier-leaders were preparing grumbling peoples to withdraw from Gravengate, moving them to more secure camps farther from the fortress walls.

"A great deal was learned when sorcery and miracle work collided," the Wizard continued, as they moved through the twilight. The South Tower was distinct in front of them, a lone, stone bulwark framed against the darkening horizon. "Of old, sorcery mastered one dimension, that of distance. Portals from one point to another would bridge distances of many leagues. We saw during the early part of our struggle how a second dimension, that of time, can be crossed when great magics collided. Yet no force on earth is master of the Timeways. Merlin himself could not by his own design have placed Sebastian and Rafir thousands of years into the future. Nor do we believe that even the Great Gods have such power. That event was powered by an unusual collision of Great Spells; thus, they were 'blown' into the future rather than 'placed' there.

"And so, distances gave way to sorcery — though what magic may open, magic may close. Time, too, is subject to sorcery, but as a barrier that can be temporarily bypassed, not a tool to be easily manipulated. A third dimension is proving somewhat more malleable, that of an alternate reality — Otherwhen, if you will, or these 'Alternaties' — we know not what to call them. Worlds exist adjacent to ours, possibilities that never came to be, yet were strong enough alternate possibilities to linger on with measured half lives. These 'Alternaties' are fading, doomed places, yet many are strong enough to last thousands of years.

"I have been foraging in Otherwhen, and I have found something that was most interesting. When I returned, I sensed that some other power was tampering with adjacent portions of the Alternaties, causing our own reality to shudder. But what did they —?" At the base of the South Tower, Balardi hesitated, and they glanced back at the darkened Plain, where torchlights flickered, as the people of the tent camps were led to the rim of Gravengate.

"What did these other explorers hope to achieve?" Balardi continued. "The intruders smelled of Demon magic, though now they seem to have fled." Balardi took a deep breath. "We need to seek shelter from the night. Come." As they entered the South Tower, the Wizard, a master of radiances of light, casually brushed the gloom of night from the darkened tower, causing the air itself to glow.

At the uppermost tower chamber, Julian lit vat candles and watched with a half-smile as the Wizard's magic faded when confronted with more natural light. Wizard and Apprentice sat across from each other at a table made from rough wood that had only recently been installed in the upper chamber; all the finely crafted woodwork that had once graced the fortress of Gravengate was now splintered wreckage strewn across the Plain, gradually being burned to feed watch fires.

"Is food uppermost in your minds?" asked Balardi. "If so, you should eat first."

Julian glanced at his small friends, then said with a smile, "Food later, my patient instructor. Power ebbs and surges at your side, and so the results of your 'foraging' are much more interesting than dinner. If our stomachs grumble, disregard them."

In answer, the Wizard placed his pouch on the table's coarse-grained wood and took from it, one by one, three gleaming Crystals. Each stone seemed unique, with many facets, glowing with colors that were far different from the surrounding vat candles. One Crystal radiated amber light, shifting slowly into gold; another blue, passing into aquamarine; while a third's red radiance grew darker, becoming a dark purple as they watched. Then the three Crystals exchanged radiances, each adopting the hues of the Crystal that faced left of them.

"Some of the gemstones of Alantéa store enchanted powers," Julian said softly, "but nothing like the forces that pulse from these things."

"I have discovered something quite wonderful," Balardi murmured, leaning closer to the stones. "Their source is organic. Some sorcerous being of Otherwhen cultured these, or formed them out of irritation, like pearls.

Their cores, I sense, are liquid, and their colors change rapidly if they are moved too quickly." The Wizard began shifting the bright Crystals around, alternately humming or whispering over them. As the stones passed from place to place their colors shifted under the Wizard's spell-words, all three fading into a dull neutral, almost grey light.

As light from the three Crystals faded, a sudden moment of understanding swept over Julian:

Here before us are three Talismans that will become critical factors in the struggle that is to come. How or why has this come to pass?

As if in answer to Julian the three Crystals rang out together with a brief, harmonic chime.

Balardi turned from the Crystals to stare at Julian. "Something about your presence provokes a reaction, a response never before encountered. What is this about?"

Julian shook his head. "Merlin sometimes calls me a 'catalyst.' Also, on occasion, some inner voice will speak to me. Now that voice tells me that your Talismans will be critical to our coming struggle with the Demon Princes. I have no idea how these keys to Otherwhen will impact us."

"These are more than just keys to Otherwhen," the Wizard murmured, turning back to his Crystals, adjusting them into a triangular pattern. "The response of the Crystals is troubling, and the probes around Gravengate are of great concern, but I am going to proceed with my original purpose.

"Here is one of our problems: the Sorcerers have become far too familiar with our Divination spells, for Thorian in his madness conspired with his ally, the Demon Prince who was hidden behind the form of Nergal. As we sought answers by spell-craft did not Alcman burst through our Vision Screen? All our old ways are suspect, and we must create new devices.

"So, before us, we have magic crafted from the stuff of Otherwhen. Beings with Sorcerous powers who are sought by sorcery may well become aware of those seeking them: for do not they themselves search in the same manner with like devices? Yet here we have magic outside of their experience, and those we seek should not readily be aware of what transpires. Now, watch closely as we try to view matters close at hand."

Ghostly images formed above the Crystals, rising only a few feet from the table. At first, the shapes were grey and shaky, as though some new talent had not been mastered. Tiny sparks raced uncontrolled through the images like lightning bolts in Earth's early storm clouds. Then slowly the images steadied, growing clearer, showing events at Gravengate: where the night watch fought off bands of assailants who were dressed only in black; where lone killers struck down single sentries; and the darkness teemed with many scores of night stalkers passing at the outer edges of the watch fires.

"As I thought, these devices will display events in progress, and those recently past," whispered the Wizard. "What of future forecast, though? Who among us will deal with this plague of vipers?" Slowly, the images above the Crystals fell back, leaving nothing but a puddle of grey light upon the table, its surface rippling as though whipped by distant winds.

Then, above the Crystals, the image of Kalanin sprang into being — effortlessly, and without hesitation. *So, it's a matter of intellect and leadership,* thought Sebastian. *I wondered about that.*

The shadow of a great wing swept suddenly over the features of Kalanin, and, as quickly, both winged shadow and captain vanished. "So does our Captain General leave us once again?" Balardi murmured, stirring in surprise. "What could cause this?" As he spoke, another image drifted into place above the Crystals, but slowly, less certainly: an image formed, that of Rostov, and the young leader's features had become older and hardened, with all his earlier humor buried under layers of stress.

"Rostov the Wily," said the Wizard slowly, "one of our most clever captains. I was searching for an answer to the plague of spies and assassins that beset the League. If Rostov is the answer, then what of Kalanin? Merlin perhaps will know. Let us leave this matter for a time. Now, for the Powers of the Mid-World and their struggle with the Isles of the Sorcerers."

Easily, as though showing matters often viewed, the Crystals flashed images of war fleets in mid-ocean, showing battles of fire and weather magic. The Emissaries of the Gods were scattered among the Powers' war fleets, while scores of lesser and greater Sorcerers were emerging from ship havens to defend their homelands. And the Sorcerers seemed to be losing, retreating from each engagement with fewer vessels that were being forced always closer to their own shores.

"So, it must be," Balardi said softly. "Though only a tenth of a tenth part of the strength of Alantéa and the Mid-World of the Truce is engaged, still it is mightier than any force emerging from the Isles of the Sorcerers. Though if Alcman and Houma of the Withered Hand were to come, would the outcome be different? We should leave these matters and see what our newly found devices might find in the future. What is to come, Talismans of Otherwhen?"

A vast tapestry of greyish black shadows filled the images above the table, but they seemed to stir and slide so that the onlooker sensed that they beheld visions of events in mid-ocean. Slowly, as though layers of clouds were picked apart by unseen figures, the grey darkness gave way, showing vast armadas sailing from waters off the Far Lands under a cover of storm clouds.

"War fleets of the Dark Lords," Julian said, suddenly intent. "Do I recognize the banners of Un-Maurag and Mordred?"

"Together with those of Haeglin," added the Wizard, "and many of the lesser Adversaries who were transformed but never reconciled to the Truce. They will sail toward the Isles of the Sorcerers to attack the war fleets of the Gods; and the Powers of the Mid-World will need to redouble their efforts to gain power over the ocean depths. Still," the Wizard sighed, "it is a narrow, almost selfish feeling, yet I am pleased with my Divinations, for I think that none of the Powers of the Mid-World will be able to view events as we have. Merlin may wish to advise the Powers — but he should be cautious, for the Gods are both jealous and proud." Once again, all the shapes created by Balardi's gems fell slowly back onto the table, becoming a grey nothingness that surrounded the Crystals.

"And now," said the Wizard, darting a glance at Julian and taking a deep breath, "now comes the greatest test for our devices as we ask them to explore strange, unknown regions: let us see how the Demon Princes fare amid their Isle that has been so recently brought to the ocean's surface. But let us hope that neither Demon Prince nor corrupted Guardian becomes aware of us."

A hesitation, a reluctance hovered over the Crystals' vision making, as though they gathered strength before attempting some monumental task. Unidentifiable shapes began to emerge, flickering at first then fading into grey smoke. As Balardi cleared his throat, ready to acknowledge failure, a shudder passed through the Crystals, and as though with a heroic effort, they cast up the image of...a circle, a dome of grey stone...was it stone or some sort of sorcerous barrier?

Julian and Balardi stood, staring down over the image, while Sebastian and Rafir rose quickly to Julian's shoulders so that four sets of eyes gazed down on an oval, polished rock face — but now it was peeling away, layer by layer, and they saw that surrounding the dome were ripples...of water, yes even waves so utterly tiny that they must be viewing them from an incredible height. Another layer of the dome's shelter was peeled away, and beneath, they could see glimpses of a vast island, where green and red vegetation ran riot, and only in the highlands were the evergreens of Alantéa and the Far Lands beginning to flourish.

Julian's eyes flickered to Balardi's, and the Wizard nodded in confirmation: from a great height they beheld an image of the Isle of the Demons; the dome itself was not truly a dome, but only a symbol of the barriers encountered by the Crystals.

With a flash, the image burst and vanished.

They sat back, trying to shed the stress from their bodies. Julian cleared his throat to speak, but the Crystals were not yet done. More images flared:

Of a Demon Prince standing on a promontory staring out over an ocean rocked by storms;

Of a princeling battling some huge adversary at the base of a twisted fortress;

Of Marids raging at the sky above them, as though it barred their passage;

Of ten Guardians standing with orb-eyes radiating red sorcery in the middle of their powerful dreams, while the world about them was slowly transformed;

Of a hunched crablike figure, scuttling down a rock face, seething with rage and frustration, and jutting from its neck was a human head bearing the features of Houma, though its eyes gleamed with red fire;

Of a lone pair of mailed feet, walking warily over a carpet of writhing red ground cover;

And lastly came the image of a great being standing on a shore where huge waves crashed and pounded against its unmoving, mighty body. Its face held the features of a Guardian, but its single orb-eye was partially closed as though it struggled with a sleep caused by powerful enchantments, and only brief flashes of blue emerged from that orb-eye as it fought its adversaries.

As an enormous wave swept over the form, it seemed to shrink, while beside it all of the earlier images crowded around the mighty figure, and each shape began to rotate, to spin and blur, passing for a moment into rainbow hues, then into grey stone until at last the barrier-dome was again restored above the enchanted Isle of the Demons, and Julian and Balardi watched it from a great height, as the Isle of the Demons passed from their vision.

Julian's eyes darted to the face of the old Wizard, and he saw that beads of sweat were slipping down Balardi's forehead.

"I..." the Wizard trailed off as he pushed his chair back. But the Divination work of the Crystals was still incomplete. Once again on the table, the gemstones cast another image before them: the features of the ram-faced Tel-Alantir, God of the Mid-World, appeared before them showing the powerful God standing on one of his broad avenues staring out into space with a look of grim determination forming on his brow.

"I feared to ask," Balardi hissed softly. "Yet if we must contend with the Demon Princes, some of the Mid-World Powers must come to our aid. Here, then — "

A tremor ran through the tower, rattling through the great Plain of Gravengate. Balardi cried aloud as within the image of the Divination, Tel-Alantir toppled and died; two immense Gargoyle shapes settled over the fallen God, ripping with talons at the dead God's carcass.

Balardi leaped to his feet, sending his chair crashing behind him. Lights fell back to the table's surface and were stilled. "Tel-Alantir assassinated! But this has not yet happened, and I will *not* permit it to happen!" A second tremor rattled the stonework of the tower.

"Why did I not wait for Merlin!" cried the Wizard, grasping his staff. More tremors shook the tower. "I was a fool to meddle unsupported in such things!"

"You were a fool," came a voice from behind them, low, quiet, and menacing. They whirled and saw that from the tower's stony surface, the head of an immense Gargoyle peered: but it was alive, pulsing with malice.

"How have you come here?!?" cried the Wizard. "I have the only keys to Otherwhen, ones you could not possibly duplicate!"

"Old fool," a second voice, a second Gargoyle face snarled from the tower's stonework, "perhaps you have keys to the front doors, forcing us to stumble down the side passages of Otherwhen, where ghosts with ruined minds mumble and weep. Yet now we will seize all three Crystals of Otherwhen. Tel-Alantir will be a dead thing in only a matter of moments."

"Merlin, attend me now!" the Wizard called out. "Thorian, I am beset!"

The second face laughed low and long as though malice slowly consumed was a dish of infinite delicacy. "Other Powers block the Portal Passages, Wizard. As for you, the Long Sleep calls."

"I am the might and the power here!" Balardi called out. Spells surging with light rippled from his staff. Gargoyle faces thinned for a second, returning as the Wizard's force of magic was shunted aside by their greater, combined powers.

"You are nothing," said one face. *I almost know that voice,* Julian thought, *almost...and the creature held itself off balance as though one portion of its body was deformed.*

"Nothing," continued the face, "nothing but a jackal-lackey of fading, would-be Gods. Behind you is a toad, attended by insects."

"Houma," whispered Julian.

"Yes," laughed the Gargoyle face, unfolding from the wall to reveal the Sorcerer, Houma of the Withered Hand.

"We are back — no longer as Sorcerers and war leaders," murmured the second voice, as its form rippled from the wall to reveal that of Alcman, mightiest of the Sorcerers. "Instead, we have become the Assassins, murderers of the Gods. But first, we must test our powers on this one feeble old man."

Unseen weapons lashed out at Balardi. As the stricken Wizard fell, a convulsion of power burst from his body, an avalanche of sorcery that embraced those around him in folds of soft, obscure, transforming magic.

Chapter Three

The Fall of the Dreamers

OTHERWHEN WAS STILL, DARK, and gloomy. Bleak desolation extended for leagues in all directions, with only moss and lichen surviving in the stillness of this fading alternate world. Perhaps hundreds of millions of years ago two possible realities had forked, with the real one, their own world, proceeding to grow and stir, alive with both natural and sorcerous energies. This portion of Otherwhen had slowed as its life force died down; even the wind seemed listless, able only to move dust and bits of dead moss during the long dark evenings.

Sebastian sighed as he rubbed moisture over the Wizard's lips. Balardi lay still and cold, eyes staring blankly into nothingness. When Sebastian held Balardi's wrist, he couldn't even feel a pulse. Julian had said that the Wizard lived on, that his form lay dying, but with all its functions slowed so that death might take months or even years.

Looking up from the stricken Wizard, Sebastian's eyes searched for Julian and Rafir. They were so far away that Rafir seemed only a small hump, a lump of ground that seemed to shift slowly over the bleak landscape. Julian was distinct as always, trudging over the cloudy horizon with his cloak held over his shoulder, his robe forming a rough sack that held fresh lichen and small mushrooms. Sebastian straightened, focusing: Julian was also dragging something — a branch, a tree limb? Where had he found it?

No trees stood upright in this fading Otherwhen. No flowers grew, and no birds sang. It would have been better, Sebastian decided, if the Wizards had confided in each another, sharing information about their secret hiding places. Again, the little Familiar sighed, rubbing moisture onto Balardi's cold, unheeding lips.

Complex spells had been woven into the Wizard's body, bringing escape and temporary safety, but now they were stranded in this remote region of Otherwhen, attending the dying Wizard, while facing slow starvation themselves, if no real food could be found.

A dry, listless thunder sounded in the distance, bringing hints of rain, but no moisture came. Julian was moving closer, and now Sebastian could see that he really did hold some sort of branch, but it was overgrown with moss and ridges of fungus that feasted on the wood's decay.

Sebastian nodded. *A fire, we might be warm again, at least for a few moments.*

Only one positive thing had happened during their confrontation with the Sorcerers: Sebastian's hand had closed over one of the Crystals before the Wizard and his allies were hurled into nothingness. Julian had hoped to affect some magic with it, open a Portal, send a message, but now the stone lay lifeless on Balardi's chest, as though neither Wizard nor Talisman might ever stir again.

Rafir was back first, sniffing around the Wizard's body as though checking for the scent of death. Julian followed, dropping the rotting limb, then he knelt beside his fallen master.

"No change?" he asked, and Sebastian shook his head.

"I found this bit of wood, Sebastian," Rafir said. "You were shivering in your sleep again, even with Julian's cloak around you."

"A fire," murmured the little Familiar. "I wonder when a fire was last lit in this forsaken land."

"Not for ages," said Julian, "and we have fuel only for a brief one, so we should wait for nightfall."

The three sat in silence for a time, nibbling on tasteless food that had little nourishment. It was useless to talk again of escape, of healing the Wizard, then turning on Houma to end the Sorcerer's treachery and terror for all time. To Sebastian, it seemed unlikely that they would die in this dismal, forsaken place: all their other perils had been so much more terrifying and dangerous. Yet in the end, wasn't death always a surprise? Did any being truly, honestly expect to die? The little Familiar moved closer to Julian, wrapping himself in the folds of Julian's cloak, as darkness and the long night's chill settled over them.

Julian let an hour of darkness pass, then reluctantly broke the branch into smaller pieces and kindled a fire with his staff. The three hunched closer to the fire; Rafir stared into the flames, curled up like a mournful kitten. The Wizard lay a full ten paces from the fire, lying as cold and still as the corpse of a dead man. Even though light and shadow moved over Balardi's face, it was hard to think of the Wizard as alive. Sebastian stared away from the Wizard, shaking his head in sorrow, but as he turned, his eyes caught a flurry of shadows that were drifting slowly across the dying landscape.

"Julian," the little Familiar whispered, and Julian came awake.

"Why didn't I sense these beings before?" The Apprentice stood, watching as the images of shadowy ghosts flickered toward them from all directions. Julian spoke the words of a brief spell, and a cocoon of white light embraced them all — Wizard, Apprentice, Familiars, and even their small fire.

Ghostly images halted, then shuffled among themselves with rustling, uncertain sounds; and they seemed to sigh, though it may only have been a distant wind.

"These things," Sebastian said softly, standing beside Julian. "They're afraid of you. How did they come here? What are they?"

"What *were* they, is a better question," Julian murmured. "I would guess that these are, or were, the ancient masters of this land — now, its fading Powers, or Gods if they chose to call themselves that." More spell-words came from Julian, but now the spell-shields vanished from around them. Julian stepped away from the flames, walking a dozen paces into the darkness. Within the Apprentice, the Gift reached out, touching the fading, shadowy forms, reacting with compassion rather than fear or reverence.

"Come closer, Old Ones," Julian said in a strong clear voice. "Share our fire, rest beside us for a time." Slowly the ghostly beings shuffled toward the flames — columns of unformed, slowly shifting shadows. Julian peered within the shadows, looking for shapes of Demon or Seraph or Mid-World Gods, but the shadows were blurred, indistinct.

"Stay with us while the fire lasts," Julian said softly, kneeling and extending his hands over the slight fire. "Later we must sleep — as you too must one day sleep, Old Ones. For the Maker has given only limited strength to his creations, so that all things must in the end sleep unless they reach the Maker, the wellspring of all energies. Yet the Long Sleep may not be our last moment — for it comes to my mind that each of us here may be touched at the Awakening when all things are made perfect in the Maker's Mind. So, rest beside us, then sleep, sleep in peace, waiting during the long quiet for the Maker's touch."

On the stricken Wizard's chest, the Crystal of Otherwhen flickered into life, glowing like a single ember from their fading fire.

· X ·

Morning brought mists of seeping drizzle, yet like all things in this fading Otherwhen, the moisture came halfheartedly, almost wearily. Shelterless, cold, and damp, they sat hunched beside the fallen Wizard. Sebastian tried to keep the droplets from the Wizard's open, unseeing eyes, while Rafir sat hunched, eyes partly closed, daydreaming about broad fields and adventures amid lush, moonlit grasses.

Still visible, the fox sped along shadowy, magic paths, moonbeams barely touching his sleek form. Ahead, in a thicket, was a creature with a strange smell — more monster than beastial creature. A touch of foulness hung in the air. And Watchers were lurking at the glade's edge. Silently, in a manner no being could ever trace, the magic fox vanished completely, and crept toward the thicket with incredible stealth.

Flurries of distant movement flashed across Rafir's partly closed eyes as the fox was shaken suddenly awake. Julian stood with a grim face over Balardi's form, staff in both hands. Sebastian was just behind him, wings flared in alarm.

"What is it?" Rafir said, peering into the mists. "Are there other creatures?"

"Portal Magic," said Sebastian. "Death, maybe, if the wrong people have come for us." The fox vanished, circling into the mist on swift, damp feet. In front of Julian and Sebastian, obscure forms came shuffling through the mist, calling out for the Apprentice. They were cloaked, hooded, but free of menace — a search party sent by their friends — and the fox found that he could almost recognize them.

"We are over here!" Julian called out from behind Rafir. *So, our friends have found us,* the fox thought, *it's a good ending, the kind that Granny would have told me not so many months ago.*

From out of the mists came Géla with her guards, numbering more than a score, all of them tall, dark haired women who had once served the Mistress of Illusions.

"Behold your rescuers," Géla said, embracing the Apprentice, "one pregnant bride, attended by a remnant of her people." She drew a quick gasp of breath as she caught sight of Balardi's lifeless face, then she knelt beside the stricken Wizard.

"To my eyes, there's no life here," she said softly, "but Merlin says otherwise, and we are to bring the fallen Wizard back with us." She signaled and four of her guards began assembling a litter at the Wizard's side. From within her cloak, she drew forth the Portal Talisman once used by Julian to return Galad from a far land. "Have you still strength to use this?" she asked.

"Yes, unless the Powers again bar the Portal Passages." Julian drew a deep breath. "But why hasn't Merlin himself come, or Thorian?"

"Spells blocking the Wizards from Portals are still holding them back," Géla said grimly. "As for other matters, I will explain some of them while you ready for our return — though if my speech distracts you, wave me to silence. Already we have endured several lifetimes' disasters, and there's no room for another."

Julian searched Géla's face for a moment: her features were bleak and tired, as though the worry lines generated by motherhood had already begun to form. With the same weariness, her guards circled around them, standing with bows held at their sides, or leaning with both hands on their long spears. Julian nodded and set the Portal Talisman beside the fallen Wizard and began to inscribe runes in the soil beside it.

"In their malice, the Sorcerers have done us triple damage," Géla continued, while the Apprentice used his staff to carve inscriptions on the soft clay soil. "First, and what seemed the greatest harm, they struck down

Balardi, one of the three cornerstones of the League. Yet their second strike has sent the most fearful chills through our people and the ranks of the Mid-World Gods: Tel-Alantir, who was becoming truly a friend to man, has been destroyed. That powerful God was our greatest potential ally, but now he drifts witlessly within the Temple of Waiting, slain by the Sorcerers with their Demon tools."

Julian looked up in astonishment. "Houma and Alcman truly assassinated a God? And survived?"

"Both of them vanished into Otherwhen, along pathways the Gods have not yet explored…. Don't let me hold you back, Julian; continue your spell-work. I'm afraid that we may be needed in our own strongholds. Yes, the Sorcerers succeeded in all their designs. The Gods of the Mid-World are retreating into their own domains, fearful lest the Assassins emerge from nothingness to cut them down.

"Further, many Powers call for the death of the Wizards and the expulsion from Alantéa of all other Mortal Magic Wielders…. No, don't stop, keep your concentration," she murmured as Julian again looked up in surprise. "This last event was one of the most subtle of the Sorcerers contrivances: in their malice, some of the Dark Gods blockaded the gates to the many Portals.

"One of these – Hiise, an obscure, secretive, dark but lesser God, barred the passage to Gravengate. In their combined fury, Merlin and Thorian hurled that being from the Gateways, not destroying, but only damaging him. The Wizards emerged before the Sorcerers could ravage the peoples of Gravengate. So, the Powers have had one of their greatest fears confirmed: that Mortal Magic Wielders acting in concert may be more powerful than many of the lesser Gods."

"We feared the disquiet of the Gods," Julian murmured, face still turned to his runework, "and for that reason the Wizards were always overly cautious. Yet the Powers could not expect the Wizards to stand aside and let one of the three Wizards be destroyed."

"Merlin has offered that explanation, with little or no success. Not since the *Wild Time* have Emissaries of the Gods appeared within our borders, yet now those beings emerge daily, full of wrath, with only the Wizard's Sendings holding them at bay.

"Several of the most militant Powers stand ready with their legions to crush us finally and forever. Kalanin and Galad and Harmadast are marshaling our tier-groups, yet they are hampered at every turn by night stalkers and assassins. For in the darkness, the intruders creep inside our camps, while our guards survive only with cunning and caution."

Julian stood up from his handiwork; as lines of power began to hum, the Portal Talisman gathered sorcerous energy toward itself.

"On that day when the Isle was raised," he said softly, "I believed truly that the Gods would arm us and join us, that together we would journey to the Isle of the Demons and put an end to the Ancient Adversaries for all time. Yet these enormous flaws, the confusion, and fear shown by the Gods have cast victory into the four winds."

Before the Talisman, a Portal with a huge arch soared into existence, leading to the tent camps at Sea's Edge, where score upon score of canvas dwellings flapped and sagged under fierce winds, against a backdrop of grey skies. Four of Géla's guards placed the old Wizard reverentially on their stretcher and waited while others closed ranks so that Géla and the stretcher bearers stood in the center. They strode through the unseen barrier, Julian passing through last; the Apprentice turned back briefly, murmuring into the desolation, "Sleep now, Old Ones, rest in the Temple of Waiting if you can. Perhaps we will meet again at the Awakening."

·)(·

For hours, one ancient but not weakened Wizard labored at the side of a second Wizard, one that was dying at a pace that might last half the lifetime of a normal human. Julian sat with his small allies, watching from more than thirty paces away. The three had taken breaks, two of them watching while the third had retreated to eat quickly then wash and refresh himself. Now they sat quietly, feeling useless, watching Merlin as the Wizard struggled over Balardi's inert, unconscious form. After more than three hours had passed, a grim-faced Merlin rose and signaled to his young servants.

"Are there more than one of these?" Merlin asked, holding the Crystal in his palm. "Are the others now held by the Sorcerers?"

"Yes — Sorcerers now hold two of the three Crystals," Julian replied softly. "Sebastian saved the third. Will the Wizard live, Merlin my Master?"

"He lies dying, and none of my labors have halted that process."

"Yet his journey toward death is so slow," Julian said, watching the somber face of his Master, "surely in time...."

"Yes, time, if there were time." Merlin looked down upon the stricken Wizard. "Time that the weak willed, envious Gods will not grant, time that the power crazed Demon Princes will not grant. There is no time.

"Julian, we confront one of the greatest alliances of power ever formed on earth; indeed, it fought the Mid-World of the Truce to a standstill, and was only overcome by the intervention of lesser, though critically important forces. The Demon Princes and their allies have been cast from Alantéa, yet their power is building once more. Will this power fall upon us? Upon the Mid-World of the Truce? Or upon a third pillar of earth's power? The last is what I fear, and we, the Wizards should be standing united with the mightiest Powers to avert such a thing. Instead, we are shifting back and forth in disarray, while the Mid-World seeks to open war with us."

Julian and Merlin were roughly the same height, so the Apprentice could stare directly into Merlin's eyes as he studied them. *What is this third force to be attacked, Merlin my Master? You seem reluctant to name it, as though the words might provoke the attack.*

"Merlin, my Master of old, let us help you," Julian said softly. "Are there no small tasks that we can help with? A watch to keep? A guard on our northern flank?"

The Wizard was silent for a moment, his features growing still, as though his mind retreated into older, more favorable times. "Take this Portal Talisman," he said evenly, staring east. "Go first to Gravengate for this day and evening. Do what can be done to hold our foes at bay. Tomorrow morning you must leave Gravengate and go to our northernmost forces where Kalanin and Galad seek to hold our borders. Counter the Emissaries; avoid damaging them, if you can, for if the Gods are given one more pretext they may — unwittingly — pass the dominion of Alantéa and the Far Lands, with all their many continents, over to the Ancient Adversaries."

· X ·

It was no longer possible to sleep in the South Tower of Gravengate, for its upper chambers had been shattered by the warfare between Balardi against Alcman and Houma. Its walls would hold only until the gales of autumn, and so Julian's tent was set well back, though his sleeping quarters still lay within the long shadows cast by the tower in the later part of the evening.

When darkness came again, Julian was lying inside his tent, listening to distant camp sounds. All through the afternoon, he had struggled to rally the bewildered peoples of Gravengate. To them, ruinous defeat had been followed by an astonishing victory; then had come a slow slide back into confusion and uncertainty, with still another disaster striking down their powerful Wizard Master.

Yet the people had rallied to him quickly. The night watch redoubled its posts, and watch fires were fed and re-fed, becoming beacons that pushed darkness to the outskirts of their camp. For the future, Rostov was needed here, or new leaders would have to come forward, people who could halt the League's decay. Julian turned on his side, his mind readied for sleep, with the Gift within him striving to reestablish the dream link with his parents.

· X ·

During the past few weeks, his control over the Dreamways had grown stronger, so that he had been able to emerge in the tower's upper chamber, seated directly across from his mother and father. Yet now, with his dream link shaken, he found himself a distance from the tower under grey skies, with cold winds and flurries of rain mixed with sleet lashing at his cloak. Several hundred paces from him the tower seemed to lean and sag, as though the winds were powerful enough to collapse its remaining stones into rubble.

In his dream, Julian raced for the tower stairs, wind and rain washing over his bare head. Inside, the base of the tower was darkened, with groaning sounds coming from above, as though supporting beams were slipping free from stone walls. Heart beating rapidly, Julian sped up the stairs, three steps to a stride.

At the top, he took a deep breath, and opened the rune covered door; it groaned like the entrance to a seldom used dungeon. Within, his parents sat surrounded by grey gloom, old and weary, with their heads downcast as though they could not meet Julian's eyes.

"Failure, once again," his father said quietly.

"To have endured so much, then to have you falter and fail," his mother murmured, face still hung downward. *"The words come hard to me but almost it would have been better had the boy never been born."*

All the details of the chamber were perfect in every respect, and yet the Gift, the Dream Warden within him, was rising in great suspicion and anger.

"You two have nothing to do with me," Julian said grimly, clenching his staff with both hands, *"and nothing to do with my parents. I was linked with them only in dreams. Why would you seek to come between me and those I love?"*

The two figures looked up at Julian, and their eyes shone bright red in the gloom, like pit fiends in a dark cavern.

"A new Lord of the Dreamways has arisen," said the figure holding the image of his father, and while it spoke, its form grew larger, and its body was coiled, like that of a snake, as though some massive serpent-being lurked within its skin.

"And our new Lord is not pleased with those forging passages through his domains," said the creature with his mother's features, and while she spoke, serpent scales rippled down long snakelike arms.

The two figures stood, becoming always larger, approaching the Apprentice with the menace of a small child's greatest nightmare: they had become monsters with the faces of his parents.

"You two seek to haunt me?" Julian asked quietly. *With his left hand, Julian waved away the tower, one that was already ruined, and it vanished. Haunters and haunted stood instead on a broad forsaken plain in the upper reaches of a mountain range, amid a stony, desolate field that was surrounded by storm clouds.*

"Next time," Julian murmured, holding his staff above his head with both hands, *"take care that you are greater than those whom you seek to*

torment." *A great wind sprang up, pushing the twin nightmares to the plateau's edge. Shrieking, they spilled over and vanished into the gulf.*

· X ·

More fierce winds whipped at Julian as he emerged grim-faced at dawn from his sagging canvas shelter. Sebastian broke off his conversation with the leader of the night watch. One look at the Apprentice told him that his worst fears were realized: after only a few months the link between Julian and his parents had again broken.

But at least he knows they live, and care for him still, Sebastian thought. *Be careful, Julian, you and Rafir are my only family. Don't do anything reckless, so you can be beside me all my days.*

"Rafir!" the little Familiar called out. Julian was clearing the ground again, making a place for his Portal Talisman. Facing north, where the danger lay, Julian was working with some urgency.

Sebastian spoke a quiet word to the head of the night watch, and the unnamed steed assigned to the Apprentice was saddled and brought forward.

"Rafir!" Sebastian called out again and this time the fox popped into view. "Rafir, don't be left behind...we might be needed to hold him back."

"So, the link's broken," said Rafir quickly, "just as you feared — but they're still alive, right? Nothing's happened that can't be fixed."

Not like Héna, your old mistress thought Sebastian. *Death is the one thing that's forever and can't be fixed.* His eyes darted to the figure of the Apprentice: Julian was nearly ready.

"Julian," Sebastian murmured as he approached the Apprentice, "what's to be done with the people of Gravengate? With Balardi gone they seem so helpless." Julian turned and straightened, staring down into the concerned eyes of his small allies — the family of a lone Apprentice.

"Rostov will come soon," he said quietly, "otherwise new leaders must arise from necessity — and they will emerge, for there is still a lot of fight left in our League. Come, ride with me as before, but we're not traveling to any safe haven. North — but you heard Merlin as well as I did: our so-called Gods are trifling with us when they should be waging war against the enchanted Isle of the Demons. Come."

He mounted, drawing Rafir up with one hand to the saddle pouch on his left, while Sebastian flew to his right shoulder, wings remaining half-lifted as though for flight. On the ground before the Talisman, a passageway, a wall of air seemed to open, a gateway more subtle than a great-arched Portal Passage. They slipped through, leaving Gravengate to its fearful, uncertain inhabitants, and to the plague of vipers that was gathering on the fringes of the ruined fortress.

·))(·

The three emerged with little sense of transition: the area to the north was as windy as the coast, though perhaps more rain was mixed with the wind's gusts and swirls. Julian gathered their lone Talisman and rode forward cautiously, the Gift within him searching for Kalanin and Galad. Open fields, grassy ranchlands seemed to rise and fall all around him, forming a land of low hills. The damp air was filled with the smell of torn grasses and horse-droppings.

After a whispered exchange with Sebastian, they shifted left, riding up an incline toward a place that seemed crowded with strife and the presence of many men, the metal of war, and beasts of burden.

Sounds came to him as he searched, heavy horse hooves pounding into ground made soft by rain. Then faces appeared over the rise: Julian looked for messengers or rangers of the League but found instead horse riders wielding bows and long lances – scores of them, and they were clad in grey or black, their insignias obscured. Half a score of them spurred their horses down the incline, aiming long lances at the Apprentice, while others drew bows, casting a volley of arrows toward the slender youth before them.

Julian's staff flashed with power, and the arrows fell, spent, to the ground. Then Julian pulled his steed hard to the right. Turning in the saddle, staff outstretched, he blasted the riders one by one from their saddles. As they toppled, their horses bolted in fear, while other riders backed from the ridge in alarm, then passed from view.

Julian rode higher, leaving the stunned riders struggling to lift themselves from the long rangeland grasses. On the hillock's far side, riders railed at one another, trying to generate courage, though they remained sheltered behind outcrops of stone, avoiding the Apprentice and his enchanted staff.

"Magician!" one called out. "Beware our Masters, the Great Gods! They will make your own death long and difficult!"

"Watch for yourselves!" The Apprentice called back. "Not many of you will draw breath at day's end, for the *Wild Time* has come again. As for your masters, they have failed to defend the Mid-World of the Truce. Why should I fear them?" He angled a little to the right, lashing the outcrop with a coil of flame that seared a patch of scrub pine; the riders broke and fled, calling upon their brethren to beware.

"The Gods!" Julian continued, but broke off, for Sebastian was pulling at his cloak, trying to calm him.

"No, Julian," the Familiar said quietly. "We'll need the Powers of the Mid-World — one way or another. But these riders have no good reason to be on League soil. Let's get rid of them, then find Kalanin and Galad."

Julian's Gift led them north and west, and like the mind of the Apprentice, the Gift had risen in anger. Outriders and other scouts ranged the countryside, but the sharp sounds of destruction that emerged from their encounters with the Apprentice made them wary. Their ranks seemed to thin as Julian rode north, and those remaining became skittish and fearful.

For a brief time, the countryside was clear of riders, then they met others who did not break when challenged; and their horsemen wore the insignia of the League. These men waved and called out encouragement to the Apprentice as he raced swiftly north; though in a brief time his horse began to tire, and he was forced to stop at the next outpost of the League to exchange horses.

"Kalanin and Galad are with the vanguard farthest north," one ranger called to Julian. "To the west are the main forces of the League, waiting for instructions."

"The Wizards are needed here, Apprentice," added another quickly, as Julian remounted. "Emissaries of the Gods appear and vanish like wild Sendings." Angry words came to Julian's lips, but he rode away in silence, with the Gift searching for their allies. As Julian rode, he whispered spell-words to the unfamiliar horse beneath him, and the stallion's stride lengthened, and his breathing strengthened.

· ◊ ·

The rearguard first noted the oncoming rider — a messenger no doubt — a youngling with dark, tangled hair, riding hard with a grim look about him — then there came shouts of command as Julian was recognized: lines parted and tier-groups pulled back, allowing the Apprentice to ride swiftly through their ranks, toward the League's vanguard, to a place where Kalanin and Galad were holding some being of sorcery at bay.

Galad stood at the forefront of their vanguard, with the Tarnished Sword, a sorcerous creation that gleamed and muttered, held with both hands, as though to restrain it.

Just behind him, Kalanin remained on horseback, speaking in soft, measured tones to the powerful Emissary that loomed in front of him. Nodding, almost casually, to the Apprentice riding to his side, Kalanin continued,

"Think again, Emissary. Doom surrounds us, for the Summoner stands before you. In Galad's hands is the weapon that first carved Marid flesh and destroyed a corrupted Seraph. We and this Magician's servants have been catalysts of fate. Is your own destiny greater than those you seek to harm?"

The being before them shifted toward a rank of pikemen that stood to Galad's left, then it laughed as those tensed to repel it. The Emissary loomed high above them, more than four times a man's height: a being not made of pure matter, one whose substance seemed formed from columns of reddish sunlight, with rays shifting and slanting as it moved.

One of the greatest of the Emissaries, Julian thought, *the one who returned — almost reluctantly — the Eye of Merlin to its Wizard-master.*

"Your insignificant 'League' might have been left to its own eventual decay, had your Wizards not trifled with the Gods." Again, the Emissary moved toward another group, red rays shifting and slanting inside its ghostly form as it toyed with them in its malice.

"The Gods!" cried Julian. He slipped from his steed to stand beside Galad. "Confused Powers who snatch defeat from victory, and you call them 'Gods'!" The Emissary drew itself up, looming above Julian, Kalanin, and Galad, then its eyes locked in spell-test with those of the Apprentice.

Julian's hands rose above his head, then he brought his staff down, shattering the Emissary's sight lock.

"To have failed," Julian called out, striding toward the Emissary, "after such a bitter, hard-fought victory was achieved by so few, and much less powerful beings!" The Emissary recoiled, but one hand reached within its own dark, red substance: a gateway lurked there and from it, wild cries emerged.

As Julian spoke his own summoning spell, calling for Kath, a winged griffin sprang from the Emissary's Portal, and soared toward them with flaring wings; but Julian's serpent-ally Kath met the griffin before it touched the ground, embracing its shrieking form in its powerful, unrelenting coils.

"Take your *Wild Time*," cried the Apprentice, racing forward, "and cast it upon your own brethren!" He smote the ground, and columns of white radiance rose to contend with the Emissary's dusk-red substance.

"Withdraw, Emissary," Julian said in harsh tones. "Tell your masters to prepare themselves, for they have helped to strengthen the foes that await them upon the Isle of The Demons."

Recoiling in surprise and alarm, the Emissary vanished, leaving only its griffin servant to shriek in hopeless desperation as massive coils tightened around its shuddering form.

· ✕ ·

Kalanin shook his head as they climbed. *Why here upon this hill? Why stop at an old graveyard on a hill's crest just as daylight is passing? Some momentous event hovers like Death tapping at the outer gates of an ancient fortress. Even the air is trembling as it did on the morning before the enchanted Isle was raised. But why stop at this place?*

In the gloom of twilight, Julian came to a halt before a tilting headstone, one that stood larger than others, better preserved than the smaller grave markers that lay toppled nearby. Sebastian cleared the ivy that circled about the stone's inscription, while Rafir used his teeth to pull back the long grasses that grew from its base. Werelight surged from Julian's staff; they peered forward and read:

A stone raised in honor
of Sentauris,
who lieth not here.
Heroine of the Wild Time,
Great Foe of Enchanters
and Emissaries.
The Wizards have chosen
not to record her deeds.

We remember and record.
W/O

"What is this place, Julian?" Galad asked, shuddering slightly as he drew his cloak against the chill. "It feels as though an army of ghosts just walked over my own grave."

"I feel a thrill of recognition, but I have no idea what it could be," Kalanin murmured, looking up into the night sky. "All we need now is a flare of comets, and a flash of bright lightning."

"At least a rumble of thunder," Galad added, "though the night's too clear for that sort of demonstration. What do you make of it, Julian?"

"This place has little to do with our present or our future," the Apprentice said, thinking aloud. "I think that it's a message from the past, from the *Wild Time*, not meant for us necessarily, but activated by the presence of raiders, foes of the League. Sebastian, do you remember what Balardi told us about the *Wild Time*?"

"He once spoke about Wylar and Orantes, maybe the 'W' and the 'O' on this stone," the little Familiar said thoughtfully, "Adepts who aided the Wizards in the early history of the League. Now we have a third name: Sentauris."

"Voices from our past," Kalanin said, "summoning us here from across an expanse of years. What would they say to us now, about our own *Wild Time*?" They read the inscription again, then turned from the gravesite, as the werelight faded from Julian's staff.

"So, Julian, what next?" asked Galad. "Do we rest here, to prepare for yet another *Wild Time*? Or are the Gods coming themselves with countless legions to crush us once and forever?"

Julian took a deep breath and sat. "What you felt earlier, an unease, is something I feel even more strongly, and it would be a sensation much more powerfully felt by the Gods because the whole of creation is trembling. We don't need to fear the Powers, not if events are taking place that will trouble them this much."

"And these events?" prompted Kalanin.

"Merlin hinted about this moment," Julian said thoughtfully. "A new *Wild Time*, three Crystals of Otherwhen, Balardi's fall, the Death of Tel-Alantir, sea-war to the south — all these may be borders on a tapestry showing one central event, something that I...." He trailed off.

Kalanin sat to the right of the Apprentice, resting his back against a side of the stone that had been raised for Sentauris. Finally, Kalanin spoke: "All these events are linked by a common thread: we are again losing." He stared upwards, where the stars shimmered from the misty heat raised by the day's bright sunlight; in the sky's corners, meteorites were beginning to slide, then flare to earth. Kalanin turned his thoughts to Julian. *Warning signs at last. What now, Apprentice?*

Julian sat with his eyes closed, but tense, reaching, as though other omens were calling to him. "Here, beside this stone," he said softly, eyes still shut tight, "is a place of strength for us, a stronghold. Sebastian, Rafir, come rest beside me. We can view events from here.

"You remember how in the Gangean Range our minds journeyed together. I don't think this journey will be as dangerous, but it would be wise to keep ourselves together in one place." He glanced to the horizon, where the soundless skyfall was destroying some distant corner of the Far Lands.

Apprentice and Charmed Knights sat in a semicircle, with Julian's back set against the center of the stone carved for Sentauris. Kalanin was on his right, Galad on his left, while in front of him Sebastian and Rafir rested, eyes studying the starlit night skies of Alantéa the Forerunner. Julian whispered hushed spell-words and in moments their seated forms slumped forward in sleep, resting beneath a decaying crown of falling stars, while their minds journeyed outwards.

· ☿ ·

The hill they lay upon grew larger in their shared dream vision, growing broader and stronger, a huge entity with massive shoulders rising from the earth around it. Behind them, the field of stones had become one monument: an obelisk of grey-black granite that ignored the changing seasons, while inscriptions upon it were being carved even at that moment, as the long history of the League continued to be inscribed.

Soundlessly, Julian gestured to the stone and the hillock, then to themselves, saying without words: here is the League, a thing we know to be fragile, yet shored up with an inner strength of Destiny laid upon it.

Other beings, Powers, searching for enchanted dreams and visions, watched them from a distance, as they also sought to view events that so troubled all of Alantéa the Forerunner. Viewed from their hillock, these other dreamers seemed no more than pools of light, or bright radiant beams of shimmering radiance, ranging over a vast darkened field. Though now, from the far corners of their eyes, to their left, came a surge of turmoil, a shuffling movement rippling through the pools of light: Julian recognized the serpent beings, who had broken the dream link with his parents; and now they led other even mightier beings, seeking in their combined power to drive the Apprentice from the Dreamways and all the gateways leading to enchanted visions.

Julian rose, staff clenched in both hands. Kalanin and Galad stood also, drawing weapons, while Sebastian and Rafir leaped to Julian's shoulders. About their hillock, white marble seemed to pulse and glow now with a green radiance in the darkness.

At Sea's Edge, Géla stirred and reached for weapons, and the child within her also grew aware, just able to perceive a fraction of the room's night images through her mother's eyes.

Behind the five, the stone of Sentauris shone brightly, eclipsing the others, with the inscription engraved upon her tombstone radiating an emerald green.

Would-be Dreamlords halted uncertainly. Before them, the Far Travelers seemed to blend, to become one mighty being of myth, while around the Dreamlords, other onlookers began to murmur in disgust, with sounds followed by thrusts of power — like heavy boots kicking away small, squealing creatures. Then the aspiring Dreamlords fled, scurrying down their night burrows, racing from destruction.

All the shifting lights around them became still, and they stood again as though on a darkened field amid many interspersed watch fires. Julian, Kalanin, Galad, Sebastian, and Rafir became as before — one of many groups of watchers seeking to behold events from afar, events that so troubled creation that onlookers flocked to behold them.

Then it seemed to all the many watchers that their own thoughts receded, that the images before their own eyes grew dim; instead, their shared vision passed through a haze of faint, watery images until they reached the interior of a vast underground cavern, with an oval shoreline surrounding a broad underground lake. Two small figures strode over the rock-strewn shoreline, their own faces lit by werelight beaming from half-open palms. And one palm was a blackened, shriveled thing: the hand of Houma, as the Sorcerer strode a half-step behind Alcman.

As though sensing Julian's intrusion, Houma turned and seemed to recognize the distant Apprentice — he bared his teeth in a wolf's grin, then turned away with a snarl of malice. As the two picked their way amid the rocks, Marids began emerging from the waters behind them, following Alcman and Houma. Marid forms dwarfed those of the Sorcerers, yet they kept several paces behind the Mortal Magic Wielders, and the humans paid only the slightest heed to the Marids, as though these monsters created by Demon Princes had become of lesser relevance.

Echoes resounded in the cavern as Marids crushed loose rocks beneath massive feet. As their procession moved slowly along the lake's side, other figures began to join them: from shimmering pockets of air came hairless, farseeing Guardians, masters of all dreams. Guardians towered over the humans, while standing only three-quarters the height of the Marids.

And lastly, as though grudgingly, reluctantly, the three greatest of the Dark Lords emerged from Portal Passages: Haeglin, and Mordred and Un-Maurag. All other creatures maintained a symmetry of head, arms, and legs, but the Dark Lords were misshapen, as though their forms had been mixed with those of monsters.

The procession moved on, drawn slowly toward an array of lights: on the far side of the lake, a range of braziers cast patterns of red light over slabs of carved granite. The stone-work was unpolished but placed in intricate patterns of power, forming an altar for the Adversaries. And before the altar stood the greatest of the Adversaries: the three Demon Princes.

Slowly the procession wound its way about the broad, underground lake, and always more figures emerged to join it: Marids, Guardians, lesser Dark

Lords, half-bewildered Sorcerers from the Isles of the Sorcerers who stared in open fear at the assembled Powers surrounding them.

As Alcman and Houma reached the altar of the Adversaries, their palms were withdrawn into long sleeves and their werelight vanished. They stood, heads bowed until the many Powers reached the Demon Princes' place of power, and all the shuffling echoes died down so that only the slightest lapping sound could be heard from the waters of the underground lake.

Then, with the utmost reverence, the two most powerful Sorcerers knelt before the Demon Princes, bowing their heads in submission. Marids also sank to their knees before their great Lords, with other lesser powers hurrying to follow. Guardians began sinking to their knees, some with open acceptance, while others seemed to stumble, portions of their beings stirring in reluctance and confusion.

Turning to stare malignantly at the darkened lake, the huge figure of Haeglin finally sank into submission, as did Mordred a moment later — though every gesture from the two Dark Lords was filled with defiance.

At the last, only Un-Maurag remained facing the Demon Princes, searching their faces balefully, as though to say, is your darkness truly greater than my own? A long silence followed; the lake grew completely still as thoughts and images sprang from the minds of the Demon Princes into that of Un-Maurag.

Finally, as though confounded by a deeper malice, Un-Maurag sank to his knees beside the forms of his brethren.

All the Powers seeking to challenge the Mid-World of the Truce now knelt before the Demon Princes and their stone altar. A pause came, a moment of stillness, then lines of light began radiating among all the kneeling forms. Faces began to lift as power shifted among them, with lines of jagged light passing from kneeling forms into the focused power of the Demons' stone altar.

Others looked up, staring blankly at the focus of power building before them. Guardians were the first to rise. These stood, bowing to their masters, then they began striding to the lake's farthest side. Marids stirred as though suddenly waking, and Dark Lords and Sorcerers rose also, to circle right or left around the lake, in a procession illuminated by gloom. At last, the lake was completely encircled by a throng of many interspersed powers, though each was linked by the power of the Demon Princes.

In the darkness surrounding the still lake, all faces turned as one to the cavern's roof: hewn, polished, or pockmarked, none could tell, for the cavern was held in a deep well of night. Power built to a low hum, as the greatest work of sorcerous power since the founding of the Mid-World of the Truce forged itself into a weapon to be wielded by the Demon Princes.

With a vast sigh, the cavern's roof vanished, and the dark lake was exposed for the first time to the light of the universe.

A full moon radiating sickly yellow light hovered over the enchanted Isle of the Demons. The lake remained still, but within, its energy seethed as it sought to drink the moon's light and all its magic. For now, in its reflection of moonlight, all the moon's features, its craters, jagged mountains, and broad plains, grew more detailed and vivid than those perceived by charters of the stars or lovers of the night.

Sounds in the cavern faded as even the low hum of sorcerous creation dimmed. Silence prevailed as the lake's surface grew still as polished glass.

Then with a vast rending sound, the lake's surface shattered. An arc of light burst from the water and hurtled out into the night: a Scimitar of radiant energies forged by the Adversaries.

· X ·

All the many watchers recoiled in fear and dismay, many breaking off their vision quest to vanish into long prepared places of concealment. Others, like Julian, Galad, and Kalanin, rose to draw weapons and defend themselves as best they could.

Those remaining in the vision watched on in horror as the weapon forged by the Adversaries hurtled over the moonlit night skies of Alantéa the Forerunner. Three times the Scimitar circled Alantéa and the layers of sorcerous kingdoms surrounding it, then it vanished, passing into a place outside of time, beyond the Mid-World of the Truce.

Such was the strength of power within the Demons' Sending that it drew all its onlookers with it, as the weapon of jagged light rose over the Hall of the Dreamers, then over the enchanted Cup of the Maker, whose sparkling waters danced in the starlight, completely unaware of the Demon Princes and their great Sending. Halfway down the mountain's side, the Hall of the Dreamers glowed dimly, glass panels passing the flickering light of many candles out into the darkness.

The Scimitar whirled through the moonless darkness, arcing high above the Maker's Cup, almost seeming to shiver in glee and anticipation.

"No!" Julian's mind shouted into the silence. ***"Dreamers defend yourselves! Send your own weapon aloft to duel the Demon's Scimitar in the starlight! Guardians of Earth, rise to defend us all! Maker, this is not Your Will!"***

But the Scimitar of jagged moonlight was countered only by the air of the darkest night. Hurtling downward, it shattered the Cup of the Maker, smashing asunder the whole of the mountain's cone.

Rivers of marble rubble, torrents of enchanted waters, cascaded down the mountain's slope, crushing the Dreamers and their Hall. Within the mountain's heart, old fires were rekindled, with lava bursting from the broken cone, spreading flames and ruin to the enchanted forests in the valleys below.

Satisfied, the Demons' Sending rose into the night, drawing power from Alantéa and its enchanted layers. Surging through the upper skies, the Scimitar took a deep draught of moonlight once again, then hurtled into deep space, to pass beyond the circles of the sun, following the path once forged by those seeking the Maker in the starry universe: The Sending had become a dagger, hurled at the Maker's Heart.

Chapter Four

How the Gods Begat Godlings

A GREAT TAPESTRY WAS forming on the south wall of the Halls of Merlin at Sea's Edge. This tapestry emerged fragment by fragment, slowly expanding down the wall as tiny strands blended together to form larger images. This tapestry was the work of tens of thousands of tiny weavers, beings so slight that human eyes could see only the movement of cloth.

From time to time, sounds would interrupt the tiny weavers' work: the sound of their master sighing. Then the weavers would pause, awaiting new patterns, yet always their master, the Wizard Merlin, stood beside another giant, one that lay motionless at the far end of the chamber. Those two huge figures were so far from the weavers that the Wizard's sighs might well have been sounds of bad weather from a distant kingdom. As the sighing sounds passed, the weavers resumed their tapestry, their great cathedral, their pyramid, the work of many generations.

At the far corner of the hall, Merlin, master of small and large magics, called up yet another shielding-spell over the dying Wizard, his ally, Balardi. In his mind, Merlin imagined Death, dressed in his darkest clothing, waiting silently in the shadows, yawning in mockery. Outside, on the third evening after the Dreamers' passing, the night watch readied again for the skirmishes that came with each nightfall.

The watch is the least of our problems, thought the Wizard, *with war at sea amid the Isles of the Sorcerers nearly as insignificant. The Gods were astonished, distracted, and they had allowed the Dreamers, one of the great pillars of creation left by the Maker, to be destroyed. Yet eventually, the jealous Dark Gods would be called off or countered by other Powers; then the Sorcerers' cunning servants would stand alone against the reordered might of the League.*

Like the sounds of distant chimes, the mind of Merlin heard or felt the passage of nearby enchantments. Casually, as though considering some new and complex thought, Merlin turned from Balardi's nearly lifeless form to stare beyond the west windows where the sky was showing only the faintest touch of red sunlight. Night was coming.

One of the Powers is coming for me, unannounced, he sent to the Eye of Merlin.

Thorian is prepared to assist you, came the eagle's answer, after the briefest of pauses.

All was silent, though the air was tight with tension.

Merlin stood, facing the source of enchantment, leaning on his staff. The air before him began to glow with a brilliant light; some of the Gods used a strong radiance to foreshadow their arrival. Merlin caused his own eyes to adjust to the light so that other dimmer portions of the chamber came to seem like shifting pools of darkness.

"Magician," came a half-mocking voice from within the pool of light. "Magician and mortal, have you at last found some healing tasks that are beyond your powers?"

"Yes," said Merlin, leaning on his staff. Either the Wizard was frozen in a half-bow before some remote deity, or he stood like an old man hunched before a storm.

"Yes," the Wizard repeated. *Yes, all of creation trembles yet you take pleasure in the dying moments of one old man, and satisfaction that another old man is unable to aid him.*

Slowly, the pool of light diminished in brightness, and Merlin was left standing in the divine presence of the Great God Thoth, a bird-faced Power known, among other things, for his strength in healing.

"What would you yield, Mortal, in exchange for my healing arts?" asked the mocking God. "A portion of your realm? The greatest of your weapons and tools of power? The Keys to Otherwhen? Guardianship of the Timeways?"

Though his words were scornful, other events revealed a more serious intent: slowly, cautiously, with his own miracle work, the Great God Thoth was shielding Merlin's chamber from any of the distant eyes and ears of the Mid-World that might seek to overhear their discussion. Merlin spoke soft, hesitant words to the Mid-World Power, while his own spell-work shielded intruders from the Alternates, and from viewers from the past or the future.

Insulated from his brethren, and from the Adversaries, Thoth spoke in far different tones: "We have dealt before, Wizard."

"You have always dealt fairly with me, Lord."

"And always — almost always — our dealings have been to my own satisfaction." Thoth stepped from his receding pool of light and strode toward the pallet on which the dying Wizard lay. Thoth, bird-faced Power of the Mid-World, stood perhaps three heads taller than the Wizard, attended still by light so that he gleamed beside the grey-clad mortal. Yet the two, so different, seemed surprisingly comfortable in each other's presence.

Thoth knelt beside Balardi's pallet, placing various devices upon the old Wizard's chest, his wrists, and forehead, then murmuring, "The same weapons that destroyed Tel-Alantir were turned against your Wizard ally. When I felt Tel-Alantir's passage toward the Temple of Waiting I knew fear,

Wizard, for the second time since my rebirth into the Mid-World of the Truce." The tall, bird-faced figure of Thoth straightened, staring down at Merlin. "I cannot promise success, yet I will take this one as a challenge to my craft, to attempt a thing never before accomplished. As for payment, I will choose the greatest of the spoils you bring back from the Isle of the Demons."

"Is your service so easily obtained, Lord?" Merlin asked softly, looking fully into the Great Power's face. "Surely, in such a great matter, there will be other voices, advice from other Gods, some bidding that you destroy this powerful mortal before he becomes as menacing as Alcman or Houma. Others might wish him half-healed, to fight one more battle before falling into the Long Sleep. Are there other voices, Lord, or has the Fall of the Dreamers left me fearful beyond reason?"

Thoth leaned back his beaked head and laughed: piping sounds that rippled through the chamber. "Wizard, had I devices that would grant you another thousand years of life, I would yield them, for then all the proud and mighty Powers might have further cause to learn humility.

"Yes, there were 'voices.' Devices were offered, so that your fallen ally might survive only in service to one of the Great Ones or live only on the sufferance of another Power. So many conflicting counsels were given, that I will be able to easily choose none of them.

"Yet I cannot remake this mortal being as though he had never been struck down. There will be a price either in life span or in strength. Which would you select, should it come to such an alternative?"

The Wizard sighed, pausing for only a half pulse. "I must choose strength, for our need is greatest now: the enchanted Isle of the Demons haunts my dreams, calling to me in the darkest hours of the night. It feels like doom."

Thoth shook his head grimly. "The Isle has been crafted as a killing ground for the Gods. May you have better fortune in that place than I might have." Then with one gesture, he caused the bier holding Balardi to lift into the air; with another, he reinvoked his enchanted pool of light. Lastly, the God Thoth stared at the tapestry that hung on the South Wall: it held an image of the Hall of the Dreamers, as it had once stood glowing beneath a vast canopy of brilliant stars. As the bird-faced God watched, tiny weavers finished another small fragment of their great tapestry.

"At times, an echo reaches out to me, a beckoning call from the Temple of Waiting," Thoth said in a soft voice. "I would choose never to sleep, to rule in my own domains forever — but if we come before the Maker, speak for me, Wizard."

"A season ago I would have assured you," said Merlin, watching as the pallet transporting Balardi vanished into a cone of light. "Now all things are called into doubt. My voice if we come to Judgment Day, may be broken, or transformed. Yet, if the Maker permits, I will speak for the Great God Thoth, the Healer."

· X ·

So many ancient magics lay within the enchanted Vale of Whispers, that only the palest rays of starshine spilled over the Vale. In the darkness, ghostbeings huddled together, speaking to one another in hushed tones: "They are coming, they are coming, they are coming," the voices murmured repeatedly in soft voices.

Above them, winged Emissaries of the Gods rode the upper currents of the night sky, marking the progress of four figures who approached the City of the Truce. Each figure came from a different direction, from east, north, west, and south; and their progress was slow, almost tentative. The Emissaries watched on, sending ripples of formidable thought speeding back to their distant masters:

Four of the Great Gods are passing through the Vale of Whispers, preparing to call down the Truce; but their plans and purposes are obscured by more than the darkness of night.

· ꓷ ·

As the Powers passed into the Vale of Whispers, a small group of humans gathered many Leagues south of the Vale, less than a half day's march from Gravengate. Kalanin, Julian and Galad had ridden from the north, while Géla, Harmadast, Harlond, and Rostov had journeyed from the south. They planned to discuss the League's many troubles a little distance from the disturbances surrounding the Wizards' fortresses. A rough command-tent had been pitched for them, with crude tables and chairs inside, and torches passed smoke into the upper reaches of their tent's canvas peaks. A few sipped from mugs of ale, while others held smaller cups of herbal brews. Outside the tent, Sebastian dozed in the starlight, while Rafir raced through the night's shifting shadows.

"And so, we seem destined to become the true rulers of the League, at least for the near future," Kalanin said quietly to the seated forms around him. "The Wizards can barely be approached to discuss even the gravest of disasters."

"Management of day-to-day events was the least favorite of Balardi's tasks," added Harmadast. "Nor did Thorian, for all his well-known forbearance, take real pleasure in the routine affairs of men."

"Thus, we have become a Council, the Council of the League," Géla said, glancing at those about her: Rostov and Harlond sat to her left,

Kalanin and Galad to her right, while Julian and Harmadast sat across from her. "What do you say, Apprentice? Will the Wizards resent us if we take charge of their realms?"

Julian sipped a tisane of herbs and stared into the distance. "Deal with them as though they were Emperors." He was too far from the Vale of Whispers to sense that the Truce Terms might again be invoked, although the Gift within him was uneasy. "Have seals forged, issue proclamations in your Council's voice, but give the Wizards a day — no, two days, to amend, revise, or overturn your decisions."

"*Our* decisions," Kalanin corrected. "You have already advised us clearly on one matter: Rostov will undertake the restoration of our security."

"That's something the Crystals, devices of Otherwhen, showed us," Julian said, turning to Rostov. "Our people should never, never be left uncertain as to the allegiance of the man next to them. Friends and allies should lie within our borders, our foes outside."

"Begin if you like with those who served the Mistress of Illusions," Géla said to Rostov. "There should be no doubt as to their loyalties."

"Nor as to the fealty of the remnant of Grey Men," Galad added.

Rostov had been drawing idly on a rough sheet of parchment, inscribing interlocking oval shapes. Now he looked up. "Here we stand in the first circle: the Council. Those who are known to us form a second circle, while those known to our brethren in the second circle form a third. Over time, it should be possible to exclude, even identify, all those seeking to oppose us."

· 𝕏 ·

"*Call it not the Isle of the Demons,*" said the one Power, "*rather call it the Slaughterhouse of the Demons, a place where the Gods are destined to be destroyed.*"

The four Powers stood upon the same ground on which the Truce had been fashioned so many thousands of years before. Each could guess, but not be certain as to the identities of the other three, for they stood heavily disguised. Even the arts of the City — forces for unbinding and revelation — were unable to master their transformations. It was night in the Vale of Whispers, and a pale starlight blinked faintly overhead, while all the voices in the Vale were hushed and muted, waiting to see if the Truce would be called down for a second time.

"Yes, the Isle has been crafted as a killing region, where the Gods will go to be destroyed," said another. *"Yet if the mortals governing the south of Alantéa make this quest alone, what will be the outcome?"*

Two voices laughed with unexpected harshness.

"Indeed, they would perish," said the fourth voice. *"These devices of the Maker may have wielded power against the Ancient Adversaries — were not all of us astounded as the Dreamers rose in might, then passed so quickly into the Temple of Waiting? We might think of the Wizards as seedlings sown by the Maker's Hand, with some power even against the mightiest of the Adversaries. Yet if they stood unsupported in the Isle of the Demons, they would have the same power that straw would have when hurled into a vast bonfire."*

"We might forge weapons of great power for them," offered one harsh-voiced power in muted tones.

"They would still be nothing more than straw, gilded straw perhaps," said the fourth voice, *"but none of our Mid-World Weapons, or Great Sendings or even well-armed Emissaries would survive conflict in the newly-risen Isle."*

Darkness seemed to gather about the harsh-voiced Power, and that being murmured, *"You two once served the Maker. Does your Godhood now make you feel guilty? Do you think to atone for the Mid-World of the Truce by sacrificing our Pact?"*

"It is true that now, in this place, at this time," said the first voice to the second, *"it was fated that some of our hidden ancestries would become known.*

If you and your darkness and your rage at the Maker speak as a transformed Demon Prince, I can respond as a being who once stood as a Greater Seraph. If I come, one day, before the Maker, I will bow my head in sorrow, acknowledging my weakness and failure. But for now, I must focus all my strength to defend the Mid-World of the Truce."

"Let us speak for a moment of outcomes," said the third voice in low, rumbling tones. *"If my innermost desires were to become realized, the Wizards would journey to the Isle of the Demons and be utterly destroyed. But, in their struggles, they would so fatally weaken the Demon Princes that all their threats to the Mid-World of the Truce would be removed forever. Might this outcome now come to pass?"* Slowly, somberly, in the gloom, the other three Powers shook their heads.

"And for you," continued the third voice, a God-being who might once have been an ancient power, a Lord of Dragons, *"you who entered the Mid-World from the Right-Hand Path, you might wish for a much different outcome, in which the Demon Princes and their allies are destroyed, while the Wizards survive, though humbled and weakened."*

"Somewhere within me," the fourth voice acknowledged, *"a strange disquiet arises when I consider the destruction of the Wizards and their League. Yet when the Wizards set forth from Alantéa, they are nothing but dragonflies assailing a host of monstrosities. They would not even reach the enchanted Isle of the Demons."*

The second voice seemed to sigh, then rumbled, *"I have known that we will be forced to take actions that stir the ancient rage that still lingers within me. We must raise a force to aid the Wizards, something much greater than Mid-World Weapons, or Sendings, or Emissaries."*

"Great Powers, Mighty Warriors," added the fourth voice.

"Godlings, beings created by Gods that will attain the strength of Gods," said the third voice.

"We must create Godlings as an initial step," said the first voice, *"and after, many other forces must be moved to support the Wizards in their hopeless quest. And all these brilliant miracles will be the combined effort of the Mid-World, passing so much of the Mid-World's malice toward the Wizards into our creation of Godlings. So be it."*

Slowly, word by bitter word, the four God-Beings together invoked the Truce Terms, and all the energies of the Mid-World began to gather again to the enchanted Vale of Whispers.

· ⅍ ·

In the night, Julian found himself awake, standing in the darkness outside of his tent. His mouth seemed to belong to some other force, and it was forming the words of power that invoked the Truce. He faced north toward the Vale of Whispers, and he could feel the force of sorcery radiating from that place of power so that it beat upon his brow like a harsh wind.

Sebastian, too, was awake, clutching at Julian's cloak, staring into the night, as though his small eyes struggled to penetrate a thousand leagues.

"Julian," whispered the little Familiar.

"The Mid-World of the Truce," Julian murmured, "invoked for a second time, but to what end?" Images were shuddering through his mind — some of them were his own memories from the Vale of Whispers, while others showed that four of the Greater Gods had gathered again to that place of power.

Now through the night sky, an arc of light hurtled overhead from the north, pulsing black hues, mixed with seams of blue. A second arc followed, brighter, filled with gold and green hues, then came a third, an even brighter silvery red, so that it lit the night sky with dim illumination like fireworks from a distant celebration.

"Power is being unleashed," Julian said. "It seems most unlikely that it will be turned against us, but also there seems little chance that the Isle of the Demons is trembling at this moment. Sebastian, if you heard those words from me — words that might call upon the Mid-World of the Truce — it is best that you forget them as quickly as you can."

The little Familiar stared up into the night sky, where starshine was returning, no longer eclipsed by glittering arcs of light. "I don't know, Julian — could I ever stand in the Vale of Whispers again and call down the Truce? And if they came, would they even listen to me? As I recall those matters, they paid no attention to you after you summoned them, did they?"

While they stood murmuring quietly in the darkness, Géla approached them, with Kalanin following, bringing Géla her cloak, and another for himself.

"The child within me woke first," Géla said, "not in fear, but with excitement."

"Your daughter has the Gift," Julian said, and he would have smiled had the night's events not been so strange. "We saw that in the Gangean Range during our vision quest, when —"

A concussion burst over them suddenly — its sound waves trailing the arcs of light like a strange thunder. A second concussion swept through the skies, then a third followed.

"When your magic was guided by a greater hand," Géla finished. Then she turned because others were rising, stirred by sounds of thunder in the night.

"North," Galad murmured, staring in the night sky, "and from the gap between light and sound, an event far beyond our borders."

"From the Vale of Whispers," Julian added somberly, "the Mid-World of the Truce has been called upon for a second time, and some power has been unleashed. But the nature and purpose of that power are hidden from me."

"A Great Sending?" Harmadast suggested. "Was it perhaps launched against the Isle of the Demons?"

Julian stared north, the Gift within him struggling to penetrate a haze of darkness and distance. "The Isle would not be so easily shaken," he said softly. "No, I think that the Gods fear the Isle of the Demons and wish us to journey there to deal with the Ancient Adversaries."

"While we of the League, even at full strength," Harmadast noted, "have perhaps a thousandth's portion of the power of the Mid-World."

Julian nodded. "The Gods must also understand these matters. Perhaps they will take steps to balance the scales somewhat."

"Even if our power is doubled or trebled," Géla said, "we are still no match for Demon Princes allied with Sorcerers and Marids and Creatures of the Darkness. Now, you know that I rarely offer cautious counsel, but one of us must eventually ask, why must we go and die upon the Isle of the Demons?"

"We are Servants of the Maker," Julian said, "entrusted with the control of Ancient Adversaries. The Maker never told us that our tasks would be simple or safe."

"It would be nice to know," Géla replied, bitterness creeping into her voice, "on which tablets of stone the Maker recorded his instructions about suicide."

Kalanin wrapped his arms and cloak around her. "My beloved, it does not feel like certain death. Also, the Apprentice has not mentioned the daughter of Thorian."

Julian turned southeast toward Stone Mountain. "When the Gift within me looks for Thorian, it sees him engaged in a passion of sorcery, preparations of magic that last well into the night. Even asleep, the Wizard's mind cannot rest, for he dreams of freeing his daughter from the Demons' enchanted Isle."

Géla's shoulders slumped. "And so, the entire League will be drawn to its doom."

"'Doom' is too strong a word," Kalanin said. "We should never forget that each time we felt devastated and defeated, we survived to fight on. Julian, what do you see as the Wizards and their servants approach the Isle of the Demons? Do we spill through enchanted mouths of Portals, or surge through the upper skies on Chariots drawn by Griffins?"

"Nothing so dramatic and dangerous," Julian said. "The journey at least begins, I think, by ship."

"An armada built for war, then?" Kalanin asked.

Julian hesitated, sifting images in his mind. "A boat, a single boat, I think, but larger, a deep-water sailing vessel."

"A construct, perhaps of metal and magic," Kalanin prompted.

Julian shook his head. "Our vessel begins, at least, as a ship of wooden beams and nails and pitch."

"Then," Kalanin said, "while you and others deal with the safety of our peoples, Géla and I will gather a small battle contingent and make our way to Khiva and the coast. There, we can at least gather resources for shipbuilding. Does the Gift within you, Apprentice, find any fault with these thoughts?"

"No..." Julian hesitated, "I believe that you were meant to nudge the Wizards forward by beginning this task. I would wait, however —" The Apprentice felt danger looming overhead. He grasped his staff with both hands and stared up into darkness. Shapes emerged from out of the night sky, three of them, drifting lower to examine the Apprentice and his allies. A hesitation hung in the night air, then the shapes surged skyward, vanishing into the night.

"I would wait for a signal from the Wizards before laying a keel," Julian finished, drawing a deep breath. Then he stared southwest toward Sea's

Edge. The three shapes that seconds ago had hovered overhead were now hurtling toward Merlin at Sea's Edge.

· X ·

Merlin seldom felt the need for sleep, though often he chose an hour before dawn to let his mind slip through the enchanted Gates of Dreams to investigate strange visions of the past or future. On this night, just two hours after midnight, the Wizard was fully awake, laboring in his topmost tower, one that looked out through glass paneled windows onto eight separate views of Sea's Edge. Great vat candles lit the tower's interior, providing an even light, except when sudden movements in the tower made those shadows shift and slant.

The Wizard was leaning over a broad basin that was filled with fluids that were darker than red wine, but wisps of steam hung over the waters, curling slowly from the basin's surface. Strangely, the vapor formed patterns, forming an inscription that read,

Wizard, your ally is almost healed. I can release him at any time now.

Merlin breathed air out and the wisps vanished, then again formed slowly to read,

Not yet, Lord. Other events transpire. Can you not feel the trembling?

Again, the wisps formed slowly, guided by the distant breath of Thoth.

The Mid-World of the Truce has been invoked. Guard yourself, Wizard.

Merlin nodded, then pushed himself back from the table that held the basin. Casually, as though whispering to himself, the Wizard summoned the first of several spells that reinforced the defenses of Sea's Edge. Then, because there was no longer any point in concealing his efforts, the great

Wizard called up the last of his devices, so that clusters of subordinate elementals, dominions, intelligences took up their posts around Sea's Edge.

Staring out into the night, Merlin watched the first of the arcs of light, dark hued, interwoven with seams of blue, then the second, gold and green, and the last of three, bright silver mixed with red. Merlin's mind considered the patterns that had been set before him:

The first creation reflects the power of the Mid-World, the child of grim Gods who have retained some sense of justice. The second, green and gold, has mixed the emblem colors of Dragon and Seraph, while the third contains silver elements of the Spirit Lords mixed with the red of Demon Princes. So, has the Mid-World of the Truce produced three great Sendings, or are these of a different order? The Sending, by its nature, has the impact of a sudden storm, but storms do not endure, so it may be that these are different creations, more permanent powers.

Distracted, somewhat puzzled, Merlin turned from his tower windows, and cast a film of dust over the same table that held the basin used to converse so discretely with Thoth. From the dust rose an image of Thorian; like Merlin, the Wizard was staring north toward the Vale of Whispers. Separated by distance, both Wizards were watching the same event, the distant birth of some new force.

Moments later the first concussion rolled over Sea's Edge; its impact was muffled, flattened by distance, and then followed by the equally diminished sounds of a second, then a third remote explosion. Merlin felt the distant hesitation, then came an abrupt decision, as the Godlings turned toward Sea's Edge, surging through the upper skies. A moment later, Merlin felt the distant communications from his closest servant, the eagle, the Eye of Merlin:

Our Portals are not challenged, the eagle sent, *and so Thorian can be at your side in a matter of seconds.*

That should not be necessary, Merlin replied. *Though the Gods are never evenhanded when dealing with the League, it is no longer in their interest to destroy our strongholds. Thorian should watch from a distance, however, for some new force of power is coming to Sea's Edge. You, too, should watch through my eyes, for they draw near.*

Shadowy forms hurtled through the night, surging over the headland, then with the chaos of magic meeting magic they smashed into the defenses of Sea's Edge. Lights flared and concussions rattled the glass panels of the tower. Energies surged back and forth, and Merlin felt his defenders give way, many drifting wounded into the night. Merlin gestured, and his invisible allies were released. Some slipped hastily away while others lingered out of curiosity or even the possibility of revenge. As they shifted, the Wizard quietly called upon a separate portion of the magic employed in his own defense.

Suddenly, Merlin was joined in the tower by three tall forms that stood ghostly, almost transparent, with mutating energies that shifted in turmoil within their unfinished figures. So slight were their forms that even the air of the tower was untroubled, and the vat candles illuminating the tower burned on with just the slightest of flickers.

"Unformed," Merlin murmured in astonishment, "unfinished Godlings. Why would your masters, the Great Gods, not have completed their work? And why have you sought me out?"

"Whispers of thought reach out to us," said one Godling with the darkest hues.

"And these whispers," added a second, a silvery red being that showed the first traces of a female form, "ask us, 'Why should the Wizard not train you, since the Godlings were created to save the Wizards from their doom.' So now, Wizard, you must show us all of your devices."

"Malice, pure malice," Merlin said, and if the Wizard was seldom surprised, here he was unable to conceal his astonishment.

"Mortal, you must respect the Gods," said the third Godling, and it lashed at Merlin with an array of gold and green radiances. As though linked to their brethren, the other two launched wild magic at Merlin, with blasting sounds echoing through the chamber. Suddenly, the Wizard's spell-shielding shuddered, then died, and the Wizard's form toppled to the floor, shook with spasms for a few heartbeats — and then it was still.

Wild shadows flashed and slanted briefly over the tower floors; then came stillness and silence as the Godlings stared down at the Wizard's corpse.

"What is this?" said the Godling that had lashed first at the Wizard. "What have we done?"

"This was not the thought we began with," said another, flopping the Wizard's body over with a tendril of force. Nothing was left of the Wizard but cloth covering skin and bones, and even as the Godlings watched, the Wizard's mass seemed to be lessening, as though decades of aging had become the process of a few seconds.

"Will the Gods now try to unmake us?" asked the third, staring into the darkness. "Must we now flee? This was not our plan."

"It was not your plan," came a voice from behind them. The three Godlings turned to find Merlin slipping through a seam in the air, whispering spell-words under this breath. "If there was a 'plan,' it involved having me expose all of my devices in order to train you; but the plan was pure malice, with little forethought."

"Wizard," said the being radiating a darkish blue color, "we know much about the magic of the Mid-World, but your sorcery was completely different. How were we deceived?"

"You have much to learn," the Wizard said, then he finished his incantation. "Here is magic you may recognize." And the three felt suddenly sluggish, slow, as though they moved no longer through the air, but swam through thickened water. Within each of their unfinished forms, both thought, and energy seemed suddenly, equally slow.

"Now," the Wizard continued, "how are you three named, and which of you leads?" Three unformed, sluggish beings seemed to glance at one another, then back to the Wizard.

"So, you have no names, no leader and no plans," Merlin said, turning away from them. "Return to me when more is known to you." As though compelled by powerful, invisible hands, the three found themselves forced back out into the night. They hovered in uncertainty for a moment, then drifted over the ocean at Sea's Edge. Above them, a clear starshine radiated pale light over their troubled forms. Power gradually returned to the three, and they fell to bickering, each blaming the others for their inability to control the Wizard. As Merlin watched from afar, lights flared and flashed, with each Godling testing its powers against the other two.

Those three Godlings are like children, dangerous children, the Wizard thought. *Or perhaps they should be compared to the offspring of basilisks, testing their destructive skills against one another, while showing great care not to fatally wound their brethren. Some of the Gods, at least, intended these to be allies of the Wizards, yet at present, they are far more dangerous to us than to the faraway Demon Princes. What am I to do with them?*

·)(·

At Khiva on the coast, the early summer air was filled with soft, moist warmth. Only the nights were cold, and the ocean kept a slight chill so that the frail and the aged, avoided swimming in it. The land curled around

Khiva, forming a natural deepwater harbor, one that had favored fisher folk, shipbuilders, and merchant traders long before the founding of the League.

In this setting, Kalanin began to learn the art of shipbuilding — and in many ways, he was learning more than he would ever have wished to know.

Each morning, Kalanin met with a council of craftsmen and navigators, discussing various design and construction techniques. Afternoons were spent assembling materials in sheds that were created for the building of boats. All through the long day, separate parties worked to clear the inner harbor. In the late afternoons, a group of armed guards stood a bored watch in the bright sun as Kalanin swam in the ocean beyond Khiva's seawalls.

After a brief meal with Géla, his evenings were devoted to studies of diagrams and other schemata. They had set aside a small dwelling for themselves and lived in modest comfort. From their topmost windows, Kalanin and Géla could see harbor waters, though their view of the eastern sunrise was blocked by the high walls of nearby warehouses. All their close friends and allies remained far from Khiva, organizing the rebuilt strongholds of the Wizards, so their evenings were quiet, and Kalanin was able to review his ship-building options long after the sun had set.

It was late one evening, three weeks into this process when Géla finally interrupted his routine. Carefully moving paper and parchment from the map table where Kalanin studied, she set two cups before them containing broths of herbs and spices, then sat across from him.

"So, is it true then?" she asked, favoring him with a slight, distant smile that suggested a caregiver visiting a slow witted, difficult patient.

Kalanin sipped his broth. "Of course, it is true. All charges are true, though it would help me if you could identify which of the many accusations we are discussing."

"They speculate that you have become so obsessed with detail that your studies of shipbuilding begin with dugouts made from hollowed logs and coracles that float upon the waters like the petals of spent flowers. People wonder how you could consider constructions made of reeds, and other flimsy craft, when a large, deep water war vessel is required, one that can slide easily through strong seas."

Kalanin looked into her eyes for a moment and smiled, feeling an enormous inner joy that he was with Géla, that he spent his nights beside her, and that she would bear their child. He also understood that beneath her half mocking interrogation, she was raising a serious question.

"Have you ever considered," he said, leaning back, "that when we come to study a process like metallurgy, or star gazing, or the naming of plants, that we can't review all the decisions that have led to that study's present state? We begin a hundred leagues into the journey and cannot retrace our steps to see whether better choices might have been made earlier in the quest."

She studied his eyes for a moment. "And now you have time, some breathing room, to look for obvious flaws in the shipbuilding of our time? That may be to the good. But you might also wish to consider our recent history. Do you not recall the great floating palaces favored by our arch-enemies, the Sorcerers?"

"It is generally considered that these huge galleys were coastal craft, easily shattered by the first great wave on the high seas. That's what all my fine builders and navigators tell me. But others have been sent to investigate these matters. They have located two of the designers of these crafts and either bribed or coerced the two back to Khiva. We should be speaking with them before week's end. Does that satisfy you?"

Géla smiled. "It does, and I will report back that Captain Hangnail is only slightly senile."

"Certainly, with my advanced years, I can use more guidance," Kalanin said, touching her hand. "Would you like to join our enterprise? The tales of the navigators are particularly confusing, and your insight would be most welcome."

Géla glanced away. "No, I think not. Already the reorganization of Khiva takes up most of my day, and as the resistance of the local elders and merchant princes fades, we can accomplish so much. By the end of next week, we hope to have the schools of Khiva again busy teaching their young. And this time of rebuilding feels, almost, like a time of peace, a respite from the struggles of the last few years."

The two rose and held each other for a long moment. "A time of peace," Kalanin murmured. "I wish it would go on forever, but it will not."

· ✕ ·

Julian emerged from their conjuring chamber in the South Tower carrying a rough sack made of jute, used by stone gatherers to carry rocks from the Plain of Gravengate. Within the sack were items of great value, both protected and concealed, though they clinked together as Julian hugged the wall fortifications, carefully avoiding the broad sunlight that poured over Gravengate.

The people of Gravengate were focused on their building tasks, so Julian was almost unnoticed as he slipped into a side entrance, and passed quickly down one set of stairs, then a steeper, darker staircase, one that coiled its way down to the chilled depths of the fortress. Wishing to avoid both the attention of the Wizards and the many eyes of the Mid-World, he made his way down into the deep foundations of Gravengate. Marids had destroyed the upper portions of the fortress, but down in the deepest base of the original fortress, the old, damp stonework remained.

In this deep place, Rafir and Sebastian had once spoken with the Ancient One, a Spirit Lord later liberated from the strife of earth. At least that much good was done, Julian thought, for first the Spirit Lord, and later, a great Lord of Dragons had broken free of the bounds of earth to seek the Maker in the starry universe.

He stared into the gloom; all traces of the Ancient One had vanished. From far above him came the *pick-pick-pick* sounds of men working to rebuild the stonework of the upper fortress. Bright sunlight was passing over the Plain of Gravengate, but at the deepest levels of the fortress, it was dark, cold, and still, lit only by the silvery grey glow of the werelight cast by Julian's staff.

Julian took a deep breath, withdrew a soft cloth from his rough sack, then began taking Balardi's devices from his sack, carefully spreading them over the soft surface of his cloth.

In the absence of Balardi, Julian was master of Gravengate. The great Wizard, however, had been healed, and would return to Gravengate before too many more days had passed — that was good because the League would be once again at full strength. On the other hand, Julian would again be reduced to a servant and advisor to the strong-willed Wizard. If there were old mysteries he needed to solve or some subtle work of magic he wished to accomplish on his own, only a few days remained to him.

He stared down at the Divination tools arrayed before him. Balardi was accounted the least of the three Wizards, but he was extremely powerful, and some of the devices that lay before Julian were so filled with latent energy that their use might be dangerous. He sorted: the remaining Crystal of Otherwhen might be linked through the other Crystals to Alcman; *The Game of the Masters* was disabled, leaving its talismans without power; a magic mirror contained a contrary intellect that obscured its insights, reporting to its master only in riddles, and Julian was not powerful enough to force his will over it, so that device, too, was set aside.

In the end, he was left with Balardi's single most powerful Divination tool. An onlooker might have seen nothing, but a poorly constructed or damaged table ornament — no more than two large hands in width, the device was constructed of layers of brass circles, the greatest at the bottom, smallest at the top; but the circles seemed to slip and slide, to overlap, and the bronze of the device was both dented and tarnished.

But within the Divination Talisman, a restless intelligence was beginning to stir.

Balardi had spoken briefly of the Talisman of concentric brass circles once before, only telling Julian that he was no longer willing to use it, because several Powers of the Mid-World had become aware of the Talisman and watched for its use. So, the Wizard had set it aside for a time, waiting for the watchers of the Mid-World to focus on other matters.

Julian closed his eyes and *reached*. He was alone; the many, searching eyes of the Mid-World were focused on the Godlings and their chaotic growth. No one was near — Julian sighed — no one was near except his Familiar, Sebastian, who was making his way slowly down a side passage, searching for Julian. No doubt an invisible fox was following just behind him as they slithered down an abandoned air shaft. The two were supposed to watch for messengers from Khiva, riders bringing lists of goods and craftsmen needed by Kalanin. But the two Familiars were so attuned to Julian's moods that they were hard to deceive.

Julian stood and backed away from the Talisman, letting the restless being within slip back into its dream world.

"Sebastian," he called out softly, "Rafir, that way is blocked. Go back to the top of the stairway, then I'll let you both in." Moments later, the three stood together at the deepest level of Gravengate, the Apprentice staring down with a mixture of pity and rebuke at his two Familiars who were covered in cobwebs and dust.

"Julian, we're sorry," Sebastian said, trying to groom his slender wings. "We thought you might need help, or at least some companionship later — you were going to look for your parents again, weren't you? You searched for them all those years, then you found them, only to be cut off again, so we thought we should be beside you."

Julian knelt and wiped webs and dust from the fur of his small allies, his friends. *These two are my real family, the family of a lone Apprentice,* he thought, *and the three of us are nothing but the playthings of greater powers.*

"Stay with me," Julian said, rising. "Keep just behind me and flee if my efforts fail. Sebastian, I don't think that I will ever again be able to speak with my mother or my father. The Powers have created such a great gulf between us. Perhaps, if by some miracle we survived, some benevolent God might again take pity on me.

"But for now, I seek something of much greater importance. I remember as though only moments have passed, how the Dreamers sat in their great Hall, and how they seemed to be part of the Maker's Design. Are they truly dead? Have they really entered the Temple of Waiting, there to drift endlessly with the other dead immortals until the end of time? A thought has slipped several times into my dreams: is Death then greater than the Maker's Will? We may learn the truth — or we might find ourselves in danger. So, the two of you must be ready to flee."

Julian sat once again in the grey gloom with the Talisman on a cloth that had been set on a stand in front of him. Sebastian was on his right, and Rafir on his left, each a little behind him. The stonework underneath the slender Familiars radiated a deep chill through their slight bodies, so they pushed closer to Julian, trying to share his warmth.

The Apprentice whispered *words.* Power surged toward the Talisman set before him and the restless entity within began to rouse itself. As a force of magic poured into the overlapping rings of the Talisman, all the silvery grey werelight in the deep regions of the fortress seemed to darken and the sounds of men hammering stone blocks grew fainter.

Coils of brass began to glow. An image formed above the Talisman, an image perhaps twice Julian's size, spectral, ghostly, of some creature that had once flown on night-black wings. A beaked mouth formed words, but no sounds came, until finally, a whisper reached them from a great distance, as though a dead thing spoke.

"So long asleep, Wizard, why have I slept so long? That was never part of our pact." The being with dark wings had eyes that gleamed amber and glared at Julian, "and yet you are not the Wizard. Have you overthrown the Master? But no, you have nothing like the master's strength."

Julian leaned forward. "I am only Balardi's ally and servant — as you are. Our master will return to Gravengate in a brief time. I know nothing of your pact or the forces that guide you, but now I need your aid, Being of the Talisman. Will you help me?"

Talons of the ghostly image began to twitch and dark wings to beat. "I am Atâh," the voice murmured, "a force within the Mid-World and no plaything of a simple Mage. Why should I not seek to destroy you and free myself?"

Julian grasped his staff with both hands and summoned power to himself. "Atâh, I must open my mind to you so you can see all that has transpired. Atâh, know this: I am not mighty, but note how many times *The Web of Fate* has cast its strands around me and yet failed to ensnare me. I do not believe that my doom lies here in this chamber."

Damp mists of cold filled Julian's mind, and he drew in a soft, deep breath. Linked to Atâh, he could feel the spectral creature recoil in shock. After, there came a moment of silence, when the gloom seemed to lessen and the three beings still fully alive at the base of the fortress could again hear the muffled sounds of work on the ramparts.

"Ancient Secrets," the ghostly voice whispered, "greater than anything previously imagined. Who might have guessed that one *Ancient Secret*, the

Hall of the Dreamers, would be employed to reveal a second, the Isle of the Demons? And then that the Hall itself was itself cast down by the Demon Princes inhabiting the Isle. Who are you, young master, to be involved in such momentous events?"

"You have seen the work of powerful forces beyond *The Web of Fate,*" Julian said softly, "and that I am only a catalyst used by these great powers." Within the shadowy energy projected by the Talisman, the wings of Atâh had subsided, and Julian relaxed his grip upon his staff.

"Even *The Web of Fate* is only a component of *The Game of the Masters*," Atâh murmured, in a voice that was less hoarse, more intense, "and *The Game of the Masters* is itself undone. Apprentice with an Adept's power, you have become enmeshed in forces that lie within the innermost core secrets of the Mid-World of the Truce."

"Then aid me now, Atâh. Let us see together what became of the Dreamers. After, I will do what I can to assist you."

"I would wish to be free," came the hollow voice, "to again be a Power, surging through the night on my own dark wings, and see with my strong sight events that have eluded even the Gods, yet it comes to me now that I am not truly alive, that within this Talisman is only an echo of the being that was once Atâh. And so, I might wish for a new life drawing on the power radiating from the Isle of the Demons.

"Yet, you are doomed, Apprentice — you will never survive your journey to the enchanted Isle. If the doomed can bring gifts to those partially alive, I ask only that you speak for me on Judgment Day. Speak for Atâh who once lived, surging through the shadows on night-dark wings."

"I swear it," Julian said. "If I have thoughts that can be formed, and a voice that can be raised, I will speak for you, Atâh."

"Then, behold," Atâh said. Images flared before them — of a sunless land ruled by the grey gloom of twilight. Just some distance before them stood an enormous building with many spires and towers formed of grey granite: the Temple of Waiting. As though gathered into a Dream Quest, Julian and his small allies were drawn into this vision.

Outside the Temple Gates stood Alanthéa, the Tree of Heaven, radiating sentient light into the gloom. Six ghostly forms circled the tree, forms that had once seemed so filled with might and majesty in the Hall of the Dreamers — Orissa, great Seeress; Nablus, binder of Creatures Indomitable; Hestaur, forerunner of the Wizards; Voll, Elf-Lord, and powerful Mage; Llara, great among the Spirit Lords; and Voritar, Prince of Demons.

Yet now as their vision drew them closer, Julian saw that the Dreamers stared vacantly into nothingness, with dead eyes that no longer gleamed with wisdom and power. And as Julian watched their images, the six shades drifted, light as feathers, away from gleaming Alanthéa, the Tree of Heaven, and passed through the gates into the Temple of Waiting. Death had claimed the Dreamers.

"Enough," Julian said, turning aside, "enough, for they are dead things, and we are all lost." But his night vision was not complete, for Julian was drawn beyond the ghostly shades of the Dreamers into the Temple of Waiting, and within, Julian felt a panic arise in his body, as though he had been buried alive beneath ten thousand tons of stone. Around him, the shades of dead immortals drifted endlessly — Demons, Dragons, Spirit Lords, Seraphs, hybrid Godly creatures, Elf-Lords — all filled with a remote sadness that was completely without pain. Julian the Apprentice stood in the middle of a great Cathedral of Sorrows, vast in height and depth, built upon a foundation of many stone crypts.

Yet now, as the Dreamers entered the Temple of Waiting, all the dead immortals halted their endless drifting, to behold the entry of Dreamers with their vacant eyes. One of the last, great echoes of the Maker's work had come to an end, and a single voice was raised in song, vaulting through the Temple's uppermost domes, singing with such sorrow that even dead immortals wept, though they could no longer understand the reasons for their tears.

Julian stood, head bowed, filled with sorrow and disbelief. He closed his eyes and willed himself far from his dream quest. When he felt again the soft damp air of the foundations of Gravengate, he drew a deep breath; and saw suddenly that they were not — or perhaps had never been — alone: one of the unformed Godlings now stood before him. The Gift within Julian flashed danger, and the Apprentice again gripped his staff with both hands.

"You should not fear me, Apprentice," the Godling said softly, and if its substance had become more solid, even now it was filled with a turmoil of red and silver energies. Vaguely feminine, its shoulders now held hints of a flowing cloak, and its eyes were as grey as a Wizards, touched by hazel.

"I have been warned, Godling," Julian said, eyes glancing around the dark chamber. Atâh had vanished, as had Rafir, while a fluttering, nervous Sebastian now came to rest on Julian's right shoulder. "Thorian has described you three as unformed, potential allies of great strength, though still a danger to us while you learn the powers of your own Godhood."

"That is why I have come, Apprentice, to learn. My brothers have reasoned that as I show feminine aspects, I would be more filled with empathy, and so I have become their ambassador to mortals. We, the Godlings, need to understand all your complexities. Apprentice, why for example, are you filled with such sorrow? Has your own mayfly lifetime ended? Why otherwise would you weep?"

Julian stood silent for a moment. The Godling towered over him, powerful, yet completely unfinished, radiating uncertainty.

"The Hall of the Dreamers has been destroyed," Julian said at last. "One of the great pillars of the Maker's Will no longer exists — I might speak to you of the Dreamers, how they once seemed so mighty in their Hall, but it might be best to ask Atâh to show you —" Before Julian could continue, a shudder rippled through the Godling's form.

"My Brother!" the Godling called out. "The Wizards call to me! My reckless brother is about to ruin us — again! No! He must not —" And the Godling leaped away in panic flight, passing through the damp stone of Gravengate into the high blue skies of Gravengate, then surging toward Khiva and the coast.

· ✠ ·

The great wave towered over him, hovering, then it crashed down. At the last second, Kalanin dove through, and all the thrashing turmoil of the ocean passed behind him and he surged beyond the surf-line, then dove again. Storms had destroyed the great saltwater predators that had once ruled Alantéa's coastline, but as the land healed, the ocean again teamed with life — crabs tumbled through saltwater undertows, while slight, silvery fish darted away from him, down through sandy waters into clumps of yellow and green seaweed.

Overhead, broad sunlight poured over bored, sweating guards. Most stood silent, while a few talked among themselves of inns and chilled ales, watching as their powerful though strange captain again challenged the strong waters of the coast. Only three of the fifteen guards had heard vague tales of Kalanin's role in the struggles of the League, but even those three were dreaming of rest, and ale, and of a time of peace that would follow the League's long struggles.

Not one guard looked up as a strange darkish shadow passed overhead. Several guards did note that Kalanin was returning at full speed, while others were surprised into awareness, watching as their captain raced toward them, and took up his sword.

"Make yourselves ready," Kalanin panted, "but do not draw weapons until I say so." He turned back toward the ocean; sword still sheathed. Where the ocean met the sand, the Godling who radiated darkness had settled over the shoreline, and now drifted toward them, taller and far more powerful than the combined force of sixteen humans standing before it.

And I hold nothing but metal, Kalanin thought, *while even the Tarnished Sword might be powerless against this being.*

"Hail, Lord," Kalanin called out across the sands. "Welcome once again to the Wizards' League." The figure said nothing, only drifting over wet sands, form filled with menace.

"Lord," Kalanin tried again, "perhaps it has not been explained to you, but the Wizards rule this land, and you should tell them of your needs, for there is little that we of Khiva can do to assist you."

The Godling loomed over Kalanin and his guards. "What you can do is to worship me, Giftless mortals. It is the way of Alantéa, that fleeting mortals with their mayfly lives must fawn and fall before the Undying Gods, and so shall you, mortals."

"Lord, whoever instructed you on this subject is an adversary of the League and is using you as a weapon against our alliance. Was not your role to be that of an ally, to grow in power and join with us in our great struggle against Demon Princes, and Sorcerers, and Marids?"

"There is a certain consistency to your logic," the Godling said, as though mildly surprised. "Nevertheless, if you will not fawn and fall, you may simply fall." The Godling gestured and the guards fell stricken to the ground. "Or you may stand and die — it means nothing to me."

Suddenly, Kalanin could not breathe; his chest would not draw air. He dropped his sword, clutching his throat with both hands as he stared at his deadly foe, a Godling only partly formed, and so very, very ignorant. *Géla, I'm so sorry. This is such a stupid place to die, a senseless way to die. Please live on, don't give up, please live on....*

A Portal with a huge arch burst over the wet sands, with warfare shuddering through its sorcerous energies. *One of the Wizards,* Kalanin thought, *and the perverse Gods will not let him through.* He fell to the ground and began to crawl from the Godling, darkness crowding his mind.

Overhead, forms were shimmering in the sky, then warfare swept over the beaches as though a second Godling had come and now fought with the first Godling.

Another convulsion of power surged through the upper skies — was that a third so-called Godling? It didn't matter much to a dying man, and so Kalanin crawled away. Voices seemed to be calling out to him...was that Dargas? Baroda? The soft voice of the Mistress of Illusions? Thrashing, he rolled, and as his back struck sand, the slightest wisp of breath slipped into his lungs, as he gasped, thrashing again, fighting for slivers of air.

Then Thorian was through, his Portal collapsing behind him. One flash of Thorian's hand released Kalanin and his guards so they could breathe again. As they gasped, Thorian spoke five words in a voice of doom, and buffets of power struck the three Godlings like backhanded slaps from a Giant. The Godlings' own magic was suddenly extinguished — flashfires blown away by a storm. The three Powers hovered in hesitation, then began haphazard drifting motions downward toward the Wizard.

Kalanin struggled to his feet and began pulling guardsmen from the ground — but two of them no longer breathed and could not be revived.

His chest and lungs ached, and an old rage stirred inside him, but Kalanin forced himself to walk across the beaches toward the Wizard and his wayward Godling allies. From long habit, he retrieved his sword but held the useless weapon at his side.

Where the ocean met the sand, three abashed Godlings stood sheepishly before a Wizard who struggled to control his anger.

"For a second time," the Wizard said in low tones, though his words lashed like whips, "twice, these three Godlings have been turned against us. There must not be, there will *not* be, a third." Thorian's hands clenched in what seemed anger, but when they opened again, they were filled with scrolls of ancient parchments, rolled, and bound and sealed.

"Here are the words I have been instructed to speak," Thorian continued. "Godlings, it may be that we, the Wizards, are partly at fault for neglecting your guidance. Therefore, we have arranged, through benevolent Gods, that the Elf-Kindreds school you in the ways of the Mid-World of the Truce. The Kindreds maintain embassies in many, even most of the courts of the Powers; with their aid, and as your own strength grows, so also will your knowledge of the Mid-World. Take these scrolls as talismans and pacts with the Kindreds. When next we meet, it will be as equals, at least in power and in knowledge of the Mid-World."

Gravely, Thorian reached up and passed scrolls to each Godling. Despite his pain and anger, Kalanin forced himself to walk toward Thorian and stand beside the Wizard. The two watched as the Godlings drifted away, reciting parchment inscriptions to one another before drifting again upward into blue skies.

Captain and Wizard stood nearly the same height, but they were so unlike that they might have belonged to different species.

As the Godlings slipped skyward, Thorian drew a deep breath, and his jaws unclenched. "And so, Captain-General of the League, did those sound like my words, those spoken to the Godlings?"

"Truthfully, they sounded like Merlin's," Kalanin said, and suddenly he wished for Géla, for Géla and wine, and to be far from the shore.

"They were indeed Merlin's. While some Power plotted and planned its malice against us, I watched my daughter Eléna, trapped in the Isle of the Demons, as she fought and died for the seventh time. Has she an eighth life? Perhaps, but these enchanted lifetimes are finite, and one day she will pass forever into the Long Sleep...."

Thorian drew a second deep breath. "Now, as to shipbuilding. All your explorations have opened my eyes and those of Merlin's; we now see more clearly what must come. Your own warship's design, large as you perceive it, will need to be more than twice as great. Six large chambers must be constructed within our sole vessel — conjuring rooms for each Wizard and each Godling, or Godlike being. Smaller quarters for two warriors and a lone Apprentice should be built higher, near the ship's upper deck. Provisions, such as food, are required for only..." Thorian stared into the distance as though studying an infinitely distant horizon, "six humans, and the two small Familiars of the Apprentice. The Eye of Merlin always hunts for itself in fair weather or in foul."

"You will seek to man this warship solely by magic?" Kalanin asked.

Thorian grimaced in what might have passed for a smile. "You and I have seen how both flesh and magic may each, alone, easily be undone. No, we will not man your warship by magic alone. You will see."

Thorian gestured; a Portal with a huge arch burst over the sands, and before he passed through, he turned to Kalanin. "Only one Mid-World Power remains as our adversary. Merlin must deal with that God. As for you, Captain-General of the League, you must heal. Heal quickly and build your warship at your topmost speed. Balardi has returned. Events now flow with the swift motions of quicksilver."

Chapter Five

Defending the Wizards' League

WEEKS PASSED. A BLAZING summer heat swept over the southern coastline of Alantéa. Shipbuilders and craftsmen flocked to Khiva and the coast, while provisions and building supplies reached the port city by both sea and land. After a well-armed raiding party attacked the city's outlying docks, Harlond led two full tiers totaling a thousand men from Gravengate to supplement the guardsmen of Khiva.

Kalanin maintained his shipbuilding routines during the long daylight hours, but many evenings he would sleep a few hours then rise late at night to check the watches that protected the huge shipbuilding loft and the warship within. When he was satisfied that the watches were intact, Kalanin would slip through the darkness, exploring Khiva's winding streets. On these forays, he was accompanied by two young guardsmen, both chosen for their swift strength, their quiet movements, and their ability to follow Kalanin as their Captain passed almost unseen through the shadows, as Kalanin watched, listened, or sometimes only stared silently up into the night sky.

On this night Kalanin again studied the night watch, looking for secretive motions, for faces that could not be recognized, or movements within the long buildings housing the warship. All seemed well at the shipyards, but then noises reached him from a distance: trouble was again rising between the guardsmen of Khiva and the soldiery of Gravengate.

He passed back into the shadows, then raced toward the disturbance, his bodyguards not ten paces behind. As he neared the waterfront, he slipped silently into a darkened alley and stood, listening in silence. Flurries of dark motion passed back and forth across the alley's mouth. Loud noises were followed by curses, breaking glass, and the sounds of fists pounding flesh, then the thud of bodies falling. Fighting spilled out from waterfront inns onto the long quays, followed by splashes as bodies toppled into murky harbor waters.

Raw wine, Kalanin thought, *plus heat, stirred by fantasies about tavern wenches — and boredom. At least their wounds had been few, and no one had died, not yet.* Shouts rang out as the night watch raced toward the fight, and the brawlers sped from the quays and the inn, fleeing back up into the hillside and the winding upper streets of the city. One man darted into the alley, passing close to Kalanin, not seeing his war leader's cloaked form in the shadows. Kalanin was tempted to reach out, to grasp the man by his throat and to ask him how his night's efforts could possibly be helping their League to survive.

Instead, he slipped further back into the shadows, shaking his head, judging that Harlond should deal with them. He listened for a few moments as peace was restored, and his own breathing slowed. Then he returned to his dwelling, to seek at least half a night's sleep. As he settled in beside Géla, she stretched, as though she had lain awake for some time.

"Listen to them," she murmured. On a distant stretch of the waterfront, more trouble had broken out. Their windows faced south to the ocean and east toward the city's walls, so it was impossible to tell whether trouble had arisen between rival guilds, craftsmen from distant cities, or the guards again.

"It's late now," Kalanin said softly. "The worst of the troublemakers will be asleep in a short while, as we should." He lay on his side next to her, one arm embracing Géla and the child within her. Both of their faces were turned toward the south window that frequently brought traces of ocean breezes into their room.

"My beloved," Géla said. "I am awake not because of this night's disturbances, but because there are things you have not yet said to me, things you may wish to say, but are still unwilling to speak. Here, beyond midnight, perhaps you should talk to me."

Kalanin nodded; Géla knew him too well. "The Godlings have passed far from League soil, and Balardi has healed," he began. "The Wizards now become far more interested in the crafting of our warship. Diagrams, sketches, notes, all appear daily on my worktable."

"And so?"

Kalanin sighed. "And so, our cargo includes provisions for only six humans."

"Six means — three Wizards, Julian, Galad, and you." Géla turned and stared at Kalanin with fierce eyes. "Were I soft, I would weep — and the child within me would weep, too. You believe that by leaving me behind, that you protect me, but think clearly on this. Might I not be safer on board your enchanted vessel? After you depart, will I be left to breathe new life into a remnant of the League? In this festival of malice celebrated by Dark Gods, assassins will claim both me and our child, while those considered 'benign' Gods all sigh and shrug and return to their many diversions. Have you thought this far?"

"I could not set sail believing you and our child in mortal danger. Yes, we have thought that far."

"So, promises have been extracted from those Gods you mostly trust, or perhaps factions of the Tanu warriors or Sidhe knights will form a guard for me. My beloved, these are barriers of thin straw against the fierce, malicious flames of those who greatly desire our deaths."

"We have thought the same thoughts you have — and perhaps a few more. Now, my lady, lie on your side again and we will speak a few more words...there...." A slight breeze rustled the thin curtains covering their south facing window. "You know that you cannot go on this voyage; deep down you understand, and you also know we will find some way to shield you. In perhaps ten days you will again feel comforted."

Géla stirred. "Am I a child to be soothed by future promises? Tell me now."

"Patience. We will know more in a brief time. But there is a second thing unspoken in my mind. Did you not sense another concealed thought?"

"Hmm...no, only one, and that thought I guessed."

"Here is the second hidden matter," Kalanin said. "Three nights ago, by an owl's light beneath the slightest sliver of a moon, I saw a familiar face, nothing more than a flicker in passing, of one who would not be seen unless he wished it. Who might that have been?"

"Likely Rostov," Géla said, "also known as 'The Wily.' Does his presence confirm your worries that Khiva is still at risk?"

"I fear so. Thorian said that one Power, at least, still actively conspires against us. Interesting, though, that Rostov wished to be seen by me, and me alone, and not to have his presence otherwise known, except by you, my beloved, from whom I can keep no secrets."

"If you had secrets," Géla said, "I would worm them from you as easily as I drew the others from you on this night." Then, with the curtains gently rustling and her husband's strong arm around her, she forced an end to the restless uncertainty inside her mind, and she slept.

· X ·

"The Wizard has always had a soft spot for us," Sebastian said. "If we come with you, perhaps he won't be as difficult."

"I was asked to come alone," Julian said. "Anyway, I will apologize for using his devices, then Balardi will grumble and mutter for a time, and after, we will speak of other things. Don't worry." He reached down and ruffled the soft fur of the fox. "This once, Rafir, it's better not to follow me. I think I'll be more relaxed if I'm alone."

The fox stopped his endless grooming and looked up. "I'll behave — though it's hard." Julian touched each of his small allies, left the chamber, descending a half flight of stairs, moving swiftly through a narrow passage, then he climbed three flights to reach the parapets of the upper fortifications. Outside in the sunlight, Balardi was waiting for him. The Wizard had returned, fully healed, all his powers intact, and yet he seemed preoccupied, remote, as though his thoughts were focused on matters far from Gravengate.

Julian took a deep breath and passed from the shadowed corridor out into the slanting sunlight of late afternoon. All the afternoon's clouds had been shuffling southwest, so the sky overhead was a brilliant blue. Instead of the difficult reception Julian anticipated, Balardi smiled at his young ally, then led Julian to a small side table that had been set in the upper ramparts, together with two chairs. Strangely, and most unlike Balardi, a crystal beaker of sparkling white wine had been set on the table, with two freshly polished silver goblets.

They sat in silence for a moment, the sun radiating warmth down upon them. Balardi poured wine for each of them, then sipped from his goblet, staring out over the Plain of Gravengate, where many hundreds toiled through the long afternoon to restore the fortress and the ruined lands surrounding it.

"First of all, Balardi, my Master and great patron," Julian began, "I must apologize for the use of your devices while you healed. It was senseless of me, and I should have waited for your return."

Balardi smiled. "What you did was entirely right — in my absence, Gravengate was yours to command. At any rate, that is not why we are here."

"Please don't be too generous, my Wizard Master. I will feel even more guilty later."

"Indeed, I have been too *un*generous," Balardi said. "Healing slowly, lying powerless, all the events of my long lifetime churning through my mind, I most regretted how I dealt with allies, with those closest to me."

"You have always dealt fairly with us, more than fairly," Julian said, feeling a strange discomfort.

"Justly, perhaps, but never generously." From within his cloak, Balardi drew a parchment scroll — one much smaller and far less ornate than those passed to the Godlings. "Sip wine first. Relax for a moment if you can, while we share the serenity of Gravengate's skyline together."

Balardi, my Wizard Master, have you truly healed? Julian took a deep breath, then glanced to the horizon, where giant billows of white puffy clouds were casually sliding southwest toward Khiva, and Merlin at Sea's Edge. On the Plain of Gravengate, the slanting sun used the complex lines of the fortress to create interesting shadow patterns on the dust of the ruined Plain. Julian studied light and shadow as he sipped wine, and let his mind relax in the silence that followed.

"First," Balardi continued, "events are drawing you to Khiva and the coast. You must leave at daybreak, leading a war party of nearly three hundred. I will speak no more of your errand, for when you begin your journey you will understand its purpose.

"Secondly," Balardi pushed the parchment over to Julian, "I have named you as my heir and fellow ruler of Gravengate. How I wish this act were more than an empty gesture! I have no legacy, no great gifts to pass to you, Julian, my great ally, and foster son! In a brief time, we must journey to the Isle of the Demons. Not even the most drug-addled Goblin Soothsayer could foretell our safe return. That was one of my greatest regrets, as I lay healing, that I had not shared governance with you in better times."

Julian felt a great wave of affection for his old mentor, his patron, and ally. "My Wizard Master, I will always be your pupil, your servant, your ally. I will now also be your foster son. May my own birth parents see this moment from afar, for their own generous hearts would be filled with joy."

Master and Apprentice rose to embrace for a moment, then sat facing the slanting sun. "I have not permitted wine to affect me for over a hundred years," Balardi said, "but tonight I will drift into the darkness comforted by wine. Sit with me for a time, until sunset, then you must prepare yourself again for danger." Balardi fell silent, sipping, staring out over Gravengate where many workers toiled on, though others were beginning to slip away to their evening meals.

"I have always thought of myself as fearless, indomitable," the Wizard continued, "but Death's reminder, Death's tap upon my shoulder, has made me reconsider all matters, and I have become nostalgic." He pulled his chair back from the parapet, to face the broad stone floors and the ramparts that lay beyond.

"Let me show you." Balardi waved his hand, a casual gesture as though brushing a small curl of smoke aside: images flashed over the stonework, showing workrooms and laboratories that had once lain at the foundations of Gravengate.

"Here is what I might once have bequeathed to you as my heir. Consider how many decades the Wizards labored apart from one another, communicating only by devious means. Working alone, I created scores of crafty devices, things of magic, with so many different purposes."

Julian peered into the image and saw darkened storerooms and alcoves where strange devices glowed, or shuffled, or whispered in the darkness, ready to be activated at a signal from their creator, Balardi.

"In the end, I decided," Balardi continued, "as did Thorian and Merlin, that it was far more important to have sorcery at my fingertips than to have stored things of magic readied for the unknown. Now, they are gone, all gone, each of them so lovingly crafted...but see how they rose to defend me when I was most beset, long ago, here in this very citadel."

Now the image showed the Wizard's devices rising in wrath, flashing lights in the darkness, calling alarms, or groaning aloud. The Wizard stared at them across a gulf of many years, then waved his hand, so that the images faded, but they passed slowly, as though Balardi was reluctant to let the memories of his old magical devices depart.

"And here," the Wizard brightened again, "here was Gravengate at its full strength, how it might have been had one of my old servants and allies been named my heir. How I wish I might have done this for you!"

Images flared in front of them, showing the Gravengate of old: untarnished, lush plains filled with farms, orchards, and vineyards. Within the image, men of Gravengate had assembled outside the fortress, legions of them clashing shields and swords together in celebration, while the Balardi of old presented an unnamed Mage to the throng outside the walls. Across the years, and the gulf of might-have-beans, Julian could hear the echoes of the throng, and even now Julian was stirred by their celebrations.

"And so, it might have seemed, had Wylar or Orantes been named your heir," Julian said softly.

Balardi's eyes showed the slightest hint of surprise. "Or even..." his fingers flashed, and letters flickered on the pavement in letters of fire — ***Sentauris*** — but so quickly did the inscription vanish that the word might have been only a reflection from a flash of light passing through the upper skies.

The two sat together through the sunset, Balardi's mood softened by wine, as the Wizard recounted the long, lonely struggle of the League. At dusk, when Julian rose to depart, Balardi reached out, touching his cloak, and spoke directly into Julian's mind.

Forgive me, but I have used your invisible ally, the fox, to stow a few small objects into your saddle pouch. You will see how they might be needed, and what they might accomplish. Every word spoken to you on this night has been the truth — except for the abandonment by the Wizards of hidden devices of magic. Farewell, my wonderful, adopted son! We will meet again at Khiva.

Strangely, all the softness created by wine had vanished from the Wizard's voice as he spoke into Julian's mind.

·)(·

The cloud patterns that Julian and Balardi had watched from a distance, had by nightfall reached Khiva and the coast. As Kalanin resumed his restless nighttime prowling, the sky overhead was dark; only distant lamplights down by the long quays could be seen as Kalanin and his two bodyguards passed through the shadows.

Far out over the ocean, a different weather system ruled the skies, and tiny radiances flickered and flared as lightning flashed over dark ocean swells. For Kalanin, the distant storm mirrored the flash and flare of danger inside his mind: he understood that the malice of at least one Dark God was again reaching toward Khiva.

Lightning, made so tiny by distance, flared again. No sounds reached him, either from the usual disorder of the dockside inns or from the distant storm. With hand motions, he called his two bodyguards to his side, whispering careful instructions to each: *As quietly as possible, rouse the sleeping guardsmen to support those protecting Géla. You must watch the watchers, for treachery is reaching again into the heart of Khiva. No, do not be concerned about me — I am moving to higher ground, so I can see, though not be touched, by night skirmishers. Go. Be wary.*

As his unhappy bodyguards raced quietly away into the night, Kalanin shifted silently through one dark street, passing cautiously over uneven paving stones, through a darkened alley, then into a wide square. As he made his way toward the upper hills of Khiva, the dim lighting from the harbor grew even less bright, though occasionally torches flickered from inner courtyards, lights maintained by drowsy servants while their masters slept.

Just a few streets higher was a vantage point, one with stone walls to guard his back. He sped up, noting that his struggles with the ocean surf had made his breathing stronger and his body more fluid.

Hints of motion could be sensed in the darkness. He hunched down, racing through the now-closed, so-called "Goblin Market," with all its shuttered stalls, then passed higher through winding, curved lanes. The slightest of breezes made wind chimes tinkle softly, and now also the muffled sounds of footsteps grew closer as men raced through the darkness.

Suddenly a large form loomed beside him. An arm reached out and Kalanin was swept from his feet, sliding over slate pavements. He pulled free, rolling twice, ready to rise with his sword in hand.

"Down! Stay down!" a voice hissed out of the darkness — a voice Kalanin recognized. He rolled again, drawing his sword, but he stayed down. Arrows lashed overhead. Cries of rage and terror surged through the night. Torches flared, two streets distant. Then horns sounded, with more arrows leaping from the darkness a short distance away, but these were arrows aimed at night stalking assassins, and they struck flesh.

"Rostov has them," Galad said, then he reached down to pull Kalanin to his feet. "Captain Hangnail — or is it now Admiral Hangnail? You proved to be far more fleet of foot than I expected, though fortunately, Rostov was right when he predicted that you would seek your hilltop overlook."

Kalanin embraced Galad. "It's good to be beside you again — we last met as strangers in the darkness of Erivan Forest, did we not? Yet then I had a much clearer sense of the struggle. What is happening?"

"Assassins," Galad murmured. "Listen...." Some distance away came muffled thrashing and choking sounds. "Now transformed into dead assassins. It was agreed beforehand that they would not live out this night. Tonight, their corpses will hang within the city walls, but tomorrow their bodies will be a feast for carrion crows well beyond the city gates."

"Assassins...after the Fall of the Dreamers," Kalanin murmured, "we thought that the Gods and all their dark devices would depart from the League and leave us to begin our astonishing, almost hopeless tasks."

"All but one Power," Galad replied. "Merlin suggested that we come here, and Merlin will need to deal with that remaining Power. Now, master shipbuilder, Admiral Hangnail, whatever you are called in this charming seaside village, all this has been hot, dry, thirsty work, but if you can rouse some besotted innkeeper, a flagon of wine would be suitable, and then I would like to see your ship."

Lame excuses of darkness and lateness came to Kalanin's mind, but he brushed them aside. "We'll send word to Géla, then find us some wine, and after, you have certainly earned a brief look at our warship."

Later, Galad's thirst partly quenched, they paced in the darkness around the enormous keel of the ship, *Alantéa the Forerunner*. Their journey around the warship's skeleton took them more than a few minutes. In a darkness offset only by their two torches, not much detail could be seen, but the sheer size of the vessel left the glib tongue of Galad almost speechless.

"It seems...somehow...overly large."

Kalanin took the wine flask from Galad's hands, drank deeply, then murmured, "When I look at it through your eyes, I see a warship manned by hundreds of warriors, prepared to carry brutal, flaming battle to the Isle of the Demons. Instead, we will have provisions for only six humans, three Wizards and their servants, and most of the ship's space will be dedicated to conjuring chambers — I think of these as spaces where spells are weaved, where Wizards and Godlings will train themselves throughout our journey. They will never be the equal of Demon Princes, but they hope to greatly increase their powers over the course of this voyage."

"And, I suppose," Galad muttered, "the three less majestic humans, and their pets, the two Familiars, will be stashed well below-decks, in dank, dark and dingy quarters."

Kalanin drank more wine before replying. "Our quarters will be a bit less grim than those you mention, but certainly smaller than those of our far more powerful companions."

· 𝕏 ·

In dreams, Julian drifted over the shipbuilding loft that housed the huge warship. The building itself was several times greater than the warship, hundreds of paces long, guarded at night by several watches. And even the watches were being inspected — on this night, Galad was studying the night watch from an overlook above the loft. So, Galad had been drawn to Khiva, as Julian himself and the warriors supporting him were being drawn.

In his night vision, Julian's ghost form passed into the loft. In the darkness, the long keel of the warship seemed endless, vanishing only into shadows and gloom. The ship's skeleton lay flat on the ground on either side of its keel — assembled but not yet raised to the ship's sides. In the corners of the loft, mounds of sawdust had been pushed together for removal in the morning. Anything — a spark, a few men with axes — could gravely damage the warship's progress. No wonder the shipbuilding loft was so closely guarded!

In his dream vision, Julian sensed the intrusion of a second dream visitor. He turned swiftly but saw nothing except a shadow of some powerful onlooker who radiated a dark, untamed malice; it was time to break free.

He woke with a start, then sat bolt upright, glancing quickly in every direction: their twin watchfires were alight not fifty paces from his sleeping roll. Overhead, stars shimmered under the haze of a summer night. All around him, members of their war party lay sleeping, except for the night watch gathered around the fires. Three days into their journey from Gravengate, they had made camp in a soft hillock, one cleared of tall growth, with fields all around them, except for a few distant, dark stands of trees.

Suddenly, Rafir blinked into view.

"Sebastian said you would be awake," the fox whispered.

Julian touched the soft fur of the fox, then stood. "As I become wiser in the ways of magic, every year it becomes a little more difficult to surprise me." Even while asleep, Julian wore a pouch lashed to his waist, and as he rose, he reached inside, touching each of the three packets Balardi had slipped into his baggage.

Here I stand, Julian thought, *the one called "Maker-Touched Summoner," but truly only a lesser force, an Apprentice with an Adept's power. Here I stand in all my weakness. Come now if you are still intent on destroying us.* The stars blinked down. Watchfires crackled. Sleepers began twisting and turning with dreams that had become very strange.

Suddenly, a great arched Portal burst into existence just beyond the watchfires. Julian raced toward it, but before his third step touched the ground, a second Portal surged over their campground, just to the left of the first. Beings of power hovered beyond the Portals' mouths, mounted, spectral, calling aloud in harsh, muffled voices.

Julian ran, hurled a packet into one Portal, spun, raced again, and hurled a second into the other opening.

Blasts hurled him from his feet, lifting him into the air then smashing him to the ground. But as he struck earth, both Portals collapsed upon themselves. With their watchfires blown dead, darkness again surged over him, and Julian lay on the ground, slowly gathering his breath. Rafir was first at his side, then Sebastian was whispering into his ear, and finally, Julian was helped to his feet by a tall, dark-haired woman warrior, one who had once served the Mistress of Illusions.

"That was an astonishing moment, Apprentice," she commented. "We had no idea that you had become so powerful." *Balardi saved us,* Julian thought, *but perhaps that understanding is best unspoken because another Portal bursting over our landscape might just ruin us.*

He looked carefully around the clearing, searching for any further hints of danger, though all that could be seen were figures huddled together, speaking of the night's troubles, while others were settling back into periods of sleep that had been so abruptly disturbed.

Julian was traveling toward Khiva with a core, incorruptible force of the League: a remnant of only three hundred, nearly half of them woman warriors who once served Géla's grandmother, the Mistress of Illusions: the other three-fifths, Grey Men of the Dragon's Teeth, who now owed their allegiance to Kalanin. These would form the core of a bodyguard that would protect Géla and her child. In the aftermath of the League's great, virtually hopeless thrust at the Isle of the Demons, mother and child might be left as the last frail hope of the League, and now they would be properly defended.

· 𝕏 ·

On the same night through Gates of Dreams, the Mind of Merlin walked beside a tall, powerful Wraith figure, one more than three times the Wizard's height. The shadowy substance of the Wraith trembled with rage, but somehow it seemed compelled to remain at the Wizard's side. Within this portion of the Dreamways, the two drifted along the banks of a dark river, whose sluggish currents made only the slightest of murmurs. Overhead, a lone pale star shone down — a reminder of lost, forgotten starlight. On the banks of the river lay the broken timbers of an enormous, ruined warship. Merlin understood that in the dream visions he shared with the Wraith, that the being beside him greatly desired the destruction of the warship Alantéa, and yet the Wizard was not dismayed.

"*You will die for this, Wizard,*" said the Wraith, "*and all those you have loved and protected will be destroyed.*"

"*Lord, I apologize greatly for my transgressions,*" Merlin replied softly, "*yet I have only sought an abandoned entity, a lost Avatar of the Great God Set. Left alone, that Avatar would have passed into nothingness; instead, I have breathed a few moments of life into your substance, Wraith, and Avatar, so that I may know the Will of Set.*"

"*The Will of Set is simple, mortal: you must die swiftly and painfully,*" the Avatar muttered, but its rage seemed to lessen, its substance to grow in darkness, and its concentration to focus, as though it had linked with some greater power.

"*When last I beheld the Great God Set,*" Merlin continued, "*we had become allies. In the Vale of Whispers, we fought together defending the Mid-World of the Truce.*"

"*Allies!*" The Wraith laughed — bitter humor, contempt, insane rage contained in a single word.

"I will agree, Lord, that we were only allies of convenience. Yet now the Wizards must set sail to do battle upon the enchanted Isle of the Demons, defending the Mid-World of the Truce. The Gods, in recognition of our efforts, have set aside their distaste for the League and ceased to intervene — all but for one Mid-World God, a Power unable to contain his malice."

"I am not that Power, Wizard!"

"Of course not, Lord. The Great God Set has more than fulfilled his bargain to leave the League to its devices for three score years. Many more years have passed, and indeed, in none of the intrusions against the League, in none of the other malignancies, could be sensed the distant hand of the Great God Set."

"So, that is why you have called me, Wizard. You wish me to name the Power that troubles you. Find some lesser God to do your jackal-work, Wizard!"

Merlin drifted along the riverbank, listening for a moment to the sounds of its sluggish, dark waters. "Lord, you have dealt fairly with us over the last hundred years, but we also have held our side of the bargain — are there still rumors of the difficulties the League once had with the Great God Set?"

"Whispers, only fading whispers. Wizard, is this a threat? Crude blackmail, that you would revive old tales unless I supply you with your enemy's name? And lastly, are you now so foolish to provoke me?"

"Lord, I absolutely have no wish to provoke you; I only offer arguments in favor of your aid. In a few weeks, either we will set sail to fight for the Mid-World of the Truce, or we will be struggling to guard our backs, and this one decisive moment will pass forever. Consider this, Lord: if we set sail for the enchanted Isle, do you think Alantéa will ever again see even one of the three Wizards?"

The Wraith floated beside the Wizard, staring up at the lone star, wondering which constellation might be left at the End of Time. "Wizard, *when we fought Demon Princes, and Marids, and Creatures Indomitable, and insignificant, scrawny mortal Sorcerers in the midst of the Ruins of Dahlak, did you note how one God was called, but would not come in full power, how his legions would barely defend themselves?"*

"Not yours, Lord, they fought with all the majesty and might of the Wrath of Set. More than a few Powers, however, did come to battle in a listless fashion."

"Wizard, you are being deliberately dimwitted! The God who would not defend the Truce was Arioch. That lesser God, Arioch, assails you, Wizard. You must deal with him, then you must depart from Alantéa forever. It seems unlikely that you will even reach the enchanted Isle of the Demons. Yet once you set sail, you will never return, never! Other Gods may one day recall benignly how subtle your puny, human mind had become, but I, for one, will not."

The Wraith stared one last time at the lone constellation above, then it whispered, twisting in pain, and finally gathered its own smoky substance to itself, shrinking, writhing, until the Avatar passed beyond the reach of all magic.

Merlin bowed his head briefly, and shifted again through the Dreamways, passing into a dream vision of Tuvan the Battleground before it was destroyed, then through the ancient Halls of Merlin as they had once stood during the early years of the League. Even now, the Wizard took comfort in what the League had once been, and what it might one day become again.

Satisfied that his progress had not been followed, Merlin then drifted into one of the greater nexuses of the Dreamways, where many Powers and their servants gathered to share their dream visions. The Wizard stood alone under starlit skies as many thousands of ghostly beings, travelers amid the Dreamways, took note of him.

"Great ones, Powers, Gods of the Mid-World," Merlin said quietly, *"it is worth noting that I do not confront, I do not challenge, I merely speak the*

truth, and that I come before you most rarely. I now name the Power that assails the Wizards' League. The God known as Arioch seeks our destruction. Arioch is the dagger that hovers over us. We cannot rise to defend the Mid-World of the Truce with this dagger poised at our backs. We cannot set sail until Arioch is restrained."

Chapter Six

The Warship Alantéa
the Forerunner

ITH GALAD, HARLOND AND Rostov all present at Khiva, Kalanin no longer felt the need to prowl the city's winding streets long into the night. Yet the many restless nights had reduced his sleep and postponed his dreams, so that in the aftermath he found himself waking later, with the summer sun rising brightly over Khiva before he opened his tired eyes.

He was dreaming again of being finally at sea, broad sails billowing under bright skies, surging through blue waters when the flapping of curtains and the sun's heat finally woke him. His eyes blinked open, and he saw Géla fully dressed, gazing out of their east-facing windows. In her hand, she held a sheet of parchment, whose shape and texture Kalanin recognized.

"Balardi," Kalanin murmured, and he rose. "The Wizard's helpful suggestions are normally left at my worktable, not at our bedside. What's happened?"

Géla turned and handed him the note. "The Wizard seems strangely polite of late."

Kalanin's eyes scanned the paper in seconds:

Master Shipbuilder:

You may wish to be at the East Gates of
Khiva some two hours after mid-day.
Through Gates of Dreams, I watch the
white sails of Alantéa The Forerunner
sweeping over a surging, white-capped ocean.

Balardi, for the League.

"'You may wish,'" Kalanin quoted wryly. "Should we fear that some imposter was returned to us instead of the old, hot-tempered Wizard?"

"Merlin is too wise to let that happen to his fellow Wizard," Géla said. "Now, Master Shipbuilder, will you not reconsider and join us this morning? Your presence would lend weight to this morning's deliberations."

Kalanin was up, dressing quickly. "I think not — you, Harmadast, Rostov and Harlond are to be regents of the League, and so the governance of Khiva will rest with you, Harlond, and Rostov, while Harmadast alternately resides at Stone Mountain and Gravengate. Let me, at least, escort you partway down to the dockyards."

They passed from their dwelling into the early morning sunlight. Dressed in light summer clothing with somber hues, the two might have been shop-owners or lesser servants of some merchant prince; but Kalanin's bodyguards surrounded them instantly, while another dozen guards, hand-picked by Rostov to protect Géla, followed a few paces behind them.

The upper squares of Khiva were used for formal gatherings, such as funerals, but whenever the core business of the city called its people together, the populace gathered in the great open spaces surrounding the dockyards. On this morning, the guardsmen of Khiva and others responsible for the security of Khiva had been summoned by Harlond and Rostov, though many other officials had followed them down to the dockyards. As they reached the outskirts of the gathering, Kalanin briefly embraced Géla, then went his own way to the shipbuilding loft housing the warship *Alantéa*.

Banks of windows provided light within the great shipbuilding loft, but, as always, light alternated with gloom inside. Hammers pounded and great saws ripped through strong timbers so that noise made communications difficult inside the loft. Kalanin called the ship's architects and foremen aside into a relatively quiet, dark alcove.

"Today is a jittery, nervous time," he told them. "This morning we will deal a decisive blow to those who do not wish us well. Be comforted, however, for none will die on this day unless they choose it themselves." Kalanin paused because in the distance came the sounds of assembled people, voices raised in anger. Throughout the great loft, workers hesitated, saws faltered, and even those pushing long brooms stopped and stared into the distance.

"And so today is a day when mistakes are made," Kalanin continued. "They are made and corrected, with every step checked twice. Speed yields to caution, for after this day is done, we will add a second shift and work will proceed with far greater speed."

They were beginning to raise the ship's exterior, lifting the great skeletal sections from the floor onto the ship's sides, so the warship seemed like a huge ghost vessel of yellowish white timbers. Work continued at a faltering pace, as periodically sounds from the dockyards penetrated the tumult of building noises. Kalanin was saddened, though not entirely surprised, when

Rostov and his guards entered the shipbuilding loft, briefly saluted Kalanin, then led away two foremen who had been suspected for some time.

Shortly after noon, Galad joined Kalanin in the loft. To Kalanin's surprise, Galad was sipping a tisane of herbs rather than a draught of wine, and he seemed unusually thoughtful.

"Not much joy in this morning's work," Galad commented.

Kalanin checked the sun's slant and put down his pen. "How many?"

"Somewhat less than two scores are sealed away as having masters outside the League. It is hoped that the Wizards can lay some compulsion upon them so they will pass from the League and never return." Galad glanced around, pulled an empty barrel that had once held nails to Kalanin's worktable, then sat. "The first judgment was the easy part — serve the League and remain with us or serve another master and depart. The second was harder by far, for those who brawled or broke watches, or stirred anger against newcomers — hotheads and such — are being exiled from Khiva, to depart to other cities of the League and make new lives for themselves. The first group was silent as ancient, lifeless ghosts, thinking perhaps of those hanging outside the walls, and glad to be alive. The second group wept and begged and wailed like children caught in a hailstorm with thunder booming all around them."

"And these numbered...?" Kalanin asked.

"More than three scores, and included, perhaps, even a few only marginally guilty."

"Even so, it was a cleansing that had to be done. Harlond and Rostov have grown."

"Do not omit your beloved, Admiral. Géla, I think, tempered some of the harsher judgments. But yes, all three have grown. Do you recall Rostov just a few years ago, as a slender youth with a wispy beard? Now his eyes look more than a little tired, and his shoulders are stooped with the world's weight."

"Speaking of weight, Géla is resting, I hope? In addition to the world's weight, she carries our child."

Galad smiled and looked away into the gloom of the shipbuilding loft. "She rests; even warrior maidens find childbearing tiresome. Yet she said she would join you at the East Gates some two hours after midday. What's that about?"

"Judge for yourself," Kalanin said, passing Balardi's note to Galad.

"'Through Gates of Dreams,'" Galad read, surprise mixed with scorn. "What will the Wizards become next — poets, mallet-wielding sculptors, designers of fashionable clothing? I'm fortunate that managing Wizards is the work of Admirals, not swordsmen with brains made soft by wine. Will you be at the East Gates at the appointed time?"

Kalanin again checked the sun's slant, then stood. "You and I both will be there, and a late midday meal will likely follow. Before that, my brother in arms, we have time for a brief daylight tour of the *Alantéa*."

Galad followed Kalanin around the vessel, listening abstractly to the detail Kalanin provided about beams and spars, and the huge chambers required by the Wizards. Yet throughout the tour, one thought returned to Galad's mind, crowding out all other considerations: *This warship is the largest, moveable construction ever imagined, and made by humans. Each day adds many hundreds of pounds to its total weight. How in the Maker's Name will they ever get it into the water?*

Aware that he had lost the thread of Kalanin's narrative, and that Kalanin's explanations had trailed off, Galad turned and smiled brightly at his longtime friend and erstwhile "Admiral."

Kalanin met his eyes and laughed softly. "We know each other only too well, and our thoughts are practical and similar. You ask, 'How by all the Nine Billion Gods are they going to get this thing into the water?' This is the same question I have raised several times, and I have been told not to worry about it. Come. Time for the East Gates."

Khiva was set against a coil of low hills, outcrops of forested soil and stone that slanted down into the ocean, forming its natural harbor. The city had begun near the water's edge, then gradually worked its way up its surrounding hillsides. The East Gates were high enough, built at a place where they could look down on the ocean's expanse, though the shoreline was obscured.

Much of the roadway leading to Gravengate and Stone Mountain was also hidden by the surrounding hills that curled and capped the nearby countryside. As Géla, Kalanin and Galad, together with chosen guards gathered to the East Gates, Julian's war party was discovered first by sound: the archers of the Mistress of Illusions had broken into song as they neared the walls of Khiva. Beneath their light voices, came deep harmonies from the Men of the Dragon's Teeth.

"My people," Géla murmured, and the child within her stirred as though she too wished to sing.

"Joined by men of the Dragon's Teeth," Kalanin added. "Now we have a force whose origin and loyalty can't be challenged."

As she realized the implications, tears slipped down Géla's face, and she brushed them aside. "Yet it also means that so little time is left to us. Soon you will depart on your lovingly crafted warship, and I will see you never again in this world."

Kalanin embraced her. "We are *not* doomed."

"I will be strong for you, strong for our League," Géla murmured. "Have them open the gates and welcome our peoples." Guards, six on each side, pulled the gates open, and streams of riders poured through, voices still raised in song. As their captains led them down into the heart of the city, Julian dismounted and approached his friends and allies. On one shoulder,

Rafir blinked into visibility, while on the other shoulder, Sebastian's wings fluttered in delight.

Julian embraced them one by one, murmuring, "It may seem as though we journey to our deaths, but my heart lifts to be with you once again. All the might of the League is gathering to Khiva. Can it be that we are part of the Maker's Will? If so, then forces far greater than our own may not prevail against us."

"What of Balardi," Galad asked, "has the Wizard truly healed?"

Julian laughed. "I, too, had my doubts, but yes, he is whole, powerful as ever, but more thoughtful, and somewhat introspective. I have been named as his heir, if you can believe that, and as fellow ruler of Gravengate."

"Ha! Then you outrank even Admiral Hangnail here," Galad said, nodding at Kalanin.

"We are all of the same rank," Julian said, embracing Géla in turn. "Now known as Far Travel...." The Apprentice trailed off, for as he touched Géla, he could feel her deep sorrow, and even then, unbidden, a healing strength passed from his own touch into Géla's warm body.

"Far Travelers," Julian finished. "And we are *not* doomed, not even when we set foot upon the Isle of the Demons. Enormous powers have been set in motion, forces that lie behind and beyond the Mid-World of the Truce."

"Will you now speak of the Dreamers?" Géla asked softly. "Have they truly broken the Temple of Waiting down to its foundations, and risen in wrath to defend us?"

Julian shook his head gravely. "The Dreamers are done, and the Maker must raise them at the End of Time. Even so...." The voice of the Apprentice faltered, and his eyes were drawn skyward, for from the northeast, in the fullness of afternoon sunlight, a Godling had emerged from the upper skies and was descending toward them.

"Guard yourselves," Kalanin muttered, stepping forward so that he stood two paces in front of Géla. Galad touched the Tarnished Sword but did not draw it; the enchanted blade woke from its endless dreams of violence and let out a soft moan.

The Godling floated downwards, glinting silver and red, vaguely feminine, face serene. Julian felt tension and hints of violence on the faces of both Kalanin and Galad, but he said nothing, only clenching his staff with both hands.

The Godling touched ground within the City gates, then drifted slowly toward them, murmuring, "Hail, Servants of the League, hail Servants and allies!"

Julian felt some of the tension lift from those around him. "Hail God-being, Power of the Mid-World," he said, bowing his head, acknowledging a being of force and power. "How might we assist you?"

"We have grown somewhat, Apprentice, and we have gained names. I am now called Phaedra, while my brother of the green and gold hues is known as Turin. Magog is the name of my darker-seeming brother, he who was used as a weapon against your League.

"I have been sent as an ambassador to make amends, for if we are to be allies, there can be no discord festering among us. But first, I am still learning; there are so many questions, with so much still to be learned. Yet I do not wish to discomfort you, and so I am willing to wait and speak with the Wizards at a later date."

"Ask," Julian said, "and we will answer if we can."

"We have begun to understand mortals better, and so I feel the violence and stress before me subsiding, but one sentience, not human, still wishes to rise and smite me. How can this be?"

Julian and Galad's eyes flashed together, then the warrior reluctantly stepped forward and offered the Tarnished Sword, still sheathed, to the

Godling named Phaedra. As it passed to the Godling, the blade let out a keening ring — a cry of hostility and alarm.

"If the Elf-Lords have taught you of *The Game of the Masters,*" Julian explained, "your hands now hold *The Mid-World Weapon.*"

The Godling peered intently at the blade. "Though the *Game* is now a broken thing, I have been advised of its many aspects — and yet this weapon is still very different." Released from her hand, the Tarnished Sword drifted back to Galad's side.

"Your blade is strange," Phaedra continued, "yet, as I regard you humans, you also seem different from other mortals, for there is a glow about you, some hint of energies beyond the Mid-World of the Truce. What is the source of this aura?"

"I could offer you one easy answer," Julian replied, "that before you stand the Summoners who rode together into the Vale of Whispers and called down the Truce against the Mid-World's adversaries. But since we are allies, I will tell you the true reason: the Wizards are the first and greatest theme of the League — three great mortal conjurors gathering together to create a haven for mortals. Those before you represent a second theme: that when the League is threatened, a band of lesser beings gathers to defend the League — warriors, captains, magicians, who become catalysts for even greater forces. Others like us have come to support the Wizards in the past, and perhaps still others will arise when we are gone."

"So much to learn, with so little time left to us," Phaedra murmured, glancing from face to face, "but I have come principally to speak with this Captain." One silverish red hand pointed toward Kalanin. "And I would do so apart from others, just for a few moments."

Taking Kalanin aside, Phaedra spoke in hushed tones, "My brother is troubled that he was used against you and your people. Too proud to feel real shame, he would still like to make amends."

"We lost only two dead," Kalanin said, thinking aloud, "and truly, the Power that used your brother, Magog, as a weapon, is to blame." He stared up into the Godling's far-seeing eyes, noting that her dark pupils seemed flecked with touches of hazel.

"Something to restore a balance between us," Phaedra prompted.

"Then, a Weregild," Kalanin said, "a payment of precious stones and amulets for the families of the two men who died. Accidents happen, mistakes are made, and gifts of treasure bridge the gaps and make amends... only...." He hesitated.

"Speak. I stand before you as an Emissary who will not be easily offended."

"Your gifts would likely include enchanted charms and potions," Kalanin said. "It would be wise to make certain that malignant Powers do not pass poisonous gifts to our people through your brother's offerings."

The Godling stared out into the distance, then fixed her eyes on a remote speck in the upper skies. "We have been used by other forces, and now must learn to be most wary. We will do as you suggest. Farewell for a time."

Kalanin stood still and silent for a moment, watching the Godling named Phaedra as she rose from the hillside, lifting like a being made of air drawn to some remote kingdom in the skies. As she rose, he noted that the speck hovering overhead was becoming swiftly larger, as the eagle, the Eye of Merlin, descended downward, coming to rest on a lower portion of the city's outer wall works, so that the eagle stood only two heads above Kalanin.

"Well met," the Eagle croaked. "All the strength of the League is gathering to Khiva. Also know this: from this time forward, you no longer need to fear the malign Mid-World Powers, for the League's hidden adversary, the God called Arioch, has been assailed by a host of Emissaries. His

Mid-World Empire has been destroyed and Arioch has fled to the Far Lands, his powers reduced to a fraction of their early potency.

"The power of the League gathers to this place, and the first Wizard, Thorian, will arrive in the next few seconds through an enchanted Portal Passage. Julian, do not seek to check this Portal, for Thorian, not some remote adversary, passes through, and he comes...even now...."

A Portal with a huge arch, suitable for a God, spilled over the soil at Khiva's eastern edge. As Thorian strode through, the Portal turned to smoke, then mist, and finally vanished with a muffled concussion. Julian watched this display, then laughed softly. *The Wizards have always been most discrete in their use of Portals, for fear of angering the Gods by such open displays of power. Thorian is now focused on the rescue of his daughter from the Isle, and so he no longer cares.*

Thorian glanced at each of them with fierce, swift eyes. "You have done much, all but the slightest fraction of it good. I have no desire to anger you or earn your resentment, but much more is required."

Kalanin and the others stared at the Wizard without warmth.

"I am not judging you," Thorian continued. "I have said that you have done well. In the same fashion, you should not judge me; only consider that upon the Isle of the Demons, my daughter fights and flees, and fights and flees again, and ultimately, she is destroyed. Yet then some Power resurrects her and each time she goes forth to battle in a new form. How many deaths can she endure? How many deaths could any of us endure? And so, within me, a fire burns to bring ruin to this malignant Isle of the Demons."

Géla turned away from Thorian so the Wizard could not read her eyes. Kalanin embraced her with one arm and said, softly to Thorian, "Work on the *Alantéa* proceeds apace. We have authorized a second shift, beginning tomorrow afternoon."

"Then plan a third shift," Thorian said. "Let each hour of each day move us closer to the Isle of the Demons."

"So, it might seem," Julian replied, "if we ruled an anthill, ordering hordes of insects to labor without rest or distraction, that their labors could be increased fourfold. Yet we know that even the antlike workers would falter and fail, while humans would tire far more quickly, then falter, then make complex errors that might not easily be corrected."

"Even more practically," Kalanin added, "the structure of the harbor passes sounds upwards into the broad streets of the upper city. With all the noise and chaos of a third shift, few would find peace at the end of each day."

"Come now," Thorian said patiently. "You have the trained workforce for a second shift. Many other craftsmen and shipwrights have been called to Khiva, and so your third shift will soon become reality. As for noises, we, the Wizards, have been cautious in the use of our power because of dark and jealous Gods. But all those old conflicts are now behind us. I will lay enchanted clouds of soft sleep over the hillsides. Soon a second Wizard will join me, then a third. Will we not bring energy and intensity and a focus to this enterprise?"

Julian, Kalanin, and Galad glanced together, while Géla bowed her head and would not look up.

"It can be done," Kalanin said, "and so it must be done."

· X ·

A second shift was begun as promised; after the first few faltering days, the pace of shipbuilding doubled. Thorian took for the Wizards' dwelling a smaller shipbuilding loft less than a thousand paces from that housing the *Alantéa*. The Wizards' place of power was no more than a rough warehouse, sealed from surrounding buildings by bands of soft smoke, a hazy substance that few cared to touch. Thorian was seldom seen, except sometimes at dusk he was visible from a distance, a shimmering Wraith that seemed to glide, utterly preoccupied, through the city's winding streets. His presence made the nights quieter, and even those lingering late in Khiva's inns sometimes spoke only in whispers.

By day, more craftsmen and shipbuilders were drawn to Khiva and were swiftly put to work. Less than a week after Thorian's arrival, the figure of Balardi was seen striding along the docks toward the place of power chosen by Thorian. The barrier of smoke surrounding the warehouse parted and Balardi vanished within. Only later did Julian learn that Balardi had passed through shifting portions of Otherwhen, choosing alternate realities — Alternates — that collapsed the distance between Gravengate and the coast; and so, having achieved a thing that no Power had ever before mastered, the Wizard was greatly pleased with himself.

A third shift was started, fitting almost seamlessly into the other two shifts. With the weather controlled overhead, the loft housing the *Alantéa* was being slowly dismantled, as the great warship gradually came to stand under broad sunlight by day, and interlacing crowns of stars at night.

On one such starry night, Merlin entered the city alone, greeted only at the gates by the eagle, the Eye of Merlin. Then, with three Wizards in Khiva, and three shifts working feverishly on the *Alantéa,* Thorian's words did come to fruition: at night, clouds of soft, enchanted sleep ascended the hillside. Clanging sounds from the shipyards were muffled, but so profound was the sorcery of sleep, that even the most vigilant guards who passed even a short distance into the mists collapsed to the ground, as their spears toppled to the pavement.

His work mostly done, Kalanin spent most of his time with Géla, speaking of the past of the League, and its future. Withdrawn to a place of her own solitude, Géla would nod distantly, though part of her mind tried to retain the essence of what was said. Other times, Kalanin would lie beside her, holding Géla and the child within her, until soft sleep drifted over their small family.

Some evenings, Harlond and Rostov would join them, sipping beer or a broth of herbs, Rostov taking detailed notes on the history of the League, and listing carefully to Kalanin's thoughts about the future of their alliance.

One such evening, with work on the *Alantéa* complete, Kalanin sat in their seaside quarters, speaking quietly with Harlond and Rostov, while Géla stared into the distance, her mind walking through the wooded empire of the Mistress of Illusions, dwelling in a time when the whispers of small birds on the upper branches mixed with the rustling sounds of soft leaves.

Muffled noises at the window interrupted their thoughts. Curtains of light cotton were being brushed aside by the Eye of Merlin.

"The last pieces are set," the eagle croaked, "for the Godlings have passed from the night skies onto the streets of Khiva. We will set sail within the next two days. Prepare yourselves."

· X ·

Two mornings later, Géla woke before daybreak and slipped from Kalanin's side without waking him. Down by the water, the ocean lapped and foamed as always, and the breezes of morning understood nothing of what was to come. The dark sky grew pale, then showed a deepening red until finally, the sun rose, seeming to tremble as all the earth's midsummer moisture stirred in the morning air.

Then Kalanin was beside her, watching the sky transform itself. "I will return," he murmured. "If any strength is left to me, I will come back to you and to our child."

Géla embraced him and forced herself to smile. "May you be given not only the power to triumph but also the strength to return. And for this day, I must be strong. I *will* be strong."

By midday, most of the citizenry of Khiva had gathered down to the dockyards, though guardsmen and the soldiery of the League kept them a few hundred paces north from the great warship. The shipbuilding loft, housing the *Alantéa,* had been torn down and the warship stood completely finished, polished and glittering under clear skies, though a network of props and large beams maintained it upright.

The crowds grew hushed, eyes drawn to the Wizards' place of power, where the protective haze embracing the old warehouse gradually thinned. Then the three Wizards emerged, and the crowd noise lessened, some speaking only in quiet whispers.

Thorian stood tallest, stern, erect, hair silver and white; even in travelers' garb, he radiated power. Balardi was also a figure of strength, standing just a hand's breadth shorter than Thorian, his flowing gold hair and beard now heavily interlaced with grey; and even in his calmer, later years a storm of emotions seemed to threaten over his eyes and forehead.

Merlin stood between the two a little hunched, unassuming, the Wizard's hair and beard completely grey. Leaning on his staff, the Wizard seemed farthest from a being of power, and as he regarded the Warship *Alantéa,* his eyes were faintly puzzled, as though the purpose of the great vessel somehow eluded him.

Then the crowd began to gasp and murmur aloud. For behind the thinning barrier that cloaked the Wizards' quarters, three other figures were emerging: the Godlings had come to support the League's great quest. A ripple of applause built into a thunder of praise. Here at Khiva the Mid-World and the League had at last forged an alliance.

The Godlings were now fully formed, filled with such open power that the Wizards seemed diminished. Phaedra stood foremost, more than two heads taller than the mortals around her, she radiated two of the forces that had been poured into the Mid-World of the Truce: silver of the Spirit Lords mixed with the smoldering red of Demon Princes. Her brother Turin was a mirror to her, glistening with Seraph Gold and Dragon Green. Magog was darker, emanating the greyish black strength of the Mid-World, tempered by blue seams showing at least a partial desire for justice.

Such was the stir and tumult, that Julian, Galad, and Kalanin passed almost unnoticed through the barrier of guards. Clutching Kalanin's arm, Géla also slipped through, holding Kalanin fiercely as though unwilling ever to release him. The three were lightly dressed for summer travel by water, with all their cloaks and armor and heavy weapons already stored aboard ship.

Galad had halfheartedly joined the rhythmic clapping, though as he did so, he murmured to Kalanin, "This is all very well, though we still have the minor problem of moving one very large warship that remains far from water."

"If I understand these matters," Kalanin said, just above the cheering sounds, "the stage has been set for an open display of power. Watch!"

Guards had been massed along the dockyards, keeping the populace to the north, so the path of the *Alantéa* to the ocean lay open. But the distance between the enormous warship and the glittering blue ocean was so great, and the path so flat, that no system of slides seemed able to bridge the gap — and none had even been started. Only pavements of poured stone and cobblestone plazas lay between the *Alantéa* and the harbor.

The Godlings shifted forward, still seeming to glide rather than walk as they moved over the heavy plank flooring of the demolished shipbuilding loft. Phaedra passed to the left, Turin to the right, each moving to a position forward from the center of the great warship's weight. Magog halted at the ship's rear.

The gathering grew hushed again, only a few of the onlookers beginning to understand what was to come. Overhead, scores of Vision Portals slid into place, as the Gods began to view events at Khiva; and as Portals crowded the upper skies, the day was no less bright, but the sunlight over Khiva was transformed, light rays reflected from many strange sources, and onlookers felt as though they lived in a dream.

Sounds emerged from the Godlings: deep harmonies, vibrating noise, groaning sounds from the depths of chasms. The great warship began to tremble. Supporting spars and beams fell one by one away from it. Finally, the enormous ship seemed to glow, radiating with a strength of sorcery, and it lifted, slowly, inch by inch from the ground, until it floated in mid-air, keel level with the height of the tall Godlings' heads.

And this is what Rostov and I predicted, Kalanin thought, *a show of force, but we thought they would need to summon the Great Gods to their aid, and so the Godlings are more powerful than we considered.*

Galad glanced at the faces of Kalanin and Julian, then back to the warship. *These second level Divinities are not even beginning to perspire. Perhaps they have become more than a feeble cosmetic effort of the Mid-World to obscure its many failures.*

Behold the Godlings, Julian thought. *See the radiance of power flashing over Phaedra's face. If they are still deferring to the Wizards, that respect will not last for long. And then they will wish to lead us, even to rule us.*

As the warship glided down to the harbor, the people of Khiva followed, beginning again their rhythmic clapping, while many in the upper hills were cheering, rejoicing. Kegs of ale and wine were broached, and Khiva embarked on a celebration that would last for days.

The great warship floated over cobblestone plazas, then over docks formed with broad beams, and quays, and finally out into the deep waters of the harbor. All the while, the citizens of Khiva clapped and called aloud, while the Powers of the Mid-World watched from afar — in silence.

At the edge of a long pier, a galley lay waiting for Julian, Galad, and Kalanin, to ferry them out to the *Alantéa*. Géla and Kalanin embraced one last time.

"Weep if you feel sorrow," Kalanin whispered to her, "but do not despair. If the Maker and his works have any power left in this world, some of us will return." Géla blinked back tears, forcing her face into a mask of rejoicing, as though she shared in Khiva's triumph. For a long moment, she clutched Kalanin as though she could never let him go, then she released him and returned to the people of Khiva in their moment of triumph.

Then Géla stood with Harlond and Rostov, watching as the great warship *Alantéa the Forerunner* surged under clear blue skies into an ocean capped with white foam. As the ship passed into the distance, and the city's celebrations became more raucous, she embraced Harlond and Rostov. Her two Captains held her for a time, each understanding the sorrow within her.

Finally, accompanied by picked guards she slipped back to the modest building she had shared with Kalanin. With evening near, and her guards mostly dispersed, Géla was alone except for the child within her, and her own true feelings.

She paced, facing her east windows, storming with rage at the Wizards, who had assumed a task so far beyond their strength that it defied all reason — and now the Wizards had drawn their most faithful servants into destruction.

Then she cursed all the Nine Billion Gods — their divisions, their selfishness, their confusion, and all their other, fatal weaknesses.

Finally, she sagged down on her bed and wept, lamenting long into the night.

Chapter Seven

A Battle at Sea

FOR A LONG TIME, Kalanin stood at the rail of the great warship, staring back toward Khiva in a trance. He grasped the railing with both hands as the warship rose and fell, surging through a restless ocean with foaming waves, watching as the spires of Khiva slowly diminished, leaving only a distant shoreline, one that vanished completely as sunlight passed into dusk.

At nightfall, Kalanin bowed his head and prayed, praying for Géla and their child, then for his friends and allies, then for guidance for himself, searching for wisdom and strength. While he stood, head bent for a time, the night sea had risen somewhat, and now it sent spumes of white foam hurtling into the night so that coils of foam lashed at him, and he took a deep breath, turning at last from the railing.

Under a sliver of moonlight, he could see that the ship was being manned, though he knew that not a single human mariner from Khiva had sailed with them. Part of his mind had recorded the sounds of ropes sliding over metal, and flapping sails being trimmed, as he stared back toward Khiva, but nothing had forced his mind to ask what sort of beings were working the sails.

Now he descended to a lower deck and stared openly at the warship's "crew," then shook his head in disbelief: the ship was manned by nothing more than constructs of flesh, rough copies of human forms created by the Wizards. Hadn't Thorian promised sailors of a much higher order? Cautiously, he drew closer to the warship's "crew." None took note of him — some seemed even to have forgotten their simple tasks and stared into the darkness and distance with lifeless eyes. And their flesh was pasty and thin, with pinkish blood flowing from scrapes on their arms and legs. What had the Wizards been thinking?

As he studied their "crew," he became aware that some being of power was watching him. He turned slowly to find himself in the presence of Magog.

"Do not fear me, Captain," the Godling said softly.

Kalanin took a deep breath, preparing — if needed — to rouse the Wizards. "Of course not, Lord," he said evenly, "we are allies at the beginning of a great quest. Why should I fear you?"

Below the main deck, they could still stare out portholes to the ocean and the land beyond. Magog spent moments with his eyes fixed on the distant shores of Alantéa before speaking. Then he murmured, "Though they were only mortals, I am still troubled by the deaths of your two guards. We have given gifts to their kinsmen, but was that atonement sufficient? It feels like such a small thing."

"The true fault lay with other Gods, Lord, and it speaks well for you that you desire justice. The League holds you absolved. Also, you should know that three others lost their lives while building this warship — all great enterprises are troubled by such mishaps."

"Absolved..." Magog said softly, "I reach for this word, and it is understood, though faintly troubling because, in the hierarchies of power, I should be absolving you, Captain. Yet when we speak of hierarchies, mortal warleader, is it then true that you of the League still worship a being called the Maker, an entity who has been gone so long that no mortal has ever beheld or even sensed from afar?"

"Lord, as an ally, I will answer you with all candor. Yes, we worship the remote Maker, and if you speak of hierarchies, he is the First Fashioner, the God of Gods and creator, directly and indirectly, of the Mid-World Powers. But please, I beg you, do not repeat my words to other Gods, for you will only anger them." Kalanin bowed and turned to depart.

"One moment, mortal," Magog said, his soft tones touched by traces of irritation. "As we grew in power and understanding, and considered our missteps, it came to mind that a debt was owed to you, also, for your wisdom and forbearance. And so, we have crafted a weapon for you." From his cloak, Magog drew a sword from its sheath; the weapon radiated a dim white fire into the night air. "This sword will have many of the attributes of your ally's weapon, though it was impossible to match the peculiar strangeness of the Tarnished Sword." Magog sheathed the weapon and extended sword and sheath to Kalanin.

Compelled by events, Kalanin bowed and stepped forward to receive the Godlings' offering. "Lord, thank you for this magnificent gift." He searched for words, diplomatic phrases. "I can offer nothing in return, and yet if ever you wish to speak with me — on matters great or small — I am at your service.

"It is the way of the Great Gods to have many sources of counsel, to hear different voices throughout the Mid-World. As your strength and wisdom grow, you may also wish to seek out the Eye of Merlin, for though the eagle may be harsh spoken, he has also traveled the length and breadth of Alantéa. Lord, I thank you again, and wish you well on your night vigil."

Kalanin bowed again and retreated to his own quarters, struggling to keep his real feelings masked. He had absolutely no affection for their Godling "allies," and he trusted his new weapon so little that he was tempted to slip the sword overboard into dark waters.

At the door to their quarters, he took a deep breath of salty sea air, then opened it, expecting to slide from starlit shadows into candlelight. Instead, Julian and Galad were seated beside a long table, on which was a gleaming model of the warship *Alantéa*, a clear image created by the Apprentice.

"I was lost," Galad said, "not just once, but twice on your interesting but overly large sailboat. Come. Sit beside us and explain yourself. How did this vessel become so complicated?" As Kalanin sat, Galad pushed a mug of ale toward him, and Kalanin drank deeply.

"Let's begin with the top decks," Kalanin said, staring at the gleaming image, "where our unlovely 'crew' members stumble about like doomed zombies." Light shifted within the Divination so that the top deck glowed with the light of dusk, and they watched tiny images of their "crew" as the constructs lurched from task to task. Above the deck, they could hear its tall masts creak and groan with the wind.

"The forecastle at the front is deliberately low, built for the forward watch," Kalanin continued, "while most of the deck is flat and clear, except for slender lockers that store sails. You have no idea how I struggled with shipwrights who wished for elaborate battle towers. A top heavy *Alantéa* would have struggled with every gust of wind. Beneath the top decks are living chambers. Ours are small, while those built for the Wizards and Godlings are immense."

In the enchanted image created by Julian, six huge chambers gleamed, though nothing could be seen inside any of the six conjuring chambers, for both Wizards and Godlings had sealed themselves from sight.

"These chambers are so large that they extend into the ship's hold," Kalanin explained. "All such large ships have masts and sails at the top, living quarters below the decks, and the ship's hold beneath them. Much of these holds are below water, providing room for storage and a base weight. For a normal warship, all the ship's supplies and weapons would act as ballast — weight at the ship's base so that the warship would not be blown over in rough weather. Since we sail light, ballast was cast in the form of poured stone, shaped to fit exactly to the ship's contours. So, the conjuring chambers form part of a higher storage area, while beneath them lies the deep hold, down to the base of the ship, forming a sub-hold." They looked down on the ship's hold, a huge, dark, empty space, with catwalks suspended above the hold, and stairs built into the warship's sides.

Kalanin sipped more ale. "At the base of the ship's hull, the keel extends downward, like a dagger, its weight balancing the warship, as it carves its way through dark waters."

"All that I can understand," Galad muttered. "Below the top decks is the sub-hold, for example, is simple — it's just vast empty spaces with webs of catwalks, or 'ratwalks,' if we become infested. But now let's look at the side passages, and the reason I was lost — not just once but twice." Julian smiled and his left palm flashed. Then all the ship's interior passageways were illuminated by blue, showing honeycombs of interior passages, staircases, and crawl spaces.

Kalanin laughed softly. "They talked, they argued, and they fought among themselves, the whole team of professional shipbuilders. In the end, I told them to decide themselves, so what you see is the work of a demented committee. However, we will learn to rely on a few main passages, and so you won't be lost again. Also, when you refer to 'ratwalks,' be assured that the Wizards have banished all rodents from this vessel."

Julian waved his hand, and the image of the Alantéa vanished. With a second wave, candles flared, and then Julian leaned forward. "All that is very interesting," the Apprentice said softly, "but that is *not* why we are sitting in this room. We need to speak of what you have left behind in Khiva, and also what you have brought as another 'presence' into this place."

"We will speak of those things next," Kalanin said. "Only give me a moment." He filled his mug with ale and sat back, watching the candlelight shift and flutter with each motion of night air. He drank deeply, and then glanced around, viewing their quarters for the first time in the shifting dim rays of candlelight.

Most of the space in their shared area was taken up by a long table with benches on both sides, while more comfortable chairs were set into corners. Three small sleeping chambers lay beyond their shared space, while an even smaller room held perishable provisions interspersed with deeply chilled ice chests. An adjoining chamber — the largest — held all their other possessions: dry food stores, war gear, and clothing fit for cold, rough seas.

Because they were well below the upper decks, set into the interior of the great ship, none of their rooms had portholes facing out onto the night ocean. As Kalanin glanced around, he noticed that finishing touches had been added at the last moments, wood trim set around doors, wainscoting suitable for master merchants rather than war leaders.

Kalanin set his mug aside, then he drew the gleaming sword and slid it carefully onto the tabletop. "Here is your other 'presence' — a gift of the Godlings," he said. "My first inclination was to steal out later tonight and slip it over the side, hoping that the shifting debris at the bottom of the sea would hide it forever. But I am ready to listen to your advice on this matter."

Galad reached out for the sword, but as he touched it, the Tarnished Sword at his side started to keen, beginning a long string of curses in its own strange sword language. On the table, the gleaming blade replied with mumbled, snarling sounds.

"That's all we need," Galad muttered, "a quarrel between enchanted blades."

"Then let's wait for daylight," Julian said. "We can have a closer look at your 'gift' tomorrow. For at this moment, with sleep coming soon, Galad wasn't truly troubled by the warship's many passageways. We were only passing the time. He and I were waiting for you, Kalanin. We cannot feel the depth of your loss, but we can share some of your pain. Even as we speak, I can feel Géla calling to you from a distance. If only one of the three of us is fated to return from the enchanted Isle, it has to be you."

"It *must* be you," Galad added, "and though I share in your sorrow, I also feel a touch of envy. Do you recall our dream visions in the Gangean range? You stood with Géla and your two children. Julian stood with an unnamed fairy princess, whom I now believe was Eléna, the daughter of Thorian. Now recall...." The warship dipped into a deep sea-valley, tilting the cabin, and Galad's swift hand caught his mug in midair a split second before it crashed to the floor.

"Recall," Galad continued, "how many shallow damsels flitted around me like insubstantial ghosts,"

Julian studied Galad for a moment. "We should have spoken of this long ago."

"A very, very small matter," Galad said, "compared to the fate of the League. But it is true that I have grown tired of the parade of merchant daughters who wish mostly to become countesses of the League."

"That can be changed one day," Julian said, "though not on this late night, at a time when we should sleep."

"Sleep — not just yet" Galad said. "Just now I spoke out of turn, raising matters that should have been kept in the depths of my own mind. You know that I am still considered a youngling, though I have been soldiering for more than ten years now, and I've acquired an old soldier's sense of danger. That sense tells me that Khiva is not secure. Even after all we've done, when my mind's eye stares back over the expanse of ocean, Khiva still seems an unsafe haven."

Julian stared for a moment into the distance. "I felt something in Khiva, an anxiousness more than a sense of danger. The Gift within was trying to warn me, but so many other events overcame its concern. Merlin must deal with this matter...there, I have sent a thought to the mind of Merlin."

· ✗ ·

Two hours before dawn, the mind of Merlin passed again through Gates of Dreams, into a vision of Khiva at night, to a time in the future where the great celebrations had passed, and the city had returned to its shipbuilding, fishing, and maritime trade. Late at night, the city was dark and quiet, all its energy spent, and the only sounds heard were of banners flapping halfheartedly in the listless breezes of late summer.

Merlin's shadow passed through the long upper streets, down broad, curling avenues that led down to the harbor. No longer was the city seething with the malice of Dark Gods, festering with spies and assassins. A time of peace had come to the city, except....

Except that, as the shadow of Merlin's mind passed from the end of each street and shifted with flowing motions into each section of the city, sharp weaselly eyes were emerging behind him, slipping from pools of darkness to stare with malice at his departing human shape.

Sighing, Merlin passed from Khiva into a long corridor leading to a major nexus of the Dreamways. This intersection was shaped like a great oval amphitheater, with ridges of stone seats rising on all sides up into the starlit skies. Gathered on these stone steps were many of the Emissaries of the Gods, or their Grey Councilors, or Avatars of the Powers, murmuring together under distant starshine.

As Merlin emerged from the corridor out onto the oval base of the amphitheater, he raised his arms wide then bowed.

"I now cast myself upon the mercies of the Great Gods. A wickedness still stirs in the South of Alantéa. I beg you, in all humility, not to let our people be taken unawares while the force of the League is focused upon the enemies of the Mid-World."

· X ·

In the last hours of the night, a tide of dark clouds swept over the ocean's deep waters, so that in the morning, the sky was overcast with raindrops dampening the upper decks. Rafir and Sebastian were first to rise, but Sebastian found the weather too cold and damp, so the fox alone prowled the decks and investigated the strange "crew" that manned their ship. Rafir had not yet dared to try his talents on the Godlings, preferring to wait until later in their voyage to slip his invisible form past their defenses and watch them unseen.

The ship rose and fell, riding over ridges with white foam at the ocean's peaks, then down into valleys where pools of dark blue water were pelted by raindrops. Rafir had just concluded that he was better off inside when the cabin doors began opening, and the Wizards emerged, followed only seconds later by the Godlings. A few moments later, Julian led Kalanin and Galad up from below decks. All stared into the distance, where the eagle, the Eye of Merlin, was slowly descending toward the warship.

As always, smaller birds surged around the eagle with his huge wings. This far from shore, only gulls were nearby, and they harassed the

Eye unmercifully, until finally the eagle seemed to *surge* through the sky, and some unfortunate seagull plummeted, with its broken wing, into the surging, rainy ocean. Other gulls cried in alarm and wheeled away, allowing the Eye to descend in peace.

Talons grasping the railing, the eagle addressed those around him without a hint of deference: "Your first great test has come, my masters. From the Isles of the Sorcerers, a war fleet has emerged to challenge you. Many of the mightiest Sorcerers of the Isles are with this fleet. If none of them are equal to Alcman or Houma, still they greatly outnumber you. And their ships are crewed by fighting men, not by constructs."

"Wizard, let this be our first trial," Phaedra said to Merlin. "Our powers have grown, and my brothers have longed to test them on our foes."

Merlin glanced into the distance, then back to the Godlings. "Can you be patient for a short while?" he asked. "We are at an intersection, where interesting matters may be revealed." As the Godlings glanced together, hesitating, Merlin added, "We may all learn much, if we choose to delay." Phaedra spoke soft words to Magog and Turin, then the three turned away as though they had lost interest in the Sorcerers and their war fleet.

"Thorian, the fire burns brightly within you," Merlin said, "while Balardi would happily break the Sorcerers' war fleet into a flotsam of broken beams and planks, left to float for decades upon a thousand beaches; but let us avoid these fools. If they approach us from the east, we must change course and proceed west. On the high seas, we may outrun them."

"Even with a proper 'crew,'" Thorian muttered, "we might...yes, now I see your devices." He turned from Merlin, clapping his hands, and suddenly their "crew" began reefing sails, tacking swiftly.

Balardi laughed aloud. "This is the first time in my many years that I have played at being a helpless maiden." The Wizard raised his voice to a falsetto. *"Help! Help! Help! Who shall save me now?"* A frown from Merlin silenced Balardi, though the Wizard continued to chuckle at his own wit. Kalanin looked to Julian for an explanation, but the Apprentice only shrugged.

All through the long morning, *Alantéa the Forerunner* fled west, surging through rough seas, as heavy rains swept over them. Whether their "crew" was inept, or whether the war fleet following them was simply swifter, by noon the war fleet sailing from the Isles of the Sorcerers had become clearly visible, and with each passing moment was closing swiftly with the *Alantéa*.

"Pretty things, are they not?" Galad asked. The sails of the war fleet had been died or tinted with many colors. Some bore banners showing emblems of the Gods, while other banners were images chosen by the mighty Sorcerer supporting that particular ship. Rain and wind pelted sails, emblems, and banners, but still, the war fleet continued toward them.

"So, Galad continued, "should we arm ourselves? Defend our beloved and charming 'crew?'"

Julian shook his head. The three stood at the ship's stern, watching the oncoming war fleet, their own heads protected only slightly by rain-soaked hoods. Sebastian and Rafir peered out from an upper doorway, while the Godlings watched with silent disdain from amidships.

As their long, losing race continued, the Wizards continued to stare at the oncoming fleet, though from time to time, their eyes glanced skyward into dark storm clouds. A shift in lighting drew Julian's eyes upward also — a portion of the cloud cover had been brushed aside so that one or more Mid-World Powers could view events more clearly.

Warships raced on. Julian could hear nothing from the pursuing fleet; all he could hear was rain pelting down over their own ship, while the masts of the *Alantéa* creaked and its sails flapped and fluttered. Overhead, skies grew patchier as other Mid-World Powers tore sections of clouds away to more clearly view events happening on the high seas. Less than an hour later, the first of the pursuing warships was within casting range. Julian could plainly view the faces of their adversaries' crews: some were laughing gleefully, while others were far more hesitant, glancing over their shoulders at the many ships following behind them, and then to the skies overhead.

A forward catapult launched a hail of stones at the *Alantéa*, intending to shred its sails. Disdainfully, Magog and Turin waved the stones aside, so they splashed into the ocean far to the ship's port side.

Phaedra frowned and turned back to Merlin. "Wizard, some game is being played that we do not understand. As allies, we need to know your plans." As Julian had anticipated, all the previous deference of Phaedra had vanished: she now spoke to Merlin as a queen might to a high ranking but negligent chancellor.

"I offer apologies," Merlin replied, "but to speak my thoughts aloud was to invite more danger than might be desirable. But now, cannot you feel the *trembling*? Behold the sky above."

And now the first challenge to the war fleet launched by the Sorcerers was mounted — but not by Wizards or Godlings. From overhead came a dark, jagged bolt of black lightning, demolishing the lead warship of the Sorcerers' fleet.

Then the sky seemed to burst open. Portals flared overhead. Columns of bright flame surged down, and ships burned. Other ships struggled to turn aside, but the sea seemed to come alive, and coils of dark water lashed over their prows, dragging the warships down to the depths. More lightning burst from overhead. And now, faced by complete destruction in mid-ocean, Portals flared as the most powerful of the Sorcerers struggled to escape.

Merlin shook his head and turned away. "The fools, the poor pitiful fools."

Magog approached the Wizard and stared down at him with arms folded as though sitting in judgment. "Wizard, it was said that the Great

Gods would not act in concert for fear of breaking their ancient pact. What has happened here?"

Merlin stared out into the wreckage, where ships were burning, sinking, while men still tumbled from their ships' sides into an unforgiving sea. "Not long ago, the Truce was invoked against the Demon Princes. It seemed possible, even likely, that any force allying itself with those adversaries might also feel the wrath of the Great Gods. And so, it has proved."

Before Magog could speak further, Phaedra intervened. "Wizard, we cannot and will not be witless followers. I saw clearly how your Wizards understood these matters first, your Apprentice next, and then we were last, together with the Giftless warriors. That process must never happen again."

"And I again apologize," Merlin said. "The first move was ours, to set sail with a mighty warship. The second move belonged to the Adversaries, to counter with a great war fleet — and we were forced to respond before fully discussing this thrust. The third move is ours, something to discuss at sunset when we are dry, and our thoughts are more composed."

· ☽ ·

"So, we are now 'Giftless warriors,'" Galad murmured over dinner, "grouped with other highly regarded creatures like 'bilge rats' or 'worthless harbor scum.'"

"A nice defining moment," Kalanin agreed, "and it almost suggests that we should remove ourselves from this council of great ones. Julian?"

The Apprentice glanced around, then spoke in hushed tones. "Welcome or not, we must always use these opportunities to study the Godlings. What did the Mid-World Powers wish when these Godlings were created? First, a counterweight to the great menace of the Demon Princes. But think: if by some miracle we were to survive the Isle of the Demons, would the Great

Gods be happy to watch the Wizards returning in triumph to their League? Or might they wish the Wizards destroyed and the Godlings alone to return and forge their own palaces among the kingdoms of the Mid-World?"

Kalanin had finished his meal and now sat back, lighting a thin curled pipe. "Of course, that's true," he said, puffing, "though somewhat obvious. The Godlings could not be constructed with betrayal as a clear instruction, because their motivations would soon become too apparent."

"The seeds would be planted, nonetheless," Galad added.

"But those seeds might not sprout in each of them," Julian said thoughtfully, "or if sprouted those seeds might not overcome fellowship built up during a long voyage, or other developments in each Godling's character."

Kalanin shook his head. "I will never again underestimate the malice of the Gods." He puffed for a few moments in silence, then carefully extinguished the embers of his pipe. "So, our insignificant bilge rat brains must continue to study the Godlings. Where do we start?"

"Not known to me at this moment," Julian said, "but if you follow me, even this feeble Apprentice should be able to find the Wizards."

"What of your small allies," Galad asked, "and the Eye of Merlin?"

"Another time," Julian replied, "when the Godlings are more comfortable with them. Come." Julian led them from their quarters far below the topmost upper decks, up a flight of darkened stairs, then through narrow passageways, taking them through a route that led them into the open air of the ship's lower deck. The ship still rose and fell through the ocean, though the roughness of the weather had lessened somewhat, and the sky to the west showed a slight break, allowing creases of sunset to illuminate the western horizon. The "crew" manning their ship had continued to lessen in strength and numbers, worn down by the stress of their ship's daylong efforts to avoid the fleet from the Isles of the Sorcerers.

They hesitated at the door of one of the six great conjuring chambers that had been created for Wizards and Godlings. No emblem or insignia distinguished the conjuring chamber assigned to Phaedra, but to Julian, her aura dominated this region of the ship. Also, beyond the sealed portal he could sense the presence of all three Wizards. As Julian raised his hand to knock, the door, untouched by Godling or Wizard, swung open.

Within the chamber, an oval table had been set, with Wizards and Godlings facing one another on the oval's greater arcs. So large was the conjuring chamber that the oval table, which might have seated more than a score comfortably, seemed little more than a small stand in a great hall. Muted lights lit Phaedra's chamber, set so low that they emphasized the natural radiance cast by the Godlings.

Merlin glanced at the newcomers, then murmured, "Come, sit." To Kalanin's amusement, he felt again like a small child coming late to a great feast, and that his arrival was interrupting some complex ceremony. He and Galad and Julian sat quickly, though to one side, as though they were onlookers, not participants.

"We remain," Merlin continued, "prisoners of circumstances. You, the Godlings are likely, even now, mightier than the Wizards. Yet we must lead for a time because we have gathered knowledge over the long lifetimes granted to us. If I sat upon your side of the table, I might be more than a little unhappy with this situation." The Wizard glanced for a moment into the distance, then turned to the taller, silverish grey Wizard beside him. "Yet in our collaborations, we are determined not to be obsessed by our own needs alone. Thorian?"

With something approaching a sigh, Thorian drew a tablet from a deep pouch within his cloak and passed it across the table.

"Thorian has long been a master of lightning," Merlin explained, "as well as other controlled forces of light. That tablet before you was created as a knowledge Talisman. In a brief time, you three will share Thorian's mastery. Only please, I beg of you, test these weapons out upon the open waters of the sea, not within your chambers."

As the Godlings passed the Talisman back and forth, their interest quickened, and the radiant light within them gleamed brighter. To Kalanin, some of the tension seemed to leave the chamber.

"Balardi will now show you a second Talisman," Merlin continued. "This we must retain for the moment, then we will leave this device with you somewhat later, to help you develop a deeper understanding of the Alternates. Balardi?"

As Thorian had done before him, Balardi reached in a deep pouch and extracted the remaining Talisman of Otherwhen, then pushed it across the table toward the Godlings.

"You are already masters of Portal Magic," Balardi said, "and so pass easily from place to place. It is also known to the Greater Gods that under enormous, supernatural stresses, there may be movement from one distant era to another, back into the past, or even into the future. Do not underestimate the Apprentice, for this slender youngling sitting at your side first lost his Familiars to a far distant time, then was able to retrieve them by drawing them back from the future."

The Godlings regarded Julian solemnly for a moment, then passed the crystal of Otherwhen back and forth with increasing interest.

"I should add that no Greater God, nor being of the Mid-World, nor mortal conjurer has mastered the Timeways," Balardi continued, "for the weight of time has proved too massive, and its structures too intricate. In our explorations, however, we have discovered another dimension, that of the Alternates."

"When a great, decisive moment has come and gone," Merlin added, "with implications for the fate of Earth, the choice unmade branches off, thus creating an alternate reality, one that may linger many tens of thousands of years before fading into nothingness."

"We, the Wizards, have explored only a few of the realms of Otherwhen," Balardi added, "yet, it is also fair to say that our great rivals, the Sorcerers, also have some mastery of these dimensions, for if we retain one Talisman, the Sorcerers have the other two."

Thorian drew a deep, impatient breath and spoke for the first time. "Alcman and Houma serve the Demon Princes, and so we believe these two have been preoccupied with organizing the Isles of the Sorcerers for battle with our warship and have had little chance to further explore Otherwhen."

A moment of contemplation passed in silence, and then Phaedra leaned back, glancing at her brothers. "These Wizards are going to propose a change in course, a journey through Otherwhen. Watch yourselves, my brethren." Turning to Merlin, she challenged the Wizard, "And why are you even raising this question? Those feeble, haphazard constructs that you created to crew this vessel are failing even as we speak — they were never meant to endure throughout our voyage; and so, you planned a Journey through Otherwhen from the beginning. Why are you now consulting us after a decision has already been made?"

"First," Merlin said evenly, "we will not embark on any change in plans without your agreement. As to our constructs, other, far more competent beings, can easily be discovered or created. Secondly, any shift to Otherwhen substantially lessens the time of this voyage and greatly reduces the chance that our adversaries will intercept our warship. Also, it may be in your long-term interests to develop a power that no God has explored. And last, we need the strength within you three to shift this huge vessel through Portals leading to Otherwhen."

Turin was listening to Merlin's words, but his fingers glowed as they danced over the Crystal of Otherwhen. Still silent, he passed the Talisman beyond Phaedra's hands toward the fingertips of Magog. After a few moments of silent contemplation, the two brothers glanced to Phaedra and nodded, though, to Julian, their gestures seemed so barely noticeable that he felt he had imagined them. But after, events changed so swiftly that it was obvious that the Godlings and the Wizards had agreed to a change in course.

Chapter Eight

Journey through Otherwhen

"Ha!" the Eye of Merlin croaked out a laugh. "These Godlings may grow daily in power, but they will never equal the wisdom of my master Merlin." The eagle was perched on the foremost railing of the warship's great prow, as it surged south and east. Sebastian and Rafir peered out into the gloom, listening as the Eye of Merlin described events in the chambers below. Just to their right, the last crease of sunset had been enveloped by darkness. Even though it was the middle of summer, Sebastian had begun to shiver. Low, dark clouds loomed overhead, though to the far west a few pale stars were struggling to bring light to a restless, surging, dark ocean.

"Now, my small friends and allies," the eagle croaked, "prepare yourselves for a change in weather. I do not believe that a sudden frost will overwhelm us; though I am ready to pull you both to safety should harsh weather threaten us. But still, you should prepare yourselves."

The ship began shuddering; heaving, groaning sounds rumbled through the air. The sky above flickered and sparkled with shifting light patterns. The sea around them became less substantial as though seawater had been changed into a foamy mist.

"I'm sorry," Rafir said in a small voice, "can you tell me again what's happening?"

"Otherwhen," the eagle replied, showing unusual patience. "We must represent some remote hazard to the Demon Princes, for they have chosen to contest our passage. Now we will vanish!"

Something like a distant explosion rumbled over them. Suddenly the sky was clear, with bright, clear starshine pouring down upon them. The air, turning suddenly chill, covered the great warship with an icy frost.

"Ha!" the eagle croaked. "I was not far wrong! Huddle together for a few moments, then we will seek warmer quarters. Welcome to Never-Was, look out upon the strange vistas of Might-Have-Been!"

Sebastian shook with the cold, but he stared out in wonder at the new, brighter, and colder world around them. If the sky above had changed, the ocean scenery had also grown more complicated: in addition to the sea's foam peaks and dark valleys, distant icebergs gleamed white in the starlight. And the sounds of their voyage had changed, too. The ship's timbers were shuddering and groaning as they struggled to adjust to the cold, but now strange, throaty voices were calling out, and oars were splashing through foamy seas. The remaining constructs were losing control of the ropes they held, then they were sliding to the ground, as the last energies of their zombie lives froze into nothingness, and frost claimed their failing bodies.

A new crew came up the ship's sides and set to man the ship. These mariners were broad and strong, dressed in fur lined clothing to counter the cold, and they crewed the ship as though they had long prepared for this task. Curled hair only partly concealed the short, pointed horns that jutted out above their foreheads. Sebastian shivered with the cold, but he was so curious, he was unwilling to seek shelter below.

"And so, life might have evolved had the Demon Princes brought forth a parallel race of humans instead of their Dragon Broods," the eagle mused, "though we may never...." The Eye of Merlin fell suddenly silent as one of the mariners had caught his eyes and seemed to hold the Eye frozen. This mariner was older, with receding hair revealing prominent, sharp horns, and he was also set apart from the others by his ornaments: unlike the other, simply clad seamen, he wore bandoliers of charms lapped over his shoulders and about his waist.

With an effort, the eagle broke the sight-lock and looked away into the darkness. "Do not trifle with this man," the eagle croaked, suddenly subdued. "Behold a Charm Master, powered by many talismans, perhaps the equivalent, in this land, of a Sorcerer. Come. It is late and colder than we wish. Time to seek shelter within."

As they descended, their eyes were drawn back to shifting motions on the broad decks. The original seafaring constructs, their time passed, had lost body mass, and now the winds were lifting their drying husks and sweeping them out into the starlit ocean.

The eagle croaked out a deep, dark laugh. "Farewell to our faithful 'crew!' Unloved and now lost forever, unless they are favored by the crabs of the shoreline or the blind grey worms at the bottom of the sea. There are legends that we, the Familiars, may choose to return and be reborn after death — and so I do not recommend returning as an unlovely zombie construct of the Wizards!"

· X ·

As the next days stretched into a week, Rafir explored the huge warship from its topmost deck down to its deepest holds. As an invisible Mid-World

Spy, Rafir had learned that he was most difficult to detect, and so he hoped to discover more of the Godlings' ways. However, this proved a difficult task, for many protective spells had been placed on the Godlings' conjuring chambers — as well as on those of the Wizards.

Sometimes when the Godlings' experiments took place on the upper decks, Rafir was able to view their intense satisfaction as they cast powerful lightning or enormous bolts of jagged black force out over the ocean, forces that shattered the upper portions of huge icebergs. Other times the conjuring chambers of the Godlings seemed to shudder with repressed violence, or even to draw light from the surrounding passageways, and then Rafir was grateful that he had not been able to penetrate further inside.

In one of the few times that Rafir was able to slip past the barriers of the great chambers, he found Turin absorbed in silent contemplation, frowning into the distance. As Turin stared, the green power-seeking portion of his form seemed to ebb, and the aura of gold contemplation seemed to grow stronger. Another time, the fox entered Balardi's great chamber while the Wizard, shaking his head in sorrow, recorded some long-forgotten event in a great leather-bound journal.

Only once did Rafir discover anything of note, and even then, the fox was unable to make much sense of the moment. Phaedra's conjuring chamber had been radiating a strange magic, and just before the chamber sealed itself, Rafir slipped within. In the chamber's center, a shallow basin had been set. Though it held only a thin layer of liquid, it was large enough for Rafir to completely bath in it — if he had dared to come closer. As Phaedra chanted, red and silver coils of smoke lifted from the basin's seething liquid, and as the smell of burning cloves filled the chamber, the coils reached out, and links of smoke embraced her.

Phaedra began quivering, twisting, then writhing in ecstasy, red and silver radiances flaring from her body.

Embarrassed, the fox slipped away and hid, waiting until other tremors on distant portions of the warship told him that the forces of magic had moved elsewhere. Then the fox fled to the upper decks, letting the chill of the night air cleanse the smell of burning cloves from his soft fur.

Another time, Rafir found his way into the warship's dark hold and walked along the catwalk suspended from above. Below him was a vast, dark, and empty space, so large that groaning sounds from the ship's passage echoed back and forth in the darkness. What were they going to do with all this space? Take treasure back from the Isle of the Demons? That seemed so unlikely, that the fox shook his head.

Even Rafir's night vision was unable to deal with the shadows and the darkness, so after a few moments, the fox shuddered and left the dark hold, never to return.

As they reached the tenth night of their voyage, strange, remote sounds roused Rafir from a deep sleep. In their chamber, Julian was sound asleep on his bunk, while Sebastian lay slumped at the bunk's base, buried in Julian's cloak. In a flash, the fox vanished and was leaping up the long stairways, then sprinting through the narrow passageways that led out into the lower decks.

It was deep into the night, but starshine glistened down from above and radiated white light from nearby glaciers. Merlin was on deck, together with the Charm Master who led the horned mariners. The two spoke solemnly for a moment, then Merlin passed to him a bandolier filled with a score of devices crafted by the Wizards for the Charm Master. Bowing, the mariner's leader then clapped his hands three times. His crew left their posts and began slipping over the *Alantéa's* side, into the longboats awaiting them.

Nothing, not even constructs, now crewed the vessel — except that the eagle, the Eye of Merlin, was at the ship's prow, ready to leap forward into the starlit darkness. Merlin raised his arms and again called out *words*. Energies flared, then linked to Wizards and Godlings below the upper decks. As before, the ship shook and shuddered, sails flapping as though entering a land of uncertain winds. Ocean waters churned with air, becoming the substance of foam.

Then the sky above became much brighter. The moon loomed overhead, seeming lower —and much larger than the moon above Alantéa and the Far Lands. If the moon was brighter, it was also more heavily scarred, with deep craters raked by lines of force, as though Earth's battles had spilled over to its airless companion.

The air was suddenly warmer, too, and the massive timbers of the warship were creaking and groaning as they adjusted to the swift change in weather. They had passed into another region of Otherwhen. The fox stared at the glowing, scarred moon, wondering what force of magic could possibly have reached that far, with such power.

Ringing sounds from remote gongs echoed out over the waters, and Rafir looked away from the moon and out over the broad, calm waters. Three ships were moving toward them, oared galleys pulling toward them over a moonlit ocean. On the upper decks, Merlin had somehow produced a small gong and was tapping out some measured response. Rafir resisted the impulse to rouse Sebastian — he could tell his fellow Familiar in the morning.

The three galleys pulled alongside. A new crew climbed aboard. These were more clearly human, though taller, and leaner than the humans of Alantéa — many stood taller even than Kalanin. Each mariner wore a necklace of seven stones, resting on a shirt of light fabric. One, an elder, with the regal motions of a king, wore only a single stone on a necklace, and this mariner approached Merlin gravely, as though equals were gathering in the night on the upper decks of the great warship. After several minutes watching their replacement crew take control of the ship, while their patrons murmured soft words to each other, Rafir yawned, deciding that the exploration of this part of Otherwhen could wait until morning.

At mid-morning, however, Rafir was still asleep, while other voyagers were exploring their new realm of Otherwhen. Finally, Sebastian shook the fox awake, bringing news.

"You need to get up," Sebastian said gently. "I'm guessing that you were awake when we shifted away from Glacier World, but now we've been invited to one of their big mumbling sessions."

"I thought we were too unimportant," the fox said, yawning, "and what's there to talk about, anyway?"

"I have absolutely no idea," Sebastian replied, "but Julian thinks we should be there."

They gathered, as before, in the great conjuring chamber assigned to Phaedra. All came to this gathering: Godlings, Wizards, Julian, and his Familiars, Galad and Kalanin, and even the Eye of Merlin was perched upon the back of a lone chair, regarding the proceedings with a hint of scorn.

Phaedra spoke first. "Wizards, I have no idea why you have called us to this place. I speculated before that you had some device to transform the nature of our voyage, but now I understand only that you wish to tell us something that's not to our liking — why else would you attend us in our own quarters rather than your own? But come now, master Wizard, speak your mind."

Merlin nodded. "All that you say is true; you understand us only too well. Yet we, the Wizards, for all our careful preparations, have been caught off guard. One of the Greater Gods has left aboard a device intended to speak with those of the League, some distance from Alantéa and the Mid-World of the Truce."

"And so?" Phaedra said. "Bring this device forward and let us all share in its wisdom."

"In all fairness," Merlin replied, "I do not think we can share this knowledge with you, for it deals with the far, distant past, in the remote history of the League."

"Is there power to be gained?" Turin asked. "That question cuts to the heart of the matter."

"I believe so," Merlin said, "but power only to harm the League, power to bring the anger of the Greater Gods down upon the Wizards and their League."

As Merlin spoke, Magog and Turin began staring out into the distance, as though having lost interest, but Phaedra leaned forward. "This is not a happy moment, Wizard."

Merlin sighed. "We are allies now, but in a hundred years — if indeed we survive — you three will progress upwards among the ranks of the Gods, and one of you might be tempted to use information against us, to further enhance your own powers."

Phaedra looked away, glancing left and right to her brethren, then she suddenly smiled. "Then let us put the best face that we can upon this matter, and say that we are only allies, not lovers who must share everything. Find some other gift of power to compensate us. Now, go and share your guilty little secrets among yourselves." In her smile was a glint of malice, for as beings of the Mid-World, the Godlings were destined to outlive the Wizards by thousands of years.

They left the Godlings to their contemplations and gathered in Merlin's great conjuring chamber. Equal in size to that of Phaedra's, Merlin's chamber seemed somehow more comfortable, for Merlin had decorated the larger sides of the oval chamber with tapestries. To the larger portside wall of the chamber was an image of the early struggles of the Wizards'

League, showing Tuvan of old, before its destruction many years ago. To the starboard side, a great tapestry showed the Halls of Merlin at Sea's Edge, though the coastline seemed quite different, somehow more natural, and Julian guessed that this image of Sea's Edge also reflected an earlier, more peaceful time.

Only a single armchair had been placed in Merlin's chamber, set so that Merlin could contemplate his tapestry of Sea's Edge. Braziers, stands littered with parchment, and lecterns holding open grimoires were placed haphazardly throughout the chamber. Merlin's guests stood, somewhat awkwardly, for the Wizard was unprepared for this gathering and only the carpet could be sat upon.

"If you believe that all three Wizards have conspired to bring you to this place," Balardi said, "you would be wrong. Neither Thorian nor I have any idea what Merlin will reveal to us."

"First," Merlin said, "a confession: I have been so long absorbed by my own devices that I have forgotten that we are lesser powers, that the Great Gods are capable of subtle magic beyond our own conjurations. So many times, have I inspected this ship, or charged unseen servants with such tasks, that I never dreamed that any Power would conceal anything on this warship. Yet after we made our first passage through Otherwhen, a device of power made itself known to me." He held up a Talisman, one that was set upon a necklace of silver, with a white tablet showing the open-mouthed face of a Gorgon.

"The emblem of Pallas Athena," Thorian murmured, "once, at least, a partial ally to the League."

"Tale's end," Balardi said softly, "she was a force for good at the first great test of the League, and yet she has never spoken to us since that time — she must feel that our rule over the South of Alantéa has now come to a close."

"Before further discussion," Merlin said grimly, "we must seal ourselves off." For the next moments, the Wizards busied themselves with low, murmured words, as they addressed each wall and corner of the chamber, holding their staffs aloft as they chanted. Invisible servants, some murmuring in complaint, found themselves forced into outside passages.

"Now," Merlin said, far more softly, "we the Wizards speak rarely of these events, even among ourselves, but the League in its early days fought a long, limited war along its borders. Later, that partial war burst into a grim struggle, one that almost destroyed the League."

"In our struggles with the Sorcerers and the Marids," Balardi added, "you encountered references to '*The Wild Time*'."

"At the height of our '*Wild Time*'," Merlin continued, "two Powers launched plagues of Vorrs, and Uraks, and Carags, and Creatures of the Darkness upon us, followed after by the Enchanters, a force probably greater in strength than any combination of power the Wizards and our League might have wielded. The Enchanters might well have prevailed had they not worked at cross purposes with the two Gods supporting them."

"Tale's end," Balardi said. "Do not gloss over these events."

Merlin sighed. "At the very end of this struggle, we were compelled to reveal our own strength: for the Great God Set came openly against us, and on that fateful day, we the three Wizards had the mastery of Set."

"Victory over the Great God Set," Kalanin said in a hollow, astonished voice. "No wonder that such an event has been hidden from us. But how does Pallas Athena come into this story?"

"While we fought Set," Merlin replied, "the Dark Lord Mordred attacked our greatest servants and allies. With the weapons provided by Pallas Athena, they also prevailed."

"Even so," Kalanin said, astonished, "two Gods defied the Truce, came openly against the League — and the League survived."

"We survived," Merlin said, "though we will not speak again of these events outside of this room."

"Another Power aided us," Thorian added. "Since we have come to this moment of truth, I will say this: for many decades that unnamed ally remained a mystery, but I will name him now. Wotan, mighty even among the Greater Gods, endowed a slight Familiar named 'Ghorm' with an Adept's strength, and that added strength was enough — just enough — to turn Mordred aside. And lastly, I will speak the name I never thought my lips would again form: Sentauris."

"Sentauris," Merlin said softly, "a name you will not speak outside of this chamber, yet she was the binding force, the catalyst that enabled our League to survive."

"Sentauris," Balardi added. "Every time I think of her, I rejoice in her strength. The League should have named monuments, plazas, even dedicated a great city to her, but we have found that to speak her name invites the wrath of the Powers of the Mid-World, and so, to keep the peace, Sentauris is a name we do not speak."

"We were unable to learn," Merlin said, "why the Powers detested Sentauris so greatly, though it may be revealed to us now, for Pallas Athena was once her patroness. I think now we can invoke the Talisman. Under these circumstances, it might be best if I alone spoke for us. Is this agreed?"

Each nodded. Still standing uncertainly, they turned to face Merlin and watched as he cleared a lectern. Then the Wizard carried it to the starboard side so that the great tapestry showing the Halls of Merlin formed a backdrop to the stand. On this stand, Merlin placed the white emblem of Pallas Athena, then stood back with the others.

"Great Goddess," Merlin said softly, "you wished to speak with us, and so we are here to listen."

From the open gorgon's mouth of the emblem, a white smoke poured forth, surging into the chamber until it formed a massive marble-white image of the Goddess, Pallas Athena. She stood, as in many of her temples, with her helmet back, the gorgon-emblem on her breast, a spear in her right hand, while in her left hand, she held a shield that was nearly as high as her body.

Dwarfed by the huge image, the humans bowed their heads then watched on as the statue drew breath and spoke:

"Wizards and servants of the League, the creation that stands before you is only an Avatar, a lesser creation of myself endowed with my thoughts. To this Avatar you may speak without fear, for this construct has no link to me, and when silenced, it will vanish utterly, passing into nothingness as though it had never been." A touch of crushed juniper lingered in the air like a faint incense.

Merlin said nothing, only bowing in acknowledgment, then watching warily as the huge marble mouth of the Goddess formed words.

"First," the marble lips intoned, "we must deal with a mystery. Who was Sentauris? What was her link to the League? And why are none now permitted to speak her name? Sentauris was my most beloved servant. Even Gods, however, feel the bitterness of betrayal when their greatest followers leave their service, and for long I only watched her struggles from afar. Yet when your League was attacked, I understood that she had been drawn into an enormous *Web of Fate*, and then I aided her, first as a partial friend, then more openly when I understood that her death would bring me great pain.

"In the end, you prevailed, Wizards, and thought little more of me. Yet, after, I was threatened at every step by both greater and lesser Gods. My peoples suffered, and I was forced to withdraw from Alantéa the Forerunner.

Wotan also aided your League, as did Thoth, but either they were more discrete or more powerful than I was then, and so any malice directed at them was easily turned aside.

"Still, as I withdrew, I retreated into a time of great contemplation. Among the many questions, I explored was the role of Sentauris, for I came to understand that many themes and forces underlay the fate of Alantéa the Forerunner. At last, through means both subtle and devious, I learned that Sentauris, with her great strength as a Seeress, was descended from Orissa, a mighty Seeress, who once stood as a force in the Hall of the Dreamers."

"Orissa," Merlin whispered, "who now drifts aimlessly and witlessly through the Temple of Waiting. I never guessed...."

"You thought as I did," the great statue spoke with marble-white, fluid lips, "that the power of Seers was a random subset of the Gift. Wizards, there is more. I believe that your greatest servants, those named Julian, and Galad, and Kalanin, are with you at this time, because the blood of Sentauris also flows through their veins, as it does through a number of other heroic mortals within Alantéa the Forerunner."

Astonished, Kalanin glanced at Julian and Galad. It made sense that Julian with his Gift had descended from a great lineage, but....

"That explains much," Merlin said softly. "In the remote portions of my mind, I sometimes considered that the thoughts or expressions of these three were faintly familiar to others who had aided us, though I never considered...."

"This lineage must never be discussed outside this chamber, for we must not let our servants become exposed to the malice of the Powers because of their heritage. Yet we still have not spoken of the antagonism of the Gods, and why it should have been directed at Sentauris. She was outspoken when angered, while much of the time she was cautious with her words."

"Do you not recall" the Avatar of Pallas Athena replied, "how the soothsaying would come upon Sentauris as though a greater power had taken possession of her mind? Then she was linked with the innermost machineries of Destiny and could not guard her tongue. A great vision came upon her, and she spoke of the end of Alantéa and the ruin of the Gods — and her words were spoken so publicly and replayed so many times by the Powers, that they could not be denied or defended.

"In the aftermath of that fateful foretelling, many Gods moved decisively against her, and so she vanished. I wept at the thought of an assassin's dagger striking at her great heart. Yet years later, one by one, heroes, sages, and magic wielders emerged, and I alone recognized them as children of Sentauris, for had I not seen clearly into her innermost substance? Perhaps she found her way to regions of this Otherwhen and lived out the full years of her life in peace. I chose to believe so, for even the Gods may take comfort in fairy tales."

"For what it is worth," Merlin said, "I also have good reason to believe that Sentauris lived fulfilled and died in peace. Goddess, we thank you for your aid of old, and your wisdom at this moment. Now, are you able to speak of the Isle of the Demons? Should we take comfort that our foes have attempted to turn us aside and have not prevailed?"

From the huge marble white lips came a soft laugh. "A lure only for the Godlings, to draw them to the enchanted Isle of the Demons, so that all of you can be swallowed whole."

"That is what we feared," Merlin said softly. "And yet even upon the Isle of the Demons, the Demon Princes have not completely mastered the most powerful of the Guardians. Can we not ally ourselves with this being?"

The great head of Pallas Athena seemed to bow; her eyes closed as though in contemplation. "When I seek your destinies, I behold many things:

"Such is the strength of these Demon Princes and their allies, that they have cast a great Sending, shaped like dagger surging toward the Maker's Heart. Immense with power, throbbing with malice and hatred, it surges beyond the circles of our sun, gathering a speed greater than the swiftest beams of light. Nothing in the wide universe has ever matched its dark designs.

"A place of great authority has been cast down, and a portion of the Maker's Design is no more. The Hall of the Dreamers is a lost and broken thing, while the Dreamers drift endlessly alongside the Immortal Dead in the Temple of Waiting.

"The most powerful of the Guardians snarls and struggles like some powerful but cornered beast, though he is beset by greater forces and survives only because he has taken refuge like a wounded creature in a network of enchanted caves and tunnels from which he will never emerge.

"And you, Wizards and Godlings, your little war party is no more than a band of lesser Goblins assailing a Kingdom of Storm Giants — for a time you may survive, slipping into the nooks and crannies of a great realm, yet when the Storm Giants discover the Goblin band, those intruders will be smashed to pulp, then reduced to dark stains on broken stones."

"And yet," Merlin prompted, "and yet...."

The Avatar of Pallas Athena sighed. "And yet, in all our many thousands of Divinations, always a small grey area *may* be found, where strange, uncertain events *might* take place."

Merlin nodded somberly. "Because there *might* be, no there *will* be some action taken by the Gods."

The great marble features frowned, set in gloom. "It will be no more than a gesture, though I and others will strive to strengthen the Mid-World's resolve. Now, I must bid you farewell and wish you Maker's Speed. At this, our last meeting, I must also add these words: in the innermost core of my being, sometimes I wish that I had stood beside Aui Kwan Yin, when she fought so valiantly against the Sorcerers and the Marids, for if I had fallen beside her, I would have felt more just and stronger at the End of Time."

The great marble form of Pallas Athena grew still as a statue, staring resolutely into the distance. Then, it began to quiver and slide, becoming a white smoke that poured always more swiftly back into its own Gorgon mouth. Finally, the Gorgon mouth itself wavered, its substance transformed into vapor, passing like shadows overcome by light until no hint of its existence remained. The faint odor of crushed juniper lingered only seconds longer, then it, too, was gone.

The Wizards gathered together, speaking in low voices, unable to conceal their surprise.

Galad glanced at Julian and Kalanin. "Cousins," he murmured, face filled with a strange dark humor.

Days passed, with the *Alantéa* surging forward through soft seas under clear skies. Godlings continued to stare at Wizards with eyes that were filled with suspicion, and the Wizards could only look away — because yes, the Wizards had their secrets, even from their human allies. Merlin, Thorian, and Balardi had several hushed discussions, but nothing was said to the Godlings, or even to the human allies of the Wizards.

On the third day following the revelations of Pallas Athena, the Eye of Merlin woke Sebastian and Rafir by croaking three harsh words, "Red Rain. Come!" Then the eagle turned, wings flared, hopping, and scrambling to the upper decks with all the speed he could muster in cramped quarters.

When Sebastian and Rafir reached the upper decks, they stood open mouthed in astonishment. The skies were raining red down on the warship

— not just a pink mist, but red as blood droplets were showering down over the *Alantéa*.

Godlings had gathered to the port side and stared up at skies that bled Red Rain. The Wizards were at the prow of the ship, heads bowed in sorrow, while their human servants watched the Wizards, standing under an overhang, as yet untouched by Red Rain.

"Come," the eagle said to the Familiars as he flapped strong wings and coasted over to the Godlings, who continued to stare upward, red drops spilling over their eyes and faces. Julian took a deep breath and jogged over the red colored, slick deck. Linked to the mind of Merlin, the eagle was going to explain matters of magic to the Godlings. Kalanin and Galad followed a step behind Julian.

"Here we stand in Otherwhen, in Neverwas," the eagle croaked. "We are encountering things that failed to come to pass, but we can learn from these events. The Powers of the Mid-World are wary and seldom refer to the Maker, though some have called him, 'He who never answers,' or 'The God who doesn't listen.' Here in this portion of Otherwhen, the Maker dispatched an Avatar, a mighty extension of himself, though lacking the full power of the Maker."

"And what happened?" the eagle continued. "That Avatar was attacked and destroyed, not just by Demon Princes, but also by Seraphs and Dragons and Spirit Lords, aided by mortals with magic. And so, the Maker determined that this intervention should never happen. Can any of you wonder that the skies weep Red Rain?"

Red Rain, Julian thought, *a vision sent long ago by the Maker, though He never intended that Red Rain would offer a red beacon for our foes. And look at the Wizards! They expected something different, a revelation that would aid them in dealing with their foes. Instead, they met with Red Rain!*

· ʎ ·

Through Gates of Dreams, a sleeping Julian wandered along a sandy shore under bright but overcast skies. In his dream, he was six years old again, holding his grandmother's hand as they walked in silence along the beach. They were hugging the waterline, feeling some safety on the sands, while menacing shapes and strange, wild growths lurked inland upon the Isle of the Demons.

Julian's grandmother came to a halt, her eyes staring into the distance with a benign but purposeless expression. As Julian turned toward her, he was astonished to discover that she was holding a second six-year old's hand. The two children looked at each other with quiet, grave faces. Julian understood then that dream visions had placed him beside Eléna, Thorian's daughter, and that each of them had been transformed by the Dreamways to children.

"Hello, Julian, who has come to save me," Eléna, said, smiling a soft, sad smile.

"I am not alone," Julian said. *"Your father, Thorian, leads, with other Wizards and the Godlings beside him. I will also try to save you, if I can."*

"Poor Papa! If he comes here, he will die. You might live for a while as a pawn of the Great Guardian, but Papa will die. Do not come here, Julian. I will beg my patron, the Great Guardian, to force you far from the Isle of the Demons, though he has so little power left."

They resumed their slow pace over moist sands. Soft ocean winds blew strands of hair from the foreheads of the two children. Cloud masses looming over the enchanted Isle made the day much colder. Only quiet lapping sounds could be heard, though menace lurked in the air. Julian felt as though many eyes stared down on them from the high ground above the cliffs, watching the progress of the two children and their guide — like Gargoyles watching insects in the sand.

"*Do not come here, Julian,*" Eléna said again. "*You will be trapped as I am trapped, and never released. Then you will fight and flee and die over and over again. Do not worry about me, for the Great Guardian says that I will be permitted to die again soon, this time forever, and so I will suffer no more.*"

In his dream, Julian glanced again at his grandmother, for after his parents had been lost crossing into the League, his grandmother had supplied all the love and nurturing of his early years. But his grandmother's ghost seemed completely unaware, reduced to clutching the hands of two children so they would not be swept out to sea by a rogue wave.

"*Do not die the real death, Eléna,*" Julian said, "*for we are coming with the greatest power our peoples can muster. The Wizards may have made a grave error and let us be known to our foes, but they are still strong with powerful allies. Yet are there no other forces upon the Isle of the Demons? You say you are linked to the greatest of the Guardians of the World. What of the other Guardians? Have they all been corrupted by the Demon Princes?*"

"*Twenty-five Guardians were created in the beginning,*" Eléna murmured softly, as though reciting some ancient lore, "*and for ages they had mastery over three of the most powerful Demon Princess, embracing those dark powers with transforming dreams from which the Demons could not escape. The Mid-World of the Truce came into being, transforming other Demon Princes into Gods like Set, or Ahriman, or Moloch, and still, the Guardians held the three greatest Demon Princes entranced by dreams.*

"*Then came disaster and ruin. Of the Guardians, twelve were corrupted into the service of the Demon Princess. Another twelve were overcome to be transformed into things unliving, and one, my patron, the Great Guardian, was substantially diminished and survives only by stealth.*

"*Of the twelve corrupted Guardians, two were destroyed in battle with the Gods, and so only ten remain. Yet these ten Guardians alone are greater than your small force, while behind the ten Guardians lie the Demon Princes, exiled Dark Lords, and the Sorcerers and the Marids. Do not set foot upon the Isle of the Demons, for you will not survive, much less triumph."*

"We are coming to the Isle," Julian said. *"We have faced great odds before and survived. Make ready, for we are coming."*

"Poor Papa," Eléna again murmured, *"so fierce and strong, and yet he will die soon." They trudged along the sands in silence for a moment. Julian could feel the dreaming link slipping away from the two: the sky above had become patchy, and the sea's foamcaps were becoming as still as pond water.*

Eléna pulled away from the elder's hand and slipped behind Julian's grandmother, to clasp Julian's left hand. "Wait, Julian, do not leave me yet. The Great Guardian tells me that a change has come about even as we speak. The Demon Princes in their malice greatly desire to draw you into the Guardians' dream kingdoms, but Dark Lords and Sorcerers and Marids seethe with hatred and wish to destroy you now. Somehow you have made yourself known to them. Make ready to fight, then flee. Farewell, Julian, who tried so hard to save —" The shoreline was suddenly racked by concussions and the three figures were sent sprawling onto damp sands. The dreaming link of the Apprentice was shattered.

And Julian woke to find himself hurled from his bunk. Great smashing sounds could be heard from below decks. The huge warship seemed to be tilting, its mighty frame shuddering. Clutching his staff, Julian crawled over shifting and slanting floors, through the doorway into their shared area. There, Galad and Kalanin already stood, clad in light chain mail.

"Marids," Galad muttered, bracing himself with one hand while drawing a bow with arrows meant to destroy Marids with his other hand.

"Two Marids have swum upward from the ocean depths," Kalanin said, "and have broken through the base of our ship, into the sub-hold. Torrents of seawater are flooding us, while Marids tear the *Alantéa* apart. Unless we can stop them, our ship is doomed." Julian grasped his staff and stood. Then the three raced downward through narrow passages, sliding downward as the ship tilted. Smashing sounds alternated with explosions, as Godlings hurled jagged lightning at Marids. The huge warship trembled, and great rushing sounds could be heard as ocean waters surged through the warship's shattered hull.

Down they raced through dark passages. Julian's staff blazed brightly in the darkness. Below them, Marids hooted, boomed, smashed. Great power lashed at the Demon-spawned Marids, but neither Godlings nor Wizards seemed able to stop them.

Smash! The ship heaved and the three humans were hurled down to the base of a narrow flight of stairs. Julian took a deep breath; flashed light again from his staff, and then he led them further downward.

"Shielded," Julian panted, "the Marids are shielded. We must find a counter. If not, then...." He halted as the three reached a hatch that led to the ship's great sub-hold. As one, Kalanin and Galad tore the hatch open, while Julian beamed light into the darkness below.

But lights, varied lights, were already pulsing below. In the warship's great sub-hold, Godlings hovered in the air, radiating bright light as they hurled jagged lightning at enormous Marids. Power, too, surged from the Wizards as they struggled to restrain the onrushing seas, while simultaneously trying to heal the ship's siding. But the Marids — one greater scarred being, and a second unblemished Marid — would not be controlled, smashing at the warship's center keel, hammering at the warship's siding. At the base of the warship, the ocean, in the fullness of its dark, cold power, was claiming the *Alantéa,* filling its murky hold with seawater.

"They have shields," Julian muttered. The Marids gleamed with spell-shields of such force that neither the Wizards' power nor that of the Godlings seemed able to breach them.

Kalanin peered down the hatchway: beneath them, just to their left, ran a narrow catwalk that hung suspended from the dark hold's ceiling. Swift as cats, Kalanin, and Galad swung down and drew bows. Julian floated downward just a split second behind them. His staff flared with light and power.

Galad and Kalanin loosed arrows. Marid shields hissed then gleamed with pale fire — but they held. One Marid turned on them, booming, recognizing old foes with a blaze of hatred. As Julian's staff radiated defiance, the Marid surged toward them. Galad drew the Tarnished Sword, while Kalanin notched a second arrow and backed three paces along the walkway.

The huge fists of Marids smashed the walkway into splintered wreckage, while simultaneously, Galad leaped forward and hewed at the nearest great hand. And the Tarnished Sword slashed through Sorcerous shielding, biting deeply into Demon-spawned flesh. At the edge of freefall, Kalanin buried a shaft with a force of sorcery into the crease opened by the Tarnished Sword.

As the Marid writhed in agony, Kalanin and Galad dropped like stones into the hold's dark, chilled seawater, tearing the chain mail from their sinking bodies as they fell. Julian fell more slowly, and part of his mind was struggling to understand the nature of the shadows that had lurked just at the edge of his sight.

"Watch! Merlin, watch!" Julian cried, dropping faster. "Houma has come! And Alcman —" Dark waters swallowed him for a second, then he was back on the surface, one hand grasping his staff, eyes searching for the motions of shadows.

Amid the flashing lights, twisting dark shadows swirled overhead. The Marid that Galad and Kalanin had wounded now toppled dead, falling face first into the water of the hold. The second burst through the ship's siding then surged out into the darkness of the night sea. Merlin's staff flashed and shields like great disks formed before each of the three Godlings. But out of the darkness, two clusters of shadows came together. Houma and Alcman had come. Rays of power — Demon tools — burned through Merlin's shields and lashed at Turin. The Godling had invoked his own armor — flaring green with the power of Dragons, augmented with the golden radiance of Seraphs — but that armor, too, was breached; and Turin recoiled, stricken. Houma cried out in triumph.

The Wizards, filled with anger, hurled power at the Sorcerers, though the shadowy figures had vanished as though they had never been — the Assassins had struck again. Merlin and his Godling allies gathered around Turin, while Balardi and Thorian struggled to seal the wounded warship from dark, eager waters.

Julian treaded water, turning to see if Galad or Kalanin needed help. Light flared from his staff: the two warriors had shed enough chain mail so they could stay afloat. Now, as the Wizards forced water from the hold, first Kalanin's then Galad's feet found footing — they were standing on the still submerged body of the dead Marid.

"Did they...?" asked Galad.

Julian swam toward them. "Turin is wounded, though he is not in mortal danger. It was much too close though." Suddenly they were lifting from the hold's depths. More light flashed from Julian's staff. Wizards and Godlings had departed, except for Magog, who was drawing them upward: one hand was extended, and from that hand, greyish black tendrils of magic flowed, gripping the three humans. They passed up through the hatchway and proceeded, still drawn by the Godling's power, through narrow passages toward the upper reaches of the great warship.

As they passed from the wreckage of the lower holds, Magog turned and regarded them somberly. "How is it," the Godling murmured, "that this Apprentice, least in power, was the first to sense the ambush of our foes?

And how was it that this warrior, least in force of arms, cast the lone fatal blow against the Demon Spawned Marids?"

Kalanin shivered with cold and discomfort, though diplomacy forced him to reply. "Some force of Destiny is at work, governing all of our fates. We, the Giftless Warriors, will have lesser roles, while yours will be far greater. Wait and see." *And consider this, my fancy Godling ally,* Kalanin's mind whispered, *while Godlings and Wizards developed their intricate magic, Galad and I were also improving our crude warrior skills.*

They reached the upper portions of the warship where the great conjuring chambers had been constructed. Still shivering and dripping seawater, the three followed Magog into Phaedra's chamber. Others had gathered there, but this meeting lacked all the elaborate staging of previous gatherings. Even the lighting was haphazard, with pools of darkness gathering in the farthest corners of the chamber.

Just a few paces into the chamber, Phaedra stood glaring down at Merlin, while Thorian and Balardi tended Turin closer to the chamber's center. Much of the Godling's radiance was restoring itself as Turin's wounds closed and his body healed.

"We are finished," Phaedra snarled at Merlin, "with diplomatic dances. You are by default the leader of this haphazard expedition, and you have guided us to near disaster. Explain yourself."

"Our enemies are powerful," Merlin said quietly. "We have done our best to map regions of Otherwhen and chosen sections of the Alternates that lessened the power of our foes. In this region, for example, a counterforce has risen to contest the Sorcerers and the Marids."

"Warfare surges around this stricken ship," Turin said, in a voice that was far more subdued than his Godling sister's.

"I, too, feel death in dark, icy waters," Merlin added. "It might help us if we were to view such matters. We can see many events from afar. Let us —"

"Enough of your Vision Screens, Wizard," Phaedra muttered. "It is time for the Godlings to put forth our own powers. My brothers!" Lights flared from the Godlings' forms. Suddenly, the entire chamber seemed to have been transported to an underwater portion of the ocean in its darkest night. Julian felt chilled, but it was only his earlier dampness and the memory of ocean water. They remained inside the ship — but images of the ocean had been brought within the chamber, flooding Phaedra's place of power with dark, glowing images.

Marids surged toward the ship, their spell-shields gleaming in the darkness. The shadowy images of Houma and Alcman could be seen dimly, hovering above and behind the cluster of Marids as though directing their monstrous allies toward the stricken *Alantéa*.

But powerful forces had been ranged against the Sorcerers and the Marids. Scores of huge Orca shapes had gathered around the Marids. On each Killer Whale rode a gaunt hag-rider, a figure of human stature, seeming tiny against the massive Orca flesh, harnessed to them by slender saddles; and from the palms of the hag-riders scores of jagged bolts were leaping at the Sorcerers and the Marids.

Like Witches with gills, Julian thought, *allied to sentient Killer Whales. They would rule the ocean on any world, except....*

Except that as the huge Orca shapes smashed at the Marids, they were being destroyed — relentlessly, almost casually crushed. Julian stood within the chamber, watching images from a distance. But now came motion just behind him and he ducked: a hag-ridden great Killer Whale surged past him and smashed into the ranks of the Marids. Seconds later it, too, was falling stricken to the ocean's dark depths, trailing entrails, and plumes of bloody fluids. The hag-riders, too, were dying as they hurled magic at Alcman and Houma, who struck back with deadly demon tools.

Suddenly the images surrounding them vanished. The lights in the chamber flashed back on, even in those corners previously left dark. Phaedra turned again to look down on Merlin with a bleak, unhappy expression.

"Yes, there was a defense against your old foes," she murmured, "and now it has failed. What comes next?" Merlin glanced to his fellow Wizards. Like whispers echoing from a distant room, Julian could sense traces of the thoughts that flashed between their minds.

"Come now, Wizard!" Phaedra cried out. "Enough of your secret ways!"

"We did not anticipate such open warfare," Merlin acknowledged. "We thought the Demon Princes would lure us to their enchanted Isle, and then seek to overwhelm us with their great power. One of two things has happened — either our foes no longer wish us to reach the Isle, or their complex alliances again act at cross purposes."

"In either case," Phaedra said, "this moment highlights the true imbalance of this contest. My brothers, at this intersection, we must ask ourselves this question: why must we go forward, holding on to strange roles that none of us had any part in creating?"

Turin stared at Phaedra, his radiance of gold and green now gleaming undiminished. "I will not turn aside without giving battle."

"Nor will I," Magog added, and the blue and grey darkness seemed to smolder within him.

"Then I wish that I had also been wounded or misused!" Phaedra cried out, then turned again to Merlin with somewhat softer tones. "And so, what next?"

"We must leap to the furthest edges of Might Have Been." Merlin stared into the distance as though already in flight to distant places. "As we speak, I have asked our crew to abandon us.

"Now they speed toward thin and flimsy escape vessels. Payment for their services vanishes with disaster, and they flee to uncertain fates. Maker...may you wake them also at the End of Time." Merlin was silent for a moment, and to Julian, it seemed that he could hear the nearby booming of underwater Marids.

"Our next leap," Merlin continued, "will shorten the many leagues we must still travel toward the Isle of the Demons. And after —"

"After comes later!" Phaedra said, her voice again lifting. "Again, my brothers! Once more we must use our power to cast the Wizards and their flimsy vessel into the unknown. Again!"

Julian hunched down against the shuddering, the shaking, the transforming energies, and felt rather than saw that a seafoam of air and water was gathering like a cocoon about the vessel, and then they passed once more into a distant region of Otherwhen.

·)(·

Suddenly the ship groaned and listed to one side. Julian could feel a renewed surge of dark waters as the ocean sought again to claim the vessel for its deepest underwater valleys: their repairs had failed.

Julian drew a deep breath — but the air was barely breathable. And each breath was getting harder. Spell-words passed swiftly from his lips and the air gathering to his lungs became suddenly clearer and cooler.

"Merlin," Julian murmured, "help the small ones. Even the Eye...." Merlin nodded; envelopes of clear air were expanding rapidly around both Wizards and Godlings, encompassing first the chamber, then moving outward always more swiftly to embrace the entire warship.

"My brothers," Phaedra said, "the repair work of the lesser Wizards has failed. No wonder! Yet, if we add our strength to theirs, perhaps we can travel a few leagues further before joining the wreckage of this universe at a deep-water bottom that is already swollen with death. Come, Wizard, let us view the nature of this forlorn world."

"'Lesser Wizards,'" Galad murmured to Kalanin. "That's certainly a great gob of fat to toss into the flames."

Balardi's eyes showed only a slight amusement as he followed the Godlings below. Thorian stopped for a moment to stare openly at Phaedra as she left the chamber; and he watched her depart with little affection.

Feeling again like baggage, Kalanin and Galad followed Merlin and Julian to the upper decks, emerging outside into a dying world. A bloated, reddish sun loomed overhead, glowing through a haze of dark clouds that were formed from more smoke than moisture. Their warship was riding high on shrunken seas that had grown swollen with salt. Only insects remained in the skies: dragonfly creatures larger than the Eye of Merlin floated listlessly overhead; while in the dying seas the coils of enormous worms larger than dolphins floated periodically to the surface where they feasted on the dead and the dying.

Kalanin stared out over the railing, while Julian wordlessly crossed the decking then knelt beside his small allies and touched their soft fur. The Eye of Merlin stood beside Sebastian and Rafir, breathing deeply, watching swarms of huge dragonflies as they drew closer, drawn by the last flesh left in this portion of Otherwhen.

"Death is coming to this world," Merlin said, "as well as other dark forces: the Sorcerers and the Marids are only a few moments behind us." Julian opened his mouth to speak, but he sensed the same thoughts forming in Phaedra's mind; and so, he remained silent.

"Yes," Phaedra said, turning from her study of the dying sun to face Merlin. "Indeed, you have enough enemies for a hundred times the *Alantéa*'s force: Un-Maurag is at our heels, followed closely by Haeglin and Mordred."

Merlin shook his head, eyes still watching the death of this portion of Otherwhen. "Are we ready, then?" he asked.

"Though its hull was breached, and its center keel broken, your ship is healed — for now," Phaedra said.

"So, we must leap again," Merlin said softly, "and we must give thanks for the enduring sorcerous strength of the Godlings." With another shudder, they were gone, into another distant region of Otherwhen — and far closer in earthly leagues — to the Isle of the Demons.

·))(·

Julian again shook off the shock of transforming energies and ventured a cautious first breath: the air was warm and stale, but breathable. The sun setting over the horizon seemed only slightly larger than their own; and while it was still red, its color was that of a setting sun, not the bloated red haze of a universe in the last stages of its final death.

"And so," Phaedra asked, "just how much life does this universe retain? Minutes, or days, or months?"

"Left to its own devices," Merlin replied, "perhaps five hundred years. Under our current circumstances, no more than hours. The pursuit tightens. The Gift within me brings the sounds of enormous, baying hounds. Be ready for the next leap, the last leap."

"The ship cannot be wholly healed," Phaedra murmured, then she raised her voice. "My brothers, attend me now! The last moments of this tragic adventure are at hand!"

Godlings appeared on deck. More slowly, the Wizards ascended to stare into the setting sun. The ocean lapped feebly at their warship's hull; no living thing from this dying world moved or spoke. Julian searched for words to reassure his small allies, but none came. The Apprentice spoke other words instead: incantations to shield his small friends from the oncoming storm. Gleaming mists began gathering around Sebastian and Rafir, forming cushions of sorcerous energy. Kalanin and Galad retreated quickly below to arm themselves, then returned to stand again beside Godlings and Wizards as they faced a rapidly diminishing arc of red sunlight.

"Did you have allies in this universe also, Wizard?" Phaedra asked. "What will they say to you at your End of Time after you visited such destruction upon them in the last moments of their world?"

Merlin breathed out a long, deep sigh. "Their risks were well known. They offered to aid us because they dreamed of the End of Time, and the end of their own world. Having said these words, it might be just to communicate with their spokesman, now, at the last moments of this portion of Otherwhen."

Merlin spoke soft words, and the air shimmered. An image formed before them, glistening in the oncoming twilight. The figure before them stood tall as a Godling, but albino-white and far more frail. Its eyes gleamed with multifaceted surfaces, as though formed of fragmented crystals.

The figure hovered, floating just a few feet off the ground, completely inscrutable. Standing between the onlookers and the setting sun, it showed no hint of sorrow, or anger, or even acceptance. Instead, it merely gestured with one hand as though inviting the intruders from *Alantéa* to gaze behind them, to a place where the sun had once lifted from the sea and would never rise again.

They turned. In the distance, three enormous figures emerged from the oncoming night. Each stood fifty times the Godlings' height, striding toward them, looming gigantic against a starless night sky. The three figures raised hands, palms outward: a great wall of water formed, rushing toward the stricken *Alantéa*.

"And so, Haeglin has found us," murmured Phaedra, "followed swiftly by Mordred and Un-Maurag."

"We are nearing the eastern shores of the Isle," Merlin said. "Now comes our last leap. But first...." Cocoons of sorcerous force began forming around Kalanin and Galad, and even Julian.

"Wizard, there is no time!" Phaedra cried. "My brothers, we have come to the last cast! Back to the world of our birth! Back to the very shores of the Demons' malignant Isle! Leap now, before the great wave reaches us! Farewell, my brothers — farewell, perhaps forever!"

But the Godlings had waited too long, as the waves toppled toward them, they were trapped.

Shielded by layers of translucent, protective forces, Kalanin and Galad were frozen helplessly to the deck, though the force of magic within Julian was just strong enough that he could turn and watch the great wave as it swept toward them.

The great wall of water caught them as they hurtled through the last of the Alternates. And so, through all the shaking and shivering of transforming energies, a tsunami of water was sweeping over the ship, snapping its railings, shredding its sails, shattering its high masts. For a moment, Julian was unable to breathe, then the water swirled away from him, and he drew a lungful of salt sea air.

As they emerged from Otherwhen toward the Isle of the Demons, the wall of water was still sweeping them forward, casting them to the eastern coast of the great Isle on the crest of an enormous wave. It was night, but darkness was illuminated by a brilliant moonlight. They were going to be smashed against the rocky shores of the great Isle. Julian struggled to free himself, to seek Merlin, but the Wizard was concealed by a turbulence of stormy water.

They were toppling toward the Isle, moving slowly, like horror in a dream — the ship was going to be broken into thousands of fragments by the rocks and massive flatness of the sands. And yet forces were gathering toward them, far more swiftly than the rocky shore looming beneath them.

Glistening like a haze of enchanted clouds, an empire of dreams was sweeping toward them. Minarets and lean, spiked towers loomed out of masses of clouds, while the coiled shapes of greyish dark monstrosities slithered through the lower regions of those clouds.

The corrupted Guardians had assembled an Empire of Dreams, seeking to trap the intruders forever in a great maze of tortured confusion.

The *Alantéa* collapsed onto the Isle, carrying Godlings and Wizards, who were still recovering from their efforts to escape Otherwhen. An Empire of Dreams, seething with transforming energies, reached out for them. At the last, dark lightning lashed out from the Godlings hands, while the Wizards struggled to form enormous spell-shields...and yet with only the briefest of hesitations, the Empire of Dreams swallowed them whole — Wizards and Godlings and their magic, Apprentice and Familiars, and two well-armed but Giftless warriors.

As the huge warship smashed down upon the rocky shore it was crushed like a child's toy. All of *Alantéa's* huge beams were broken, masts as tall as pillars shattered, its shredded sails swept away by surging seawater, its decking reduced to splintered wreckage. All of the Godlings' and the Wizards' potions, and weapons, and charmed devices, and amulets and records, and grimoires stained by age, and hopes and plans were consumed by sand, and salt water, and a tide of transforming energies rising from the Isle of the Demons.

The warship *Alantéa* — the great, brave *Alantéa the Forerunner* — had been demolished.

Chapter Nine

In Labyrinths of Shattered Dreams

CROAKING DEFIANCE, THE EYE of Merlin fled, seeking the upper reaches of the moonlit night. Below him, a wall of water was carrying the *Alantéa* to its doom. *Merlin! I obey you now, but I would never have left you willingly! If you die, I will die too!*

From moonlit heights, the eagle watched the *Alantéa* crush itself against the rocky eastern shores of the Isle of the Demons and the eagle cried aloud. Then came a terrible straining sensation followed by a deep *shudder*, as the Eye lost his connection to the mind of Merlin. Corrupted Guardians had mastered Merlin with their transforming dream energies and the Wizard was now separated from him.

A heart-rending sense of loss swept over the eagle, yet he turned from the Isle, powerful wings taking him higher and further out to sea. It was then that the eagle found that he was not alone: more than a score of the Gods' winged Emissaries were following events from the upper skies.

A Griffin hovered to the eagle's left, and beyond the Griffin, winged serpents were distancing themselves from the more powerful Emissary in its Griffin form. Centermost, a winged horse bore a slender armored figure, a being that had turned away from the Isle, touched by shock or sorrow. To the eagle's right, an enormous, winged Gargoyle floated, a being made of coiled smoke, darkening the night sky. Other Emissaries had chosen not to be seen; their presence was only betrayed by distortions of moonlight created by forms that were shielded by magic.

The Eye of Merlin caught an updraft, then glanced down below: the wall of ater that had destroyed the *Alantéa* had halted its passage inland and was now washing backward, carrying the remnants of the *Alantéa* out to sea. Otherwise, all was serene on the Isle of the Demons: riots of wild growth seemed to bask in sensuous moonlight. But with a second sight attuned to magic, the eagle sensed concussions of sorcery, and flares of magic, like ground lightning, flashing with power. The Isle was consuming his master, and his own friends and allies.

The Eye of Merlin turned back to the Emissaries of the Gods as they hovered just outside the sorcerous reaches of the Isle of the Demons.

"Hear me!" the eagle cried. "If the Maker heeds me, all these Gods will be reincarnated as maggots and millipedes! The few Gods that are righteous and honorable can work their way through torturous reincarnations back to sentience! The rest can all squirm and struggle and die forever in the dust —"

Almost casually, the Gargoyle shape raised a talon: a shock of magic surged at the eagle, and the Eye of Merlin dropped like a floppy dead thing down to moonlit, churning seas.

· ✳ ·

Three male Harpies coasted downward on their buzzard wings, heading toward a clearing on the moonlit hill. As they struck the ground, they bounced, jostling each other, so that they snarled and snapped at each other with jagged, yellow teeth.

Each of the male Harpies was bald, gaunt, and hideous. Though their heads were hairless, tufts of hair jutted out from wattled chins: one Harpy had tufts of grey, the second, tufts of silver, and the third Harpy's tufts seemed flecked with gold; and these strands of hair, insignificant remnants, alone distinguished three of the greatest mortal magic wielders ever to dwell in Alantéa or the Far Lands.

"You had it!" one Harpy snarled, filled with menace. "It was given to you because your need was greatest!"

*A second Harpy joined in: "There was a **fire** in you, a **fire**! Where have all the flames gone now?"*

*The third Harpy recoiled from the other two. Turning its gaunt face to the moon, it cried in agony, "I cannot remember! I can recall **nothing**!"*

But then the discourse of the Harpies came to a sudden end, for out of the night sky the Winged Gargoyles — their everlasting foes — surged downward to resume their unending battle. The Harpies lifted again into the air, putrid breath steaming in the humid night air.

Guided by the malice of the Demon Princes, the corrupted Guardians had ensnared their adversaries in a dreamscape of eternal warfare — Godlings contending forever with their former allies, the Wizards, as Gargoyles fighting Harpies.

· X ·

Even in its middle slopes, the hillside was craggy with ravines. Large stony gaps could be seen from the air, but for the most part, the forest canopy overhead hid both the ravines and their nearby cave systems. The sky was clear today as was the surrounding air. On darker, more turbulent days, dank gasses seeped up from deep cavern vents, and the hillside was choked by the stench of death.

Jarl leaned back against one of the forest's shaggy trees, puffing on his pipe while gazing upwards; through a break in the forest cover, he watched as Reptile Birds floated overhead then skimmed through the forest's upper reaches as they sought their prey. In the distance, a cluster of these creatures with leathery wings had dropped down into the forest. Jarl was too far away to hear the desperate struggle, though a *shock* of death reached out to him, and he knew that yet another lifeless adventurer was having his carcass picked clean by sharp, brutal beaks.

One more treasure seeker would never reach the Temple at the Mountain's peak. Puffing on his pipe, Jarl allowed himself a slight smile.

It might be best, he thought, if the Reptile Birds pecked to death the two humans who were following him. The two were surprisingly determined, having evaded all his snares and traps. On one hand, Jarl wished them gone, but on the other hand, he was curious. And they were nearby, a pair of rangy, tall humans who were capable of considerable craftiness. Maybe a discussion with the two would be interesting. Maybe.

As the two thieves came closer, they made just a little more noise than necessary. Were they trying to announce themselves? Jarl clutched his Talisman; if they were just trying to kill him and eat him — Jarl had seen it happen more than once — he would fry them first.

"Sir," came a voice, "your thiefness, we just want to talk. No harm to you, no harm to us."

"So, talk," Jarl called out, "but stay where you are."

"Just a little closer," said the voice, "but not too close. It's a parlay, and everyone needs to relax." Two men emerged from around a stony outcrop, advanced to about fifteen paces from Jarl, then they sat. Each clutched some sort of weapon, though they were wary, not threatening. The tension in Jarl's body eased somewhat, and he puffed more deeply on his thin pipe.

"So, talk," Jarl said.

"Yes, and it's certainly a fine moment meeting you, too," the man said, "here in this lovely glade of a forest. I'm Ged, and the one beside me who does not speak will respond to Koln. And you, your illustrious thiefness, they call you...?"

"Jarl."

"And so, Jarl, you have made some sort of sorcerer of yourself, have you not?"

"A thief mage," Jarl said, eyes glancing periodically to the upper skies, then into the forest, watching for danger, and finally returning to stare at his two fellow thieves.

Ged nodded. "A specialist — that's good. So how does the quest fare these days? Getting closer to the mountain top and the Temple every day, are we?"

Jarl's eyes flashed menace at the two thieves. "You've been tracking me, so you know that I've been forced back more than a half league downslope, just in the last few days."

"We're not doing so good, either," Ged admitted. "Another twelve days and we'll be forced down into the valley. Not very pretty in the valley."

Jarl exhaled a coil of smoke. "Only the defeated and the dying live in the valley, and then not for long. What exactly do you want?"

"An alliance," Ged said, eyes gleaming. "We think that the three of us might be able to fight our way up, get to the Temple, and grab the treasure. Then it's time to celebrate, to find a place where the women dance naked on the tables and the wine flows like an endless fountain."

"Typical," Jarl grunted. "What possible use would you two thugs be to me?"

"Might teach you a bit of diplomacy," Ged muttered, then he took a deep breath. "First, you're losing. Second, you're still limping, because the snake thing almost got you two days ago — even though your skinny shanks were being guarded by your dimwitted spying creatures."

Jarl extinguished his pipe and reached behind his back for a sack. As he opened it, two Implings emerged, blinking in the overcast daylight.

"So, tell me again," Jarl said to the Implings, "which one of you was supposed to be watching when the snake thing nipped me?" Each Impling grinned idiotically and pointed to the other. Jarl resisted an impulse to crush them once and for all: unreliable guards were better than no guards. Maybe.

"So, you've got good eyes," Jarl said to Ged. "That's not enough."

Ged nodded again. "Then we'll list two more reasons. Here's one." Ged extended his hand and placed a coiled whip on the ground. "You don't have the only magic on this hillside. When this weapon lashes a Cockatrice, or a Basilisk, or a Reptile Bird, they go *poof* and vanish. This thing," he motioned to Koln, who extended a lean trident onto the forest floor, "will reach whatever I can't, except that things don't go, *poof*, they sort of explode." Ged grinned. "Noisy, messy work, that, with the explosions."

Jarl looked at the two as though seeing them for the first time: each was broad shouldered and strongly muscled, though they had become leaner and rangier with their long struggle on the slopes. Koln seemed younger than Ged, but his eyes were greyer, as though aged by equal measures of wisdom and fear.

"Does it talk?" Jarl asked, nodding at Koln.

"I speak for both of us," Ged said patiently, "but Koln can sound the alarm when the nasties come slithering into the cave." Ged smiled, radiating false heartiness. "So now we're a band of Thieves, right? Brothers in arms, with equal shares at the top, when we reach the Temple?"

Jarl shook his head: no.

"And how many times," Ged snarled, "were you dropped on your head as a child? Two-thirds of nothing is nothing! Nothing!" Ged then took a deep breath. "Right, then — first of all is there a way out at the top, a way for three people to escape this cursed hillside and the doubly damned valley beneath?"

Jarl nodded slowly. Even this far down the hillside, he could feel *power* radiating from the Temple above them.

Ged sighed. "Then you take half, and we can share the other half — whatever it is, it better be worth it."

"Done," Jarl said, somewhat surprised at the outcome of their meeting. His left hand slipped from the Talisman and instead, he drew a small dagger. Making a slight incision in his left palm, he casually flicked the dagger to Ged, but Koln's swift hand caught it in mid-flight. The two Thieves made similar incisions on their palms, and the three exchanged a blood bond, each thief knowing that it would mean little in a real crisis.

As drops of blood slipped to the floor of the hillside forest, the Implings began whispering and gibbering: something, some creature activated by the smell of blood, was coming for them. The three stood, Jarl clutching his Talisman, Ged, and Koln their enchanted weapons.

A Basilisk scurried into view, just to their left. Koln aimed his trident at it, but Ged held him back: they were still well outside the Basilisk's range, whereby its glance might stun or kill them; and most unusually, the menacing creature had taken no interest in them.

Instead, it was scuttling into the forest, moving farther from them with every step, its breath steaming from exertion, scrambling down a slight incline on its stubby lizard legs. Then, to their astonishment, the Basilisk, exhausted, tumbled to a halt and turned as though confronting an invisible foe.

The Implings beside them gibbered in fear. Just thirty paces to their left, some huge, coiled creature was surging through the forest in pursuit of the Basilisk.

To Jarl, the God of all Snakes had just passed them by, but his mouth, completely out of control, whispered, "Kath?" Where had that thought come from?

The Basilisk glared with menace at the enormous snake creature, but the Basilisk's fearsome death gaze gained it only a split second's reprieve — then it vanished with a single swift gulp into the snake's mouth, all its sorcerous power and menace gone forever.

The enormous, coiled monstrosity then turned and regarded the three humans with considerable interest. Its forked tongue tested the air as though already savoring their taste. Koln mouthed a single word, but no sound emerged.

"I agree," Ged muttered. "Run!" And so, they turned and ran, speeding through the forest, dodging fallen tree trunks, leaping over branches, skirting stony outcrops. The snake creature surged first to higher ground, then pursued them, in an almost leisurely fashion, herding them always further downslope, always closer to the valley, where fear ruled.

Koln was fastest, followed closely by Ged. An older Jarl struggled to keep pace, gasping, as his heart shuddered with the strain, while his foot throbbed, still pulsing with snake venom. Each of them could feel a force of hatred and malice, and something like joy radiating from the coiled monstrosity: it was herding them, certain that it would shortly feast. The Basilisk had been no more than an appetizer.

As they raced around a fallen trunk, Jarl's leg seized up, blazing with pain from his bite-wound — and he fell. *Gone, he thought, another dead thief.* But then, unexpectedly, Koln turned and stopped. Raising his trident, he lashed at the monstrosity with lines of force. Jagged blue fire struck the great serpent, and it twitched in pain, tumbling off to their left.

Clutching his Talisman, Jarl rose to his knees, murmuring harsh spell-words. A wall of flame raged at the serpent, and it recoiled, writhing in agony, retreating as the wall of fire burned its flesh. The three Thieves stood, regarding one another in surprise: they had not expected to survive.

"See what I mean?" Ged murmured. "With the three of us...." He trailed off as their wall of flame began hissing, faltering. Venom, mists of snake poison, were reducing their barrier of fire to a smoking haze. The serpent's head pushed through the smoke, eyes blazing in triumph. The three Thieves ran, then ran again, struggling to keep from being pushed further downslope.

Twice Ged hid behind a rockfall, then leaped out, lashing at the Snake God's coils with his enchanted whip, while simultaneously, Koln's trident sent surges of magic at the creature's eyes and nostrils. Once, Jarl filled the nearby forest with the smell of death, so that the enormous Snake's tongue thrashed in confusion until it caught their scent again. Each time one of them seemed cornered, the other two attacked or diverted their powerful opponent. But the chase seemed to go on forever.

Toward nightfall, Jarl turned the full power of his Talisman against their foe. Jagged bolts of force blazed into the Snake God's coils, but Jarl's magic barely scraped its rough scales. Again, they fled, seeming to be always herded further downslope. At sunset, the three sought shelter in a gorge, on a rocky slope that the Snake God might find treacherous. Also, within the gorge was a cavern with a narrow mouth: if the creature forced its huge head into the cavern's narrow opening, its eyes could be blasted and blinded.

Above them, they could hear the monster thrash in frustration, setting off a rockslide as it investigated the gorge. Then it jerked back, making alarmed, hissing noises: night was coming, and the Snake God needed to find its own shelter. As the monster retreated, the three Thieves stood together in near darkness, glancing into each other's faces: although they were much further from their goal, at least they had survived.

Suddenly Jarl felt hot tears surging down his face: he had lost the Implings. "Gone," he murmured, "the little ones are gone. How did I let that happen? And why should I weep over such a small matter when I am still alive?" Wordlessly, Koln reached out and clutched Jarl's arm. The thief's grip was firm, but when Koln shook Jarl's arm, his motion was gentle.

"Yes, I hear them," Jarl said, voice lowered to a whisper. "The Kul-Ghouls are coming. I will be silent." Strange tears still streamed down Jarl's face, while Koln again shook his arm as though saying, *That is not what I meant.*

"What?" Jarl whispered, then he sensed other movements, furtive scurrying rather than the heavy leaping motions of the Kul-Ghouls. It was dusk, almost nighttime in the forested hillside. Jarl raced outside, wounded leg wincing as he scrambled up the slope. Some distance from the gorge, Kul-Ghouls were speeding through the forest, bounding, leaping, sniffing the night air, eyes glowing red as they sought warm flesh. Their forms loomed large in the oncoming darkness — each of them was taller and bulked nearly twice the mass of Ged or Koln, and they moved with the swiftness of feral beasts.

But there on an upper ridge of the gorge were Jarl's two Impling sentries! Jarl climbed. The two Implings slipped down the side of the gorge, then each of them clutched one of Jarl's upper arms as he scrambled back down into their bolt hole. Once inside the two Implings wept and babbled tales of horror and woe in a language only Jarl could understand.

"Together again," Ged murmured, unable to keep the dark sarcasm from his voice.

An anger mixed with shame surged through Jarl's mind. "One day you will see —" Shuddering, thrashing sounds came from a distance and the ground overhead shook, then a slight rain of debris slipped down from above.

"Yes, yes, yes," Ged chuckled. "The Master of the Day has met the Masters of the Night — the Snake God is fighting packs of Kul-Ghouls. What could be better?" He lowered his voice, turning again to Jarl. "And you, with all your magic, are you master of the Kul-Ghouls?"

Jarl shook his head, still cradling an Impling in each arm. "Two times, separately, I've killed a lone Ghoul when it came at me with eyes of fire in the darkness, blazing with hunger. In packs, though, the Kul-Ghouls are far too much for me, far too much even for our small band."

"Maybe too much even for the Snake God," Ged muttered, listening to the sounds of battle. "But tell me this, Thief Mage: when they died, did the Ghouls go, *poof*, like the Reptile Birds?"

Jarl again shook his head. "No, they fell dead...and to answer your next question, yes, the Kul-Ghouls ate their own dead brethren, and yes, they tore open the bodies, broke them apart, and stripped the marrow from their bones."

Ged fell silent, listening as the sounds of struggle in the upper forest grew less, but Koln was clutching Ged's arm, and the thief nodded. "Our silent partner wants to ask if you have ever mastered the Wraiths. Can you turn them aside or blunt their haunting?"

After a split second of hesitation, Jarl shook his head. *Sadly, I am master of nothing in this land, and yet....*

"Then, ready yourself," Ged said heavily, "for with the night, our good friends the White Wraiths are coming by for a little visit."

Jarl hunched down, clutching his Talisman. *If the Kul-Ghouls are masters of the night above us, the White Wraiths are masters of the night in the world below ground. Already beads of sweat form on the foreheads of the Thieves, while my own pulse rattles through my veins.*

"So, your own sorcerous weapons," Jarl whispered, "have failed against the Wraiths, while my own fire and cold and spells of transforming energies have done nothing. What else is there? What else can we do?"

"Too late," Ged muttered, and indeed it was too late. White Wraiths, lean and insubstantial, were seeping down through the roof of the cavern, whispering words of torment into their minds. Then a Master Wraith entered slowly through their entrance, filled with menace — and wrath.

"You were supposed to be catalysts," the Wraith blazed at them, "hidden forces that would undo the secret powers of your foes. Now, look at you! Scum!! Worthless, feeble, scum! A Summoner who cannot even speak his own name! A Warlord whose own voice will not obey him! A Weapons Master unable to draw his own sword! All of you scrabbling on a hillside in search of a Temple you will never reach, seeking treasure you will never find or even understand! Look at you!"

As though lashed by pain, the three Thieves recoiled, while the Implings hid their faces in their master's cloak. But worse — at least for Koln — was yet to come. A second Greater Wraith pushed in front of the White Wraith Sorcerer. This Wraith held the image of a tall woman, a lady both beautiful and strong, and in the Wraith's arm lay a lifeless child — lifeless though its dead eyes radiated horror at Koln.

"Why did you leave us?" the Wraith moaned to Koln. "Abandoned to the malice of our foes, your daughter now lies dead, while the bolts and darts of our enemies will soon claim my life too. Why would you leave us to seek false treasures on a hillside of horror?"

Koln sank to his knees, the hot tears surging down his beardless, seemingly young features. Yet at this point Jarl took sudden action: he placed the two Implings on his shoulders so that their hands clutched his neck. One of Jarl's hands reached out to the kneeling Koln, the other reached to Ged. He then whispered harsh words to Ged, and Ged's other hand touched Koln's shoulder. The five were linked.

As Thieves and Implings connected, a force seemed to build within them. Where fear had prevailed, a quiet strength began to grow, and the sounds that the White Wraiths made as they lashed at the minds of Thieves and Implings seemed to recede, to become no more than voices filled with hatred echoing from distant rooms. They could still hear the Wraiths' words — if they wished to — though now they could also choose not to listen.

This is what I found, came a thought from Jarl's mind, *that when I linked together with the Implings, the pressures from the White Wraiths began to lessen. When the five of us are linked, that shielding becomes far stronger.*

As the force of the Wraiths fades, Ged thought, *the fog that grips my mind also begins to lift.*

Yes, my mind is also clearing, came a thought from Koln's mind, the first open communication from the voiceless thief, in thoughtful tones that were surprisingly clear. *While the confusion fades for a moment, do any of you have histories? When I reach for my past, I find only grey mists. Were you ever children? Did you even have parents? Was there ever a life beyond this hillside?*

No. None. Thoughts came from the two other Thieves. *Once I could fly,* came a soft, tentative thought from an Impling.

I could not fly, but I could run like the wind, thought the second Impling, *and I was very difficult to discover when I didn't want to be seen.*

Interesting, came Koln's response. *The forces that have tampered with our minds have been thorough with the Thieves, but somewhat careless with the Implings.*

The hillside, Ged's thoughts had become more urgent. *The hillside and the Temple above. Now, as our minds clear, I must ask again: if we seize the*

Idol from its pedestal upon the altar of the Temple, can we free ourselves from this place?

Yes, came Jarl's thought. *I can almost touch the Idol with my mind. And see, we did not even know before that it was a thing, an ebony dark Idol that rests upon an alabaster pedestal in a place of power that we call a Temple. One day that Idol may free us. And with sudden clarity, I can see more: I reach for the White Wraiths, and they are gone. I search for the hillside, and with our joined strength the Sight within me grows stronger. I think, with our linkage, I can even share these visions. Watch!*

Images flooded the minds of the five and they watched the hillside at night from a distance, yet the images were vague, as though banks of thin mist obscured their vision. Bands of Kul-Ghouls bounded through the night, drawn to battle with the Snake God. That monstrosity had found shelter, though not swiftly enough. Now it fought at the mouth of a burrow, with the corpses of envenomed Kul-Ghouls mounding slowly at the burrow's entrance. Lesser snake monstrosities had also been drawn to the battle, though they were far more cautious, with serpent heads emerging periodically from crevices to tear chunks of Kul-Ghoul flesh. Overhead Reptile Birds gathered in the moonlight, swooping down to slash at the eyes of unwary combatants.

Most interesting, Koln thought. *Are we now sharing the same concept?*

A night passage up a hillside of horror? Ged's thought was first tentative, then became stronger. *Then let us go now! Swiftly, before I lose my courage.*

They made considerable progress that night. The next night their "distraction" failed, and they fought Kul-Ghouls at the entrance of a cavern long into the night, with Implings hurling stones at the Kul-Ghouls' gleaming red eyes, while White Wraiths called upon them to fail and die, and caverns beneath them vented gases made putrid with the stench of death.

On the fourth night, they slew several large snakes at dusk, so that flocks of Reptile Birds and bands of Kul-Ghouls fought each other for the flesh of dead serpents, while the Thieves and Implings climbed always higher up toward the mountain's peak.

· X ·

"Pull, away, pull away," the Harpy panted to the others, as the three surged through dark, moonless skies. "Pull away and follow me!"

"Why now," panted the second Harpy, "why now, when we control the upper skies?"

"Fool," the third Harpy gasped, "doddering old fool." But the two Harpies followed their leader as he passed into a cloud bank so that folds of mist that were dark as night obscured them from their winged Gargoyle foes.

"It comes to me now," said the first Harpy, struggling to stay aloft, "that we planned for this moment. We were...different, foreseeing a time of danger...." Speech came in spurts as the Harpy gasped for air. "I was to pass a stone, a thing that held power over a place called Otherwhen." He nodded to the second Harpy, a winged, damp flier barely visible in the cloud masses, "and yet I did not. Somehow, I must still have this stone, somewhere embedded in this strange body."

"And you both blamed me!" The Harpy with tufts of silver hair blazed at the other two. "You called upon a fire, a fire that still rages inside me, yet it has no fuel!"

"A time may still come," panted the third Harpy with its gold flecks, "for the pressure upon us is lessening. Why would the force that governs our lives suddenly reduce its pressure?"

"Something is happening," murmured the first Harpy. Strangely, his flight now seemed easier, his breathing less of a struggle.

"Something is happening," agreed the second Harpy. The flickering fire within him seemed to glow. A force inside him was compelling him to fulfill a destiny that he could not yet remember, though thoughts were growing slowly in his mind, like tiny seeds newly sprouting in moist, dark soil.

·)(·

Indeed, the corrupted Guardians had become distracted, letting slip the mastery of their Dream Empire for a time, because their masters, the Demon Princes, had come together for one of their infrequent convocations. All beings of power — Gods, Mage Beings of the Mid-World, Sorcerers, Dark Lords, Guardians — could feel *The Web of Fate* grow tighter. Even the raggedly clothed Shamans and Hag-Witches of the Far Lands turned to stare in wonder toward Alantéa the Forerunner.

Three Demon Princes gathered in their citadel upon the Isle of the Demons, a place carved from the same granite and basalt that formed the foundation of the Isle. This citadel was set deep belowground where no light shone, and nothing grew. Only gases venting from deep fissures gave hints of a future life; and so, the Demon Princes had created a subworld, where they imagined themselves the first beings to rise to sentience, destined to become their world's First Fashioners.

Three thrones formed from the same granite of the citadel were set into the Demons' place of power, equally distant from each other. Between these three thrones stood a dais, a place of enchantment that would show the Demon Princes matters they wished to see from afar.

Now, on the dais, an image had formed, portraying the Great Sending event that the Demon Princes most wished to view: their Scimitar and Dagger of Destruction, speeding toward the Maker's Heart. As it surged through the dark emptiness of space, the Sending was being assailed by far distant Powers, Dominions, Intelligences — beings from other portions of the wide universe who perceived its dark designs and were determined to deflect the Great Sending.

All their efforts were being swept aside as the Sending surged from star system to star system, leaving destruction in its wake. As they watched, the Demon Princes laughed, and puffs of grey smoke emerged from their mouths. When angered, that same smoke was touched by sparks, and when utterly enraged, torrents of fire surged from the mouths of the Demon Princes.

Now, only gentle grey smoke emerged then subsided as the Demon Princes turned from their Great Sending to their long struggle to supplant the Maker and rule in his place.

"And so, begin," Iblis said, deep Demon voice rumbling through the stone chamber. Satanis and Iblis each thought himself as greatest among the Powers of Alantéa and the Mid-World, though after a time of bitter, destructive warfare, the two had postponed their claims of overlordship to a time when all other Powers had been subjugated.

"I will begin," Zikar said. If Zikar was accounted least of the three Demon Princes in raw power, his cunning was unmatched. "We have accomplished much: the Guardians of the World have been subjugated or compelled to join our cause; the hidden force of Dreamers now drifts mindlessly through the Temple of Waiting; and we have cast the greatest of Sendings into the very Heart of the Maker."

"A lesser plague of Wizards and Godlings," the voice of Iblis rumbled through the chamber, "has been consigned to a universe of nightmares, yet they were overcome almost too easily."

"It was your hope," Satanis spoke directly to Zikar, and smoke touched by sparks began to slip from his breath, "that the Mid-World of the Truce would be drawn piecemeal to the Wizards' rescue. Then we could destroy, one by one all the greater and lesser beings who call themselves Gods. Or even if those Powers formed coalitions, we could destroy them easily because of the lack of cohesion in those alliances."

"That might still happen," Zikar said evenly, "though these so-called 'Gods' have become most cautious and coy."

"And if," Satanis persisted, "if we confronted these Gods and brought warfare again to the shores of Alantéa, how would we fare?"

"We would be defeated for a second time," Zikar said flatly, and his own breath now flashed sparks.

Satanis stared away from the other two, recalling the triumph he had felt when he strode again over the enchanted soil of Alantéa the Forerunner. "So, we must again attempt a new act of creation, something different and greater than either Dragons or Marids."

"To achieve such a thing," Iblis said softly, "we will need more power. To obtain power, we need to again study the arts of the Maker."

"It was always the case," Zikar said, "that if we wished to supplant the Maker, we would need to acquire his powers."

"I will agree," Iblis said, voice trembling the stonework of the hall, "to invoke again our three simulacra, replications of the Maker, though we must make this invocation the last effort, for our attempts to recreate the Maker as three separate constructs were among the least successful of our endeavors."

"I too, agree," Satanis spoke with some reluctance, for the outcome of his efforts was also an embarrassment.

"And I will also agree," Zikar added, "though it is possible that one day we may discover a device that will transform these failed simulacra into tools of enormous insight and power."

In their efforts to mimic, then surpass the Maker, the three Demon Princes had each created a simulacrum of the Maker. Each of the three separate constructs was endowed with the characteristics and powers of the

Maker as seen through the eyes of the Demon Princes. Their memories were ancient but vivid, for they had walked and spoken with the Maker many times after he had first raised the Demons from Earth's then lifeless crust.

Iblis frowned, for the first construct drawn to the dais before the three thrones was that of his own simulacrum of the Maker. In ancient times, the Maker had appeared before Demons and Seraphs in many guises; the one selected by Iblis was that of an elder Demon, a wizened, venerable Power, features showing a veneer of aged wisdom.

As the simulacrum appeared before the Demon Princes, it immediately abased itself, murmuring, "Great Ones, how may I serve you?"

"Arise," Iblis rumbled, sparks of flame flashing from his mouth. "Garb yourself in the subtle mastery of the Maker. Since you have departed from Earth, leaving us to our own devices, we wish only for an orderly transfer of power. Tell us how to acquire the majesty and the might you once wielded."

"Nothing," the wizened Demon rose then bowed deeply, "nothing will ever equal the power and the splendor of the Demon Princes and their creative energies. For with such brilliance —" Iblis waved a hand in dismissal, and the image vanished.

"A failure," Iblis acknowledged. "Under unrelenting pressure, my construct learned only to fawn and grovel, and speak untruths that I would take pleasure in hearing."

"My own construct is even less useful," Satanis murmured. "Behold." On the platform dais before the three thrones emerged a second image, that of an elder Seraph, though taller and of less luminous substance. Yet its eyes were askew, and it babbled happily in a sing-song voice, speaking in a language none could understand. The eyes of Satanis radiated hatred at the construct, and still, it babbled on, heedlessly and without fear.

"Insane," Satanis rumbled. "Under torment and torture, this thing's mind has broken, and now I wish no more of it."

The second construct vanished, and after only an interval of seconds, was replaced by a third. This simulacrum appeared as a sheet of radiant energy, a pane of white light that pulsed and flashed, and was attuned to some other source of wisdom, beyond the Isle of the Demons.

"Upon this construct," Zikar explained, "I placed neither compulsion, nor pressure, nor pain of torture. A geas alone required this thing to speak nothing but pure truths. It was unable to lie, and so I thought, thereby, to acquire from this construct insights peculiar to the Maker's Mind. However, when it speaks, I can make no sense of it; and so, I have also failed, even after using the most subtle of approaches. Listen while it speaks."

Invoked, the construct upon the dais — still retaining its image as a sheet of radiant energy — spoke in clear tones. "Just as the Zeroth and First Laws implied the existence of properties called temperature and energy respectively, the existence of a property called entropy, which can serve as a measure of how close a system is to equilibrium, can be deduced as a consequence of the second law. Neither energy nor entropy can be measured directly. Through the judicious application of thermodynamic relations, how —"

"Enough," Zikar rumbled, and the smoke emerging from his mouth was touched by fingers of flame. "Enough. Every word this thing speaks is most likely utterly and completely true — yet I can gain nothing from its speech. It is useless and so we must seek other devices."

"Is it still possible," Iblis spoke with unusual softness, "that Wotan or Thoth or Pallas Athena might yet attempt to rescue their beloved Wizards from this Isle?"

"An entertaining thought," Zikar said, though as he sighed, soft smoke emerged. "Yet such an intervention would be most unlikely." He paused, glancing at the other two; their convocation was ending.

"Let us not end on this note," Satanis rumbled. "Instead let us view again the Dagger, the mighty Sending of the Demon Princes, then we can return to our tasks."

"Watch for me, also," Zikar said, rising. "I have postponed a lesser task for far too long."

Iblis and Satanis sat for a time with gleaming eyes, watching as their powerful Sending, a Dagger destined for the Maker's Heart, accelerated, speeding into the distant depths of the starry universe, intent on destroying the First Fashioner.

While two Demon Princes drew strength from their dark designs, Zikar passed from the citadel, to stand just beyond its entrance. Their citadel was set so deep below ground, that fissures vented dark vapors into the cavern's upper skies, forming its own internal climate. Zikar glared at the corrupted Guardians through this haze, over a distance of many leagues, but also a separation formed by many levels of complex sorceries. Zikar's mouth opened, and he breathed a torrent of fire at the corrupted Guardians: they had neglected their oversight of transformed castaways, and Zikar was most displeased.

· X ·

Passing through a bank of wispy, high clouds, the Harpies again felt a surge of heaviness and a shortness of breath. They began sinking lower, struggling now even to stay aloft. The three glanced at one another, unable even to croak out brief words. Each Harpy understood, though, that their unseen overlords had returned; anger expressed as bright sparks of white radiance pulsing through the night air.

Then, from above, came disaster. Surging downward from even greater heights, three huge, winged Gargoyle shapes hurtled through the night. Ripping and tearing at Harpy wings, Gargoyles sent their opponents cascading downward, fluttering hopelessly to the forest floor; then the Gargoyles themselves — driven by fear and hatred — dropped down to attack their foes on the dark, dank soil of the forest. Though their onslaught was overwhelming, the Gargoyles' own wings were torn, bones broken by heavier male Harpy body structure. Dark mouths of Gargoyles choked on fetid Harpy flesh, while the yellow teeth of the Harpies were darkened by greyish black Gargoyle blood.

With all the thrashing violence, gasps of pain, and shrieks in the night, the creatures of the night began to take note of the disturbance. Clusters of Reptile Birds, and Dusk Snakes, and Basilisks, and Kul-Ghouls began to slip toward the intruders.

·))(·

The sky was moonless but bright. They were far enough up the hillside, and the air was clearer. Below them, all the vented gasses had slid downslope and were choking the valley with a stench of decay. The five intruders stared up at the crown of the hillside, where the Temple gleamed in the starlight. The Temple's dark stonework seemed to simultaneously absorb starshine, then transform starlight into a different form: its granite radiated darker rays, emitting a fusion of radiant light and sorcerous energies.

"I can almost sense," Jarl whispered, staring at the Temple, "that this *thing*, this Idol upon a pedestal, is calling to me."

"Let's go, then," Ged muttered. "The whip is sending out much different signals — it's throbbing and pulsing *danger, danger, danger,* into my mind. It's shaking now as though the whole hillside is ready to fall apart. Let's go now!" As always, Koln said nothing, but he pushed forward, leading them along a steep track that curled upward to the top. The night was silent, tight with danger; all the forest's deadly feral inhabitants had hidden themselves in their deepest bolt holes.

The three Thieves climbed, excitement beginning to overcome their fear, while their Impling allies followed more slowly and cautiously, whimpering softly to themselves. Just then, out of the starlit night, a jumble of broken winged creatures tumbled to the forest floor, less than a league below them. Jarl felt, rather than saw, that Reptile Birds were swooping down in pursuit.

"What was *that*?" Ged muttered.

"Just another distraction," Jarl said quietly, but he felt as though his heart had been stabbed to death by a thin, dark, blade, and deep inside he knew they would never reach the top, never reach the ebony, dark idol and free themselves from this cursed land. Not more than twenty paces ahead of them Koln had reached a small clearing, where he could again see the Temple as it gleamed in the night. But instead of pushing onward, Koln drew his trident and turned to stare back at his fellow Thieves with a look of everlasting sorrow.

Ged and Jarl scrambled higher to stand with Koln. Their fearful Impling allies hung a few paces back, while the three Thieves stared up the steep slope, watching as a sea of White Wraiths gathered around the base of the Temple. First, a few score Wraiths foamed around the Temple's base, then there were hundreds, then many thousands. The Thieves drew weapons and braced themselves in defiance.

Then, like a great wave, a tide of White Wraiths swept down the hillside, casting the intruders down from the heights. The Thieves' weapons and their magic and their defiance gained them not a second's reprieve. They were swept aside like gnats by a Griffin's wing. Tumbling, always carried downward, embraced by transforming energies, rendered senseless by constant blows and by brutal changes within their own bodies, the five were battered down the hillside into the valley below, to a place where fear and death ruled.

Late at night, five small figures lay senseless in the valley. One might once have commanded powerful armies, another might have wielded the weapon that first wounded the Demon's most fearsome offspring, and the third might have called the Gods to battle. Even their lesser servants might have roused the Last Magic at the End of Time. Now they lay senseless, reduced by transforming energies into insignificant beings, completely undefended except by the malice of the corrupted Guardians, who had been instructed to inflict further pain and torment on the intruders before destroying them.

· ✕ ·

Each day was like the rest, as it had always been, would always be, until death claimed him. Hours of watching were followed by furtive scurries outside. Once each day he would race out into the valley through a stench of glowing fog, fill his water skin, then race back, eyes searching frantically for scraps of flesh overlooked by Dire Cats or Basilisks. After the Kul-Ghouls came late at night, there was never anything left. Hunger was forever, and he could feel his body consuming itself. Soon he would be so frail that the Dire Cats would force their way into his shelter, then the Dire Cats would feast on his gaunt flesh until the Kul-Ghouls swept them away and consumed his body, down to the thin strips of marrow left in his bones.

He edged out from the wedge-shaped stones of his makeshift cavern barrier, then slid outside. Out in the valley, it was late afternoon, hot and damp. Fog had slipped downward from hillside vents, drifting deeper into the valley, so he could see better than on most days — almost thirty paces in several directions.

Clattering sounds came from a distance to his left and he grinned to himself: the two brothers were smashing away at each other, and their warfare sometimes generated a source of food.

He scampered through the trails on the valley floor, gaining height as the trail rose up over a slight hillside. From here he could look down on the brothers and their constant warfare. He kept his body flat so that only his head lifted over the peak. Then he peered down: the two brothers were battering each other with cudgels. Bleeding, wounded by their own warfare, the two shouted at each other in blind rage. Three Dire Cats had sought to feed on the fighters, but the brothers' cudgels had smashed the Dire Cats' spines, and the cats' furry carcasses lay sprawled like broken things, saber toothed mouths gaping open in death.

The flesh of Dire Cats was most difficult to chew; even so, his stomach grumbled with hunger.

Movement came from overhead, and two Ravens settled on branches above the battle. As the brothers fought on, the Ravens jeered down, then began cawing and pecking at each other. Specks of black feathers began spiraling to the ground, followed by droplets of Raven blood.

He slid further back, easing himself out of sight. Always, he had hidden, sought food and water, then watched the brothers fight while Ravens called out in malice. From time to time, another victim would find his way into their section of the valley, fall prey to Dusk Snakes, or Dire Cats, or Basilisks. Sometimes they were taken at night by Kul-Ghouls, but always he survived as did the brothers and the Ravens.

Whenever the brothers caught sight of him, they tried to kill him. If the Ravens found him, they made wild noises until Dusk Snakes or Dire Cats came hunting for him, and then he ran, racing, as always, for his life.

He slid further back. Already he had been out too long. What had he been thinking? He had neither the brothers' strength nor their recklessness. Instead, he survived by craft, cunning, and speed.

Racing back, he hesitated at the pond. Kneeling, he pushed aside some of the pond scum and filled his water skin with grey fluid. Now for food. Swift steps took him into a pool of yellow fog, then he slipped to the ground. He peered out warily: two Dire Cats had been tracking him, circling, but his scent was now obscured by the smell of death.

Now, one Dire Cat sniffed the ground, then stared directly into his pool of fog.

Trapped! As his hand grasped the stone hatchet at his side, the saber-toothed Dire Cats — large as wolves — stalked toward him. Each was gaunt with hunger, making them unwary; one cat pressed too close to the mouth of a Dusk Snake's barrow. A snakehead filled with menace and fangs leaped out, and one Dire Cat was dragged down, shrieking, into the burrow. The second Dire Cat fled, losing itself in the yellowish fog that coiled along the valley's floor.

Food. He had been out too long. He ran on thin, spindly legs, eyes searching for scraps. Motion swirled overhead and again he dove into a patch of fog. Just to his left, something fell from the skies, twitching as it struck the ground. He leaped up, racing toward it. The tail segment of a young Dusk Snake had been dropped by some winged creature, likely a Reptile Bird. He grasped the thrashing tail and raced back to his cavern.

Sliding back through the cavern's narrow opening, he carefully filled the gap with wedges of stone and chips of bark. Only once had a Dire Cat forced its way through, but as it struggled with the lower stones, he had crushed its head with his makeshift stone hatchet.

Inside, he lay back and tried to slow his breathing. Just to his left, the snake segment still moved — twitching, rather than thrashing, until finally, it grew still. It had been a good outing, all in all. He closed his eyes, listening to the sounds of the valley outside his cavern. The Ravens had grown silent; no doubt the brothers had retreated to their own bolt holes, where they set broken bones and otherwise licked their wounds. Now everything was quiet, except every few minutes a panicked shriek would squawk out, as some barely living creature joined the ranks of the unliving.

Then came a faint grating sound that chilled his blood. Some creature was fumbling at his stony barrier! He leaped up and stood beside his stone crevice. He had kept a loose stone at eye-level so he could peer out from his hiding place; now he slipped that stone free and peered out.

His eyes were met by the glare of a Basilisk. He toppled back, frozen, falling to the ground like a creature made of stone. He was alive but paralyzed. His eyes could not even produce tears. More sounds came as the Basilisks fumbled at his barrier. They would gain entrance and begin to feed, not even bothering to kill him first. Eventually, as they ground and churned through his body, the thin red blood would run out of him, and he would join the ranks of the unliving.

Was death simply an opening to a new beginning? He had not even mastered this brief and brutal life, and now he was expected to undergo some new challenge? The thought enraged him, and he struggled to rise and smash the intruders with his stone hatchet. But his body would not even quiver; nor could his eyes produce a single tear of frustration.

Something strange happened then. A shadow slipped over the cavern, then passed outside, obscuring even the dim light filtering through his eye level portal. The Basilisks grew still, then snarled at each other in annoyance. Finally, they began drifting away, as though their small, malignant minds had grown confused and forgotten their prey. Then all was silent.

Was he simply going to die slowly rather than being eaten? He struggled again to rise, and this time, his body managed the feeblest of twitches.

As he twitched, a faint, soft voice spoke into his mind:

Julian?

Who? his mind whispered.

You were once Julian, a wonderful hero who came to save me and now you cannot remember your own name! I told you not to come!

I'm sorry, I remember nothing.

Do not apologize for I should not be angry with you! Even my own father, once so fierce and strong, has forgotten everything, reduced to a furtive, broken creature, a Harpy with a lone tuft of silver hair, a being that emerges from his cavern's hiding place only at dusk. All the saviors that I once wished for have been reduced to nothingness. But that is not why I am here. What are you called now? Do you even have a name?

Once I was called "Jarl," but that seems like a distant, lost dream.

Yes, and in the dream that lies outside of that dream, I was once called "Eléna." Now listen, Jarl. The touch of the Basilisk is easing, but you must not sleep, for, on this night, we will rise and fight for you. You must gather the brothers and the Ravens and leave this valley, this place of death, forever. Make your way upslope. In the malice of their own devices, the corrupted Guardians have placed a Talisman of great power upon the hilltop. You must reach it and gain strength from it.

That was part of the dreamworld when I was Jarl, that an ebony dark Idol rested upon an alabaster pedestal in a place of power.

Gather the brothers and the Ravens, ascend the hillside, and grasp the Idol. Whether you abide in a dreamworld or dream within a dream, to ascend the hillside is your task.

I will do as you say.

With that thought, the voice within his mind was gone, and he was again alone in his shelter, listening, frozen, to the silence. After a time, he was able to groan and roll over onto his side. Finally, at dusk, he rose on shaky legs then took a ration of grey water to clear his parched throat. Chewing methodically, he consumed every last scrap of food, including the foul-smelling segment of snake that had stopped moving just a few hours earlier.

Night came, initially accompanied by clear skies and a sliver of moonlight. A brief time later, vent gases gathered to the valley floor, obscuring everything in a yellow, evil-smelling fog. At its worst, the fog became putrid with the stench of sea life that had been dead for ages — as though the land had once been underwater, and great sea serpents had been suddenly trapped when the ground was torn from the ocean floor.

He covered his mouth with a scrap of cloth, drawing a deep breath, then he stood, stone hatchet in his right hand, water skin in his left, waiting for...for what? Was it possible that the Basilisks' dark magic had produced false images in poisoned dreams? Still, he readied himself, clearing enough of his barrier that he could slip swiftly outside.

He waited. White Wraiths came and went; as always, he was shaken, kneeling, and weeping until their hatred of him was fulfilled by his pain. Sometime after midnight, the fog slid further down the valley, and the air grew clear again, with a night sky populated by thousands of tiny, distant suns, and one sliver of a crescent moon.

The dark quiet of the valley was broken as Kul-Ghouls emerged, racing through the night to feast upon stray Dire Cats, Dusk Snakes, and unwary Basilisks. One Kul-Ghoul passed not thirty feet from his entrance, and he slid further back into the shadows. It was time to secure himself then sleep. Nothing was going to happen; only death would free him from this dark, grim valley.

Then suddenly the ground around him began to shake, and explosions burst through the night air. The caverned subworld beneath the valley was shaken, and all its hidden monstrosities — creatures of the underground crevices — were dying in their bolt holes or fleeing out into the night.

His stone sanctuary heaved again, and he raced outside. Reptile Birds were wheeling overhead, calling out in harsh, voices that were filled by fear. Dire Cats were shrieking, and even the Kul-Ghouls paused in their forever quest for food and prepared for battle.

The ground trembled again, hurling him from his feet. As he tumbled, his mind raced; when he rose, he sought again, almost instinctively, his overlook — a high ground where he might see, yet not be seen. As he ran, speeding over shaking, uncertain ground, a voice was raised against the clamor of the valley's fear.

"Hear me!" Was it the same voice, that of the young woman who called herself Eléna, who had reached into his mind as he lay frozen, waiting for death? Now it was much louder, filled with strength.

"Hear Me! In the Maker's Name, I call upon you to free yourselves from this place of death!" Overhead, the sky was changing: warfare in the heavens raged as star systems collided and sought to consume one another. Swirling streams of White Wraiths were being challenged by a lesser swarm of Blue Wraiths. Starlight no longer gleamed; instead, the light fluttered, as the dreamworld of the corrupted Guardians was challenged.

He ran. Dire Cats passed in front of him but ignored him. He reached the modest heights of his slight overlook. The brothers were advancing toward each other, but tentatively — as though their hatred had faded but ancient habits still drew them to battle.

"No, no, no!" he called down from his overlook. "We must seek the heights! Come to me!" The brothers stared up at him, not fifty paces distant. As he called down, the ground again heaved, casting all three of them from their feet. Again, he stood. The brothers also rose and began walking toward him, though slowly, as though stumbling through a dream.

All through the valley, Dire Cats screamed and fled, Basilisks scuttled back and forth uncertainly, Dusk Snakes slithered in the darkness through long grasses, and Kul-Ghouls bounded through the forest in confusion, dodging falling tree trunks, sometimes staring at the warfare in the skies above them. Overhead, Reptile Birds wheeled and called out as the stars above them swirled in tumult.

Two Ravens had been fleeing from a flock of Reptile Birds. Now they dropped to the ground and began moving toward him, heads darting back and forth, searching for foes. As the ground heaved and shook, and warfare swept the skies, the five were gathering again, drawn by a force none of them could understand.

Again, the valley heaved, and again they were swept from their feet. This time as he rose, swift bounding motions to the left caught his eyes: a Kul-Ghoul was racing toward him, eyes blazing red. He glanced down at his small hatchet, then back to the brothers and their cudgels. Even three of them were no match for a lone Ghoul.

"Get away!" he called to the brothers. "Climb the heights and seek the Temple!" He turned back to face the Kul-Ghoul. As it leaped for him, an arrow sped out of the night, catching the creature in the throat. Puzzled, the Ghoul sagged back down, pulled the arrow out — then fell dead as dark red blood spurted from its wound.

Astonished, the three stared beyond the Kul-Ghoul to the source of its destruction. Just a few hundred paces from them a slender figure stood in a small clearing — a figure made slight by distance but gleaming in the chaotic night. From every direction, the predators of the valley were stalking toward her, and calmly, she sent arrow after arrow into those closest to her so that they fell and died, each of them dying in silence.

"Jarl!" Eléna called out, voice charged with power. "Flee now! Seek the heights!"

But he could not, would not, let her fight alone. The brothers, too, gripped their cudgels and readied for battle. First one Raven, then a second settled on each of his shoulders.

In the distance, Eléna stamped her foot in frustration, then called out words of power into the night sky. Just behind her, the air seemed to part and an enormous figure, a colossus of pale grey flesh, emerged, bearing a great metal quarterstaff. Only vaguely from a distance could they see that the bald grey head of the colossus held only a single, huge orb eye.

Reptile Birds dropped from the heights. The Great Guardian's staff smashed and scattered them as though they were a cloud of tiny insects. Dusk Snakes surged up from dark crevices and were crushed by enormous heels. Kul-Ghouls surged forward, leaping, and bounding out of the night. The Great Guardian was merciless, crushing each foe that came within reach of his staff.

"Enough," the youth once called Jarl spoke softly. "We would add little to their strength. We must be gone."

"The heights," one brother intoned.

"The heights. We were told to seek the heights," the second brother coughed, as though his voice was choked with dust.

And the Ravens cawed loud in unison. Then, as one, the five raced from the valley floor, bodies weakened but desperate. Every few hundred steps they paused to let their panting bodies draw deep breaths. Stray Dire Cats, and Reptile Birds and Dusk Snakes darted at them, then sped away. All around them the predators of the lower hillsides were bounding or slithering, or scuttling downward, intent on destroying the Great Guardian, and the Wizard's daughter, Eléna. Overhead the sky still streamed in battle, stars shuddering as Dreamworld Empires collided. Yet slivers of moonlight flashed in the darkness, guiding their passage up the hillside.

As they reached the lower crests of the hill's great slope, some of the weakness left their lungs, and their breathing steadied. Then they climbed, or scrambled, or pulled themselves up the steep incline by the branches of seedling trees. Thrashing noises from upslope forced them to hunch down to the hillside's forest floor. As they hugged the damp earth, some huge, churning creature passed to their left, and they saw that the Snake God, larger in mass even than the Great Guardian, had been drawn to the battle below.

They scrambled upslope, sensing violence in the valley beneath them, but it was distant, soundless bloodshed, reduced to a quivering of the earth beneath their feet, and tumult in the skies. Then a great roar rose from the valley: the bellows of Kul-Ghouls, and shrieks of Dire Cats, and the hoarse calls of Reptile Birds, and the hissing of Basilisks calling for their champion, the enormous Snake God.

The five were too far from the battle to see or hear or sense how the Snake God coiled around the Great Guardian and buried huge, savage fangs in the Guardian's chest, while Eléna slashed at the Snake's thick coils with her slender sword.

Only Eléna beheld and recalled forever how the Great Guardian tore the Snake God's coils from his body, ripped the creature's jaws asunder, and then used the Snake's enormous coils as a whip to crush scores of Kul-Ghouls whose menace would not allow them to flee.

Only Eléna saw the Demons' Portal Mouth flash into existence on the valley floor and remembered how she raged against the Adversaries as Zikar, Prince of Demons, surged from the Portal, boiling with rage. And only Eléna felt the Great Guardian gather her in folds of darkness, and felt her own consciousness flee as the two of them escaped into the most remote hidden places of the Isle of the Demons.

· Ж ·

Jarl woke, his mind sensing that night was ending, and in an hour, dawn's light would peer over the horizon. His eyes flashed open in the darkness. He had changed and then changed again; and so, some magic he did not understand was guiding them. No longer was he a pitiful youth living out his last moments in the bottom of Death's valley. Now he was again the old, embittered Jarl, a Thief Mage. Jarl's hand brushed his chest, and in doing so discovered both that he held a staff and that his Talisman was gone. He turned to glance at the two Thieves: gone was Ged's flashing whip, instead, his sleeping hand now touched a strange, sword formed of mixed metals and many colors. As well, Koln's trident had vanished, also replaced by a sword. Both blades radiated power.

Jarl sagged back, closing his eyes, and *reached*.

The three Thieves and their two small allies seemed somehow stronger, more formidable, but now the hillside and its creatures had become aware of them. He could feel the hatred and malice of the hillside pulsing all around them. It would be a long way to the top, and every step would be contested by forces far more powerful than their own small band.

Chapter Ten

Island in the Sky

SOUNDS OF THRASHING WATER and heavy, beating wings woke the eagle. He was still alive after spending a night in the ocean. Light surged all around him, though he kept his eyes deliberately closed so that his own awareness was concealed. Some force had kept him from drowning, kept him from freezing in the ocean. From the sounds in the water, that force was now fighting off undersea predators. But now came the motions of heavy, beating wings and a stench of carrion breath — death was hovering overhead.

It will be a fighting death! Using the magic within him, the eagle surged upwards, talons extended, and seized its predator, then surged again, to press a croaking, squirming Reptile Bird with its leathery wings down into the ocean. His opponent was larger, with a beak nearly half the eagle's length, seeming far deadlier than the eagle, but on the surface of the ocean it was no match for the Eye. With powerful talons, the eagle crushed the creature's throat, then used its thrashing carcass to launch himself into the morning skies.

Some being had rescued him. Was there a hint of crushed juniper, a scent associated with Pallas Athena? Likely, he would never know. Battered but defiant, surprised to be alive, the eagle labored up into the overcast skies of late morning. In the water, unseen and unsensed, the Reptile Bird vanished with a faint *poofing* sound.

Even the eagle with his wide wings could range over no more than a portion of the Isle's shoreline, but the eagle swept back and forth over the Isle's northern beaches until it was clear that none of his fellow voyagers sailing on the *Alantéa* had escaped. They were gone and the eagle floated on the winds for a time until his mind cleared.

Toward day's end, the Eye foraged for food, skimming over the ocean's surface until some unwary ocean creature passed too close to the ocean's sunlit upper reaches; then the fish became the Eye's first nourishment since the disaster of the *Alantéa*. After, the eagle settled on a spar of wood, a broad beam left from the *Alantéa*. Strength had been given to the Eye for such purposes so that the eagle could sustain himself for a long while in the most difficult of circumstances.

But not forever.

As sunset passed and dusk loomed, the Eye reached again for the mind of Merlin. *Vanished, gone.* Merlin's mind had been so completely transformed by the corrupted Guardians that the Wizard might as well have been dead. The Eye of Merlin's wings flared in anger, then he tried to clear his mind for sleep. Nothing could be done now, while next morning at least he could continue to search the fringes of the Isle. It seemed so unlikely, but perhaps one member of their war party might escape from the Guardians' dream empire, and then...the eagle was unable to make plans beyond that remote possibility.

Overhead, the clear skies of sunset gave way to dusk, and the earth was turning slowly toward a starlit night sky. The eagle forced his breathing to slow, his mind turning to long flights over Sea's Edge; but then from a lone cloudbank to the north, came the gleam of a strange light, and the eagle came suddenly wide awake.

Other clouds drifted slowly westward, sliding toward a vanishing sunset. This cloud was somehow fixed, forming an island in the sky; and it radiated a light that came neither from sun nor moon. Before the eagle's mind even imagined the idea of an island in the sky, his wings had lifted his body into the air and he was moving swiftly toward that island, as an updraft of wind carried him almost effortlessly into the upper reaches of the evening sky.

As he neared the cloudbank, the eagle saw that other fliers were coming and going, landing on a shelf of white cloud that had been transformed into a firmer substance and anchored like an island to one portion of the sky.

The Eye kept well clear of the Cloudshelf, wheeling back toward the Isle of the Demons, where night and dark magic reigned. As before, bursts of sorcerous energy radiated across the breadth of the Isle like ground lightning. His people had been swallowed whole; if they lived, they existed only as transformed playthings of corrupted Guardians and the Guardians' masters, the Princes of Demons.

The Eye turned back to the Cloudshelf. Stars were ranging above it, with a sliver of moonlight rising overhead. The Cloudshelf itself gleamed brightly in the darkness, mostly with white light, but touched in some portions by hints of blue and black, and in others, subdued shades of a temperate forest in early autumn: green and yellow touched by orange and red.

As the eagle drew closer, he could feel the pulse of Portals opening and closing, and he could sense that many fliers, both seen and unseen, were arriving and departing. The Mid-World had fashioned a hub, a place of power, where its Emissaries could gather, just beyond the reach of the Isle of the Demons. But was this hub a place for watchers only, or was it a place where resistance to the Demon Princes was being organized?

Suddenly the eagle was buffeted back, down, and away from the Cloudshelf. A hidden Emissary flashed into view: the winged griffin, a being formed of smoke and magic, had swept through the darkness, and battered the eagle. The Eye wheeled in the sky, talons flaring, ready to give battle; but then he swept higher, moving beyond the griffin's reach. If the Emissaries of the Gods did not wish him to approach, he could not fight them all. And even if he defeated them all, what would be gained?

"Mocker of the Gods!" the griffin cried. "You pronounce doom upon the Gods and then seek to approach them? Ha! Even...." The Emissary broke off, turning in the sky as though some unseen but greater power had interrupted him. Then, with a snarl, the griffin forced its own powerful wings to rise from the Cloudshelf as it sought some distant portion of the night skies.

The way was open for the Eye of Merlin. The eagle floated cautiously down to the edge of the Cloudshelf. Unseen creatures radiated hostility toward the eagle but gave way as he descended. Surrounding lights seemed to fade everywhere, leaving only one lone pathway across the shelf. The eagle settled down at the island's edge then passed over the pathway warily. The substance of this island in the sky was softer than soil but easily held his weight. Sounds of conversation could be heard across the breadth of the Cloudshelf, but wherever the eagle passed, the voices around him fell silent.

The Eye of Merlin flew into a section of the shelf that had many layers. As he entered these tunneled passages, the starlit sky vanished. He then passed through a series of chambers, and in each hall, the chamber's walls and ceilings began radiating light as he continued, then returned to darkness as he departed. If they wished to trap the Eye of Merlin and destroy him, the eagle was finished. Wings flaring with anger at the thought, the Eye pressed forward.

At the last, the eagle found a larger chamber, empty except for a slight, gnarled figure, who sat, face turned from the eagle. The chamber's light was muted. Nothing could be heard except the scratch of quill on parchment as the Gnome figure made his notes. The eagle stood frozen during a long silence as the Gnome-being finished his comments, then began scratching on a second document. During this interval, the Eye tested the spell-shields and intricate enchantments that sealed the chamber from any intrusion: the sorceries surrounding him were both complex and powerful.

"Come no further," came a raspy, thin voice, and the Gnome-being turned to face the eagle, still holding his quill, features radiating distaste. "And say nothing until you are asked to speak. Our masters, the Great Gods, are most displeased with you. Indeed, it is more than strange that you still live."

The eagle stood still as a statue but very carefully sealed his mind off, so that stray thoughts could not pass unbidden to the Gnome Mage who had summoned him. With his thoughts sealed, the eagle allowed himself to consider that this Gnome was among the least attractive creatures he had ever encountered, with compressed, gnarled, thick, dark flesh. But the Gnome's eyes were bright, flashing with intelligence.

"And yet," the Gnome Mage continued, "while you still live, what is known to you is of interest to the Great Gods. I do not wish for, *must not,* be given details, but we need an answer to one question. As you approached the Isle of the Demons, was there a plan? By reputation, Merlin was thought to be both subtle and wise. That he was overcome so swiftly surprises the Gods. Again, was there a plan?"

"There were two plans," the Eye answered evenly, leaving unspoken his thoughts: *And both plans were swallowed by disaster.*

The Gnome Mage frowned. "Again, I do not wish for details, but you must expound somewhat, provide just an overview."

"One set of tasks was assigned to the Apprentice and his allies," the eagle said quietly. "A second set of tasks were to be undertaken by Godlings and Wizards."

Again, the Eye, left his thoughts unspoken: *The Apprentice and his allies were instructed to seek Eléna and the Great Guardian, while Godlings and Wizards raised a threat of counterforce that would enable Thorian to pass into Otherwhen, beyond the reach of the Demon Princes, then return suddenly back to the Isle where he might free loyal Guardians and restore some balance of forces within the Isle. All in all, these were the plans of demented insects seeking to destroy a tribe of Firedrakes.*

The Gnome Mage stared carefully at the Eye, as though the eagle's mind was leaking stray thoughts. "I see," the Mage said after a time. "It is not surprising that the Apprentice was put into play as a separate gambit, for in all your struggles the Apprentice has been a catalyst, a weaver within the *Web of Fate*. Was he not the Summoner, the stripling who called the Gods to battle? Yet now he has been swallowed whole, transformed, unable to recall even his own name or any aspect of his life in Alantéa. Did you know that, Eye of Merlin?"

The eagle suppressed the hot wrath that rose in him. "I did not. I know only that they have all been placed far beyond my reach."

The Mage put aside his quill, focusing intently on the eagle. "Why are you here, Eye of Merlin? What do you think is happening in this place?"

"We were told," the eagle said carefully, "that the Gods would mount a counterstrike, that they were unwilling to let the Demon Princes conspire against the Mid-World of the Truce without feeling the retribution of the Great Gods. As for the reason that I stand before you, I believe that you summoned me to this place."

"So." The Mage's eyes glinted with amusement, then hardened. "So, if such a counterstrike was mounted, might it free your allies to continue with their plans?"

"It might," the eagle said evenly, "depending on the level of force the Gods brought to bear."

The Mage nodded gravely. "I feared that you would speak those words."

· ⅓ ·

Days passed, with the eagle keeping himself some distance from the Cloudshelf overhead and from the Isle of the Demons. Drinking water became his greatest challenge, with the Eye sweeping down periodically to streams that flowed seaward from the Isle. Each time he neared the Isle, a force of magic reached out to grasp him, and each time the eagle escaped by a margin of seconds.

Rain and heavy winds swept over the Eye on the sixth night, and only the eagle's strength and willpower allowed him to survive, as his spar of wood was smashed by waves then completely flipped over with the ocean's turmoil.

The next night was calmer and clearer, with masses of clouds surging westward, leaving the sky filled with stars. As the eagle readied his mind for sleep, a bolt of alarm shot through him. He turned toward the Isle, where ripples of sorcerous energy rose and fell with unusual force. From over the dark night skies of the Isle, clusters of Reptile Birds were assembling, milling in the air. Then they surged toward the eagle, one, lone adversary who floated in waters that lay no more than two leagues from the Isle.

The eagle turned and studied the overhead Cloudshelf for a moment, where all was silent and nearly frozen. Then the Eye took a deep breath — for the headstrong eagle, almost a sigh, and he rose to fight his last battle.

But if the Gods were slow to assault the Isle of the Demons, they were not willing to let the Demon Princes extend their reach beyond their Isle. Portals in the sky flashed, and from those gateways, the raptors of the Alantéan heights surged overhead: falcons, and eagles, ospreys, hawks, owls, sea-hawks, kites, harriers, buzzards, merlins, goshawks, and condors.

More Reptile Birds gathered over the headland of the Isle. At the Isle's edge warfare raged, with raptors and Reptile Birds tearing at one another in fury, ripping each other from the heights, many falling helplessly into the moonlit night ocean.

The Eye of Merlin rose higher in the night sky. *An ending! Some creatures die slowly in witless states, but I am the Eye of Merlin!* The pent-up rage at his enemies exploded, and he swept down upon them.

The eagle dove down, talons shredding one wing, then a second, then a third. As Reptile Birds toppled from the sky, their huge beaks croaked moans of woe. The eagle *surged*, leaped through the air, then ripped apart a fourth leather-winged adversary.

The Eye of Merlin crested from his dive, crying aloud in triumph. Then came disaster. A cluster of Reptile Birds had climbed higher, wheeling farthest from the Isle. Now they swept down, beaks pointed at the eagle, and though the Eye surged, and dove seaward, beaks stabbed, talons raked, and the Eye's lifeblood began leaking into dark ocean waters.

The eagle spun away, again seeking the heights. The pain was nothing — he could at least die a fighting death. Though now, as the eagle weakened, he found the nature of his struggle strangely changed. Instead of facing sharp talons and beaks, he was buffeted repeatedly by scores of tiny blows. He could not strike back. He could not see his foes. And yet he was no longer being wounded — he was being herded away from the battle.

The eagle gave one cry of frustration, wheeled higher in the night sky, then called out into the gleaming darkness, "Show yourselves!"

An array of smaller raptors flashed into view: harriers, merlins, owlets.

"You may wish to perish," one called out, "but the Gods are unwilling to let you pass into the everlasting darkness. Some Gods foresee a future role for you, while others perceive little justice in your death."

"What is that to me?" The eagle cried, wheeling in the skies, circling back toward the sky battle. "I am the Eye of Merlin, serving only the Wizards and their League, and so the Will of the Gods means little to me."

"Your master still lives," called out a second small raptor, "and he will need you again before the end. You must follow us, for a place of refuge has been created for you."

The eagle floated back toward the Isle of the Demons where more Reptile Birds surged toward the sky battle. The Eye could feel the life's blood seeping from his wounds; rest would bring healing, but to what end? He *reached* for the mind of Merlin. Nothing — except was there the faintest of whispers, a gasp echoing from some lost dream kingdom?

Taking a deep breath, the eagle followed a flock of lesser raptors, as they led him north, away from the battle, back to the Cloudshelf. There, at the outermost edge, farthest from the Isle of the Demons, a small section of grey cloud matter had been created — a safe perch for the Eye. But if the eagle was secure there, he was also isolated; a barrier had been formed so that the eagle could not advance further into the Cloudshelf's interior, nor could he see or hear anything of the shelf's activity.

The Eye of Merlin still seeped red blood onto the grey Cloudshelf, but he closed his eyes and struggled to heal. Sleep came after a time, though his night visions brought images of the continuing battle. Many thousands of raptors from Alantéa fought Reptile Birds beneath flickers of moonlight. Those from both sides, whose wounds included broken wings, fell helplessly down to the moonlit ocean where sharks gathered and feasted. So, the eagle's wings flared, and his talons clutched grey cloud-matter as he dreamed of slaughter through the long night.

· X ·

Late that same night in the caverned labyrinths within the Isle of the Demons, other creatures stirred. One, a wingless Harpy, explored the darkness carefully, foot by foot — for if he fell, he would be separated from the other Harpies, and all hopes of withstanding the White Wraiths and emerging from the caverns would vanish forever.

Claws extended, he touched something strange, smooth, so unlike the pitted stone of the labyrinth. Bone, it was made of bone, the Harpy decided. Was it part of some huge Dusk Snake? But no — it smelled of salt water, like much of the underground labyrinth. A thought emerged from the depths of his mind: a sea serpent had died here, a monstrosity trapped when the Isle was raised to the surface.

Carefully, segment by segment, he made his way around the sea serpent's skeleton, hands and feet testing each step. As he shuffled along, he heard soft noises just in front of him, though somewhat to his right. He stopped and listened carefully: Dusk Snakes seldom ventured this far down, and made sinister, slithering noises when they passed. The sounds before him were similar to his own: testing, step-by-step motions. And so, his dream vision had proved true: a broken Gargoyle was seeking him.

He crept closer, testing each step. No light passed into this low-level cavern system, and only soft sounds reached his ears. Would the Gargoyle seek to destroy him as before? It seemed unlikely — if the Gargoyles were at all like the Harpies, then all the rage had passed from them with the destruction of their wings, and the breaking of their bodies, and the endless darkness of their new, underground universe.

Sounds grew closer. When each was able to smell the rank odor of the other, Gargoyle and Harpy came to a halt. Silence settled for a moment, as the two listened for the intrusion of other creatures. No sounds came.

"Once," whispered the broken Gargoyle into the darkness, "once we flew through the night sky and fought endlessly with you and your Harpy brethren. Before that, we were very different, so much so that I cannot remember that time. But I would like at least to fly again."

"Flight first," the Harpy said softly, "then after flight, something greater, something beyond our ability to imagine."

"We have had dreams," said the Gargoyle, who might once have been Phaedra, speaking hesitantly.

The Harpy replied swiftly, as though to forestall this conversation: "The Gates of Dreams are passages filled with strange thoughts; and no wonder our dreams are forever tormented because we are trapped down in a dark universe in broken bodies that will not heal."

"Yes," said the Gargoyle, nodding in the darkness: the two understood that each had been approached in a similar fashion, that further, it would be unwise to speak openly of their experience. Yet there was one hazard that had to be discussed openly.

"Under no circumstances should we pass into the lower sections of this place," said the Harpy, "for danger, not refuge, lurks below."

"In dreams, I have beheld a great chamber filled with liquid fire," the Gargoyle said softly, "as though a forge lies beneath us, a forge of such power that I recoil in fear."

"Such power lies beyond our dreams," whispered the Harpy, "and yet a small strength of magic is left within me and within my brethren."

"A trace of power remains also in our broken forms," the Gargoyle agreed in hushed tones.

The Harpy nodded in the darkness, then whispered, "If we join forces, we might gain enough power to heal these broken bodies."

"That was my thought also," the Gargoyle said softly, "but what of the White Wraiths?"

"They come only once each nightfall. We can gather after they depart and separate each afternoon before they arrive."

Now came the briefest flicker of light, for the Gargoyle's eyes gleamed in the darkness. "If we were to heal, then the White Wraiths would perceive the growth of wings and call down destruction upon us for a second time."

"That is among many hazards," the Harpy murmured softly, thinking hard, "and yet these caves and galleries contain the clothing of many dead wayfarers — tattered cloaks and spare bones are all that remain of their adventures. We can gather rags to shield our healing forms."

"We must appear to suffer from the cold."

"When the Wraiths assail us, we must shiver and weep," added the Harpy. "One day, perhaps, we will gain enough strength to turn upon the White Wraiths and their masters."

"May that moment come to pass before the End of Time." Then the two turned away from each other, inching their way back through the darkness. They had been reduced to broken, helpless beings, yet now they moved with a new purpose. Hope had come from an unexpected source: through Gates of Dreams, the Great Guardian had made contact with them. Appearing as a slight Blue Wraith, the Great Guardian was guiding their steps, striving to return to the Gargoyles and Harpies at least a portion of their strength.

· X ·

That same night, Jarl dreamed. As before, he stood in the Temple, with its vaulting, distant ceiling, and muted night radiance. Just before him stood the ebony dark Idol, a mound of black, bloated plaster that stood a head higher than a tall man, with a grimace fixed on its face. Though the statue was filled with mockery, inside it radiated imprisoned power and repressed purpose. As before, the Blue Wraith, a wispy phantasm less than half Jarl's height, hovered at Jarl's side.

"*So,*" Jarl muttered, "*it's Captain Hazard again, or Lord Peril, whatever your real name is. What is it this time?*"

"*First,*" said the Wraith, in its faint, remote voice, "*you must decide whether my advice has been of use or not. Gratitude may be beyond you at this time, but you must at least acknowledge the truth.*"

"*You have helped,*" Jarl said grudgingly, for even though they had remained in the lower portion of the hillside, still they had reached a third of the way toward the top — despite brutal resistance.

"*Then I will provide additional assistance,*" the Blue Wraith whispered into Jarl's dreaming mind. "*On this night when I wake you from sleep, you must rouse your band of thieves and speed upslope. I will pass into your mind your next place of refuge, and so you will steal a march on our foes, beings who sometimes lose focus on their tasks — a fact that I learned once, at great expense, so many ages ago.*"

"*Tonight! Now?*" Jarl exclaimed. "*What of the Kul-Ghouls?*"

"*No more than a score stand between you and your next haven.*"

"*A score! Even one is too many!*"

"*That was then,*" murmured the Blue Wraith, "*this is now. You have grown stronger, much stronger. With the enchanted swords of your brethren and your own powerful staff, a score of Kul-Ghouls are no longer a match for you.*"

"*We have grown stronger, but a score....*" Jarl hesitated then turned from the Idol and faced the Blue Wraith directly. "*Let me ask this once, and once only. For a moment, let us suppose that you truly wished us ill, wanted us dead so badly that you were willing to help us for a time, to bait a trap for us. Say that instead of a score of Kul-Ghouls, there are a hundred of them, backed by the Snake God, lying in wait for us. In short, why should we trust you?*"

"*My foes are your foes,*" said the Blue Wraith. "*As for the Snake God, as you call him, I destroyed him with my own two hands — what you see before*" *you is nothing more than an image suitable for dreams, and the Colossus fighting beside Eléna is my true form. For many years, Eléna has been my lone ally on the Isle. Do you recall the words she spoke when she counseled you? 'You came to save me and now you cannot recall your own name! I told you not to come!' Yet you did come, and now we are allies. We will never triumph, but a prolonged resistance might be possible."*

"*Enough,*" Jarl muttered, stung by the memory of Eléna's voice. "*Enough. I'll get them up. Just give me a moment.*" In their dream, he turned back to face the ebony dark Idol as it rested upon its white pedestal, formed of an almost translucent alabaster. "*So, this unhappy looking mass of dark plaster is going to help us escape from the hillside? What exactly is it?*"

"*The Idol before us will release you from this hillside,*" the Blue Wraith said softly. "*As for its nature, I will tell you another time, when your mind has grown more able to consider complex thoughts. Go now. The Kul-Ghouls are ripe for harvest. Scythe them all to the ground.*"

And with that thought, Jarl woke. As always, he listened carefully to the sounds around him. The Ravens' chests made soft purring sounds as they slept. Ged was quiet, hand as always clutching his sword. Even this late at night, Koln twisted and turned, haunted, even tormented by strange dreams. Overhead, and outside their underground retreat, Kul-Ghouls bounded and cried out into the darkness, voices like hyenas filled with insane glee.

As he lay back listening to the sounds of dark unquiet, Jarl realized that images had been left from his encounter with the Blue Wraith, visions so strong it was as though they had been etched in his mind. Higher on the hillside, Kul-Ghouls were rampaging through the night. Greater Dusk Snakes lurked just to the left of the hillside, and so the Thieves would not turn left. A flock of Reptile Birds would descend upon them, and yet a single flock was no match for his staff. And their next sanctuary was even more secret and protected than their present one.

Jarl stood in the darkness, reaching out so that he could touch both Koln and Ged, then he spoke clearly and strongly into their minds:

Rise. We must rise and give battle.

Have they found us? Ged's mind asked, coming instantly awake.

In the darkness, Jarl shook his head. *No. It has come down to this: recall the warrior princess who slew our foes, and the Colossus who fought beside her? That Colossus is a Power. Now he guides us in dream visions; and so, we must steal a march this night, and race up the hillside.*

A trap? Koln's mind asked, and Ged's thoughts added, *What of the Kul-Ghouls?*

Jarl took a deep breath. *All choices contain risks; all matters are subject to fortune. In less than one chance in ten, we are betrayed. As for the Kul-Ghouls, have you noted that the Dire Cats and Dusk Snakes and Reptile Birds are no longer a match for your swords and my staff? If we are to ascend to the peak, we must take our battle to the Kul-Ghouls.*

Then let it be now. Ged's mind murmured, and he rose.

Koln and Ged armed themselves, while Jarl woke the Ravens. A stone slab shielded them from above-ground intrusion, and it took the joint strength of Koln and Ged to force it to one side. Overhead, a full quarter moon gleamed in a sky populated by bright stars, but to the west, a massive cloud system, choked with dark, stormy wrath, was sliding toward them. They needed to move quickly.

The five scrambled to the surface then stood straight, listening to the night. On the hillside above them, a band of Kul-Ghouls leaped unchallenged up and down the hillside, feasting on wayward beasts, Ghoul voices calling in triumph and in glee. All was silent around them — except that their Raven sentries called out an alarm as they rose, wings flapping in fear.

Ged spun and slashed, and the head of the Dusk Snake stalking them was severed. Jarl was right — their new weapons were far more effective than the old.

They moved upslope slowly at first, then at greater speed. Jarl was foremost because their pathway had been grafted to his mind. The Ravens took turns, one circling overhead while the other watched from a perch on Jarl's shoulder. Above them, much of the sky still gleamed with moonlight and starshine, but masses of clouds were sliding toward them, and a dull thunder rumbled in the distance.

The slope grew steeper as they climbed up a narrow ravine populated by shallow-rooted shrubs. They climbed hand-over-hand over stony outcrops, with clumps of soil and small stones slipping down the slope into the ravine below. Noises of Kul-Ghouls grew louder. At the top of the ravine, the hillside's slope grew gentler, with some shrubs growing into trees, but now the first of two Kul-Ghouls sighted them, and then the second turned and stared at them, transfixed.

Both sets of Ghoul eyes gleamed red in the darkness. *Fresh meat!* Hyena voices crying in glee, the Kul-Ghouls bounded down toward them. Drawing swords, Ged and Koln pushed past Jarl. First one sword then the other began moaning in anticipation.

Kul-Ghouls bounded down, timing their leaps so that they descended with maximum violence down onto the two warriors. Jarl watched on in amazement, for in swift choreographed dance steps, each warrior slipped beneath a Kul-Ghoul and slashed upward, then slashed again as the Kul-Ghoul descended. Swords flashed a third time, exploding in violence, with dark smoke trailing from each blade. Jumbles of legs, arms, torsos, heads, bounced down the slope, finally toppling into the ravine behind them.

"The League!" Jarl's voice rang out. "One stroke for the League!" *Where had that thought come from?* His cry of triumph drew more Kul-Ghouls. A cluster of five bounded down toward them. Ravens circled in the air, calling out in defiance. The Thieves climbed a slight distance upslope from the ravine, so they would not be forced back down.

The lead Kul-Ghoul charged toward them, abandoning its leaping motion in favor of pure power and speed. Jarl raised his staff; with his arm extended he called down three harsh *words*. A single jagged black bolt of force smashed into the chest of the lead Kul-Ghoul, and it slid backward and sideways, spurting bright red fluids, dead before its body reached the ground. Other Kul-Ghouls leaped over its dead body, eyes gleaming with red menace.

Slashes! Explosions! Death! Three Kul-Ghouls fell dead, carved into spurting fragments that tumbled down the hill, then dropped into the ravine. The last Kul-Ghoul veered right, vanishing into deep woodlands, hyena voice wailing in horror.

Jarl stared at the others: they all breathed hard, but they had found the violence intoxicating. Koln nodded, and the three Thieves broke into a run. As they raced up the slope, Reptile Birds swept out of the night skies. Ravens pecked at the eyes of their foremost assailant, but the Ravens were no match for the monstrosity, and they dropped to the ground, cawing in frustration. But now Jarl's staff lashed at the overhead flock, bolts of force breaking wings, slashing necks from leather-winged carcasses. Reptile Birds flapped and fled, then regrouped for a second pass at the intruders.

The Thieves scrambled up the slope, though the way grew steeper as they pressed higher, and Jarl felt the first touch of rain. As the eldest, Jarl gasped with effort, heart thudding, though he forced himself to keep pace. Overhead, Reptile Birds circled, just beyond the reach of Jarl's magic.

Traces of red could be seen now, slowly gathering in the darkness. Ravens cried out: Kul-Ghouls had circled behind them, as well as to their left and right, while a barrier with gleaming red eyes had formed in front of them. The Thieves were surrounded. A dozen or more Kul-Ghouls circled around them, red eyes flaring in menace. Ravens fell silent. Reptile Birds flapped dark wings downward, hovering closer. More rain droplets swept over them, as the skies rumbled in menace.

The Ravens gathered to Jarl's shoulders. Koln reached out and touched both Ged and Jarl so that the five were linked; then he spoke into their minds — a plan. The circle around them tightened, then lightning flashed, and the creatures of the night recoiled in blinded surprise. Jarl swept his staff at the flock overhead, lashing out with bolts of force, then the five raced to their right, slashing down the Kul-Ghouls in their path.

At the place chosen by Koln, the five turned back to face their attackers — boulders and slabs of stone now lay behind them. Reptile Birds swept down at them, but now Jarl was killing them by threes and fives, and swords slashed through those who drew too close. Ravens pecked at wounded, crawling creatures as the rest of the flock wheeled away from the battle, crying out in harsh, tormented voices.

Then the Kul-Ghouls were upon them with renewed ferocity. Blades flashed and Ghoul limbs and heads flew into the night, spewing red fluids. When Koln's sword arm was pinned in the press, Jarl's staff pushed into the mass of Ghoul flesh and blasted them back. As Kul-Ghouls leaped high, the five shifted sideways so that the thrashing limbs of Ghouls shattered on the stones behind them. Enormous beaks of Reptile Birds pecked at them, but as they came closer to the Thieves, their beaks belonged to dead things.

Then lightning flashed again and almost simultaneously thunder burst overhead. Rain followed: a wash of water swept over the battle as the skies emptied. Both sides of the conflict were soaked, but only the Kul-Ghouls recoiled in surprise.

One by one the eyes of wounded, slumped Kul-Ghouls dimmed, red gleams flickering, then blacking out. Three remaining Kul-Ghouls backed away — or tried to back away. One toppled, discovering that its right leg had been almost completely severed; the other two stared down at deep wounds, and then their paws flapped feebly at wounds until surging, red fluids passed forever from their bodies. Then they toppled down the hillside, their eyes no longer gleaming crimson, only the grey of death.

Rain lashed down over the living and the dead, hard and cold and filled with retribution. Streams were forming, surging down the hillside. The Thieves were soaked, but the heat of battle drove the chill away.

"Wounds?" Ged asked. Jarl's cheek dripped blood from a dying Reptile Bird's beak, while Ghoul talons had slashed the flesh of Koln's shoulder, but considering the violence of their battle, it was nothing.

Ged stared up into streaming skies, then murmured: "Koln understands that the Colossus provided good counsel. Yet Koln asks: should we not steal a second march on this night? The pathway seems open."

Jarl shook his head, wiping fresh blood from his face. "Not on this night. The force of magic underlying this strange hillside is trembling. If we push too hard, a tide of White Wraiths will again be called down against us. Come. We grow stronger, but now rest and a night of deep, dry sleep is waiting for us." Jarl led them up the hillside a short way, moving cautiously. With the rain and the sudden wash of streams, their way was becoming increasingly treacherous. Finally, Jarl found the place shown to him by the Blue Wraith: the rock face on the hillside seemed almost seamless, but a crevice shielded by layers of ancient ivy led to a substantial stone cavern, one easily defended against intrusion.

"On this night," Jarl said quietly, "this once, I think a fire is warranted." The three Thieves gathered dry kindling from within the stone chamber. With kindling lit, larger, long-fallen but wet branches were dragged in from the outside. Then Jarl laid a force of magic over the mound, and they had a fire that smoldered but provided some warmth.

They dried slowly, and gradually the fury of battle died down inside each of them. Ravens approached the fire cautiously, wings extended to catch the drying heat. Sleep beckoned; Jarl leaned back against the cavern wall and closed his eyes. At last, he was warm, and all the madness of battle had stilled within him. Jarl willed himself back to the Temple, to stand again before the ebony dark Idol, with the Blue Wraith at his side, a being who had guided them with surprising foresight. Should he thank the Wraith? The notion was foreign to him, but still.... He fell into a deep, dreamless sleep.

Jarl woke slowly and in stages. He had been dreaming, not of the Blue Wraith, nor of the Idol, but of many, small points of pain. In his sleep, he twitched and turned. Pain resumed, mostly in the same places. Again, he twitched in pain — in his dreams, a hundred small monstrosities were chewing him to pieces! He struggled to wake.

But when he woke, the pain was still with him! Jarl leaped to his feet; more than a score of tiny, furry creatures fell away from him. He cried out in anger and disgust. Koln and Ged were also on their feet, sweeping rodents from their bodies, snarling and stomping.

Their fire had burned down to embers, but Jarl grasped his staff, and light surged over the chamber. Sheets of rodents — thousands of tiny voles, each about half the size of a mouse — were scrabbling up the sides of the cavern, while hundreds of others picked at the Thieves' meager food supplies. Scores of the tiny intruders lay dead, crushed by the warriors' feet.

Rage burned bright in Jarl: his staff blasted sheets of flame at the intruders, who fell blackened and dead by the hundreds. Other voles fled in panic, scrambling down lean crevices into lightless cave systems below. Finally, the stone chamber grew silent, while outside the cavern, the rain remained heavy. Though it no longer stormed, the sounds of water surging over loose stones now replaced the previous sounds of thunder. Grumbling, the three Thieves spent more than an hour stacking additional firewood within, then sealing the many vents where voles had emerged.

As they worked, their Raven sentries, somewhat furtively, gulped down the carcasses of crushed voles. After their sanctuary was restored, the Ravens were told to keep watch, to alternate in shifts, while the three Thieves struggled to compose themselves for sleep in the last few hours before the dawn.

Now, as Jarl reached out for the Blue Wraith in dreams, all thoughts of gratitude had vanished. Why had the Wraith not told them of the voles? Why had the Wraith allowed them to be chewed by rodents in the middle of a storm?

· ⅩⅩ ·

The Blue Wraith was otherwise occupied, for the Great Guardian had slipped into the sleeping mind of the foremost Harpy. The Great Guardian recoiled in pity and horror as he regarded the Harpy. This being had once been the most powerful Wizard ever to wield magic in Alantéa the Forerunner. Now it was reduced almost to nothing, a broken creature; but wings were sprouting on the Harpy's shoulder, and it might one day at least take flight again unless its enemies discovered its secret ways.

"You must wake now," the Blue Wraith was saying, "for the voles have arisen from newly flooded caverns, and will gnaw upon your form until you shake free of them."

"Is there a real danger?" asked the Harpy.

"No more than discomfort." And now the Wraith hesitated. "And it is interesting that a portion of your intellect recovers, an outcome I did not consider possible. We must speak again after you have dealt with the voles."

"First, tell me of these creatures, the voles, and their place in this world."

"The Demon Princes have created hybrid forests," the Wraith said quickly, "with growths that feed equally upon sunlight, moonlight, and the force of magic that rules this Isle. Few creatures have learned yet to feed upon these growths, and so most of the beings of the Isle feed first from the sea and the shore. Within the Isle, Dusk Snakes feed on blind worms and mulch grubs. In turn, lesser snakes are food for other predators until the snakes themselves mature. The third pillar of this perverse ecology is formed by Vent-Voles who feast upon Rock-Mites, and only emerge from the depths when floods of rainwater force them to the surface."

"You have sent visions to our dreaming minds," said the Harpy, "and so we have visited the length and breadth of this Isle. We have only glanced briefly at its depths where there lies a pool of fire, a furnace. What is that place?"

"The Forge of the Demons, a place of power where the Marids were fashioned, then tempered in boiling, churning salt waters. Do not go to that place; do not even let your minds travel there. Now you must rise — much is happening aside from the discomfort of the voles, and the fury of the Forge."

"A storm is coming," the Harpy murmured, at the edge of waking.

"A storm of magic," the Blue Wraith agreed, staring into the distance.

Chapter Eleven

A Storm of Magic

FROM AN EVEN GREATER distance, Zikar, Prince of Demons, stared into the oncoming storm, and he again breathed fire at the corrupted Guardians. As before, the Guardians abased themselves and swore to visit great pain and humiliation upon the intruders held captive in the Guardians' Empire of Ruined Dreams.

Then Zikar turned from his chastisement of Guardians, back to the northern Cloudshelf, where their adversaries plotted war against the Isle of the Demons. Zikar no longer emitted sheets of flame, though when he breathed, the smoke of his smoldering wrath was dark and heavy as he paced in frustration.

The Demon Princes had anticipated a counterstrike, perhaps something more than a token, whereby the Gods would satisfy themselves that they had done what might reasonably be expected of a congress of conflicted Powers. Then they should have gone back to their worshippers, their intrigues, their endless amusements. And yet now the Demon Princes watched on, while some greater event was being planned. Now, uncertainty eroded all foreknowledge, and the future could not be known.

Zikar's mouth flashed open, and flames surged out, leaping for a few hundred feet toward the Cloudshelf. Then the flames tapered off into the darkness. None of the efforts of the Demon Princes to dislodge the Cloudshelf had succeeded. If the Isle of the Demons had become the most powerfully defended bastion upon Earth the Battleground, the reach of the Isle had become considerably lessened. Had it been a mistake to have launched the Great Sending at the Maker's Heart? Satanis would never acknowledge faults or flaws. Torrents of dark fire would rage from the mouth of Iblis at any such thought. It could never be discussed, but the Cloudshelf could have been swept away by a single stroke from the Great Sending.

As Zikar struggled to control himself, his enchanted mind called upon images of the Demon Princes' greatest acts. First had come the Dragons, gleaming with power. Then the Marids had been birthed, mighty weapons created to destroy the Gods in battle. After the Marids had been turned aside, the Dreamers had helped to raise the Isle of the Demons. In response, the Scimitar, the Great Sending, had destroyed the Dreamers, and after, the Sending's final thrust was to hurl itself at the Maker's Heart.

A fourth act of creation was being readied. Now, as his brethren sought new dimensions of power, Zikar was forced to become a sentry. Yet soon Iblis and Satanis would wake to find their own heartland, the Isle of the Demons, trembling with uncertainty.

· ✕ ·

As the Harpy woke, and the Demon Prince Zikar breathed fire at the Cloudshelf, and the Great Guardian again slipped into the dreams of the Thief Mage, Jarl, violence shook the Cloudshelf in the sky, and the Eye of Merlin woke. His wings flared, then he sagged back in the darkness. The Eye still struggled with deep wounds and blood loss, but the forces of magic all around him were compelling him to take flight. He toppled from the edge of the shelf and forced stiff wings to deal with the chilled night air.

A chilling rain drenched the eagle as he wheeled in the sky. Lightning lashed down over the Isle of the Demons, and rainwaters were washing a tide of dust, dead forest matter, and broken bits of dark magic out into a foam-capped ocean. Currents of sorcery still swept like waves over the Isle, but somehow the pulse of magic had become more erratic, less certain. Had his allies begun to resist, or had the recent surge of fresh rainwater diluted the force of magic within the Isle?

He turned back to the Cloudshelf, sweeping closer to its strange cloudy matter. Powerful voices were raging against one another, and so the Gods were struggling to reach some sort of consensus. Or they might — in the treacherous, self-serving, dissembling way of the Gods — choose to let their Cloudshelf drift off into the sunset and do nothing.

As the eagle turned from the shelf, back toward the Isle, a thought reached into his mind from out of the darkness: *Nothing will happen on this night, but two nights from now, a Storm of Magic will be visited upon the Isle of the Demons. Pray that your master and his allies are prepared.*

· X ·

As rainstorms lashed the Isle, the Blue Wraith again summoned the dreaming mind of Jarl to stand in the Temple before the Idol. The Temple, formed of gleaming black marble, so imposing and filled with dark energies, was now leaking with rainwater, with a steady drip-drip-drip spattering down beside the two insubstantial figures.

"A Storm of Magic is coming," the Wraith was saying. "I judge that two nights from now, the sorcery that rules over the Isle will be severely shaken. At *that moment, you must race toward the Temple and grasp the Idol that stands before us. Then a new future will take hold."*

"That's all very well," Jarl muttered in his dream encounter, *"but first things first. When you guided us to our last sanctuary, did you intend that we should be food for rodents?"*

"I do not govern all the creatures living upon this Isle. Is it known as the Isle of the Guardians? It is not, and so you must take your complaints to the Demon Princes, not to me."

"But still," Jarl grumbled in his dream, *"to overcome a tribe of Kul-Ghouls, only to be chewed by rodents in the dead of night, is asking much."*

The Blue Wraith struggled to control his irritation. After all, Jarl was no more than a transformed construct, unable to speak the true thoughts of the Apprentice. Out of malice, Julian had been transformed into a lower level, aging Magician, with only a small portion of the power of Julian, and almost none of his heroic ideals. And yet a force of destiny within the Apprentice was struggling to break free from the essence of Jarl, adding to the Thief Mage's inner conflicts.

Taking a deep breath, the Blue Wraith murmured, *"I regret the damage done by the voles. If you have wounds, perhaps I can help to heal them."*

"Scratches only," Jarl muttered, *"but 'regret' doesn't make for much of an apology, does it?"*

"Enough," the Wraith murmured.

Suddenly the two figures were swept from the Temple to stand upon the shoreline of the Isle in the middle of a rainstorm, with lightning flashing in the sky overhead. There, the Great Guardian appeared once again as a Colossus, dwarfing Jarl's figure, so that the Thief Mage reached only a bit higher than the Guardian's ankles. And so, the Guardian wished to make Jarl understand that the Great Guardian was a Power, one greater than many of the Gods of

Alantéa, while the Thief Mage was puny, insignificant, and short lived — so Jarl should be a supplicant, not a critic and complainer.

Then a slow transformation occurred, an astonishing event even within the perverse Isle of the Demons. The figure of Jarl seemed to alter, to lose its beard and scraggly image, and it grew, to become nearly half the height of the Colossus. The image of Jarl only ceased its growth when it turned to contemplate the forces of magic surging over the Isle.

The Great Guardian recoiled in astonishment. Had some force been hidden within the transformed Julian? Was this indeed the Summoner — the stripling who had once called the Gods to battle — and did he represent some hidden force left by the Maker?

Abruptly, the two dreaming entities stood again in the Temple as the Thief Mage Jarl, and as the Blue Wraith counseling a scraggly Thief. A split second later, the air within the leaking Temple seemed to slide apart and a third figure joined them in their assembly of dreaming minds: the Guardian had called upon the dreaming mind of Eléna to join them.

"Julian," Eléna whispered, *"Julian, what have they done to you!"* She reached out to embrace the rank, wretched form of Jarl, but it was only a meeting of mists, with each encountering only dampness from the other's touch.

Jarl slumped, face turning to the floor of the darkened Temple. *"My eyes wish to weep, though no tears will come."*

"It was never intended," the Blue Wraith said softly, *"that you would weep, or feel pity, or speak with a loved one. You were transformed into a bitter being, one who would fight and struggle, then die filled with sorrow, after a prolonged nightmare of failure."*

"Yet we are here to change that fate," Eléna said. *"Julian — who is now Jarl — I have been called upon because you might understand through me the wisdom of the Great Guardian."*

"Why...." Jarl murmured, then he fell silent, humbled in Eléna's presence.

"Because my image evokes old memories," Eléna said. *"Now listen to me, Jarl, for every word I will speak to you is the utter truth, the whole, and complete truth. The Idol before us, so dark and restless as if wishing to break free from its pedestal, this Idol is a transformed Guardian, a former ally of the Great Guardian who stands beside you. If you grasp it and call upon the Guardian within to free itself, this imprisoned Power will take its ancient shape, then it will restore you and your brethren to your original forms and finally, take you far from this hillside. Do you understand?"*

"A Guardian?" Jarl murmured.

Eléna's eyes flashed to the Blue Wraith, then back to Jarl. *"In the beginning, there were twenty-five Guardians, led by the Great Guardian who aids us now. Twelve became corrupted and freed the Demon Princes. And so Satanis, Iblis, and Zikar now rule this Isle. Twelve Guardians remained loyal, and were imprisoned, like the dark Idol that stands before us."*

"It sounds...." Jarl trailed off.

"I understand that it sounds like a fairy tale, lacking only a wicked stepmother. But now at the heart of this transforming moment, you must know the truth. Two Guardians died in battle with the Gods. Ten Corrupted Guardians remain. Three are assigned to the control and torment of the Thieves, while three others govern the Wizards and Godlings and their chastisement. The remaining four govern the magic that rules this Isle."

"Wizards and Godlings," Jarl mumbled in a soft monotone.

Eléna turned back to the Blue Wraith. *"It is as you feared — all this detail is too much to comprehend for Jarl's transformed and twisted mind. Can you not place me with this band of Thieves? I can defend myself against their lusts and their other dark needs. Then I will guide them to the Temple."*

*"The Demon Princes would rise in fury, and so it must **not** be done,"* the Great Guardian said flatly.

Eléna turned back to Jarl. *"If allies — strange seeming allies — appear suddenly out of dark skies to fight your foes, can you deal with that event?"*

"I can deal with strange allies," Jarl said, glancing at the Blue Wraith.

"Good, then we will speak no more of Wizards and Godlings," Eléna continued. *"If we tell you that Guardians have great power in this land, that they will take shapes of their own choosing and come against you. Can you deal with those beings — more intelligent, more powerful monstrosities?"*

"If our weapons have power, we will cut down all those who oppose us."

"Yes, that is part of the problem," Eléna said, her mind racing. *"If you show your power too early, they will again cast you down into the valley — let us say that you go to battle this afternoon and reach half of your last lap to the mountain's peak. When the Guardians take different shapes and come against you, your band must go to ground — you cannot reveal that your weapons have power against your foes. Then you must hide and wait, for a Storm of Magic is coming. You will know when it strikes, and then you must fight your way to the Temple."*

"And these 'allies'?" Jarl asked.

"Not until the final moment," the Blue Wraith murmured. *"When Gods lash at Demons, and the fabric of the Isle trembles and Guardians contest your passage to the Temple, then you may look for allies — but be warned: these allies will be even stranger than your own Band of Thieves."*

· ✕ ·

When Ged woke it was late morning. Both Ravens had fallen asleep, but Jarl was standing watch, staring into the cavern's depth, where seams in the stone roof allowed thin shafts of light to penetrate. To Ged's practiced eye, Jarl seemed unusually preoccupied.

"So, more counsel in dreamland?" Ged asked, and as he spoke Koln's eyes blinked open, and both Koln and Ged stared at the Thief Mage Jarl.

"More counsel," Jarl muttered. "An old saying comes to mind — 'When your dreams come true, then the Dark Lords dance with glee.' When and if we reach the Temple, we may no longer wish to celebrate."

"A trap?" Ged asked as he stood.

"No. But the haggard and bitter Jarl that stands before you, and the Koln who always listens so closely to us yet never speaks, and the Ged who prompts me with foolish questions — all those people may well become something quite different."

"Better?" Ged asked softly. "Stronger?"

"Maybe both," Jarl said quietly. "But is that to be wished for? I recall the time that you spoke of your heart's desire — 'a place where the women dance naked on the tables and the wine flows like an endless fountain.' And I snarled, 'typical!' Now, after this long, grim struggle, your heart's desire seems like a fine place to be, and I would willingly join you. Though what if we reach the Temple and become so incredibly pure of heart that we no longer wish for such things? What then?"

Koln rose and brushed past Ged to stand outside in the sunlight. The silent warrior drank from fresh streams and studied cloudless, blue skies.

"Koln believes that we have no real choice," Ged said softly.

"We have no choice," Jarl agreed, resuming his study of the muted light rays in the cavern's interior. Jarl did not speak of his last dream before sunrise: sometime in the not-too-distant future, Jarl was lying on a battlefield, a broken gigantic thing, longing for death, while an eagle, tiny as an insect, croaked nonsense words at Jarl the broken giant; and then Jarl the broken giant was dead.

A troubled Ged studied Jarl's features then looked away. When Koln returned, Jarl told them both of their plans, how they were to speed halfway to the peak, but give way when confronted by greater powers.

"Hard to believe," Ged murmured, "of monsters more powerful than the Snake God."

With a grim face, Jarl shook his head. "The Great Guardian tells me that the Lord of Coils is a broken, dead thing. Everything we've been told has proved true, but my mind struggles to imagine a dead Snake God."

The rest of the morning they dozed or sat silent, then at midday they slipped from their cavern into bright sunlight. Reptile Birds soared in the distance, leather wings catching updrafts, but otherwise, all was peaceful. The Ravens were unusually silent. Thieves drank from fresh-flowing streams, allowing themselves a moment of quiet stillness, then the three nodded together and began to climb.

Jarl led them because their pathway was fixed in his mind. The Thieves followed him through a series of stony meadows where only stunted brush flourished. To their left lay ravines and rock-cliffs, while to their right, thick bands of forest ranged up the hillside as far as their eyes could see. Up they climbed, unchallenged, with a bright sun beating down on them. But then they felt the first numbing effects of the Basilisks' gaze and they slowed, staring up the slope.

A cluster of small monstrosities stood on a stony outcrop, radiating menace down at them. Jarl stared back at the Basilisks, hesitating. They were no more than fifty paces away, and it would be a simple task to blast the creatures from their path, but that solution was too noisy. Instead, he held his staff forward, radiating a hard, dark chill up toward the Basilisks. Nothing happened for a moment, but then the Basilisks began scrambling and gobbling with increasing discomfort and finally scampered into the shelter of the forest to their left.

Jarl could feel the mood on the hillside shift — sleeping Thieves were of little consequence, while swiftly moving Thieves wielding magic created a different challenge. Clouds of Reptile Birds began to lift into the afternoon skies, searching for intruders. Ravens retreated from the skies, croaking muted sounds of distress. As the Thieves sped uphill, fliers clustered overhead and their battle began.

Waves of Reptile Birds surged down at them. Jarl blasted more than a dozen from the skies. Swords slashed repeatedly, dark smoke lifting from enchanted metal, blades moaning as they carved. But the onslaught was relentless, and the Thieves took wounds. No longer were they fighting a single flock — now it seemed that whole species had come to battle against three lone Thieves. With red blood beginning to discolor their grey, tattered clothing, Jarl led them to the right into the deeply forested hillside.

Twenty paces into the forest, their struggle was transformed. Now, Reptile Birds thrashed through the forest's upper canopy, crying out in frustration, while the humans slipped swiftly over the forest floor. In the forest, the great wingspans of the Reptile Birds made them clumsy intruders rather than rulers of the skies.

Thieves raced up the slope, slipping past huge tree trunks. Mossy patches were treacherous, and they quickly learned to avoid them. It was darker and cooler in the forest. Ravens rose in flight, fluttering from branch to branch. Periodically, stray Reptile Birds penetrated the forest canopy, then, almost casually, Jarl blasted them into floppy dead things.

As they scrambled up the hillside, packs of Dire Cats gathered on the forest floor, and the Ravens called out in alarm. First one, then a second Dire Cat dropped upon them from upper tree limbs, saber teeth gaping in menace. Each fell dead to the forest floor, slashed by a smoking blade.

Then another pack of Dire Cats attacked, more than a score of them hissing, trying to slash and rip at human flesh. Enchanted swords flashed, their power seeming to build with every thrust, while Jarl's staff radiated death in several directions. Ravens gathered to Jarl's shoulders, shrieking down at dying cats.

Finally, the Dire Cats sprang back, still surrounding the Thieves, some hissing in menace, while others howled in frustration. Then suddenly, the pack fell silent. Dire Cats were quiet and motionless for one brief second. In another swift second, they were fleeing in all directions: huge Dusk Snakes were coming, surging up from underground caverns, ripping through roots of trees, flattening the forest's undergrowth as they surged toward the Thieves. Jarl halted; Koln and Ged stood still, one pace behind Jarl.

Dusk Snakes circled around the three Thieves, casually consuming dead and wounded Dire Cats as well as broken Reptile Birds. Then came a pause, as the mass of huge snakes stared at the intruders with a mixture of menace and satisfaction. Snake eyes were greenish jade, tongues grey, skins patterned in diamond tartans of black and green; but all their colors were muted on the shadowy forest floor.

Jarl turned and touched his fellow Thieves. With the Ravens still perched on his shoulders, the five were again linked; power and a new sense of purpose radiated through them.

Thus far, Jarl spoke into their minds, *in earlier struggles, you two have carried the weight of battle, but now only support me for a moment, and this will be my round.* Then Jarl wheeled, turning to the front ranks of Dusk Snakes. Arm extended, he blasted the eyeballs of the foremost snakes, striking at least one eye of each of the surrounding snakes.

Recoiling in shock and pain, the snakes flailed and thrashed and struck one another. Only one large snake reached the Thieves' circle, and a single stroke of Ged's sword slashed the life from it, though its headless coils still thrashed mindlessly.

Ravens called out in triumph, but Jarl hushed them. Then as the carcass of the foremost dead Dusk Snake stilled, Jarl leaped up on it and hurled magic down at the next rank of their opponents. Wherever an eye could be seen, Jarl's staff sent jagged dark bolts, blasting each eye from its deep socket. Blinded snakes lashed at one other. One huge blind snake began to consume a smaller snake, both snakes thrashing, rolling, in a brutal death struggle. A greater mass of unwounded Dusk Snakes watched the carnage with astonishment, then finally turned, slithering, and thrashing back into the depths of the forest.

The three Thieves took deep breaths then resumed their ascent, bypassing thrashing, dying Dusk Snakes. Behind them, Dire Cats ventured out, tentatively, some feeding on dead snake carcasses, while others ripped and tore at the thrashing forms of blinded Dusk Snakes with sharp saber teeth. The Thieves picked up their pace, climbing hand over hand up steep inclines, then jogging wherever the hillside grew less steep.

Under the forest canopy, the Reptile Birds were no match for them.

With their shield of enchanted swords, packs of Dire Cats were no match for them.

And Dusk Snakes were vulnerable to swift, harsh magic, and so they, too, were no longer a match for the three Thieves.

Then came the Kul-Ghouls.

Daylight was muted in the forest, and so the eyes of Kul-Ghouls still radiated red menace in the forest's shadows. Now, as scores of them gathered, their hyena voices were stilled, reduced to panting, *huffing* sounds. Ghouls no longer leaped like insane creatures, but moved toward the Thieves with a common purpose, jostling and snarling at one another as they grew closer.

What now? Jarl's mind thought out.

A shielding of trees behind us, Koln's mind responded. *Broad trunks backed by saplings so they cannot come at us from behind.* His mind transmitted images of what was required, alternate combinations of cliff rock faces, stands of trees. And in Jarl's enchanted inner vision, images flashed as though the landscape of the hillside had been inscribed in his mind.

Back, Jarl thought, and they retreated step by step, weapons extended.

Two Kul-Ghouls could not restrain themselves and burst forward, leaping into the air. Jarl's staff lashed at them, and the two fell dead to the forest floor. Other Kul-Ghouls stepped casually over their jumbled forms.

The Thieves backed. Kul-Ghouls drew closer, their eyes flashing red with menace. But they remained silent, except for the coarse *huffing* sounds of their breathing. Jarl sent thoughts into the minds of Ged and Koln: *These creatures are not truly alive, yet they cling to their partial lives and are most unwilling to slip into final darkness. Show them the swords, invoke the power of your weapons.*

Both power-charged blades were extended, and the swords moaned in anticipation, then began trailing wisps of vapor. Kul-Ghouls slowed, staring in fascination at death by enchanted metal.

Except for one — a lone Ghoul leaped high above them — its hyena voice was instantly silenced by Jarl's staff. It flopped dead on the backs of its brethren, then was spilled casually to the ground. As the Ghouls shuffled forward, staring with puzzled expressions at the swords, the Thieves backed downslope to a stand of trees. As a shield for their backs, this thicket was far from perfect — it had gaps where Kul-Ghouls might come at them from behind.

Jarl shrugged and the Ravens leaped from his shoulders into the thicket behind. Then Jarl touched each of the Thieves, linking with their minds. *We have become daggers in the bellies of monstrous beasts. It is time now to rip these creatures apart!*

Koln and Ged leaped forward, swords moaning as they carved Ghoul flesh. Swords smoked; limbs, heads, torsos were blasted back against the press of Kul-Ghouls. The two swords wove a forward shield of steel, while Jarl guarded their flanks. Ghouls backed, crying aloud in fear and astonishment. Then fear turned to rage. Howling noises burst from deep throats as they pressed forward. Kul-Ghouls died but their onslaught could not be stopped. Grey walls of dead Ghoul flesh began to shield live Ghouls as they pushed the three Thieves slowly back against the thicket.

Jarl searched for an opening as the press of dead, grey, bleeding flesh pushed them back. Nothing living lay within his staff's range. *It was not supposed to end this way!* He took a deep breath, expecting to find his own heart shuddering. Instead, he found new strength — and the Thieves were also tireless, with residues of new power. Jarl reached down inside himself, discovering a pool of unexpected magic. Was this the work of the Blue Wraith or some other force?

Jarl spoke *words*: shields created by magic formed about himself then around Ged and Koln. They had been pushed back against the thicket, but the mass of Kul-Ghouls could no longer harm them. Walls of dead Ghoul flesh slowly came to a halt.

Shrieking in rage and frustration, two Ghouls leaped over their dead fighters, but could not penetrate Jarl's spell-shield. Almost casually, swords swept overhead, striking the life from both Ghouls.

Jarl leaned on his staff, taking deep, slow breaths. Ghouls were growling in frustration, some bounding high in the air outside the swords' range. Overhead, Reptile Birds thrashed through the upper branches of the forest canopy. Again, Jarl reached down into the pool of strange magic that lurked deep inside the core of his being, and again he spoke *words*.

Spell-shields shifted, to form a spear-point that surrounded the Thieves — Koln and Ged toward the forward point, and Jarl at its base. The spear-point gleamed with silver fire, then began quivering, vibrating, churning its way through walls of grey flesh. Kul-Ghoul voices shrieked in fear and horror. Overhead, a cluster of Reptile Birds had trapped themselves in forest's upper reaches and Ravens rose to peck at them, while the enchanted spear-point formed by the Thieves churned, carving through both flesh and bone.

Suddenly they were free, confronting a press of astonished Kul-Ghouls. As one, the Thieves' minds shouted: ***Now! One stroke for the League! One stroke for the League!*** And they leaped forward, a whirlwind of destruction, swords smoking as they slashed, blades moaning as they carved. Jarl's staff hurled patterns of death in rapid pulses of jagged black bolts.

Scores of Kul-Ghouls lay dead or dying around them. Ravens fluttered overhead, making jeering noises. Finally, the stunted minds of the Kul-Ghouls understood that they faced death — death with no purpose, death without a final feast — and they began backing away. After a last split second of hesitation, they fled, racing from the hillside in all directions, howling in fear and frustration.

Jarl extended his staff, ready to destroy those last, fleeing Ghouls, but something held him back. He snarled, struggling to control the anger inside himself, then he turned to the others.

"Well fought," he murmured, though the words seemed strange coming from his mouth. "Wounds?"

"None," Ged murmured, "though something stirs within me, yet I cannot guess what is happening to my mind — and Koln's lips flutter at the edge of speech. I cannot call these changes 'wounds.' What comes next?"

"The Temple," Jarl said softly. He turned and gazed up the slope. The Temple could be sensed though not seen, and within the Temple, some force or power seemed to stir. "It will not be this afternoon — though if we are ever to stand within the Temple and grasp that ebony dark, restless Idol that stands upon its alabaster pedestal — if ever that time is destined to come, it will be on this night. Come. The hillside trembles with rage and sunlight soon will fade."

They began to climb again, expecting to be slowed by fatigue. Except now a fire had been set alight in their bodies, and they were able to increase their pace. All the predators of the hillside had grown silent, slipping into deep bolt-holes as tension built within the hillside — gone were the cries of Reptile Birds, Dire Cats no longer snarled, nor did the hyena voices of Kul-Ghouls shriek with insane glee. Yet Jarl could feel the shift of sorcerous energy, like pulses of ground lightning, as dark magic gathered to an intersection.

They climbed up the forested hillside. Now and then a hint of red could be glimpsed as the setting sun gathered to the west. Overhead, breaks in the forest canopy showed blue skies that were almost empty of high, floating Reptile Birds. Jarl felt magic pulse all around them, but he could sense neither its purpose nor its source.

Then the ground shook. The Thieves kept their balance but came to a halt. Off to their left, some great disturbance caused a small avalanche of stone and debris to cascade down through the ravines. *Monstrosities,* Jarl thought, *as once foretold to me — winged, and enormous.* A second concussion shook the hillside, then came a third with great shattering sounds as sections of forest growth were being crushed. This last came from a short distance before them, blocking their passage up the forested hillside. The third creature had landed somewhat to their right. An arc of monstrosities was forming, blocking their passage to the Temple.

"Big," Ged muttered, "very, *very* big. Are these the things we're not supposed to wound? Maybe your charming friend the Colossus should be dealing with them."

More crashing and thrashing sounds came, each time a little closer.

"I can sense them," Jarl said quietly, "but we need to see at least one. Come." He led them to their left, toward the forest's edge, toward the meadows and the ravined, stony portion of the hillside beyond. When they reached the tree line, the three Thieves hunched down and peered out.

Again, the hillside trembled, and more boulders bounded and crashed down the slope. Further up the hillside, an enormous creature with the wings of a drake was searching through the rubble. On its great grey dragon-like body was grafted a long, coiled neck, and to this neck was fixed a huge head, easily the size of the Snake God's. But this head was shaped like that of a Guardian's, with one single orb eye, and a huge, gaping mouth.

From this mouth poured out not fire but transforming energies. As the Thieves watched in fear from a distance, the mouth breathed over a boulder — and the stone took shape, transformed into a stone ogre. Before its creation could fight or flee, one huge, taloned foot crushed it into rubble. Then the transformed Guardian took wing, floating then crashing down the hillside, coming always closer to them. Two other smashing sounds were also coming closer, and the hillside was shaking from the tremors. An arc of transformed Guardians was gathering, forcing the Thieves back down the hillside.

Koln turned and stared at Jarl and Ged — here was the same look of complete sorrow that had passed over his face when a tide of White Wraiths had cast them from the hillside. Jarl shook his head, snarling, then took hold of the others, pulling them back deeper into the shelter of the forest.

"We were warned," Ged whispered, "that we should not wound one of these? Was your advisor insane?"

"We need to find shelter," Jarl murmured, "deep, dark shelter — and quickly." They sped downslope, hugging the tree line. Tremors shook the ground. The crashing noises of flattened forest sounded like nearby explosions, coming always closer. Boulders bounced as they hurtled down the hillside. Three huge, grey drake-creatures were hunting the Thieves, and all the Thieves' triumphs over Dire Cats, Dusk Snakes, and Kul-Ghouls were rapidly fleeing from their minds. If they focused on staying alive, they might survive one more night.

Down they scrambled. Finally, Jarl halted, taking deep breaths until the Guardian moving down the meadow's slope was distracted by the shadows of stray Reptile Birds passing over the upper forest. Then Jarl led the Thieves scurrying to their left, hunched over, using a slight depression in the meadow to shield the Thieves from view. When they reached the stony ravines of the hillside, Jarl led them down into a lower hollow, one that passed deeper into the caverns of the hillside. Underground, the light of dusk vanished. They felt their way through the cave system in the darkness, shuffling in silence, except when the tremors shook stalactite matter free from the cavern's roof, so that stony debris cascaded down over them.

"Rest here," Jarl whispered, and they came to a halt, Ravens flapping from Jarl's shoulders to the ground. "I must weave a deep sleep over all of us," Jarl continued, "together with as many cunning illusions as I can muster. We must become one with the stone, think like the stone, dream as stone dreams."

Guardians — beings who had become monstrosities — ranged up and down the hillside through the long evening. Under their enchanted sleep, the Thieves dreamt strange night visions of vastly different beings that walked freely over the sunlit south of Alantéa, as Apprentices and Charmed Knights. In the late evening, the Guardians moved higher, ringing the Temple, preparing for a Storm of Magic.

An hour before midnight, the White Wraiths finally discovered the Thieves, shrieking and raging at them for hours. As always, Thieves and Ravens when linked could shield their minds from the Wraiths' onslaught. But this time, Jarl peered out from behind his shield, studying the Wraiths with some interest, for within their cloudy white forms, tiny grey spidery creatures seemed to be sucking on the life force of the Wraiths.

Jarl's eyes grew wide in astonishment. *The White Wraiths are being punished. They have failed to paralyze Thieves and Ravens with fear. Now even the ghosts of this forsaken land are being haunted.*

·)X(·

The Eye of Merlin slept through the long afternoon. Before the disaster of the *Alantéa,* he had perceived events both near and far through the mind of Merlin. Now he was so completely separated from his transformed master that not even the faintest image of the Thieves' battle reached into his sleeping mind. He woke at sunset, then stared out from the Cloudshelf until the last rays of sunlight gave way to the gloom of dusk. As night came, the eagle slipped from the Cloudshelf, ranging high over the shoreline of the Isle. As always, waves of sorcerous energy were rippling over the Isle of the Demons like ground lightning. If anything, the force of magic had strengthened and become more focused.

Recoiling in disgust, the eagle turned from the Isle, back toward the Cloudshelf. *The Demon Princes have stirred and have prepared themselves. And indeed, what have they to fear? For the Gods have become feeble with their internal conflicts, and with their long, endless self-absorption. Maker, if they wish to achieve true Godhood, let them behave as Gods!*

The eagle returned to his resting place, struggling to calm himself. He watched as a cloudless night gathered overhead under a fullness of starshine, amplified by a thin, Sickle of the Maker Moon. All was peaceful in the skies, yet as night gathered, the Cloudshelf seemed to radiate tension. The Eye of Merlin had a sense of muted voices rumbling in conflict, though no sounds reached his ears.

Nothing will happen, thought the eagle. *If my people are lost, then I will challenge a host of Reptile Birds just outside of the Isle's reach and give them such an ultimate battle that our warfare will become a legend...if those Reptile Birds truly have memories...if they are even able to think for themselves. The eagle shook with frustration.*

The first hint of magic seemed no more than a tiny point of light, slowly expanding as though a distant star was hurtling toward the earth. Then the star pulsed and shook, becoming a full Portal in the sky, bristling with power. The eagle's wings flared in hope.

One of the Great Gods of Alantéa, Wotan, perhaps, has come. Now we will see who will be the master of this moment!

Yet great power was concentrated within the Isle, far too much for a single Portal. A torrent of dark flames, raging with even darker energies, surged up from the Isle. The Portal exploded, fragments of its magic substance fluttering downward, cascading like huge ashes through a star-filled night sky.

· ☓ ·

Jarl's staff flashed bright radiance. "Up," he muttered. "It doesn't feel as though we're winning, but it's fight or die time again. Come." He led the partly awake Thieves and Ravens back out into the night, where the Isle of the Demons surged with magic, though it was focused on events in the night sky.

· ☓ ·

"Is that *all*?" the eagle cried out into the night. "One lone Power with only modest courage and —" Again the eagle broke off, for many scores of Portals were forming swiftly, and blasts of power hurtled down upon the Isle of the Demons.

A Storm of Magic raged over the Isle. Lightning flashed, so powerful and brilliant that stray Reptile Birds were blinded, while others were paralyzed and lost all their powers of flight. Down came whirlwinds of powerful energies, lashing at the sources of magic that ruled the Isle. Huge bolts of electrical force blasted at the stony headlands of the Isle. At higher levels, fire raced down, and forests flamed, while in coastal regions, weather magic brought sudden storms, with wild waves lashing at the coastline. The foundations of the Isle were challenged. The ground shook, and thousands of hidden monstrosities were crushed by sliding and crumbling slabs of stone.

·)(·

The Thieves ran in spurts, dodging boulders that bounded down from above. Lightning blazed down, burning sharp afterimages into their minds. Every few moments the hillside convulsed, hurling them from their feet — then they would tumble, roll, struggle to their feet and continue their race to the top.

Cavern systems were being crushed by earthquakes. Wildfires raced like thickening ribbons of flame through the forested hillside. Only in the middle portions of the hillside was passage possible, where thin strips of meadows led to the summit — but now the meadows were filled with Dusk Snakes, Dire Cats, and Kul-Ghouls, all trying to flee downslope into the valley beneath.

Yet even the Kul-Ghouls were attempting only to save themselves — with one sight of an enchanted blade, or of Jarl's staff, then the monstrosities would veer away from the Thieves. Overhead, disks in the night sky were again opening and closing, raining magic down on the Isle. While from the Isle, bursts of dark energy ripped into enchanted Portals.

"Wildfire!" Jarl gasped, "a Storm of Magic comes to the Isle!" Panting with effort, the Thieves raced up the meadow's path toward the summit. Whenever the shaking ground hurled them from their feet, they rose, quick as young felines, and raced forward. To their left, an empire of lightless caverns was being crushed, while to their right the forests blazed with fire. Even though the maddened creatures were blundering into each other, seeking only to escape, the larger ones became targets for lightning bolts; and so, the twisting, smoking carcasses of Dusk Snakes and Kul-Ghouls became another hazard as the Thieves raced upward.

Somehow Jarl's body no longer struggled with the climb — some new strength had been given to him. Was it possible that they would truly reach the Temple and triumph? Would he still be Jarl, or would Jarl become nothing more than a husk, a snakeskin outgrown by events, a thing left drying in the dust? Or would he be left on a battlefield as a broken, gigantic creature, longing for death?

As Jarl raced up the slope, filled with hope — and fear — another portion of his mind saw that the storm around them was lessening. He glanced to the upper skies and came to a halt. Where hundreds of Portals had gathered overhead, now they had been reduced to a few scores. The forces that had come to their aid were retreating. Powers had taken wounds, or grown weary, or had lost focus on this lesser conflict, one that had only a minor impact on their long-term interests.

"Once," Jarl murmured, staring up at the sky, "once I had the power to call these beings to battle. Or is that memory just a dream, a dream within a dream?

· ☿ ·

"Once!" the eagle cried from the heights, "Once you were called to battle and fought for your own lives! Now, the Demon Princes need only threaten you with harm, and you slink away! Rabble stealing away into the night! And you call yourselves Gods!" The Eye of Merlin then halted, for a cloud was forming above the Isle of the Demons. This cloud was more than a Portal, greater than sorcerous passageways that could open and vanish in an instant. This cloud pulsed with dark energy and powerful, unrelenting purpose, and the Eye realized that he was seeing some great transformational event.

A Great Sending, I understand that. Yet what force could it bring to the Isle of the Demons?

Power sped upward from the Isle, lashing at the dark, boiling cloud, yet the Sending only seemed to pulse with even greater strength. And now from the mass of energies overhead, emerged only a single sound, clear and loud, echoing over the horizon.

A Word.... The eagle's mind recoiled in shock. *What was that sound? Once I knew that Word from the Mind of Merlin.*

A Second Word.... *These are the Truce Terms! One of the Great Gods has stirred! Yet if the Gods are called to battle, they will be brought to the very shores of the Isle, and then be destroyed!*

A Third Word.... *Greater than all the lightning, and all the columns of magic, one of the Great Powers invokes the Truce. But to what end?*

A Fourth Word.... *Once I was linked to the mind of Merlin, and he knew those tones, that voice. Set is speaking! Dark Souled Set! In his pride he tells the Gods to bring greater force to battle or Set will compel them to come and be destroyed. Set!*

A Fifth Word.... *And then the sky exploded with thousands of Portals, all hurling torrents of magic down upon the Isle. Lightning blasted down, and waves of fire, with whirlwinds of dark sorcery, smashing at the intricate sorceries of the Isle. From the oceans came mists, billows of transforming energies, and all creatures that those mist droplets touched struggled to retain their forms.*

· X ·

The night sky was filled with light — flashes of powerful magic were flaring over the hillside, and now Jarl could see the first outlines of the Temple. They raced upward, with convulsions of magic shaking the hillside, while miracles and magic and dark sorcery raged in the night sky. Just as Jarl glanced up to the Temple, they passed through a bank of dank mist, one that was charged with transforming energies. Convulsions shook both Thieves and Ravens and they tumbled to the ground.

One Raven spilled over and over, becoming for an instant, a blurry figure with red fur. The second Raven slowed, then landed sloppily, its body shuddering with conflicting magics.

Jarl was changed; suddenly he was an old woman, then just as quickly, a stripling youth, then the old bitter Jarl again. Were these past or future versions of himself? Why was he seeking to be something other than a strong Thief Mage?

Koln became older, then much older, twitching on the ground, as though a dying ruler was convulsed by poison. But then Koln forced his aging body to stand. Shuddering with transforming energies, Koln spoke for the first and last time: "None of these changes matter. Our destinies remain at the pinnacle of this hill. Come."

Then Koln, bent and twisted with age, led them as they struggled up the last portion of the hillside. Their way had grown steeper, though the Temple itself, at the hillside's peak, was set on a gentler slope. Warfare in the skies raged on, while the hillside had grown still, becoming a silent, waiting entity.

They climbed. Magic stormed all around them but left both Thieves and Ravens untouched. Gradually, all the transforming energies lashing at them fell away and they became, again, no more than Ravens and Thieves.

Koln's throat constricted as though he would never again be allowed to speak. Jarl's mind struggled with dark fears and faint hopes, while at the same time, a force like wonder began to grow inside him.

The outlines of the Temple grew more distinct as they climbed. Columns of black marble glistened with magic. Slabs of dark stonework arched overhead to form a roof, though the upper stonework had been transformed by time, becoming a lodging for sparse shrubs, and long, trailing ivies that flapped and flailed with each gust of wind.

A brilliant flash of bright light illuminated the night sky and they halted. Now they could see that Guardians in Grey Drake form ringed the Temple. The heads of Drakes were turned skyward, and all the magic hurled down at their Drake forms was being transformed into vapor and ash. Yet now, as Thieves and Ravens approached, one long neck turned, and its Guardian's face regarded them with an everlasting malice...the Thieves slowed and halted, Ravens settling on Jarl's shoulders.

"Come now," Ged muttered, "it's fight or die time — again."

"One more moment," Jarl said softly, and he reached deep down inside himself, into that well of internal knowledge that had produced hidden understandings.

"One more moment," Jarl said again, leaning on his staff and taking a deep breath while staring upwards. "We can — perhaps — deal with one of these creatures. It will come at us with transforming magic, and I can forge a shield against it — a shield that will last for a fleeting time only. At a critical moment, you must strike at it with your enchanted weapons. Slash at its neck, not its orb-eye. As for the other monstrosities, the forces of destiny must align themselves toward this encounter and remove the other two from our path. Now it's again time to fight or die. Come."

They climbed slowly toward the peak. The face of one Guardian regarded them with detachment, then a second coiled neck turned from the skies, and finally the third turned to watch them with remote amusement. Overhead, the force of magic assailing the Isle continued to pound down, though the Guardians had been released from its onslaught — for the moment.

As the Thieves approached, the Temple gleamed with always greater intensity. Ravens hunched down, clutching Jarl's shoulder in fear, though they did not flee, as the tiny figures of the Thieves advanced slowly toward the monstrosities. Jarl's staff was extended. Koln and Ged drew blades, but all hope died as they drew closer. They were glowworms in the dust, advancing on a pride of demonic lions.

Then everything changed in a matter of seconds.

From overhead, great focused power raced down, like bolts of jagged, black lightning, converging on the bodies of the great Grey Drakes. Coiled necks twisted skyward. Transforming energies tore into the power overhead.

But not all the Gods' power was turned aside. Drake forms took wounds. One great Drake wing was shredded. The second Drake howled and writhed in agony, its back ripped and scoured by greyish black lightning. The third Drake's orb-eye was struck by a stream of white fire, and the substance of its eye turned opaque, still smoking from the blast. Maddened by pain, the third Drake thrashed, tumbling from the hillside. Then its wings extended, and it lifted into the air, huge mouth moaning out transforming sorceries, blended with sounds of woe as it flew blindly through the night.

Jarl shifted forward in nervous, half steps. One Drake had been driven from the field. The other two had been wounded. It was not enough. But it would have to do — then flickers of motion in the night sky brought him to a halt.

From out of the night, lesser flying creatures swept down — not one of them was even half the size of a human — and they smashed down on the back of the second Guardian.

Harpies and Gargoyles thought Jarl. The words emerged in his mind with only shadows of their true meanings. *Were these the "strange allies" promised to us? They are more than strange, yet they have brought a force of magic to this battle, Harpies raking the Drake's wounds, while Gargoyles ripped at the orb-eye of the creature.*

In agony, the second Drake took flight, while the last Drake sprang at the Thieves, breathing transforming, destructive energies down upon them. But its shredded wing made its leap unbalanced, and it landed heavily to one side.

Jarl spoke *words*. A shield of silver radiance formed around Thieves and Ravens; and the shield held fast so that the Guardian's transforming energies passed over them. Their shield held, but the shield's particles were failing, like dewdrops burning away from the heat of a summer's sun.

As the Drake took a deep breath, preparing to transform Thieves into dead things, Jarl, called out "Now!"

Koln and Ged raced out; leaping forward they each struck to either side of the creature's coiled neck. Koln's sword would not bite, and it fell back, moaning in frustration. But Ged's sword bit — and it slashed deeply.

The Drake reared back, its wound spouting pale fluid. Its coiled neck spasmed and it rolled away from them, howling, tumbling downhill. Pale, spurting fluids caught Ged's sword arm, and the blade fell from his hand.

Ged's hand and arm were transformed — like the wild snake's neck, Ged's arm became a coiled thing, a creature that would not obey Ged. Filled with venomous destruction, the snake-like arm gathered around Ged's neck and its coils began to tighten. Ged could not breathe. Koln dropped his own sword onto the grasses of the slope and struggled with both arms to tear the coils from Ged's neck.

Overhead, a great jagged bolt surged down at them. Jarl pushed the two Thieves away from it, but the shock of powerful magic still hurled all three of them to the ground. Jarl rose, staff lashing at the coils choking Ged, so that the snake-arm spasmed, loosened, and Ged could gasp deep gulps of air.

"And now," Jarl called, struggling upslope, "destiny — or doom summons us. The Idol is calling out to me...while other voices are warning me...." As Jarl shambled toward the Temple, Koln was still wrestling with Ged's thrashing coil-like arm with both hands. Finally pinning the arm with his left hand, his right hand fumbled on the ground for the two enchanted swords and awkwardly slid the Tarnished Sword into Ged's sheath, then his own enchanted blade into its own sheath. Finally, the two Thieves were able to follow the Thief Mage clumsily up the slope, still struggling with Ged's thrashing snake-arm.

Broad shadows loomed above them, and as Jarl hunched down, a huge wing swept overhead; but then more magic smashed down over the blinded Drake, so that it again veered away from the Temple, moaning in agony.

Jarl's shambling motions slowed as he neared the Temple. Then the Mage came to a complete halt at the very base of the Temple. Only five steps separated the Thief Mage from his destiny. His body shook in conflict — he could not force his feet to take the final steps up the five black marble stairs that led to the Temple. Jarl turned to the Thieves coming up behind him.

"I cannot go forward," he choked out. "After entering this Temple, I will become a broken dying giant on a battlefield of death, and so my feet will not obey me." Ged's snake-arm leaped for Jarl's throat. Almost absentmindedly, Jarl tapped it with his staff and the coiled thing fell back, limp, at Ged's side.

"Koln thought that it might come to this," Ged said softly. "Great mysteries lie at our journey's end. But now, just try not to fight us, and we will help you with these last, brutal steps." Ged took one of Jarl's arms, Koln the other arm, and they half carried, half dragged the Thief Mage up the final five stairs and into the Temple.

Then from out of the stormy night, two Ravens swept through the temple's entrance, one settling on Ged's shoulder, the other on Koln's. Both Ravens were suddenly silent, as though they had been struck by a strange sorcery that robbed them of sound.

It was dark inside the Temple, dark and wet, with air that was still as a tomb's. They dragged Jarl through shallow pools of standing water until his feet began to obey him at last, though he could manage only the feeble shuffle of an ancient shaman. Rainwater, driven by wild winds, had been trapped in the Temple's upper reaches. Now, water poured down onto the stonework, sounding, strangely, even louder than the forces of wild sorcery that still ruled outside.

Magic beat against Jarl's brow like pulses of dark energy. He was in the presence of some Power, a restless force barely restrained. Yes, there it was as it had been in his dreams, the Idol, a squat, misshapen thing, made of plaster that had been stained black, thick lips trapped in a grimace — almost a parody of ancient, stone gods. It pulsed with real magic now, its plaster form beginning to twitch. The Idol, black as the dark marble of the Temple itself, rested on a broad pedestal of almost translucent, white alabaster, an altar set above the Temple floor with one last stairway leading up to it.

Arms released Jarl, and he shuffled toward the Idol, counting the final set of stairs — there were twenty-five of them. What did that mean? Eléna had mentioned twenty-five as the count of Guardians — whoever, or whatever those beings were.

Seven, eight, nine, ten. Even the dripping sounds seemed to dwindle as Jarl ascended. Though now came motions in the darkness. They were not alone in the shadowy Temple. Jarl ignored them, shuffling up more stairs.

Koln and Ged drew weapons and turned back to the Temple's entrance. Ravens hopped away, wings flaring.

Yet no weapons were necessary. Creatures, no more than half human height, were passing warily through the shadowy entrance — six creatures made faltering progress as they stumbled forward. All had battered, stunted wings. Three had twisted human faces — partially human Harpies, while the other three had the gnarled features of Gargoyles.

Thieves and Harpies and Gargoyles turned toward Jarl as he ascended the last steps. All of Jarl's inner warfare was slipping away. It seemed almost that hands of some other being were reaching toward the ebony dark Idol that rested upon its dais of nearly translucent alabaster stone.

"Great One, you are released," Jarl heard his own voice say, though it seemed to belong to some other person.

The Temple shook. Blocks of dark stone fell from overhead but crushed no living thing. The Idol burst into a thousand fragments, then the fragments themselves dissolved into swirling smoke, and finally the smoke reformed into something infinitely greater than a stone idol.

Standing more than twice Jarl's height, its mass many times greater than Jarl's, stood a Guardian, master of transforming dream energies, with a single blue orb-eye that looked down with detachment on Thieves and Ravens, Gargoyles, and Harpies.

"I am released," murmured the Guardian. "You will argue that I, in turn, should release you from the tormented designs of my corrupted brethren. Yet in doing so, I would be joined forever to your alliance — and your cause looks far from promising. Why should I take your part in such an unequal contest?"

"Are those the words," Jarl said in a voice that now belonged wholly to another, "that you will speak to the Great Guardian who leads our cause? Indeed, will you speak those words to the Maker at the End of Time?"

The Temple was silent for a moment, as the Guardian stared into the distance, and only the *drip-drip-drip* of rainwater could be heard as it spattered over white stone.

Then the Guardian's orb-eye blinked once. Suddenly, Jarl was no more, and Julian stood in his place. Then the Thieves vanished; Kalanin and Galad replaced them. Ravens were hopping toward the altar; in the middle of its hop one Raven became Sebastian, the other Rafir. Then Harpies and Gargoyles shook free from their crooked forms and became again Wizards and Godlings. With this last transformation, the Storm of Magic assailing the Isle began to lessen, as though its time had passed.

"Merlin!" Julian cried out. "We, the former Thieves, must join forces with Eléna. She can guide us through the innermost secrets of this Isle!"

"We cannot reach them at this moment," Merlin said quietly, then he turned to Godlings and Wizards. "Matters change — this Storm of Magic is fading way. Search with me."

Godlings and Wizards, and the lone Guardian reached out beyond the temple's slabs of stone, to study the night sky. Portals were fading. Clouds still blocked the night sky above them, but starry patterns were forming on the low horizon. Drake wings were flapping high overhead, circling like vultures above the temple — not only had three Guardians been healed, but three additional Guardians had taken Drake form, ready to engulf the interlopers who stood, restored, in the Temple.

And farther in the distance, a torrent of White Wraiths was racing toward them. Bands of Blue Wraiths had emerged from seams in the night. Battle was still raging in the skies, but Blue Wraiths were vastly outnumbered by White Wraiths.

Merlin turned back to the Godlings, and to his fellow Wizards. "We must break free of this place. Guardians descend from above, stung by fear and rage, seeking to reabsorb us again into their dream kingdoms. If we do not fight them off, we will reenter the nightmare labyrinth, with Demon Princes rising in wrath against us, and we will wish that we had never changed from our roles as Harpies, Gargoyles, and Thieves."

Wizards began whispering *words*. A massive Portal surged open in the Temple's center. More stonework collapsed down from overhead. The Portal shook as transforming energies grappled with its substance. But then power, a force only partly trained, radiated from the Godlings, and the Portal was restored. Behind the Portal-mouth, a labyrinth of tunnels lit by strange lights beckoned, leading down to the foundations of the Isle, down to the Demon Princes' place of power, down to the Forge where Marids had been fashioned.

The freed Guardian passed first through the Portal-mouth, followed by Godlings, then Wizards, then finally their servants. As Julian passed through, he could no longer restrain himself.

"Merlin, my master!" he called out. "Had we landed upon the beaches of this Isle, unchallenged, we would never have reached this place. We are passing into the innermost hidden reaches of this perverse Isle of the Demons. And now we are free!"

Chapter Twelve
"Set a Thief to Catch a Thief"

"ET A THIEF TO catch a thief," Houma said to Alcman. "You and I will lead a band of the Demons' followers and destroy the interlopers on this Isle. That will bring an end to the Wizards and their lackeys, and all their bizarre misadventures. When we speak to the Demon Princes, will you have anything to add?"

Alcman nodded, staring out into the distance. "Only a few thoughts, nothing compared to what you will be telling them. Houma, we now have a moment to consider the devices of our masters. When you look out over this 'kingdom,' what do you see?" The two Sorcerers stood on the highest parapets of the Citadel created by the Demon Princes, staring out over the cloud covered, barren fields that lay on all four sides of the Citadel. Occasionally, the wind would move small clouds of dust back and forth over the fields, but the dust clouds seldom moved beyond the hills that lay beyond the fields.

"I see that this fortress has been surrounded by dead plains — killing grounds — and beyond those killing grounds lie steep ravines that lead up to a ring of high, stony hills. This Citadel, and its surroundings, form a standard defensive configuration, one that is possibly unnecessary, given the power of the Demon Princes." Houma turned to look up into the taller Alcman's face. "Why are you so interested in their devices?"

"We are servants, not allies of the Demon Princes," Alcman said evenly. "To understand them better is to be able to serve them more effectively."

"In this matter, you may be right," Houma acknowledged, and he took a deep breath. "I understand why they built these killing fields, and to indulge you and answer your next question, I will speculate on the smell of death that surrounds them."

Alcman nodded, only partially surprised, for that indeed had been his next question.

"Let us say," Houma continued, "that the Demon Princes are capable of many creative efforts. Perhaps they were not completely satisfied with the Marids and sought other monstrosities to assist them in ruling this planet's oceans. Then something went wrong, possibly a revolt, and the Demon Princes destroyed their own offspring."

"Not only death surrounds these killing fields," Alcman added, "but a sense of violence still lingers over these barren fields."

"And so dead Sea Monsters or Sea Dragons lie buried all around us," Houma again turned to look up at Alcman. "Now, does that satisfy your curiosity?"

"Not completely," Alcman replied. "Some other extremely powerful force is being created by our masters. I can sense their hidden efforts. I dream of tongues of fire lifting from the underground lake that lies beyond those hills, just to the north and a little to the west."

"In the direction of the Cloudshelf," Houma said. "Yes, I have also dreamt of tongues of fire lifting from that lake. But all these discussions are meaningless, for our masters are now calling to us. We must serve the Demon Princes with all our cunning and all our strength."

"Agreed. We must serve the Demon Princes with all our cunning and all our strength," Alcman repeated, though he was beginning to believe not a single word of that statement.

·)(·

"Set a thief to catch a thief," Houma said, speaking in humble tones to the Demon Princes. "Mortals should deal with the ways of mortals, while your great majesties contemplate matters beyond our comprehension."

Houma and Alcman stood in the Demon Princes' place of power, a great oval underground chamber within the Isle of the Demons, where three Demon Princes stared down over a circular court formed of black basalt poured over grey granite. Their huge thrones were set equidistant around this circle. Deliberately, the diameter of the court was overly large — from long experience, the Demon Princes had learned to space themselves far enough apart so that the flames could not reach one another when torrents of fire burst from their mouths.

Houma and Alcman had been called upon to reveal what they knew of the Wizards and their ways. As they entered the chamber, both Sorcerers had bowed deeply, then remained hunched in reverence, although Houma had become increasingly energetic as he spoke at length of the long struggle of the Sorcerers and the Marids against the Wizards and their League. Now he wished to summarize his understanding of the Wizards, then move on to a second, somewhat more sensitive topic, the nature of the Godlings.

"And so," Houma continued, "we have noted that hierarchies exist even within the lesser order of Wizards — Merlin retains somewhat greater than a third of a God's power, Thorian has an even third, and Balardi has amassed less than a third. Also, unless they can be replaced, the Wizards have always been a short-lived phenomenon, with the Mid-World returning to its ancient ways after their death in battle or when the Sickle of Time removes the Wizards from the South of Alantéa."

Thus far, Zikar considered, *they have acquitted themselves adequately, yet they do not understand how closely my brethren watch them, and how dangerously they dance along a precipice.*

"Now, as to the Godlings," Houma said, growing increasingly animated, "these entities are most fascinating to study from afar, for they represent all the confusion and compromise inherent in the Mid-World of the Truce. Imagine the creation of the Godlings. How powerful should they be? The Gods would never contemplate the creation of beings with the Gods' own strength, yet Godlings must be strong enough to give battle upon the Isle, and so we have beings with powers greater than the Wizards, while their lack of wisdom reduces their strength.

"Let us consider for a moment the components of each of these strange Godling constructs. Magog is dark-hued, touched by seams of blue and white, showing the force of dark Gods, with other colors supposedly reflecting a sense of justice. Turin mixes the gold of Seraphs with the green of Dragons. Often when seen from afar, the aura of gold dominates as Turin stares into the distance, dreaming as Seraphs once dreamt — whatever those strange dreams were. When warfare surges around him, he gleams with the green of Dragon force.

"Phaedra is the most intriguing, taking the silver essence of female Spirit Lord blended with the deep red of a Demon Prince. I will guess that the silver portion enables her to communicate with humans, while the smoldering red would contain a great desire to rule, to dominate all of creation."

As Houma described the nature of Phaedra, the Demon Princes leaned ever so slightly forward. *By all the Nine Billion Gods,* Alcman thought, *has the Mid-World in its malice fashioned a possible lover for three otherwise sexless Demon Princes?*

Unaware of the reaction of his masters, Houma continued his discussion of the Godlings. "Now, how closely should these strange creatures be wedded to the Wizards' cause? They must have some sense of allegiance to the Wizards, otherwise Godlings would hesitate to risk themselves in battle; instead, they would slink back to Alantéa and seek to build their own sorcerous empires within the Mid-World of the Truce. Yet what sort of outcome would suit the Gods best? Let us imagine the unimaginable for a moment — let us say that somehow Wizards and Godlings prevailed. What would the Mid-World wish at that moment, what would the Powers of the Mid-World desire?"

Houma rubbed his hands, laughing softly to himself as he continued. "Obviously, the Gods would wish for the mutual destruction of both Godlings and Wizards. Thus, in the aftermath of even a partial victory, the Godlings would be provided with a second set of instructions to turn upon the Wizards and destroy them. Yet the Godlings themselves would not understand the hidden purposes embedded within them, though the seeds would sprout as they ventured across the Isle."

Here Houma glanced up into the impassive features of Zikar, then added hastily, "*If* they were permitted to venture across your Isle. Great Ones, I do not wish to try your patience. My small insights may be so trivial as to prove worthless. Is it your will that I proceed?"

"If we are to rule this world," Zikar said evenly, "and the universe beyond it, we must at times show patience. Proceed." *You are going to show us something, little insect. I wonder what your insignificant secret might be?*

"Once again," Houma continued, "I hesitate to use my trivial magics in your presence, but it has always been more interesting to show than to tell. When we revisited our skirmish with Wizards and Godlings, here is what we found — first, now, as a brief overview."

Houma stood back, his dark, withered hand surging with power. Images flashed in the chamber's center, showing the hold of the *Alantéa*, as Sorcerers and Marids clashed with Godlings and Wizards. The images in the Divination flashed forward swiftly at an accelerated speed, ending as the Sorcerers and the remaining Marid fled the great warship.

"We were not happy with this outcome," Houma said softly, "but we were determined to learn from it." Now, Houma displayed images of the skirmish again from the beginning, though with painful slowness, and focused on the Godlings. At each moment in the conflict, the Godlings' faces flared with confusion, then hesitation, before the Godlings finally acted. So faint was the delay, that it could only be noted when events were slowed to less than a tenth of their true speed.

"This hesitation," Houma continued, "we attribute to the Godlings' instruction — at each critical junction they must ask themselves, 'Should we continue, or is it time now to turn upon the Wizards'?"

Houma rubbed his hands together gleefully, animated once again. "Yet this was a significant conclusion, and we had no way to test it — except, what of the swords? The Godlings had forged a second semi-sentient blade to pass to that Giftless blockhead they call a 'Captain.' What was that sword's nature, what could be learned from it if we watched closely?" Again, Houma's withered hand surged with power.

Now, as the Demon Princes watched on, images of battle flashed before them — the enchanted swords of Koln and Ged slashing simultaneously upon a lone Kul-Ghoul caught in the middle of its leap. In seconds, the Ghoul was reduced to a jumble of bleeding segments, destroyed by swords that flashed and smoked with power. Then the onlookers watched again the same event in agonizing slowness. Each sword struck virtually simultaneously, but with each slash, Koln's sword hesitated — ever so slightly, but it did pause before slashing Ghoul flesh.

The eyes of Iblis, Prince of Demons, stared down intently. *We intended to simply dispose of these Sorcerers eventually as useless vermin, but perhaps we can pass their enchanted brain matter through the Forge and extract some of their cunning.*

As Alcman studied the expressions passing over the face of Iblis, he struggled to shield his own thoughts. *All the binding spells protecting us from the malice of the Demon Princes are now utterly void and powerless. We rely solely on their need for us, and on their benevolence. I do not like our chances. Is there perhaps a hiding place in Otherwhen where we might live out the rest of some miserable partial existence?*

Houma waved the images away and they vanished. "In summary: three Wizards together contain the power of a middle-ranked God, while the three Godlings constitute something greater in strength, though untrained. And so, in their dreams, the Powers hoped that battle would transform the Godlings into lesser Gods, and then as Powers, they would turn upon the Wizards. All this, of course, was nothing more than confused dementia, but you wished me to pursue the nature of those dreams — and so I thank your great majesties for your indulgence."

Houma bowed, then withdrew to the shadows, and Alcman stepped forward, taller and broader than his fellow Sorcerer, though his long struggle against the League had left him somewhat stooped and haggard, his white hair trimmed raggedly so that when it was tucked behind his ears, it failed to reach his shoulders.

"Great ones," Alcman said, bowing, "your cause is our cause. We wish only for your complete victory. In the aftermath of your triumph, you may wish to reward us — or you may not. That will be your decision."

The words of this maggot are humble, Satanis thought, *while he has the manner of a wise and ancient elder forced to convey unfortunate truths to his powerful rulers.*

Alcman glanced at Satanis as though reading traces of his thoughts. "My searches happened in this manner: as we began to review the devices of our foes, I understood that your servant Houma was more than equal to that task. And so, I asked myself, how can I best serve my great masters? As I contemplated our long struggle, it always seemed to me that perverse or hidden factors had always favored our foes. Might there be Ancient Secrets at work, hidden designs? Had the Maker deliberately planted stumbling blocks in our paths? What were the designs of the Maker? What, indeed, was the Maker thinking?"

Again, almost imperceptibly, the Demon Princes leaned forward. Alcman paced slowly, eyes glancing into the upper reaches of the Demons' place of power, where volcanic gases gathered like tiny cirrus clouds.

As Alcman spoke, it was as though he murmured to himself: "I have no wish to be forever human. To be human is to live a short life, struggling for many of a mortal's later years with the afflictions of age, and then to die, with so much left unknown and unlearned. Yet consider this thought for a moment: humans are waking upon the shores of the Far Lands — not lesser Demons or a lower-level Seraphs, or other immortals, or some entirely new race of beings, but humans are waking in the Far Lands."

Satanis leaned forward and interrupted, hints of fire flashing from his mouth: "If you leave the carcass of a serpent in the sunlight, maggots will breed."

Alcman bowed again. "Lord, you suggest that I misspeak myself, and so I am likely to be completely in error. Unless you wish me to proceed, I will be silent."

"Proceed," Zikar said, a hint of flame also emerging from his mouth, and he glared at Satanis, while the mouth of Iblis formed a sardonic smile.

"So, if," Alcman continued in a small, barely heard voice, "I asked myself, if the Maker wished to pass power to mortals, he might plan for a sequence of events — a progression that ultimately produced humans, set in motion on the Far Lands. This process would produce a race of mortals virtually identical to those found in Alantéa. Secondly, he might well have activated that talent called the Gift, a forward shield of power that might assist in the survival of mortals during a time when Demons and Seraphs, then Mid-World Powers held true power...."

Alcman's voice had trailed off, and now he hesitated, searching for some uncomplicated way to end his discussion of difficult and unwelcome truths.

"You must speak up," Zikar prompted, striving to keep the smoke and flames from his own mouth, "and you must fully speak your mind — I have dealt more frequently with mortals than have my brethren, and I sense from the motions of your human form that you have at least one other thought to share with us."

Alcman sent a surge of cold through his body so that its agitation would not again betray him. "Yes, of course, Great Ones; I feared only that I would speak the obvious and so waste your time, yet now I will continue.

"Two other thoughts are aligned with the possibility that the Maker sought to favor mortals with their brief lives. If the Gift was a shield for humankind, then a weapon might also serve their cause. And so, I believe that an enchanted sword blade might also have been fashioned for mortals who still revered the Maker.

"The foremost edge of that blade would be the Wizards and their League, while a secondary edge would be formed by the band of heroic mortals gathering to the League's defense at its time of greatest need. I believe that this theme has been repeated several times in the South of Alantéa, and we are now seeing its final example."

"Lastly," Alcman said, his voice again trailing off, "in line with the Maker as a remote patron of mortals, He might also have looked to a time beyond the force of magic, when the energies of miracle work might fade, and all the Powers relying on those forces would be doomed." Alcman glanced up to the tiny wisps of clouds gathering to the chamber's heights. "I cannot foresee myself living to see such a time, but for the immortals of that age, it would be most interesting to learn whether the comets and meteors surging through the airless void, whether those bodies are rich with sorcerous energies. If that is so...." Alcman trailed off, while staring into the upper reaches of the chamber where wisps of clouds continued to gather.

The Demon Princes were leaning forward intently. Zikar signaled to Alcman by flexing huge fingers toward the Sorcerer, and thus prompted, Alcman continued: "If such energies were stored in the heavens, it might be necessary for the Powers of that time to drag comets and meteors earthward, to assure a steady stream of sorcerous power at a time when earth's own natural force of magic had weakened or failed. Those Powers controlling such a flow of heavenly debris would truly be masters of this planet. Now, I must thank your great majesties for hearing the wandering thoughts of a doddering old man." Alcman bowed, and withdrew from the center court, seeking arcs of shadows that would obscure him from the attention of the Demon Princes.

He has dared to consider matters, Satanis thought, *that my own mind remotely understood, but refused to acknowledge. Even now he shields his mind because other unfortunate truths are better left unsaid. He must die, but not until a test by torture squeezes the last, unruly thought from his overly agile mind.*

And Alcman in the shadows caught something of the mostly shielded thoughts of Satanis and his mind recoiled. *Otherwhen beckons, though not yet, not just yet. Would it be possible to become allies of the Dark Lords? Might some sort of counterweight to the Demon Princes be fashioned? It does not seem likely at this moment, but still....*

Oblivious to the hidden thoughts of Satanis and Alcman, Houma again stepped forward. "Set a thief to catch a thief," Houma repeated, "though we have had enough of 'catching.' We must kill them all, slaughter them, assassinate them one by one if necessary. If that sneakthief of a fox falls within our grasp, we must destroy it. If one, lone Giftless blockhead of a warrior stands for a split second vulnerable, kill that mortal. And so, each small death will weaken the whole more than we previously understood. Your Majesties, allow us, the Sorcerers and the Marids, to complete this task. Only arm us with a lone Guardian to seek out hidden places within the Isle. Then we will kill them all, kill them forever, one by one if necessary."

"Kill them all," Satanis agreed. "I do not readily admit to failure, but we should have exterminated these vermin when they were helpless. Now we will set matters right. The cunning of the Sorcerers and the raw power of the Marids are both useful, though not adequate to this task. We must draw upon the Dark Lords, the mightiest of our followers.

"Haeglin and Mordred will lead one party, with Houma as the hound, the questing searcher. To that party, we assign a full third of the Marids, together with a lone Guardian. The second party is assigned to Un-Maurag, who not so secretly believes himself the equal of the Demon Princes. Let him prove himself now. Alcman will be his mentor and guide. To this group, we assign two Guardians and the balance of the Marids.

"It does not matter to us which group is victorious — but to that group goes glory and honor, and greater power. It is only necessary that we kill them, then bring their broken dead bodies here, that we might view them and rejoice. But first, kill these interlopers, kill them all — and swiftly."

·))(·

Those referred to as "interlopers" were deep belowground now, passing through twisting labyrinths, moving downward toward the Forge of the Demons. Godlings, lighter beings formed partly from sorcerous matter, were swifter than others and had passed to the forefront, beaming light in front of them, radiating illumination into darkened tunnel passages as they moved swiftly downward.

Bulking larger, their lone Guardian ally came next, moving hastily, as though anxious not to be left alone to face enraged Demon Princes and their servants, the corrupted Guardians.

The Wizards, too, passed swiftly through the labyrinth, their senses beginning to feel the force of the Forge, its great magic pulsing through the stone. Lights from their staffs flashed and flared. A stench of death was also reaching up toward them, the odors of long dead enchanted creatures whose flesh yielded slowly to decay only after many scores of years had passed.

Last came three humans and their small allies. Their passage was less bright, almost deliberately dark, with Julian's staff providing only dim illumination. They, too, had begun to smell death in the air, though they were distracted by the keening noises made by the enchanted swords.

"The Tarnished Sword," Galad murmured, "wishes to know why it alone cleaved Guardian flesh, while its companion blade could not. Ha!" *Maker's Touch! It feels good to be alive, to have my old mind and body back!*

Kalanin drew a deep breath, inhaling more death fumes. "I think we both know the answer to that riddle," he said quietly. "It's best not to speak openly, for we do not wish to offend our Mid-World allies." As they passed a sealed chamber on their left, the stench of death grew stronger, as though activated by the presence of trespassers.

Several levels down and many paces from them, Phaedra heard the warriors' words and did not completely understand them. She was nearing the Forge of the Demons and most of her enchanted mind was focusing on the rhythms of great magic; nevertheless, she carefully set aside the warriors' comments to be considered at some quiet time in the future.

Now, before her, she could see shadows on the stone of the labyrinth — lights that came not from the Godlings, but from the Demons' Forge. As they came around the final bend in the labyrinth, the Godlings halted. Gleaming like lava, the Forge stretched out before the Godlings, perhaps seventy paces wide, its liquid radiating orange and grey radiances, passing shadows over the surrounding walls and ceilings. As the Godlings gathered to its shores, the Forge began to seethe, and dark, choking gases rose from its surface.

A place of great magic lay before them, but its power could be invoked only by Demon Princes.

"So, from this source, the Marids emerged, flaming hot" Turin said softly, "and after, they were tempered by chilled sea water."

As the Wizards came up behind them, Magog circled to the left of the Forge, where a chamber had been walled off. Wherever Magog passed, dark shadows mingled with his own inner hues of blue and grey. He reached the chamber and halted. It had been sealed with a massive slab, but with the power of his enchanted body and the force of magic within him, Magog ripped the slab from its foundations. Then the Godling recoiled from the stench of death within.

Inside lay the carcasses of huge, long dead, winged creatures, made of a light, almost translucent, substance.

Thorian circled behind Magog; ignoring the stench, the Wizard peered within. "Wraiths of Dragons," he murmured, "perhaps one of many failed experiments, before the Marids were birthed." At the far-right side of the Forge, Turin had ripped open another sealed chamber, his body radiating green hues as power surged through his form. Mold and decay billowed out like a soft cloud of grey ashes. Deliberately, Turin let the cloud settle around him, obscuring his green and gold radiances; but he did not breathe in its particulates. Holding his breath, he stepped inside the chamber and inspected a jumble of enormous, but long and lean bones. What had these been intended to accomplish? A thousand possibilities flashed through the Godling's enchanted mind, but he could reach no conclusion.

Balardi had followed Turin but now the Wizard pulled back from the chamber, turning to stare at the Forge, concealing his own thoughts. *Vampiric Giants,* Balardi decided, *nightmare beasts that could only rival the Creatures of the Darkness. As they could not challenge the Gods, they were cast aside. It no longer matters, and for me to offer an interpretation would only antagonize the Godlings. You should know your own place, Lesser Wizard, and be silent.*

Merlin had been staring into the seething Forge in silence and when he finally spoke, it was in a subdued voice, almost a whisper: "Some great act of creation is taking place here, something completely evil. For the creation of Marids was aligned with a quest for power, a forging of weapons, while here a new dimension is being formed, and already that dimension radiates pain and horror."

Phaedra spoke: "Nothing can be done to counter the Demon Princes now. For Un-Maurag is coming. The Dark Lord surges toward us, leading a force several times our own strength." Face grim, she turned to face the Wizards. Staffs flared with power and a great Portal again flashed into view, an arch that framed itself against the wall of the cavern, forming an enchanted opening to a distant portion of the Isle. Beyond the Portal, light, misty rains, and gusts of wind swept over the stony beaches of the Isle. Above the coastline, the sky was heavy with spent storm clouds; but lightning still surged from cloud to cloud, and stars could be seen in the far distant northern and eastern skies, radiating starlight down over Alantéa the Forerunner.

Rafir lay just a few paces from the Forge, panting softly. Sebastian was on Julian's shoulder, staring into the Portal. Julian, Galad, and Kalanin spoke quietly to one another, glancing back and forth between the Portal and the seething lava of the Forge.

These three men are really not much different from me, thought the fox. *We have had enough adventures for ten thousand heroes, and more than enough danger for the hordes of Familiars trailing behind them. Just a few hours ago I was a fluttering creature with a brain tinier than a peanut. Somehow, we broke free, but now Un-Maurag — "delightful and charming Un-Maurag" — is after us again. Whatever happened to the Gods? When will this —*

Their Portal began to tremble, then to shake and shiver. As before, the Godlings extended their power to stabilize the gateway's structure, though this time the attack upon the Portal was redoubled. The Portal shook, and its magic groaned. Images beyond the gateway blurred and lost focus.

As they raced through, the Portal collapsed around them. Julian was the last through, and fragments of shattered magic lashed at him as he was smashed down onto a rainswept, darkened beach.

· X ·

Consciousness fled for a moment as Julian lay senseless on a beach of polished stones, but then the strong arms of Kalanin and Galad drew the Apprentice to his feet. Concussions of thunder boomed overhead, and Julian came fully awake, standing beside a churning ocean, while heavy rains pounded down on both shore and sea. Waves were crashing onto stony beaches, and foam lapped over his leather boots. Arms still held Julian; now they turned the Apprentice gently so that he faced inland. Framed against the forests of the Isle, the outlines of another Portal were forming.

"Not even a moment's breath," Magog murmured, then he raised his voice. "Yet now the time has come! Time to give battle!"

"My brother," Turin cautioned softly.

"Another of the Wizard's devices is revealed," Phaedra called out. "Why do you believe that Merlin has brought us to this shore? Behold!" She pointed to the horizon, where the Cloudshelf, an Island in the Sky, was looming closer to the Demon's place of power.

A concussion of thunder burst overhead as Julian watched the Portal reinforce itself. Behind the Portal's mouth, two huge figures loomed. *Now Mordred and Haeglin have come for us,* Julian thought. *So much for the "prolonged resistance" as foreseen by the Great Guardian.*

Power lashed from the Godlings into the Dark Lords' Portal, and the gateway seemed at first to recoil — but then it grew stronger. *Two great warriors face three striplings, and the end of this contest cannot be in doubt,* Julian thought. *Time to be gone!* He could sense now, from a distance that Marids, and at least one Sorcerer, were pressing toward the gateway. Behind Julian, he could hear the Wizards chanting feverishly — another Portal, another brief escape.

"My Brethren!" Phaedra called out, "this is a matter for the Gods we will become!" As the Godlings renewed their focus on the Portal, its outlines blurred and shook.

As they fought back and forth for control of the shuddering Portal, the Guardian moved toward it from the beach, and then a few hundred paces from the Portal's outline, the Guardian's power extended into it. Transforming energies grappled with the forms of Haeglin and Mordred so that they began to shiver and shake under the stresses of multiple sorceries.

Then, from the looming Cloudshelf, came the final blow: energies, waves of dark and light power, billowed toward the Portal — and the enchanted gateway collapsed, exploding in the night, sending fragments of broken magic hurtling in all directions.

Phaedra turned upon Merlin, her red radiance flaring in anger. "This was *your* device, Wizard, to bring this Cloudshelf, and the Emissaries of the Gods, into play. How many other stratagems have you hidden from us?"

"Not enough to save us from our foes," Merlin said flatly. "Now we must make ready to flee once again, for Haeglin and Mordred were caught by surprise. Next time they will be prepared."

Julian turned, for a second Portal was forming, this time with firmer lines. Behind him, Julian heard Thorian whispering to Eléna, but somehow the Wizard could not reach his only daughter.

A before, the Godlings lashed at the Portal with their evolving force of magic, and as before, the Guardian launched transforming energies into the Portal's center. Yet now a second Guardian — one aiding Haeglin and Mordred — rebuffed the magic of its fellow Guardian. From the Cloudshelf, again, came billows of destructive energies, though these, too, were now turned aside.

From the shuddering Portal emerged one lone Marid, armored against sorcery, wielding a massive club. Kalanin and Galad edged forward with Julian only a step behind, but then a second and a third Marid slipped through. Other Marids loomed in the Portal's dark recesses, struggling to force a passage.

"Too late for swordplay," Merlin called out. "Come, we must pass from this place." Thorian, still calling to his daughter, passed through first, followed by all but the Godlings, who hurled one last burst of power at the Dark Lords; then the three Godlings passed from the shoreline into distant regions of the Isle.

· X ·

In dreams, Julian found himself again in the Temple, though now much of it lay in ruin. Many pillars had toppled, and most of its roof had been reduced to rubble, stonework scattered over the floor and the hillside beyond. Rain spattered over the weightless spirit form of the Apprentice as he stood astonished, again, before the broken alabaster altar that had once held an ebony, dark Idol. Julian shook himself, struggling to focus.

Why am I drawn to this place? First, we escaped Un-Maurag, and then Haeglin and Mordred fought through to the beach. Godlings and Wizards raised brutal magic against them, even invoking the Emissaries of the Gods from their Cloudshelf haven, but Dark Lords were greater than all our devices, and again we were forced to flee. We remain in flight, and I have no time to dream!

"Julian," came a voice from behind him. *He turned and the ghostly image of Eléna swept into his arms; as before it was a meeting of mists, but now these mists gleamed brighter than they had during previous encounters between Jarl and Eléna.*

"Julian, the Great Guardian has gained a respite for you, only a short one, but first....." Eléna whispered words. *Suddenly the images of Galad and Kalanin, together with Sebastian and Rafir, approached the altar. As the two warriors became suddenly aware of their circumstances, they reached for swords, weapons that were no longer at their sides.*

"I have left the enchanted weapons behind," Eléna said to them. *"I believe you understand why. Now, we have only a brief time together, so I cannot dwell on your own bravery, on how brilliantly you have given battle, on how strong and fierce and wonderful my own father has become. The Great Guardian has asked me to raise three matters:*

"Firstly, as you give battle upon the Isle, the Great Guardian's own strength increases, and so he is able to interfere somewhat with the Portal magic of your foes. And so, a few fleeting moments have been gained for you.

"Secondly, he is now activating the latent powers of the Godlings, and so greater awareness and cunning and knowledge will flow to them. From this time forward, they will be more powerful than the Wizards. Though they are allies, you must watch what you say in their presence — even when speaking casually to one another."

"I am the least cautious of our little group," Galad said, "yet I have already grown concerned about their long-term allegiances."

Julian's form was fading as though his mind was being called back from sleep. Eléna reached into his body's mists and steadied them. "Only a brief time remains," she murmured. "To counter the imbalance within your alliance, the Guardian Julian freed will now — under instruction from his leader — align himself with the Wizards.

"Thirdly, the Great Guardian asks why the attention of Demon Princes is drawn back now to Alantéa the Forerunner? Even though a Storm of Magic has released potent forces to oppose them in their own domain, why would they now turn to Alantéa?"

Fear swept suddenly over Kalanin's face, then he stared into the distance, toward Alantéa and the League before speaking. "Alcman and Houma have counseled the Demon Princes concerning the Maker and the forces of destiny that have aided the League. That line of destiny runs through the Seeress Sentauris to the three of us in our own time. The last of this line has now been born into the League: a little child, an infant, my only daughter."

Chapter Thirteen

A Prisoner is Freed

ON THE FARTHEST REACHES of the Isle, the sea had eaten away at the limestone foundations of this corner of The Isle of the Demons, and tidal caverns had formed. Worn down by a long night's flight, the Wizards and their allies had gathered belowground and spoke together in low voices. Kalanin let them drone on in the darkness, while he stared out through a gap where the limestone had opened to the sea. Daylight was coming slowly to the Isle, accompanied by mist and drizzle. With the new light of day, both barnacles and seaweed were revealed, growths that flourished inside the cave system; and so, at high tide, the cavern was reclaimed by the ocean. Now, as the tide sank back from the shore, their limestone recess made soft, seeping sounds; and these blended with the droning voices of Wizards and Godlings as they murmured together in the darkest regions of the cavern.

Kalanin listened, nodding. *Their voices are muted, so they are not arguing, and that's to the good. We need to open a new battlefront in this unequal struggle with the Demon Princes. Then our enemies may turn their attention away from Géla, my beloved, whom I may never see again, and from our daughter, Serena, whom I may never meet in this world.*

"We are done." Merlin's soft voice was raised, just enough so that all might hear him clearly. "Balardi will yield the Crystal of Otherwhen to Thorian, who will journey through adjacent realities and seek to re-emerge close to his daughter."

Without further ceremony, Balardi took a leather thong from around his own neck and gravely placed it on Thorian's. The thong held a leather pouch, containing their lone Crystal of Otherwhen.

Thorian stood straight, his eyes gleaming with an inner fire. Yet he hesitated. "For so many years I have longed for this moment, to seek Eléna, then to hold her again, as I once embraced my only child. Yet one small, clear voice whispers in my mind, and it says, 'You must take the Summoner with you.' That would be you, Julian."

"The Summoner only journeys with two bodyguards," Galad added, stepping forward to stand with Julian.

"And two sets of small but very sharp eyes," Sebastian said. His wings flapped, and he came to rest on Julian's shoulder.

Merlin watched them gravely, blinking slowly as though waking from sleep. After a slight smile and a nod from Balardi, Merlin turned to the Godlings. "It feels right to me, and to you?" Turin and Magog nodded while Phaedra simply turned away and stared out into the overcast ocean.

"Come, then," Thorian said. "I will make our entry into Otherwhen as gentle as possible. Yet it is more than likely that one or both of the other two Crystals, those held by Alcman and Houma, will be stirred, and so, your brief moment of peace may well be coming to a close."

"Do not fear for us, Wizard," Turin said. "The power within us is growing. One day, perhaps we shall turn upon our foes and astonish them." Merlin's face held a slight, grim smile, and Kalanin knew from long experience that Merlin's inner mind was whispering, *Not yet, not just yet.*

They stepped from the cavern out into a grey morning that was filled with mists and soft rain. Thorian led Julian, Kalanin, and Galad from their limestone retreat, walking slowly along the shoreline as he invoked their Crystal. Rafir scampered along the ground, while Sebastian, as always, rested on Julian's right shoulder. Godlings and Wizards watched as Thorian led the humans and their small servants slowly into Otherwhen: after perhaps fifty paces, Thorian's party became vague and insubstantial, and after a hundred paces their forms seemed to have merged with the mists.

· X ·

"Otherwhen," Alcman murmured, "they have passed into Otherwhen. Lord, this may be the moment we wished for. Their party is split into two factions; only a few have passed into Otherwhen on some unknown errand, and this may be our chance to crush one portion of their strength, leaving the whole far weaker. Lord, is it your wish to pursue the lesser or the greater group?"

"You hold a device in your hand," Un-Maurag said, unable or unwilling to conceal the malice in his voice, "it is my desire that this Talisman becomes mine. You may pass it to me and gain favor, or I may take it from you and punish you later."

Alcman turned and straightened, staring up into the features of the Dark Lord: the enormous face of Un-Maurag was gnarled and twisted, radiating malice. "Lord, I must ask this one brief question: how has our alliance become so one-sided that I am obliged to surrender each potion, each spell, each talisman, based simply on your wishes?"

"It is simple: I am a God, and you are nothing but a maggot. But you have responded, and so I will take the Talisman now, and punish you later."

Alcman felt the spell take hold of him and his body became immobilized — everything froze except his one hand holding the Crystal of Otherwhen. Alcman invoked the Talisman's magic; he had sensed the malice of Un-Maurag and had been prepared. Now, as the great hand of Un-Maurag reached down for the Crystal, the Sorcerer's form became strands of mist, and his true form was transported elsewhere.

Deliberately, Alman chose a branch of Otherwhen closest to this world. He stepped into a wooded area, some distance from the shore. A brilliantly blue sky with the full sun of summer radiated down on him. Dragon-wings swept through clear skies, while in the distance he heard the hooting and booming sounds of Marids. Alcman sat, leaning against a mossy tree trunk. It felt strangely peaceful here. Perhaps in this world, the Demon Princes had fought free from the dream-world prisons of the Guardians, raised their Isle with their own powers, and allowed Alantéa to remain a plaything of the Gods. If only the universe had been that simple!

He looked up and drew a deep breath. Butterflies flourished in this world! They fluttered through their brief lives, seeking moisture and comfort from the mosses of the trees while the bright sun beamed down on them. Alcman watched their passage for a few minutes, then he rose and began walking, carefully staying hidden from the winged creatures overhead, invoking a passage from Otherwhen, back to the tangled reality of the Isle of the Demons.

Back in the Isle, Alcman drew on sorcery to conceal himself. He peered out from the tree line. Un-Maurag had erupted in rage. Lacking other victims, he had sought creatures concealed from within the hillside, and so now the carcasses of huge Dusk Snakes and fearsome Kul-Ghouls lay crushed around the Dark Lord.

How did I ever dream that the Dark Lords might form a counterweight to the Demon Princes, and that Houma and I could forge an alliance with them? My soul is drenched by rivers of blood. I sought enormous power and life everlasting, and so I was prepared to do anything to attain those ends. But to be completely evil is to be insane. Houma has kept so much of that madness, but almost all this lunacy has passed from me. What am I to do now?

Taking a deep breath, Alcman let his body become visible. Warily, the Sorcerer slipped from the tree line and approached the Dark Lord cautiously. Strangely, Un-Maurag had become more philosophical. "Do not fear me, Sorcerer. All alliances of Gods and Powers are essentially unstable, as is mine with the Demon Princes. In the end, there can be only one ruler, one master of this planet, and if it is not to be me, then I must adjust."

"Lord, there is still time to pursue our foes into Otherwhen," Alcman said quietly. "You have only to speak the words."

"That task has already begun, by Haeglin and Mordred," Un-Maurag said. "Our party gathers for the main assault on Godlings and Wizards. We were only waiting for you, Sorcerer."

· ✸ ·

Julian took deep breaths of failing air, and held himself motionless, for to move was to waste oxygen. Rafir lay on the stony ground, panting, tongue exposed to the moistureless cloud cover. They had journeyed to the farthest reaches of Otherwhen, waiting while Thorian examined his Crystal. As though sensing their discomfort, Thorian knelt and held the Crystal out so that all could see it.

The Crystal showed an image of Alcman, seated in some sunlit portion of Otherwhen. To Julian's surprise, Alcman's worn but powerful and intense features seemed unusually peaceful.

"We have learned," Thorian whispered, "how to view other forays into Otherwhen from afar so that when one Crystal is in use, the others can perceive its viewpoint. I do not think the Sorcerers know how...ahh! Now Alcman leaves Otherwhen and his image fades. I sense conflict within the Sorcerer as he returns to his many masters — alliances are never easy, particularly with Demon Princes and Dark Lords. Come!"

Thorian led them over a stony beach where barnacles that had been dead for years had been crushed into a chalky powder. After the briefest of *shudders*, they shifted to an alternate reality where ancient barnacles and stones were transformed into sandy beaches. Their breathing grew easier as they passed into more habitable regions where Otherwhen retained more of its life force.

"It feels as though I am navigating an enormous sea," Thorian whispered to them, holding the Crystal before them so that all could see. "Otherwhen is like an ocean teeming with many islands. But which island should I choose? And they are coming behind us now. Houma leads them, with Haeglin and Mordred, together with a lone Guardian, and many Marids. We are no match for them, and so we must be far swifter than they. Eléna, Eléna, where has the Great Guardian concealed you?"

Julian said nothing, though his mind whispered, *Eléna! I do not think you can sense me here in Otherwhen, but still, I am calling to you!*

"Houma is coming," Thorian murmured, "and I must now choose. I thought to pass back and forth between the Isle of the Demons and its false realities, and then give Eléna several opportunities to reach out to me. We should be swifter than our foes, so that each passage would increase the gap between us, leaving them farther behind. Alas! They are speeding toward us all too quickly. And which island of lost destiny do I choose? There are so many, each with its own complexities — and so I will begin with a place where we are unlikely to prosper, while the hazards should be surmountable."

Thorian stepped forward tentatively, then more swiftly and decisively. With the briefest *shudders*, they passed from dark shadows into a forested hillside, baking under the heat of a midday summer sun. This portion of

Otherwhen was filled with croaking and growling voices, while the land's heat was so intense that their foreheads beaded instantly with sweat.

"In this portion of Otherwhen," Thorian murmured, "only the beast constructs of the Demon Princes survive. Were all the Demon Princes and Guardians and Marids destroyed in battle? I cannot imagine how such a devastating event might have occurred. We will never know what events forked to leave this possibility behind, and we will not be forced to remain here long. Only let them be drawn here and —" Thorian jerked away, for a Dire Cat had been caught in the middle of its leap by Galad, and its shriek was silenced by sharp, enchanted metal that smoked in the sunlight.

As the Dire Cat's twitching form stilled, Kalanin knelt and examined it. When he rose, Kalanin stared into the skies where Reptile Birds gathered overhead. Not far from them the hyena voices of Kul-Ghouls were being raised in hunger. Kalanin glanced back to the dead Dire Cat.

"Larger," Kalanin murmured. "Left unchallenged, they have grown greater in mass. Dire Cats were once the size of leopards, and now they rival sleek lions. Even their saber teeth seem larger."

"If the others have grown larger," Galad said softly, "imagine the Snake God."

Thorian's face was set with its old remote hardness. "We must draw Houma and his masters to this place, and if that means giving battle to a rabble of brainless beasts, so be it." The Wizard let the Crystal sag back to his chest, held there by a leather thong, then he drew his staff.

Enchanted swords began to moan. *Huffing* sounds from Kul-Ghouls were drawing closer. Shadows gathered overhead, then more Dire Cats sprang down at them, seeking to overrun them with their collective mass. Swords shrieked and smoked and carved effortlessly through flesh. As Reptile Birds surged down upon them, jagged bolts of force raced from Julian's staff, and creatures with broad wingspans began crashing down into the forest's upper canopy.

Now, on the hillside above them, the first of the Kul-Ghouls bounded down toward them — the creature seemed huge, and the earth shook. A jagged bolt of force from Julian's staff only seemed to stun it, and it tumbled to the forest floor. As it picked itself up, a tribe of more than two dozen Kul-Ghouls gathered to it, each with the bulk of a massive bear.

"Yes," Thorian murmured grimly, "Houma and his Dark Lords draw closer — and this should bring them even more swiftly!" Lightning from Thorian's staff sped into the ranks of Kul-Ghouls. Flesh smoked, and trees surrounding the tribe were struck and burst into flame. Kul-Ghouls toppled in ruin, crying woe, but others emerged behind them, shoving dead Kul-Ghouls before them as shields.

Thorian laughed and lashed with lightning at the trees in the Kul-Ghouls' path so that the progress of dead Ghouls pushing downslope was halted by burning deadfall. Then, suddenly, Thorian's dark laughter halted — for in the distant hillside above the Kul-Ghouls and the burning forest around them, the Snake God was sweeping downslope with eyes that gleamed with magic and malice.

"The master of this subworld approaches," Julian said softly. "Do you think we might let the Lord of Coils be dealt with by Dark Lords and their Marid followers?"

Thorian drew a deep breath. "We need only a few more moments. I do not normally give ground before great beasts, but at this strategic moment —" The Wizard began to shift backward, moving carefully downslope, step by step. The others did likewise, slowly, as though hypnotized by fear, while the Snake God casually crushed the forest in its path, eyes gleaming in amusement and cruelty as it drew closer.

Then Thorian shifted them, with the slightest of *shudders,* from Otherwhen back to a windswept portion of the Isle. And so, they never beheld, except in later dream visions, how Haeglin and Mordred emerged from the Isle moments later, and how their Marid allies surged toward the Snake God, and how it put forth its enormous physical might and its powerful battle magic, and how those mighty aspects only extended its death agonies by a few, brutal, minutes.

No mountains towered high above the Isle of the Demons, but Thorian had taken them to the highlands, a region least touched by the Guardians' dream magic, and the perverse ecology of the Demon Princes. Young pine forests ranged over the highlands. In some sections of the forest, pine trees were holding on, while other areas had been exposed to windstorms, and trees lay toppled like broken straw. Other trees had been truncated by gales, leaving broken lower portions bristling with young pine needles as the stumps of trees struggled to survive.

Thorian stepped over a jumble of broken branches, calling "Eléna! Eléna!" Julian's mind called silently, but nothing stirred except Thorian's voice, and the hushed whispering noise the wind's passage made through the pine needles overhead.

Sebastian fluttered nervously overhead, while Rafir followed closely behind Julian, determined not to be separated from the Apprentice.

"Eléna!" Thorian called again, then murmured in lower tones, "Can it be that the Great Guardian is not willing to release her? Why should that be? Eléna, we have come so far...." Thorian trailed off, while no response came except that Julian could feel the power of their foes gathering to the highlands.

Thorian also felt the pressure of Houma and his Dark Lords, and his voice was urgent as he called out again, moving swiftly from a clearing in the forest toward a shelf of cliffs that marked the highland's edge. From this height, the Wizard could look down to the distant ocean. Thorian called again, out into an expanse of sky, then down to the sea below, but still, no answer came. Except now, they could hear the shuddering sounds of Portal Magic, and the air in the woodland glades behind them was beginning to shimmer.

"This does not feel," Galad muttered, "like a winning strategy."

Thorian's face was grim. "Houma has mastered travel through Otherwhen quickly — far too quickly."

"A council," Kalanin said softly to Julian, "a brief council of war."

"My Wizard and Master," Julian added, "can you take us back into the Alternates? Back to a place of long ago and far away so we can speak together? Breathable air would be helpful."

Anger flashed over Thorian's face, and he muttered dark words under his breath. But then he led them along the ridge, staring down into his Crystal as they shifted from the reality of the Isle back into a dying realm of Otherwhen. As they passed from the highlands, none of them noticed that a cluster of shadows had gathered beneath the pines or saw how those same shadows fled when Houma and his Dark Lord Masters, and the Marids serving them, surged through a massive Portal, crushing the pine forest before them as they ranged through the highlands seeking Thorian and his allies.

· X ·

"We grow closer," Houma murmured. "Because they are shifting fewer and less powerful beings, they believed that their passage into and out of Otherwhen would be swifter than ours, but I am almost matching their speed. Ha! Whatever they are seeking to accomplish, we will deny them the time to finish their little schemes."

The Dark Lord Haeglin looked down at Houma, towering high and menacing over the Sorcerer as though a mantis stared down at a tiny ant. "Sorcerer, this pursuit has become wearisome. I was mildly entertained by the destruction of the Snake God, yet I am a Dark Lord, more powerful than all but a handful of Demon Princes and Greater Gods, and now I feel like clumsy baggage. It is time now to catch them and destroy them, then claim the rewards promised by the Demon Princes, those who have become our masters."

"You must give me the Crystal," Mordred rasped, "and I will bring this farce to a swift and brutal end."

Houma laughed silently to himself, then glanced up into the gnarled features of the two Dark Lords. "Of course, Great Ones," he said easily. "You had only to ask." The Sorcerer then hesitated. "Since the Great God Mordred was the first to request the Crystal, perhaps it should be passed to him first, yet the Great God Haeglin should also be offered an opportunity when his fellow Dark Lord is done with it. Is this agreed?" Houma beamed up at the two as they stood perhaps five times his height, looming taller even than the Marids, though they were not as broad shouldered.

Mordred and Haeglin examined each other with open antagonism, then finally nodded in agreement. Mordred reached down and extended an enormous hand. Houma smiled as he placed the Crystal of Otherwhen into the Dark Lord's palm; but he did not glance again into Mordred's mantis eyes or focus on the Dark Lord's gnarled and twisted features. Even the Sorcerer, who took considerable pleasure in the grotesque, found the features of the Dark Lords unsettling.

Mordred stared into the Crystal for a time, while Houma studied cloud patterns overhead, and Haeglin seethed. Marids stood stone-still, while the lone Guardian assigned to the Dark Lords stared into the distance, transforming remote portions of the Isle with the power of his dream visions.

Finally, Mordred spoke: "How does this thing work, Sorcerer?"

"Of course, Great One," Houma said, animatedly. "The Crystal is no more than a gateway, a simple Talisman leading to subworlds of alternate universes. You have only to think like the Crystal, to become one with it, and then you will be transported to those regions chosen by our foes."

Dark powers surged to the Dark God as Mordred struggled with the Crystal's magic. The highland sky shimmered, with puffs of greyish black smoke slipping from seams in the air, while the ground trembled beneath their feet. Finally, Mordred snarled and passed the Crystal to Haeglin.

As Haeglin struggled to control the Crystal, Houma continued to study the shifting sky patterns overhead, seeming completely unconcerned. Many days ago, Houma had foreseen this moment and had reordered the Crystal's magic, so that only his withered, transformed arm could invoke its power.

After a brief time, Haeglin placed the Crystal on the ground before the Sorcerer. "We are not deceived, Magician," the Dark Lord muttered. "You have obviously prepared for this moment. We will find some way to deliver everlasting pain to you."

Houma did not respond, but he allowed himself one thought as his withered hand grasped the Crystal and invoked its magic: *Pain, what pain will you deliver to me if I leave two great Dark Lords adrift on the farthest shores of Otherwhen, never to return to the Isle of the Demons?*

·)(·

To match his somber mood, Thorian had chosen a portion of Otherwhen where darkness and silence prevailed. This subworld was also a deeply chilled one, and Julian could feel Sebastian shiver as the Familiar struggled with the cold. Pale starlight shone down upon them, as a preoccupied Thorian stared out into the distance. Kalanin sat, with Rafir in his lap, while Julian and Galad stood, waiting patiently for Thorian to compose his thoughts. The air was clear, though no life stirred around them as they gathered to a rock shelf in the middle of the ocean — for at this moment in Otherwhen, the Isle of the Demons had been reduced to lifeless stone.

"Why would Eléna not come to me?" Thorian asked again, staring out into the darkness.

"Time, my Wizard-Master," Julian said. "I felt forces *reaching* for us, but there was simply not enough time."

"It should have been so straightforward," the Wizard murmured, "we journeyed over thousands of leagues, passing through sorcerous realms, transformed in mind and body, then we were reconstituted, surviving powers that nearly brought down the Mid-World of the Truce, and now this last small step frustrates me."

A brief smile flashed over Julian's features. "I have often counseled patience to Balardi, but never to you, my Wizard-Master. Our solution is at hand; I can almost sense the thoughts forming in Kalanin's mind. But here, at this remote time, we must first listen to Galad, for a different understanding forms in his mind."

Galad sighed and turned to face Thorian. The Wizard stood as tall as Kalanin, half a hand's breadth taller than Galad, but the lean, bearded, aging Wizard might have come from a race of beings so very different from the two warriors.

"A great seer's sight flares within Julian," Galad said. "Are there other forces stirring? I cannot tell, but the old dream, one recounted to you several times, comes back to me like a Sea Hag's haunting. In the Gangean Range, some great hand showed us visions of triumph — and in that vision, Julian stood beside Eléna. And so, my great Wizard-Master, this tale, the one we are living at this moment, this work of destiny, may be the tale of Julian and Eléna, not the story of a great Wizard saving his daughter from the darkest of destinies."

Thorian's face was grim. "When I set foot upon the Isle of the Demons, I knew that my life was forfeit. If I can free Eléna, I will pass willingly into the Long Sleep."

"May you pass from the League only when Eléna is free, at some time far in the future," Kalanin said, and he put down Rafir and stood. "As for your daughter, we may be almost at her side. You wished for time, time that we needed to delay those seeking us, leaving them adrift in Otherwhen while we venture back to the Isle. First, is there a way to interfere with their Talismans, render their sister Crystals of Otherwhen dysfunctional for a time?"

Thorian shook his head somberly. "We can see with our sister Crystal much that our adversaries see, but we have not learned how to reduce the powers of the other two Crystals."

Kalanin nodded gently. "Then the equation changes from a dimension of time to that of counterforce. If the Snake God held our foes only a few moments, in what realm of Otherwhen would Houma and his masters meet serious resistance? What portion of Otherwhen has sufficient power to defend itself, to give battle against the Dark Lords and those following them?"

"Of course, of course," Thorian muttered, "in several strands of Otherwhen, the Guardians remained uncorrupted, apparently still controlling the Demon Princes in their dream visions. One of those strands seems particularly potent, though it is strangely obscured from me. We believed nothing could be gained from that portion of the Alternaties, yet surely the Guardians of that region would give battle! Why did I not come to that understanding myself?"

"You would have come to it," Julian said softly. "You would have reached it when you took a deep breath and fought free of the haunting of this land. Let us pass to Otherwhen first, then we will reach your daughter, your heart's desire."

Thorian studied his Crystal for a moment, and then he let out a deep breath.

Now the Wizard guided them without hesitation. He led them up a ridge of this darkened remnant of Otherwhen. As they climbed, they shifted with a brief *shudder* to another portion of Otherwhen. A few broad steps took them from a ridge filled with rubble to a broad plain.

Suddenly, the air was brighter, though neither sun nor moon nor stars could be seen — the air was glittering as though diamond dust had been suspended in the air, reflecting unseen light. Beneath their feet, the ground had become firmer, formed of soft stones and crushed earth.

Julian stared into a land of gleaming mists. No living things could be seen, but motions swirled in the haze, as remote forms coalesced, spun, and writhed for a brief time, then merged again with shimmering, hazy matter. Some of these ghostly creatures formed coiled shapes, others grew ragged wings, while a few had heads crested by horns — but they all dissolved into mists after failing to come to life.

"Listen to those sounds," Rafir blurted out. "*Things* are moaning, like lost souls trying to be born, and they can't quite make it."

"I can feel waves of sorrow," Sebastian said, "but they're not dangerous. None of these ghostly things are going to stop Houma for two seconds."

"There's power in this subworld," Julian murmured, "but it's behind us, not in front of us."

They turned, and in the distance, one powerful image stayed solid in the shifting mists, and it dominated the landscape: a single broad, dark tower, so tall that its peak disappeared into banks of high clouds. When gleaming mists tried to embrace the tower, cloud matter fell away from its dark stone, dissolving into raindrops that slid down the tower's polished stonework. Faint whispering sounds were coming from the mists: more creatures struggling to be borne were making soft, weeping noises when they failed. A deep hum came from the darkened tower, of complex machineries, groaning as they powered a lost world.

As Kalanin and Galad listened to the weeping noises and the darker sounds of metal mixed with magic, their hands drifted to their sword hilts.

Thorian drew a deep breath and came to a halt. "Julian," he said in restrained, seldom-used tones, "on several occasions you have been in the presence of the Great Guardian. Does this feel at all like a kingdom that he might rule?"

"There's no hint of the Great Guardian that I once encountered," Julian said softly. "Something's wrong. We failed to ask *why* this branch of Otherwhen forked away from its main branch. Why has this realm concealed itself? What portion of reality was transformed here? What —"

Julian fell silent, for one by one, enormous spectral Wraiths forms began coalescing around them in the gleaming mists.

All these towering shapes were greyish hued but flecked with dark red, as though rust had gathered great power in this world. When Julian counted spectral Wraith shapes beyond twenty-five, he understood that they had entered a realm of great hazard.

Kalanin, too, was counting, and as he reached beyond twenty-five, he muttered, "Oh, oh...."

"You were counting," Galad said. "What's wrong with the count?" Both he and Kalanin had drawn swords, but they were backing away.

"Our friend the Guardian spoke of twenty-five Guardians at the beginning," Kalanin muttered.

"Twenty-eight is not a good number," Julian said softly. "It means that the Guardians of this subworld were joined by Demon Princes. That's not rust were seeing in those images, it's bits of Demon Princes." Julian, too, was backing away, though the spectral forms were drifting closer, and Thorian's war party was running out of space.

Thorian looked grim, his powerful Wizard's mind struggling to understand the fusion of Demon Princes and the Guardians created to govern them. *How could such an event come to pass? Images struggled to form in his mind, but only one clear thought emerged: Let us imagine that Demon Princes freed themselves and confronted the Guardians. Two Great Spells might have collided; each spell determined to transform the other race of beings. These spells might have merged, forming a metaspell; and so, both Guardians and Demon Princes were transformed. So now we have grey shapes — flecked with red. With the enormous power of a metaspell raging over the Isle, nothing living survived. Indeed, we seem to be the only creatures of flesh and blood intruding upon this portion of Otherwhen.*

And now, from out of the mists, a single, enormous spectral hand was extending toward his lean Wizard's body, reaching — for his Crystal of Otherwhen. Thorian drew back, one hand holding his staff, the other shielding the Crystal. Kalanin and Galad stepped in front of the Wizard, swords extended, but Julian waved them to lower their swords.

Suddenly, the spectral hand withdrew. Twenty-eight spectral and ghostly giants straightened and turned away from the intruders. Something like growling noises emerged from soft throats formed of mist. Then suddenly the Wraith forms vanished.

"Houma is coming," Julian whispered.

· 𝕏 ·

Houma was murmuring softly to himself as they entered this new portion of Otherwhen, passing from the windswept highlands of the Isle into a much different landscape. But when banks of gleaming mists began gathering around them, the Sorcerer fell silent and then came to a halt. He could feel the impatience of the Dark Lords just behind him, but strange powers were stirring in this region of Otherwhen, and the Sorcerer became suddenly cautious.

Houma stood frozen, staring up at a dark tower, an enormous shape, the only solid feature in these strange, glistening mists. Forms, soft hazy creatures, were struggling to be born in those mists — they took shape, then they were gathered back into the mists, whimpering as they vanished.

"I should have foreseen this moment," Houma murmured. "They have drawn us into a region of Otherwhen that has sufficient power to contest our passage. Great Ones, I beg you not to lash out. If the Powers of this place challenge us, let me speak for our side."

"Ghosts," Mordred spat out. "Why should I fear the Ghosts of Neverwas?"

"Ignore the ghosts, Sorcerer," Haeglin muttered. "Where has Thorian hidden? Find the Wizard and this farce will come to a swift and brutal ending."

Words died on Houma's lips as the first spectral Wraith flashed into view, looming tall, higher even than Dark Lords or Marids. Dark flames lashed from Mordred's hand, and the ghostly form groaned and was gone. Mists gleamed brighter. Suddenly, they were surrounded by more than a score of Wraiths. Houma counted more than twenty-five, and fear surged within his slight Sorcerous body.

Again, Mordred lashed out with dark fire, but this time it had no impact. Haeglin shouted powerful, sorcerous words into the haze — gleaming mists shuddered, struggling with dark shadows, then they renewed themselves.

Spectral Wraiths advanced, floating toward them, dark grey, but flecked with red, filled with menace. The lone Guardian assigned to their search party groaned and sank to his knees. Marids fell to the ground as though in agony, and began pounding upon the ground's lifeless soil, seeking to batter their way from madness.

"You must shield them," Houma said in a soft monotone. "Forces of sorcery remain to be tapped, both from the Marids and from the Guardian. Use their energies to strengthen your shields. Do not waste your own powers by striking out at our adversaries."

Mordred radiated both power and hatred. "And what of you, Sorcerer? Will you not add your own feeble power to our 'shields?' If you attempt to flee, we will destroy you first, whatever happens later to our shields."

"I am going," Houma said evenly, "to get help."

· X ·

No words were spoken as Thorian led them from the embattled portion of Otherwhen back to mist filled beaches of the Isle. They walked along the shoreline with the ocean on their right and the haunted interior of the Isle to their left. Soft rains pelted down on the restless ocean beside them, and their boots made crunching noises as they passed along the pebbled shoreline.

As they walked, all four humans and their two small servants noticed that a swirl of shadows was beginning to form just to their left, and after a time, all six noted that a fifth set of boots seemed to be passing in a slightly less noisy fashion over the pebbled beach just to their left.

For a time, no one was willing to look; even the overly curious Rafir forced himself to stare straight ahead.

"I am almost afraid to turn," Thorian murmured, his voice shaking.

"Father, do not fear," Eléna said. "I am fully present, in my old flesh, though I have lived so many years like a ghost caught in an endless windstorm."

"Eléna, Eléna, Eléna," Thorian murmured, turning to embrace his daughter. Father and daughter wept, and the skies seemed to weep down upon them, adding soft raindrops to their tears.

"Father, how brilliantly you have fought! The Mid-World of the Truce threw your lives away, for the Gods never dreamed that you might survive. And now you stand here embracing me, against all odds!"

"Eléna, my life was forfeit when I set foot upon this Isle. I do not begrudge payment of one life for another. If I can keep you alive, I am more than willing to pass from this world."

Eléna clasped her father again, then turned to the Apprentice. "Does that remain true, Julian? Is my father's life still committed to be sacrificed? I believed that true once, yet I now ask you, Apprentice with a Seer's Sight — is my father's death a certainty?"

Julian opened his mouth to respond but instead turned to stare down the shoreline. A Blue Wraith was drifting toward them, and on its shoulder was perched the eagle, the Eye of Merlin. The Great Guardian's Avatar had emerged; acknowledging the moment, the eagle gave out a great cry of triumph. His croaking sounds were met by the alarmed cries of many scores of seagulls as they lingered in offshore swells, obscured by a haze of rain.

"Endless possibilities have been flashing through my mind," Julian said softly, "yet this intersection has never been among them."

"We sought only a few additional moments," Kalanin murmured, "and now we have time for a full parlay. It would be nice to know how this moment came to pass."

When the Blue Wraith reached them, all bowed, for the Great Guardian was mightier than all but the Great Gods and the Demon Princes; yet they did not kneel.

"Great One," Thorian said, "my everlasting thanks to you for preserving my child. If I were holy enough to convey the Maker's Blessing, I would do so."

"To draw her from the Demon Princes was the right choice, the only choice," the Blue Wraith said, "and while we were hidden for so long in dreaming wastelands, Eléna and I formed the only resistance to the Demon Princes upon this Isle, and she alone gave me hope.

"Now, hear me, and do not celebrate even this modest victory, for we still represent only a fraction of the power that the Demon Princes have gathered to themselves. As we speak, the Three, seated upon their thrones of dark granite, are at the edge of discovery, where even greater power will flow to them. I cannot yet perceive their plans, yet a force of creation, as powerful as the birthing of the Marids, has been building.

"Yet now, if you listen to my advice, I will yield Eléna to guide you through the Isle, and you will allow your Familiars to come to my side. For even this creation, this Avatar, draws my attention from the greater struggle. From this point forward, these three, the Eye, and the two servants of Julian, will be my messengers, emissaries who will speak my thoughts to both your dreaming and waking minds."

Humans and Familiars glanced together, then all nodded.

Eléna pulled away from her father and spoke to the Great Guardian. "Great One, they will wish to know why or how we have gained so much time. What has become of our foes?"

The Wraith turned toward the inland depths of the Isle. "As we speak, a second party led by Un-Maurag and Alcman has joined Mordred and Haeglin and Houma in a nightmare realm of Otherwhen. In that portion of the Alternates, Demon Princes and Guardians have merged into a different order of beings. Now, the spectral phantoms of Demons and Guardians are being destroyed by the combined dark powers of our foes. Would that they each consumed one another, so that Dark Lords and Sorcerers and Marids and corrupted Guardians would also perish! Alas, that outcome will never happen!"

The Great Guardian turned away from the Isle's haunted, misty forests, back to the humans as they stood waiting. "Two last matters, then we must be gone, for the pursuit will begin again in moments. First, as we speak, Alcman and Houma whisper in low voices, wondering how to escape the malice of the Dark Lords after your group has been destroyed — and so the alliance against you is maintained only by the cruel oversight of the Demon Princes. I will ask Eléna to raise the second matter."

She nodded gravely. "It has been left to me to raise this last issue. Father, my magnificent father, a Seer's Sight grows strong in Julian, so strong that if he wields the Crystal, that Talisman becomes far more powerful in his hands." Thorian drew back, face hard, body stiff with displeasure.

Eléna laughed and again embraced the Wizard. "Yes, that is the father I knew, so harsh with power, so soft with love."

"Great Wizard," Julian added, "I will never begin to equal your mastery of magic, yet I have seen myself in fleeting visions, staring down into the stone, studying the many gateways provided by the Crystal." Thorian began to speak, glanced briefly at Eléna, then as his daughter again embraced him, the Wizard slowly passed the Crystal over to Julian.

The Apprentice held the Crystal in his left hand, staring down into its depths, while his right hand placed the leather thong around his neck.

When he looked up, Eléna was still with them, while the Blue Wraith had vanished, drawing his two Familiars with him into the innermost hidden reaches of the Isle.

"The Eye will soon join Sebastian and Rafir," Julian murmured. "For us, we must now move swiftly. Come." As Julian led them back along the beaches, returning to their original limestone redoubt, he invoked the Crystal, and with a slight *shudder*, they shifted back to Otherwhen, to a time when it was dark with fog, and colder, so that an icy frost was gathering on the upper levels of the beach.

They passed swiftly over chilled sands, the icy crystals from their breath adding to the shore's mists. Julian was at their forefront, leading them below into a larger limestone cavern, and in this realm of Otherwhen, that cavern led downward through passages taking them towards the Isle's foundations. As they descended, Thorian's staff flared with light, and immediately after, they could hear deep groaning voices as dwellers in the depths gathered to feast on the intruder's warm flesh.

"We have no time for this," Julian whispered, and again they felt the *shift, the shudder,* as they passed into a different portion of Otherwhen. After, the growling sounds were replaced by slithering noises, and now the creatures of the deep stone passages were fleeing whenever bright lights approached. As the creatures slipped into deeper caverns, Julian came to a halt, just at the curl of a dark labyrinth.

The Apprentice took a deep breath before speaking: "Now we are returning from Otherwhen back to the Isle. I hope I am right; my mind *sees* what lies beyond, but I know nothing for certain. Come."

Kalanin and Galad glanced at each other, eyes filled with questions, though they said nothing. Julian had led them through several regions of Otherwhen, and now they were returning to the Isle. But to what purpose?

The briefest of *shudders* shook them as they turned the corner and entered a broad but low cavern. They had returned to the Isle. Kalanin straightened — he was able to stand easily, but a mass of stalactites, like menacing stone daggers, hung from the cavern's roof. They stood staring as Thorian's staff flashed light over the erosion and ruin that water left when it flowed for ages over ancient stone. Finally, the staff's light came to rest and focused on a long boney shape resting in the center of the cavern's floor.

It was a skeleton, the size of a whale, but elongated, with the teeth and jaw of a long-dead dragon of the depths. Kalanin shook his head. *Some sea monster was trapped here when the Isle of the Demons was raised from the depths, and so it had died. What was Julian going to do, resurrect it? What would be accomplished?*

Julian stepped swiftly but warily over the cavern's floor. Placing one hand on the skeleton's great rib cage, he spoke four words. "Arise and follow me."

The skeleton's great bones shook and blurred. White bone became covered with grey flesh — and the being grew much taller. The creature rose from the ground, shattering stalactites overhead, and stared down at Julian with its single orb-eye.

A second, long hidden Guardian had been freed.

Demon Princes seldom allowed themselves to dream, for night visions outside their control brought back memories of their long imprisonment in the dream worlds of the Guardians. On this night, however, stunned by the surprising release of a second Guardian, they deliberately sought refuge in their place of power and secured themselves against interruption. No words were spoken

as they gathered darkness and silence to their great oval chamber. Sitting on equidistant thrones formed of grey granite, the Demon Princes closed their eyes, then forged a passage through Gates of Dreams into enchanted night visions.

Within the Mid-World of the Truce, all night visions were linked by magic, forming an immense Empire of Dreams. Yet so mighty were the Demon Princes, that all dreams fled before them and the three found themselves floating alone in a lifeless void.

"When we rule!" Satanis snarled, and flames flashed from his dreaming mouth.

"Then all things will be reordered to our liking," Zikar added softly, *"but for now, we must adjust, as we have done before."*

Suppressing the rage and the fire that surged within each of them, the Demon Princes transformed themselves, becoming far less powerful Avatars, lesser beings that might drift unnoticed through the Dreamways, seeking through hidden ways to view the night visions of others. As they drifted from the void, they returned to the Empire of Dreams, a subworld nurtured by Gods, creatures of magic, mortals born with the Gift, and immortals, and the great network of power that gathered to the Mid-World of the Truce.

The Demon Princes were seeking hints of the Maker's many creations, strands in the enormous tapestry of night visions that had been woven by the Great Fashioner who had first discovered their partly alive forms in the dust of earth's unliving crust. Easily perceived were the clear designs of the Greater Gods, deep, black hues from the visions of Dark Gods. Dream fragments from Creatures of the Darkness and Tanu and Sidhe and Elf-Lords and Sorcerers formed lesser threads. Nothing of the Maker's designs could be observed; if any design had once existed, many billions of night visions seemed to have overlaid any previous weavings left by the Maker.

"It is not enough," Satanis spoke in somber tones.

"Pain is only a gateway to understanding," Iblis murmured.

"It must be done," Zikar said.

The Demon Princes then fused their intellects, recoiling in agony. They were blind for a brief time, but as their vision cleared, they were able to search the Dreamways with far more powerful insight. Now, glints of Maker's light — gold of sun, silver of moon, blue of sky — seemed to radiate through the Empire of Dreams. But these were lesser strands, tiny by comparison to the glistening tapestries woven by the Great Gods — except to one side, in dreams that lay beyond Alantéa and the Mid-World, a great theme of the Maker's had once stood: the Hall of the Dreamers — now utterly destroyed.

"An ancient creation of the Maker that lies in ruins!" Satanis called out, radiating satisfaction.

"Now less than nothing," Iblis murmured, more quietly, and Zikar was silent, for all three felt pain whenever great emotion surged through their joined intellects.

The Hall of the Dreamers was gone, vanished forever. All the remaining strands within Alantéa contained no consistent patterns, and the one major design of the Maker had been destroyed. The Demon Princes relaxed, their minds beginning to pull back from their painful union. Then they paused; a second, far smaller line of dreaming strands had now become evident. Tiny by comparison, lines of power designed by the Maker had passed through the center of Alantéa in the Gangean Range. Less than two circles of the sun had gone by since a cluster of lines of Maker-force had gathered to Alantéa, yet these were so slight, that to rush up upon them would ruin this portion of the Dreamways like a trail of petals scattered before a great wind.

Within their dream voyage, the Avatars of Demon Princes became phantoms, mists that could only behold, and not influence dreams. Slipping back a short passage in time, they passed through the numberless dreams of the Mid-World Powers. Finally, they reached the sleeping forms of the feeble

Apprentice and his Giftless allies as they lay dreaming in the Gangean Range, almost two circles of the sun ago.

"*Why are we here?*" Iblis whispered. "*These are the least powerful of our foes.*"

"*The Maker has always been our true foe,*" Satanis hissed, "*yet soon his last devices will be exposed.*"

Zikar was silent, only watching intently as the humans lay still as death, while their eagle sentry stared into the distance. The Wizards' League had been destroyed, and the Vale of Whispers barred to them. In the aftermath of defeat, the four humans and their two small allies had retreated into dreams. Yet now as the Demon Princes watched on, strands of gold and silver and blue — hints of Maker-Work — seemed to embrace the mortals as they dreamed.

They were dreaming of a triumph that lay sometime in the future. Somehow the mortals had survived! They were gathering at a river, where a newborn child was to be washed, held by the Gift-born daughter of the Captain named Kalanin. In dreams, the daughter had grown to twelve years or more. Zikar snarled: Maker-work was showing the humans a scene of triumph, a time where they had prevailed. Sunlight held this scene for a moment, then the dream shifted slowly into grey mists and darkness.

"*If that was the Maker's dream,* Iblis murmured, "*now comes the brutal truth.*"

Within the mortals' night visions, great power gathered to the far side of the river opposite to them: the Sorcerers and the Marids, followed by the Demon Princes. To the Demon Princes, it was fitting that the Sorcerers had been reduced to spewing Gargoyles — after all, mortal magic wielders were no more than clumsy tools; and so, the dreaming Demon Princes laughed quietly to themselves as they watched the shrunken, spewing forms of the Sorcerers.

As darkness and destruction gathered to the river, all the allies of the four mortals vanished. Then the infant child of Kalanin faded, as did the other Captains of the League. Finally, the daughter slipped away, though she struggled desperately to remain. At the last, the four mortals were left — armed, defiant, but vastly overmatched.

Then the mortals turned and removed themselves, though they did not fade, but were simply drawn to another battle. Only Sorcerers, Marids, and Demon Princes remained, looming over a fouled river and its ruined landscape.

"And so, all the devices of the Maker have come to nothing," Iblis murmured with satisfaction.

"We must watch," Zikar whispered, *"for we have seen only the old dream, and now the old dream merges with its aftermath, a vision showing us one of many futures."*

In the dream's aftermath, the sky overhead slowly cleared, with shafts of sunlight radiating a bright light over a ruined landscape. River currents began flowing cleaner, passing masses of foul waters downstream. Mists lightened. Marids holding shrunken Sorcerers stepped back from the river's bank, while the dream images of Demon Princes held firm, grim faces studying first the sky and then events unfolding upon the other side of the river.

Two figures approached the opposite bank. One was a Sorceress, radiating great power — a queen of middle years, while the second was a decade younger, a Captain and leader of armed hosts. Neither showed the slightest concern that Demons, or Marids, or Sorcerers on the opposite bank might ever have troubled them in the past or might threaten them in the future.

These are the children of the one called Kalanin, Zikar thought. *Only one of these two is now born, nothing more than a blob of corrupted human flesh. Yet they regard us from the future with an utter lack of fear as though it is we, the Demon Princes, who have become dead things! If this is one of many futures, this alternative future must be reduced to nothingness!*

The Sorceress sighed, and with the motions of a servant clearing a long-overlooked storage room, she began transforming the dreamworld surrounding the river. Behind her, the warrior and captain watched on with only obscure interest, lips forming a vague curl of irony, while his right hand rested easily on the hilt of a mighty sword that remained sheathed.

Rays of bright sunlight burst over the scene so that even the Demon Princes on the river's far side grimaced at the sun's brightness. Then the river began to run completely clear, and the mists hovering above the river slid downstream. The hands of the Sorceress danced in the sunlight and her mouth whispered **words.** A radiance like gleaming starlight gathered to her.

On the opposite bank, where Marids held Gargoyle-like Sorcerers suspended over the river, the images of Sorcerers were transformed into limestone statues. Then those statues shuddered and fragmented, becoming shards of stone that slipped into the river's shallows and were gone. Marids shifted in slow stages, to become gnarled, twisted willows that extended roots and branches into the river's eddies; while beyond the riverbank, Demon Princes were transformed into toppling stone pillars, pitted with age, green with moss, ancient remnants of some ancient temple that had been long forgotten.

"What has happened here!?!" Iblis recoiled in astonishment.

"A dream within a dream," Satanis spoke, and now fire emerged, even from his lessened Wraith form, while power gathered to all three Demon Princes, as they began to discard their Avatar guises. "And this dream that will not be allowed to stand, for we will destroy it!"

In the nightmare of the Demon Princes, Kalanin's daughter turned to face the intruding dream images of the Demon Princes. Palms extended, she forced a wall of air toward them, followed by a slight gust of air from her own mouth. And then the dream-voyaging Demon Princes dissolved into puffs of smoke.

Chapter Fourteen

"We Must Destroy the Child"

"**WE MUST DESTROY THE** child," Satanis said, leaning forward intently. "To your mortal minds this step might seem nothing more than a diversion, but we have each of us on several occasions, encountered undesirable visions of a distant future, with this mortal infant as its source."

"A lump of puking mucous," Iblis said quietly, though smoke and fire slipped from his mouth, hinting at deeper emotions. "Why we should be troubled by a mortal creature defies all reason, but a swift death will remove these dark visions completely."

Seated on his throne, Zikar alone looked down to meet the eyes of Houma and Alcman.

"At first, I argued for delay," Zikar murmured, "seeking time to explore the strangeness of this situation. This child, this clump of corruption, may be only the symptom and not the source of our problem. Yet you have explored Otherwhen, where realities fork and branch; and so, we require no more than a simple pruning of one branch — a knife, a cup of poison, then one future is utterly forestalled and we can clear the pestilence infesting our Isle, and then finally destroy the Mid-World of the Truce."

"Consider it done," Houma said. "As always, we rejoice in serving your great majesties. Enormous pressure has been placed upon our assets within the League, though we have concealed two of them for just such a purpose. Now I will activate them, put them into play — as assassins."

"Do it now," Satanis said. The two Sorcerers stood in the throne room, with Houma nodding enthusiastically, while Alcman stared into the distance, face grim and set, as though he contemplated other, far more important matters.

Something like a smile flashed over the face of Satanis. *How interesting! We believed that the Sorcerers would do anything to fulfill our wishes — but one of the two remaining maggots still has scruples! And over nothing except a lump of flesh belonging to our foes!*

Alcman sent waves of cold radiating through his body so his reactions could not be sensed, though his mind still seethed. *We are doing it again! I do not understand why the Demon Princes have become so troubled, but so many times their rashness has provoked events that we might otherwise have avoided. How it will come back upon us I do not understand, but it feels like all those other terrible decisions made during this conflict: poorly considered, reckless, and stupidly counterproductive.*

The Sorcerer's eyes closed to further conceal his thoughts. *And not all the foolhardy choices have been made by Demon Princes: I learned through spies and Divinations that Houma wasted many of our assets within the League in a strike against their Captains Harlond and Rostov. Houma the Insane! What was he trying to gain? Even though Harlond lies dying and Rostov may recover, what was the point? We have become prisoners of our own malice.*

Alcman's eyes flashed open. He bowed and left the chamber, face frozen as though deep in thought. His body was beginning to shiver from the cold, while his mind struggled to restrain wild thoughts. *Keep silent, you old fool! Already you have said too much, told your masters far more than they were willing to hear. In this matter, if you had a trace of logic you could reason with them. Even Demon Princes listen to logic. Sometimes, he corrected himself, sometimes they listen to reason.*

Alcman's hand slipped to his chest, where he had bound the Talisman of Otherwhen onto a necklace formed by links of steel, with each link reinforced by powerful spells. He took a deep breath and tried to reassure himself. *You have become senile, you old fool. Soon the infant will be dead, and your masters will destroy the interlopers. Then we will see whether Gods or Demons will rule this portion of the universe.* But still, his hand would not release his Talisman of Otherwhen.

· ☼ ·

Serena was crying again. Géla woke from a deep sleep that had been filled with dreams, and began nursing her, staring out the window into an overcast night sky. Normally untroubled, her daughter had been born with the Gift, and she stirred when the matrices of magic surrounding her became disturbed.

Several months ago, when Serena was only a newborn, something terrible had happened to Kalanin, and the child had wept and wept. Then somehow Kalanin — no doubt aided by Julian and Galad — had fought his way free and Serena had smiled again, returning to peace at nighttime. Now, as Harlond lay dying, and as Rostov struggled with deep wounds, Serena's rest was again disturbed.

They are coming for us next, Géla thought. *I do not know what to do.* Serena's nursing mouth slowed and finally stopped; then she stared up at her mother with grey, searching eyes. Géla rocked her gently until Serena's eyes again slipped closed. After, both mother and daughter slept.

Their sleeps were restless, with night-visions swirling through their minds. An hour before dawn, both Géla and Serena were drawn through Gates of

Dreams and found themselves in the presence of a Power, the Goddess Pallas Athena. The Great Goddess sat upon her marble-white throne with wispy curls of incense lifting around her. In her left hand was a shield, while her right hand held a spear. On her chest was the necklace bearing an image of the Gorgon's head.

"And so, you both look up at me with such large, unafraid eyes," the Goddess said softly. *"The blood of Sentauris flows not in your veins, Géla, as it does in your daughter, Serena's — yet Sentauris would be proud of both of you."*

Géla bowed, then glanced back into the eyes of the Goddess. *"Holy Mother, my beloved has spoken of Sentauris, as a great, hidden force in the early time of the League, yet to me, she is the slightest of legends, less than a ghost. Now you speak of Serena as kin of Sentauris, and that means?"*

Pallas Athena nodded gravely. *"Orissa, the great Seeress, who once sat among other Powers in the Hall of the Dreamers, was a foremother to Sentauris. Lost in time, hidden from the Gods, this essence of heroes comes down from Orissa through Sentauris to your own child. Kalanin and Galad and Julian are all distant cousins, with Sentauris as their foremother."*

Géla hesitated, then asked, *"Holy Mother, was Sentauris, then, also a servant of yours, a follower?"*

The Goddess again nodded. *"She was my most beloved, yet wayward, follower. Each time I think of Sentauris, my heart fills with equal measures of joy and sorrow. The joy flows from her strength and wisdom, while in sorrow I understand that she lives now only in my own memories."*

"And so, you have come to save this child, this final echo of Sentauris."

"I have come for both of you. Daughter, you must gather your child and then I will draw both of you into my own enchanted kingdom, there to rest under my protection until the Wizards and your beloved return. Only nod your head, then safety and a nurturing filled with gentle wisdom await Serena."

"You were present at the beginning of the League," Géla said softly, *"or so the Mistress of Illusions once instructed me. And now you are drawn to the last moments of our alliance."*

On her throne, the dream-image of Pallas Athena leaned forward, face filled with sorrow. *"Daughter, nothing fashioned by humankind will last forever. Even the Great Gods may one day falter and fail. Yet if you seek sanctuary with me, I will defend both you and your daughter until my own immortal form lies dead and I am cast into the Temple of Waiting.*

"Hear me, child! Many Gods came to battle in the Vale of Whispers with reluctance. Yet I came fully armored, leading thousands of mortal warriors, and dangerous Sidhe, and mighty Tanu, and enchanted constructs of my own making, all rising to defend the Mid-World of the Truce.

"Filled with righteous wrath we surged toward the Demon Princes, the fashioners of that day of misery. On my left, Amon-Ra led his legions, while forces loyal to Tor-El-Baldur fought on my right flank. Yet we broke like water against a granite cliff as we faced the Dark Lords and Marids and Sorcerers and Creatures of the Darkness. Behind these potencies ranged the Demon Princes, their feet passing for the first time in ages upon the shores of Alantéa the Forerunner; and so, they cried aloud in triumph, torrents of fire flaming from their mouths.

"These Demon Princes were not content to merely turn us aside, for they launched a storm of dark energies against Amon-Ra. This shield that I hold now in my hand, deflected those energies, and so Amon-Ra was preserved. Then I sped forward into a wild melee. I could not destroy or even damage the Marids, while they were not swift enough to grasp me as I danced among them. Creatures of the Darkness, twice the height of my own form, sought to bludgeon me into ruin and dark death. I cut them down and they died thrashing in the dust.

"Then I stood with nothing before me but a lesser creature, a lone Sorcerer, Cronar, in my path. Yet this Sorcerer had grown so mighty that he wielded

a God's power. He lashed at me with his Demon Tools, and I took wounds. Astonished, I fell back. Then a desperate stroke lashed out. Cronar stiffened with a look of utter bewilderment forming on his lined, ancient features, and then he died swiftly as mayfly humans do, in that same brief second.

"Tor-El-Baldur had fought to my side, dragging Marids into the melee. Though Marids had him in a death grasp, with his last stroke Tor-El-Baldur struck down my foe. I was free, though the Marids grasping Baldur's form began to tear it asunder. How had we, the Greater Gods, become so fragile? Yet then, on Baldur's right, Ahriman pushed his Urak tiers forward toward our melee; all his servants perished like straw in a firestorm, while Ahriman recoiled in horror at the dismemberment of Baldur. Gathering himself, the Great Dark God launched grim and powerful energies at the Marids, and their substances seemed to struggle to retain their shapes. I do not understand what happened next, but I believe that the transforming energies of the Guardians intervened, converting all things into the texture of dreams, and the Marids again turned their power against the Gods.

"Then I slashed at Marids with the same weapon that rests in my right hand, but the spear would not harm them — it was straw matched against stone. In a great rage, I hurled this weapon against the Demon Princes. This spear, my mightiest Sending, was casually cast from the upper skies by the great power of the Demon Princes. After, the tide turned against us, though I fought on and will never give way."

Pallas Athena took a deep breath, glanced away as though clearing thoughts of battle from her mind, then turned back to Géla and Serena. *"Also, since that time, I have strengthened myself, and should any Greater God or Demon Prince seek to assault me in my place of power, that being would be most surprised. I pledge my increased strength to your defense. Come to me now and rest. Please come to me, for a soft, untroubled sleep will reign in my kingdom."*

Géla leaned forward, her own eyes radiating compassion. *"Goddess, if I have speech at the Awakening, I will ask the Maker to acknowledge your great heart. Yet still, I should ask of you, what might Sentauris have said, should she have stood in my place?"*

Pallas Athena paused, then sighed. *"She might have said — that she could never abandon her people. Your own heart is strong, strangely similar over the passage of years, to that of Sentauris. Yet mortal hearts are the devices of mayflies, flickering only briefly, then they are forever dead. I will further consider your destiny, though I do not know what other steps I might take. Farewell, and may your Maker provide you with greater wisdom than I have."*

·)(·

Passing through the Dreamways, Sebastian slipped into Julian's sleeping mind, where the Apprentice was waiting for him. The dreaming mind of Julian gathered Sebastian into his arms and embraced him.

"It is better to be a ghost than not to be alive," Sebastian said.

"Ghost! You are simply a messenger journeying through dreamland." Julian beamed love into his Familiar and Sebastian smiled.

"It is strange being at the side of a Power like the Great Guardian," the Familiar whispered. *"Every second, a thousand thoughts race through his mind — I'm linked to him and can follow some of his lesser thoughts. Then, with every minute, some of those thousand thoughts lead to action, and scores of magical forces leap from his mind to counter the Demon Princes. Other portions of his mind search endlessly for the ten remaining, hidden Guardians, the ones who remained loyal to him. But these seem to have been so completely transformed and hidden, that they might just as well have never existed. Anyway, only a few of the Great Guardian's thoughts focus*

on you, with your increasing ability to navigate Otherwhen, and I've been sent with only one reminder, so the Great One must have given you at least a passing grade."

"The Wizards have thought of everything!" Again, Julian's sleeping mind embraced Sebastian's. *"What could possibly have been forgotten?"*

"The Great Guardian says that you didn't respond to Eléna. If Thorian's death is certain, what he calls "a destiny unforgiven," you should speak to her. The Great Guardian sees a most difficult moment when Eléna's hopes are suddenly ruined, and she herself becomes far too willing to die."

Julian took a deep breath. *"If only I were certain. Let me sleep, let me dream, and then perhaps I will know more."* Julian turned on his side and Sebastian vanished, though the dreaming adventures of the Apprentice did not end.

He closed his eyes, then suddenly felt motion swirling through the Dreamways. His eyes blinked open to find Eléna beside him.

"Hail, Julian," Eléna whispered. *"Did you think to escape from me so easily? You can embrace me now, freely, here in this empire of dreams."*

The sleeping, ghost form of Julian pushed nearer to Eléna, and their ghostly mouths met.

"In one way or another," Julian whispered, *"I have been seeking you all my days."*

"My quest for you came later, for all of my early steps were guided by a most powerful, intensely focused father. Yet, did I once dream of you as Julian the child? Your hair was dark, and you were perhaps five, splashing across a river in great haste."

"Such was my passage through the borders of the League," Julian said softly, *"though it was the passage of many others, too."*

"I believe that there was a line of destiny between us, even then, Julian. And now that I have you trapped here in dreamland, with no convenient interruptions, I will ask you again: is my father doomed?"

Julian turned and stared into the darkness. *"None of us seems likely to survive, yet visions of your father's death — in one last burst of power, he will rise to smite our foes — and then, he will die — these visions have been so numerous they cannot be denied. It may be that the frequency of visions confirms a destiny."*

Julian could feel Eléna pull away from him, and he again embraced her. *"No, wait, there is more. When your father first declared his doom, speech sped to my lips, seven halting words —* **'this fate may not come to pass,'** *though I did not speak those words because my understanding was so incomplete."*

"So, perhaps one chance in a thousand, nothing more than a seam in fate," Eléna whispered, and again began pulling away.

Julian released her, murmuring, *"Much more than a seam in fate is opening before us, more like a shift in land masses, unleashing forces that cause the earth to shake, or forge mountain ranges."*

Eléna also turned to stare up into the darkest regions of their shared dream vision. *"My father always counseled me that the Powers were somewhat wary of the Maker, never speaking his name, letting lesser forces crush his peoples and his temples. Perhaps the Demon Princes should never have attempted a Great Sending, hurling a dagger into the Maker's Heart."*

"I do not believe that the Maker would fear any such dagger," Julian said softly. *"Also, this shift in fate has come only recently, long after the Scimitar of the Demon Princes struck down the Hall of the Dreamers and was launched into the heavens. Perhaps other, more subtle devices have been left to confound the Maker's Adversaries. Might the Demon Princes have invoked some hidden device without understanding its nature? Might their misstep free your father from his doom? That, at least, is my hope."*

"A chance, that is all I could wish for, a chance," Eléna whispered, taking a deep breath, then settling back beside Julian. *"So, my great and wise fortune teller, night is turning into day. What will daylight bring?"*

"Daylight brings more flight from our foes," Julian said in a remote voice. *"Evening takes us to the greatest of the underground caverns on this Isle, one with a lake at its center. There we will fight the greatest pitched battle since we landed upon the Isle of the Demons."*

· ⅄ ·

Mother and daughter slept beyond sunrise, so deeply that the guards became concerned. Finally, Anthera, senior among the remnant of woman warriors who had once served the Mistress of Illusions, cautiously unlocked the chamber door and peered into the bedroom. In a few moments, she re-emerged, to confirm that mother and daughter were well, that they slept untroubled.

Géla finally rose an hour before noon. Food was set before her, but she ate only a portion, for with the coming of daylight, the old sense of danger was slowly returning. Serena's afternoon nap was restless, so it was late in the day before mother and daughter set out into the overcast streets of Khiva.

A carriage had been constructed for Géla, and with the increasing sense of danger, she no longer complained about its ungainliness. At first, planking had been added to a simple carriage, creating a more elaborate coach. Then, when Rostov had forcefully demonstrated that planking was no match for powerful, reinforced bows, overlapping sheets of tin had been attached to the wood. So, their simple coach was no longer merely unsightly, but also stuffy and dark and heavy, requiring a team of four horses and two drivers as it made its way through Khiva's winding streets. Guards, some alert, some fatigued, led the carriage, while others followed behind it.

The hospice sheltering Rostov was set against the upper hillside of the outer city, facing south, so that those healing within could watch the sun arc across the sky, and view the passage of the many ships moving through the busy seaport. On this day, the skies were overcast, and distant rain clouds were shedding moisture over the surface of the southern ocean.

Rostov was sitting up in bed, initialing scrolls that had been prepared for him. His nightstand was covered with signed documents. However, quill and parchment were set aside when Géla entered. He took Serena in his arms. The child glanced apprehensively at her mother, then smiled shyly up at Rostov.

"We are safe enough," Rostov called out to his guards. Géla nodded to her people, then both sets of attendants reluctantly departed. They were left alone for a moment. Géla reached out to reassure Rostov, while the Captain clutched her left hand with one of his own, closing his eyes in grief. Each felt that of all the people in the League, they could be completely certain only of each other.

"I was told that Harlond still lives," Rostov murmured, "but then I heard bells ringing, and voices chanting. What was that about?"

"A prayer vigil," Géla said quietly, "though it was more like a funeral. Word came from the Great God Thoth that he could not heal Harlond. I was at that vigil, sitting in the darkness of my caravan, weeping as I nursed Serena."

Rostov released Géla's hand so he could cough quietly into a towel — the towel's fabric was red with blood, and Géla shook her head grimly.

"And so Harlond is doomed," Rostov said in a choked, hoarse voice, "and yet still he lingers. I hope Thoth, at least, is controlling his pain. In Harlond's place, I might still wish to hold on, waiting for word from the Isle of the Demons, to hear — one way or the other — about the fate of our League." Rostov was silent for a moment, sinking back into his bed and closing his eyes before continuing.

"The League has been struggling for such a long time. You never met Envar, but he was the first of our Captains to die. I was just beginning to understand him and his soft humor when he led a force of pikemen against the Dark Emissary, and then he was dead, seconds later. Dargas and Rurak perished before Gravengate during our warfare with the Sorcerers and the Marids. Somehow, I hoped that the Fates would overlook Harlond and Rostov, perhaps even allow them to retire to small villas, where they might write memoirs that glorified their own contributions while exploring the lesser qualities of the Wizards."

"It may still come true for you." Géla smiled, and she pulled up a chair so that she could sit eye level with Rostov. "Now, the last time we spoke, you had only tentative conclusions about the attack on Harlond and yourself. Do we now know more?"

Rostov took a deep breath. "A Wizard could peer deeply into this matter and speak with a clarity that I can't offer. However, I am satisfied that Houma is the author of our misfortunes — Houma and the forces within the Isle of the Sorcerers." He handed Serena back to Géla and continued in hushed tones.

"From several sources, we've learned that the war fleet sent from the Isles of the Sorcerers was destroyed in the middle of the ocean by the Gods, but the Wizards were blamed for arranging this trap. For years, Sorcerers from the Isles have maintained networks of agents within the League — with Houma at the center of these plots. We learned that many of these agents lost close family, and so, prompted by Houma, were willing to sacrifice their own lives to gain revenge. Because you and Serena are protected by men of the Dragon's Teeth, and archers who once served the Mistress of Illusions, they attacked their Captains, Harlond and Rostov."

Rostov coughed, then wiped the blood from his mouth. "The assassins' plans for escape were almost nothing. Only one of seven called out an invocation to Houma to save them. All the rest expected to die, and so the attacks were for revenge."

Rostov sat up in bed, peering around Géla to confirm that they were alone. Then he reached for his quill from the side table and wrote swiftly on Géla's palm: *Danger! Get away from Khiva!*

Géla nodded, carefully rubbing the inscription from her hand until nothing was left of it. Then she spoke a few reassuring, meaningless words to Rostov, and passed from the hospice back into the overcast city.

·)(·

Within Khiva, Houma's dormant magic had been activated for less than half a day, but already his two hidden allies had exchanged shifts with other guards, and so had made time to develop plans that would fulfil the Sorcerer's designs. When, as instructed, they met in Khiva's broad open-air, so-called "Goblin Market," each responded with surprise.

"Zur!" Alcayna murmured, smiling. "I had no idea that the people of the Dragon's Teeth would seek curios from the 'Goblin Market,' joining a gaggle of bewildered seamen, lost travelers, and distracted housewives."

"As humans, we share human vices," Zur said evenly. "Mine are entirely normal — rich, red wines from high slopes south of the Gangean Range are a delicacy found only here in what this simple village calls the 'Goblin Market.' Come, join me for a moment, then you may judge for yourself."

Zur and Alcayna sat together on a wooden bench, at an old, stained table placed at the outskirts of the market, watching as streams of people bought fish, meat, garden vegetables, or curios. Other stalls offered pottery, clothing, and jewelry. One small stall contained ancient, tattered books that promised discrete access to the lesser powers of Wizards and Adepts.

Indeed, almost all goods were available at this "Goblin Market," except Goblins and the handicrafts of Goblins, and the many items of magic available far to the north, in the outskirts of Far Avalon, where the real Goblin Market thrived. The market in Khiva had been created mostly to lure visiting seamen, and to capture their money.

Zur was tall, black sculpted beard showing the first touches of grey, though he seemed, otherwise, something less than thirty years of age. Only a few of the guards, those who spoke with him for more than a brief time, noted his remote, almost haunted eyes. Alcayna was also tall, hair long and dark, perhaps in her early thirties, a woman with a ready laugh, but prone to long silences, as though preoccupied with remote thoughts. Citizens of Khiva carefully avoided both of them as strangers, for Zur was one of the men of the Dragon's Teeth, a force once numbering ten thousand, now a remnant reduced to a few hundred. Alcayna was part of an even smaller residue: the women warriors serving the Mistress of Illusions now numbered less than three score.

Neither Zur nor Alcayna wished to be the last of their kind.

Zur sat, drinking rich red wine, staring down into the hazy, overcast harbor, considering his future sourly: he and Alcayna were to be lovers, though obviously neither was attracted to the other. Then murder was to be followed by a desperate flight into a future transformed by riches and power promised by the Sorcerer.

How could I have ever trusted Houma? Perhaps I should just allow the beast within me to rule, then slip into the forest and be gone. But where would the rich red wine come from then?

"Come, come," Alcayna tapped his hand, and sipped again at the heavy red wine, grimacing at its strong flavors. "Our struggle has gone on forever, and so we are entitled to some solace. Be content, live for this moment."

Zur forced himself to smile. "I suppose that my first moments were the happiest. We of the Dragon's Teeth were born unto a battlefield, fully armed, surging across the Plain of Gravengate. That was a great moment, though there have been other triumphs as well."

Alcayna nodded to herself: Zur spoke his lines in flat tones, and so he was not an accomplished actor. She would need to act for both. "My greatest moment came when the Mistress of Illusions emerged from her domain, bringing war to our foes. We burst into song then, and victory seemed not just possible, but a force of destiny." *Indeed, I forced myself to sing,* Alcayna considered, *driven by ambition and hatred and desires I could not fully understand.*

Zur stared at her evenly: not one false note had emerged from her voice. She had only winced briefly at the wine's flavor; otherwise, her performance was perfect. He would need to improve his own acting skills if they were to survive.

He rose from the table. "Some among the guards find the wines of the Gangean Range overly flavorful. What is your true preference?"

Alcayna beamed at him. "Something white, touched by fruit and with a hint of sparkle." With fresh wine set before them, they sat through the long hazy afternoon, speaking in low voices, quickly developing a rough code: when they wished to convey matters relating to their enterprise, their feet brushed together; otherwise, their conversation dealt only with trivial matters. Their goblets were refreshed several times, and skewers of meat were set before them. If the service at the Goblin Market was not entirely warm, none of their silver was rejected.

At dusk, they slipped into Zur's chambers on the upper floor of an old inn. Their lovemaking was brief, filled with more obligation than passion. After, Zur turned from her, still lying on his bed, eyes staring out into the night.

"We can speak here," Alcayna whispered. "If I have only the slightest touch of the Gift, I am at least warned when we are overheard. Now I will tell you why I am here and then ask from you the same truth.

"I have grown to hate them, Wizards and Far Travelers, hate them with a great and secret passion. I disliked — and feared — the Mistress of Illusions. I scorned her tepid lover, the Grandfather of Géla, the spoiled child. From her childish beginning, Géla grew quietly powerful. Then came Kalanin, the so-called Far Traveler, this languid lover to the Mistress of Illusions, a hero who spent much of his time staring into remote galaxies. I caught his eyes once, and I could read his response — 'Ah, an unhappy archeress. Why does she linger here?'

"My hatred redoubled, yet I did ask myself, why did I linger? And the answer was something beyond hatred. It was a desire for power — if I wished power, I needed to study the ways of force in the courts of those who wielded true power. Now, at least a portion of their power is within our grasp." She nudged Zur, adding, "Speak now the tale of Zur, the truth, for once."

Zur stared out into the overcast night. "It is dark. I lie in the forest and the beast comes for me. We rise to battle, I with a club in one hand, a dagger in the other, while the beast lashes at me with brutally sharp claws. Each time, I prevail, though every encounter leaves me weaker. The beast was close to triumph until Houma intervened, and now a charm protects me, shields me from the beast within."

She massaged him gently, fingers flowing first over his neck then over his stressed, tight shoulders. "Strange fates followed the men of the Dragon's Teeth. Some became gaunt and spectral, while others grew beastlike. You are a victim of yet another of the Wizards' desperate, hazardous, half-witted magics. Yet you must also speak to me of the merchants' daughters, so that I may fully understand you."

Zur laughed, though both his neck and back stiffened. "To those daughters, I am nothing more than a rite of passage — as maidens become women, they seek me out to test their bodies against my flesh. I have become a trophy of sorts — and a perversion — for in moments of passion I growl like a great beast, and they shiver in delicious fear."

Alcayna took a deep breath and turned from him, to stare up into the chamber's shadowy upper reaches. "So, you bring both fear and weakness to this enterprise. Those two things are not enough."

"They are not enough," Zur agreed, staring out into the night, the beast within him quickening, stirred by strange desires. "What are we to do now?"

"You believe that we have come to an end?" she asked, rising. "We are not even at the beginning." She stood and fumbled in the darkness through her satchel. Zur was forced to admit that her naked form was shapely and trim, though she was almost twice the age of his young lovers.

Alcayna spilled powder from a pouch into a wine goblet, added wine, then she drank half and passed the balance to Zur. He sipped, stared into the darkness, realizing that he was trapped in events he could not control, and drank the potion down.

Zur glanced into Alcayna's eyes, then a fire of lust raged over each of them. Sometime before midnight, they pulled apart, bodies exhausted, the sheets spilling around them soaked with sweat.

"We have not yet truly started," Alcayna panted. "*That* was only the beginning."

Zur steadied his breathing; deep within him, an imprisoned panther paced unquietly through its narrow cage. "The potion?" he asked.

"Yes, another pathway to power," Alcayna murmured. "If magic is the ultimate force, can only magic wielders control it? Not so, for even I, with the slightest touch of the Gift, have acquired a wide range of charms and potions."

She rose and again rummaged through her satchel. "This brings us to the second phase of our alliance." She drew forth a thin vial that was stopped by an equally small cork; the container itself was formed from dark glassware, and the substance within was even murkier.

"If I have only the slightest touch of the Gift," Alcayna said, again sitting beside Zur on his bed, "you are a being of magic, filled with latent power. *This* will activate that talent."

She pulled the cork wedge from the vial; after a brief second of hesitation, Zur drank its substance down and nearly retched — even with sugar and brandy, the vileness of the potion's flavor was barely masked. Had the potion been formed from the secretions of scorpions and spiders? But seconds later, he grew suddenly more alert. All his senses became stronger; although it was dark, he could see more clearly, and his ears caught distant sounds as his senses reached beyond the curtained windows into the night world outside.

And, with a sense beyond sight or sound, he felt the *hum* of sorcerous energies that powered the Mid-World of the Truce; and the night around him was alive with the force of magic.

To Alcayna, Zur seemed suddenly more intense and focused — something restless, bestial, was stirring inside him. And faintly the ridgelines on his forehead grew more prominent, to press outward, as though a restless panther within was seeking to burst through Zur's flesh.

"Good, good," she murmured, struggling to keep traces of fear from her voice and from her mind. "Now comes our first, great test. I have with me the three Talismans passed to us by Houma. The first is a sleeping potion to still the guard. Here...."

She passed to him a simple cloth pouch of dusky silk; unseen within the pouch was a fine, chalky powder. Zur held the pouch for a moment, then murmured, "Yes, they sleep. Dark visions cloud their minds. Terror begins to consume them. With breaths growing shorter, they struggle to wake, but suddenly they are dead, never to breathe again."

They glanced together, and Alcayna shrugged. "Every great enterprise involves at least a few casualties," she said softly. "Here is the second of Houma's Talismans — an enchanted gateway is to form, taking us to Far Avalon, the greatest distance from this failed League and its doomed Wizards." This Talisman was pentagonal, formed of tarnished silver, small enough so that Zur could hold it comfortably in the palm of one hand.

Zur's eyes closed as he focused. "You lift the Talisman, as instructed, from your satchel and invoke its powers. Suddenly from a thousand directions, slivers of dark lightning swarm and seethe. Two figures, the assassins, Zur and Alcayna, seeking desperate escape are now truly free — free because they are dead, with nothing left of them but ashes." He passed the Talisman back to Alcayna, growling, "The third device, no doubt, will be the same."

In shock, Alcayna wordlessly passed the third Talisman to Zur. This device seemed no more than a simple cup of porcelain inlaid with small jewels, though Houma had sworn great oaths to grim Dark Gods that incredible riches would flow from it. As before, the warrior focused on the Talisman, eyes closing as he spoke: "We have been wary, using others to activate the escape Talisman. Now, with our flight blocked, our one chance is to obtain great wealth, then bribe our way free from Khiva. We invoke our third Talisman. Instead of riches, we are transformed into stone statues, instantly dead. Later, the enraged people of Khiva smash these stone statues into tiny fragments with hammers of steel, but it does not matter, for we are long dead."

Zur rose, lithe and naked, quick as a hunting wolf, and with one motion, swept a dagger from beneath their bed. "Where is Houma? Let us see if this Sorcerer can magic himself away from cold steel!"

"Hold on, wait — and lower your voice," Alcayna muttered, struggling to control the moment. "Were we not wise to test these devices? But Houma is exceedingly crafty, the most cunning being I have ever encountered. He will have prepared for this eventuality, holding other Talismans in reserve. It would be more convenient for him if we perished, but now he must deal with a new reality — there is a moment where I can reach for him, speak a few words, just two hours before dawn. We have several hours before that time. I have secured a second bonding potion for us — if anything, stronger than the first."

While Alcayna poured wine and prepared her second potion, Zur paced like a caged beast. A brief time later, when Zur growled as wildly as a creature of the night forest, Alcayna moaned and writhed like the mate of a demonic beast.

·)(·

As the hazards mounted, the Gates of Dreams were cast open for Géla while she slept in her daughter's room late at night. Above their chamber, the infinitely remote and uncaring stars gleamed and glittered through the long night.

Her first night vision showed her many of the events of the past months: the warship Alantéa *surging over a foaming ocean, battles at sea, journeys through Otherwhen, and finally the great disaster, as the warship* Alantéa *collapsed upon the Isle of the Demons, hurtling Godlings, Wizards, and their allies into the corrupted Guardians' dream empire.*

Then came the long, grim time when her beloved could not even recall Géla's name — or his own. A slow, bitter, brutal time of recovery ended with the freeing of the first Guardian. Then the Great Guardian delivered Eléna to her father, and finally, the Apprentice located and freed yet a second Guardian. Then the images faded as though the Gates of Dreams had yielded its final vision.

The League! Géla exulted. We will not be put down so easily! Yet these are matters that have already happened. I feel it now, in the restless dark night, that momentous events are happening even as I lie here! Great one, great benevolent power, whoever has intervened on my behalf, will you now allow me to perceive events as they occur this very moment? She could feel a hesitation in the air.

Please, her mind called out again, I beg of you to show me what is happening now, at this very moment, in the darkness!

Her dream visions shifted slowly, reluctantly. She was floating in midair in the night sky, high above the Isle of the Demons. Beneath her, magic pulsed over the Isle like ground lightning. Drifting lower, she watched the Citadel of the Demon Princes as it trembled — some great act of sorcery was being forged, and the Demon Princes would not allow her to watch their work.

Géla felt herself drifting north from the Citadel, floating in the sky. North of her, the Cloudshelf gleamed in the moonlight, while below her lay the killing fields that surrounded the Citadel. Even in her dream visions, she could smell death below her. Ravines lay at the edge of the killing fields, then she passed over a range of stony hills, drifting always closer to the ground.

Startled, she found herself to the north of the fortress, pressing down through the earth, down through the roof of a stone cavern that closed off starlight and moonlight. Moisture was rising from below her — she glanced down, and the surface of an underground lake, made dim by darkness and vague by distance, lay beneath her. She looked away from the water, staring into the distance; now, on the far shore, lights flared, and cries of wrath were interspersed by explosions, sounds echoing across the great cavern. The lake's normally placid surface was beginning to shiver, rippling with the concussions of great violence.

In her dream voyage, Géla drew closer to the battle. Lightning flashed, while magic burst over the shore. Power surged to Houma as he fought at the lake's edge. Houma led a force of Marids, though the Marids seemed to be struggling with some enchanted barrier. Wizards were holding them back by magic! Houma was shouting counter spells, though the lone Sorcerer could not overcome the power of three Wizards.

In the shallows, her beloved stood, raising his longbow, and notching an arrow, waiting, watching...then a shaft was loosed sliding through the shields crafted by Sorcerers...a lone Marid recoiled in pain. Galad was beside Kalanin, loosing a second shaft. Then Galad notched a third arrow, while at his side the Tarnished Sword was moaning for battle.

While the warriors fought from the shallows, the Wizards held the ground at the water's edge. To the Wizards' right, some distance from the shoreline, Godlings glistened with light. The three Godlings had taken flight, radiating power — though they faced not just one, but two Godlike beings, the Dark Lords. Haeglin shimmered with power. Mordred spoke incandescent words. But the Godlings were holding them! Dark Lords were struggling to break free and crush both Godlings and Mortal Magic Wielders, and they were being turned aside!

The Godlings could not hold forever! Where was the Apprentice? Where was Julian, always at the intersection of great events? Ah, indeed Julian was at the center. To the left, in the lake's shoals, were the warriors, with Wizards beside them at the shoreline, contending with Houma and his Marids. To the far right, Godlings matched battle magic with Dark Lords, while at the center, Julian was dwarfed by two Guardians, who were locked in a battle of transforming dreams with a third, corrupted Guardian opposing them.

Behind Julian, Eléna also stood in the shadows of the Guardians, almost deliberately obscured, holding a bow, notched with a partly drawn arrow, a small slender weapon, half the size of the great longbows wielded by Kalanin and Galad. Magic, it must reek of spell-work, but to what end? Julian and Eléna were hidden, passive, waiting, but for what?

In her dream visions, Géla turned: out in the depths of the lake, an enormous Portal was forming, with Un-Maurag and many Marids looming beyond it, and somewhere beyond the Portal's gateway Géla sensed the dark presence of Alcman. Géla wished to cry out to her beloved — go, get away, perhaps you have held your own in this skirmish, but in the greater battle, you are overmatched!

Yet even then, power lashed out from the Wizards — powerful, focused magic with the concentrated power of a Great Spell. That power smashed into the Portal, and as the enchanted gateway collapsed, rolling concussions boomed through the underground cavern, cascading shattered stones from the cavern's roof down into dark waters.

At that moment, all of Julian's hesitation vanished. He turned to the warriors, calling instructions to them, and in one motion, Kalanin and Galad notched greyish-hued arrows and wheeled to face the lone Guardian opposing them. Both shafts lashed simultaneously at the Guardian — but its orb-eye pulsed with power and both arrows were transformed into harmless beams of light. Yet, while arrows were still in flight, Eléna raced from behind her Guardian allies, launching a third darker-colored shaft — and this one buried itself in the grey flesh of the Guardian serving the Demon Princes. Their opponent stumbled backward, grimacing in pain, astonished.

Eléna's Guardian allies turned right to face two Dark Lords with their own powerful sorcery, launching transforming energies at them. Haeglin and Mordred cried aloud, in pain, huge, gnarled bodies shimmering with dark energies as they struggled to maintain their forms.

Then suddenly the Godling named Magog was at Julian's side. The Apprentice invoked his Crystal, then both he and Magog vanished.

Géla found herself drifting from the battle. She was floating away from the light, back into shadowed regions of the caverns, but to what destination *and to what purpose? The Wizards had brilliantly orchestrated their battle, and so she was at the end of this segment of the tale. If there is more, let me be beside my beloved! She could not even recall if he looked worn or strong — he was powerful and resolute, a warrior called to battle, she told herself.*

Now she was floating into dark and deep regions of the Isle, guided by some unseen hand, drifting down a coiled passage, leading to the depths of the Isle. Was she following the Apprentice? Where had Julian and the Godling Magog gone? They had slipped away, passing into Otherwhen, and perhaps, perhaps in dream voyages, she could not travel through Otherwhen...and so, what was being shown to her?

Weightless, floating downward, she smelled death in the air, the ancient and strange deaths of so many, different, sorcerous entities. Her descent halted, and she leveled out, with hints of light beginning to glimmer through the darkness. She turned a corner and recoiled in horror before the Forge of the Demons, a great pit filled with substances that seethed like lava, radiating orange and grey hues, its own substances disturbed by the warfare in distant caverns. A forge, she thought, a place of nightmares, reeking of dark magic. Were the Marids birthed here? What was created before the Marids, and what will come after?

Motion swirled in the air. With the briefest **shudder***, Julian and Magog emerged from nothingness. They had taken side passages through Otherwhen to arrive back at the Forge of the Demons. But why were they here and not enmeshed in battle? Magic pulsed around Géla — but it was Demon magic, not any force that the Apprentice could ever use.*

Now in swift movements, Magog was speeding toward a section of the Forge, where a chamber had been walled off by a massive stone slab. With the power of his own form and the might of his magic, Magog ripped the slab from its foundations. Julian raced into the chamber. Within lay an enormous, dead creature, with a massive, pitted skull — had some Ghoul Giant been created by the Demon Princes, Géla thought, then abandoned as a failure? Now it had been dead so long that only fragments of decaying flesh still stuck to its enormous bones.

Julian reached out and touched the great white bones of its skull and spoke five words. "Arise. Follow me — to battle." In flowing motions, massive white bones reshaped themselves, and grey flesh began covering the creature. Finally, it stood, staring down at Apprentice and Godling with its single orb-eye.

On this dark night, a third Guardian has been freed! Géla exulted. The League! The League will not be put down so easily! Now let us see what shape the battle takes in the great cavern. Perhaps even the malignant Houma might reach the end of his many lives. My beloved, launch a sorcerous arrow into the Sorcerer Houma's dark heart!

Instead of returning to battle, the air around her grew still. All the sights and sounds of her dream voyages slipped away from her. She could smell the salt of the sea air as it reached through the window into her daughter's chamber. A dreamless sleep lapped at the shores of her mind.

Wait, now wait, her mind called into the darkness. Please do not abandon me now. I am forbidden to worship you, but I will love you and your peoples all my days! I am grateful, so grateful, for I have been shown the past — what an incredible journey! You have shown the present to me — beyond all belief, we have opened battle upon the Isle of the Demons! Through Gates of Dreams, we can view the past, the present — but also the future. What of the future, please, a hint, I beg of you!

A moment of indecision hung in the air.

Please, I beg of you, Géla's mind called into the Dreamways.

Then, through Gates of Dreams, she was drawn far from the Isle, back to Alantéa, but high above it, floating down from banks of upper clouds, passing slowly through rain and mist. Below her, as she slowly descended, she recognized the spires of Khiva in the rain. The city seemed strangely still, with the only motion that of water sliding down roofs and through the side gutters of the city's winding streets.

So, her mind whispered, my senses tell me that I've been watching **the past** — and now it seems that I'm encountering the most **likely future**, touched by a shimmering glow that suggests something probable, but not certain. And so, what is to come?

Then, as she drew lower, she could hear the tolling of low, grim bells, and she could see that the populace had gathered together, as it had when they learned that Harlond could not be healed.

No! Her mind called out, not Rostov, not — a sudden thought struck Géla, and her mind became grim and quiet, while she peered forward intently. As she descended, she could feel the moisture seeping all around her. Then, as she drew closer, she could hear more than the ringing of bells and the rushing sounds of water passing down drainpipes, for there were soft, weeping sounds coming from Khiva's central square.

In dreams and in horror she drifted downward, passing through narrow, rain-soaked streets. In the city's square, surrounded by mourners, were two caskets, one that of a warrior, though covered in ruler's purple. The casket beside it was tiny, that of an infant. Between the two caskets stood a haggard Rostov, unable to speak, shaken with grief.

I am dead! Géla's mind cried. Serena is dead! No, wait, her sleeping mind cried out into the darkness.

Now I have been forewarned! We will move into a stronghold. We will be fully armed, and wary, with doors that are barred at three levels. The future has changed — the sun shines down upon Khiva, and its populace goes about its many tasks. Am I right? Tell me that I am right!

The scene shifted and Géla again found herself drifting downward. The day was still mournful, filled with rain. The bells still tolled, endlessly and *grimly. Two caskets, one substantial, one tiny, still lay in the square's center. Rostov was still shaking with grief.*

Yet there was one change: at the square's edge, two figures had been hung on gallows, dead and sagging with gusts of wind. They had been so brutally hacked and hewed that they were now covered in burlap cloth. Rainwater seeping from their nearly bloodless forms was only slightly touched by pink, for most of their blood had drained away.

Retribution! We can destroy the assassins after we ourselves are dead, and that is all that can be changed. We are dead things! I must flee, yet I cannot flee. I must change this — but how?

Géla woke, still in the darkness. She rose and paced, struggling to discover an escape from her destiny; but still, she could not keep the tears from sliding down her face. With her motions and the slight sounds of her grief, Serena began to stir. Géla forced herself to stand beside the window and stare up into the uncaring night sky.

Maker, she prayed, *I understand that you do not intervene in events of the moment, but guide me to one of your servants, or to some other force of destiny, so that I may at least save my daughter's life. Please, please, please, I beg you.*

Behind her in the darkness, Serena's eyes opened, and seeing her mother in supreme distress, her tiny, enchanted mind also formed a prayer. Had Serena the power to form words, her mind would have called out, *Help my mother, help us, please help us.*

· ✕ ·

Now, while the Gift within mortals was strong or weak, it was normally only able to focus shortly after speech came to the child born with the

Gift; and so, all the early spells of young magic wielders were formed from spoken words, invoking, and focusing the sorcerous energies of the Mid-World of the Truce. In the oppressive night darkness, however, with the pain radiating from her mother's grief, and with the brief intense focus of her own, powerful Gift, the focused prayers of Serena formed an infinitely small, though potent *Sending*.

Unseen by mother or daughter, a slender image of a butterfly formed on the child's forehead. Like the ghost of a butterfly, translucent, with hints of blue and gold, *The Sending* lifted upward, gleaming faintly as it flapped its ghostly wings through the rafters and wooden shingles of the roof, passing out into the starlit night skies of Khiva.

Under bright starlight, *The Sending* reveled in brilliant moonlight, gaining strength from the moon's magic, so that its blue and gold hues gleamed in the night. A night raven caught a glimpse of flickering blue and yellow, though as the raven wheeled through dark skies toward its prey, *The Sending* slipped effortlessly from Alantéa into the Mid-World kingdoms of the Powers, searching for guidance and wisdom from the Gods.

Seeking allies and guided perhaps by the collective memories of those serving the League, *The Sending* flapped its enchanted wings first into the realm of Tel-Alantir, to discover an empire in decay. Abandoned, unsupported by its dead God, the sorcerous, transformed matter of Tel-Alantir's domain could no longer even sustain primitive vegetation. Buildings lay toppled. Dust clouds drifted over ruined temples, carried by listless winds. The grey soil of the lifeless ground was separating as though heavy cloud matter sagged apart.

Translucent, gleaming wings flapped through layers of enchantment. As *The Sending* passed into Thoth's kingdom, neither that God, nor his servants, looked up to recognize *The Sending* and its quest.

Wotan's remaining one eye failed to focus on *The Sending* as it passed through his great Hall, though the Ravens attending Wotan became slightly unsettled. Only in the Temple of Pallas Athena did the Goddess stand suddenly and stare into the distance. *Was that the voice of Sentauris calling to me from an enormous distance of time and space? But no, it is only some phantasm that called out, for when mortals died, they were dead forever.*

The Goddess turned, and would no longer harken to remote, fantastic voices.

Translucent, almost invisible, the butterfly image drew a deep breath, sighing as it slipped far from the palaces and temples of the Powers. Now *The Sending* passed into darker regions, seeking one of several Kingdoms of Death.

The way was hard, and *The Sending* faltered. Finally, exhausted, it fluttered down toward the Temple of Waiting, settling down upon Alanthéa, the Tree of Heaven, whose foliage gleamed as the Tree dreamed great visions of Earth's past, its present, and its future. On its branches *The Sending* refreshed itself, gaining strength, its purpose finally made clear; then it swooped down from its branch, passing easily through the massive doors of the Temple of Waiting.

The Sending fluttered overhead into the shadowy reaches of a great Cathedral of Sorrows. Below it, tides of dead immortal Wraiths shifted in shadowy masses over the Temple's polished marble flooring, never at rest, never in torment, lost in dreams, waiting, waiting perhaps forever.

Wraiths of Dragons floated without taking wing. Demons no longer gleamed with red menace, nor did Seraphs and Spirit Lords glisten with gold and silver radiances. And all the frowning, dead Gods had lost focus and power, for their eyes stared into the distance and could see nothing of the past or of the future. All was grey and dim, except that the butterfly's form gleamed anew with hues of blue and gold.

Fluttering downward, *The Sending* sought out the least in stature of all the dead immortals, the human Seeress, Orissa. It paused one split second, then passed effortlessly into the forehead of Orissa. Its epic journey complete, the ghost of a butterfly became one with the mind of the Seeress and was still.

Orissa's eyes blinked twice. She ceased her floating motions, and her feet touched the polished stone flooring of the Temple. She drew a deep breath of stale air — air that could not sustain herself nor any truly living creature for long. The Sorcerer, Hestaur, was needed. Where was Hestaur? She closed her eyes, invoking her Seer's Sight.

Carefully shifting from one milling mass of phantoms into another, she allowed the streams of dead immortals to guide her to the Sorcerer. Then she *reached* within Hestaur and brought him carefully awake in slow stages.

"I understood that we might find ourselves in this place," were the first words of the great Sorcerer, "but only after the last of Earth's magic had become exhausted."

"Yes, I too looked to the Long Sleep, perhaps far in the future," Orissa murmured. "Yet here we are — and now, my great-granddaughter, Serena, many times removed, is calling to me. We must acknowledge that our work is unfinished."

"Air," Hestaur said softly. "I will strengthen the air around us, then we must arouse the other Dreamers."

"An age ago, we sat as Powers in the Hall of the Dreamers," Orissa said, "and now we have become reduced from agents of the Maker's Will, into fading ghosts."

"Ghosts with only tiny vestiges of power," Hestaur replied, "and yet later, perhaps we will become something greater than ghosts."

· X ·

It was done. Night had fallen, and a slow poison was gripping the guards. Alcayna was fully armed. Zur, too, was shielded by metal; his armor clanked as he paced back and forth. He was also slowly changing — a ridge, like some strange beast's now extended from his forehead, and his helmet no longer fit properly.

We must part ways, Alcayna thought. *I do not care much for the man, and though I lust for the beast within the man, we must part ways. Soon, far from here, with riches beyond measure, all matters will come easily. I will treat him to one last night of ecstasy, then there will be an ending, whether he wishes it so or not.*

Houma had stormed and cursed, and threatened, though, in the end, he had yielded two vastly different spells — real magic, not the treacherous devices initially provided. Only one of the original spells remained, and now as they neared the modest three-story dwelling that housed Géla and her child, Alcayna could sense that Houma's potion was spreading death among the guards.

Death. On the first floor Anthera, senior among the guards, lay slumped, dying, face filled with horror. Alcayna brushed past her with a grimace — they had never cared for one another, though Anthera had struggled to appear fair.

Let us hope your Maker appreciates you, Alcayna thought, *for I never did.*

Taking stairs two at a time, they reached the first landing. Guards were sprawled around a great dining table, goblets and dishes cast on the floor as the poison gripped them. Kitchens and guardrooms were maintained on the first floor, dining rooms on the second, with sleeping chambers at the top, where night breezes swept the summer's heat from the building.

Zur raced ahead. She could not hold him back. Panther-like leaps took him beyond the dying guards at the topmost floor. An armored foot smashed open the sleeping chamber. Alcayna panted, racing to keep up with Zur. *Now! Now the bitch would die!*

But within, Géla was fully armored. Something in the shadows — it looked like a tall grey ghost — was holding Serena. Neither the ghost nor the infant seemed at all troubled by the assassins.

"Time to die!" Alcayna shrieked. Zur sprang, growling. Géla darted, sword sweeping through the night air. Zur landed heavily, in two portions — body spurting plumes of blood, while his severed head bounced along the floor.

Counterstroke! Alcayna's sword swept down at Géla. Blades clashed, then clashed again. *Pain!* Alcayna glanced down at the red blood surging from her side. How had her armor failed her? How had her counterstroke been so easily turned aside?

"My life!" she shrieked. "You, who have always had everything, now want to take —" Then Géla's sword swept before Alcayna's eyes, and in a flash of blinding pain all her inner conflict, and knowledge, and awareness passed into an everlasting darkness.

· ☿ ·

Weeks later, many of the citizens of Khiva referred to that night as "Judgment Night," while others called it "The Night of Ghosts."

First, the guards were stirred from dreams of horror. Poisons drained from them; they rose to hear Géla calling down to them. In her chamber, they found the corpses of two fellow guards. These two were traitors who would be quietly buried far outside the city, and all who had dealings with them were questioned carefully.

Not all the citizens of Khiva were as fortunate as the guards. Twenty-seven men and women were found dead in the morning, lives effortlessly ended by the whispers of ghosts. Some of the dead were of dubious character, while others were beyond reproach. What linked these twenty-seven? Rostov would not comment, though he shook his head in disgust as he read a roster of the dead.

Also, two merchant princes, who had quietly, but consistently, cheated the government of Khiva, found themselves awake before midnight, drenched with perspiration, feeling a terrifying need to flee from the city. Servants were woken, families roused and clothed, caravans assembled. It was deep into the night when the two merchants passed beyond Khiva's outermost limit. The pressure on their minds only eased when they could no longer view Khiva's topmost towers, and then the city passed forever beyond their gaze.

Finally, Khiva returned to sleep. Moonlight and starlight gleamed peacefully overhead. Fishers returning from nighttime seining, their holds filled with whitefish, noted a rustling of waters, a stirring of shadows, as a small tide of ghosts passed from the city, traveling swiftly south over the great ocean, following in the distant, vanished wake of the warship, *Alantéa the Forerunner*, toward the Isle of the Demons.

Chapter Fifteen

"We Must Build a Lake of Fire"

"**WE MUST BUILD A** Lake of Fire," Iblis said, and his pronouncement was accompanied by smoke, clouds of particles that showed only traces of flames.

"We have labored long for this moment," Satanis murmured, deep voice rumbling through the Demon Princes' place of power. "No doubt those beings calling themselves 'Gods' have whispered among themselves about our passive stance, why we allowed interlopers to fester upon our own Isle. Now they will encounter a new dimension: Hell will be born, a place of the damned, where all dead magic and dead beings of magic will be drawn — to feed our own power. Should any creature of magic, Kobold or Urak or Sidhe, pass into darkness, there will be no Temple of Waiting for them. Hell will claim their essences, and they will forever twist and turn in torment, while their former power passes to us."

"Sooner or later the Mighty will fall," Iblis added, and now flashes of fire brightened the smoke from his mouth. "Lesser and Greater Gods will perish and pass their core powers into our Lake of Fire. Then this portion of the Universe will understand what a true Greater God is, for we will dampen or destroy the fires of nearby suns that mar the darkness of this planet's nightscape with starlight."

"As always, I have counseled caution," Zikar said evenly. "As we developed the Hell Dimension, we also sought to hold the souls of mortals to prevent them from passing forever from this planet's domain, yet at this moment Hell cannot hold them."

"As Hell gains strength," Iblis murmured, "its reach will grow. One day even the essence of that miserable conjuror Merlin will writhe in a Lake of Fire."

"There is the matter of our 'allies'," Zikar said, though his lips curled in malice as though anticipating the response of his brethren.

Satanis laughed, a low, dark rumbling noise that trembled through the stonework of the chamber. "We will no longer need 'allies' when their essences pass into the core center of Hell, and so their power will become our power."

Iblis nodded. "Hell is calling to us. We must build a Lake of Fire." The powers of the Demon princes fused. Miracle work focused on the great underground lake, that same place where the Demon Princes had launched their Scimitar against the Maker, and the place where the interlopers had fought the first pitched battle of their struggle.

In the great underground dark cavern, tongues of flame began to lift from the lake's surface. At first, nothing but ripples of fire raced along the water's surface, but then the heat rose, and water began to be transformed from a purifying liquid into an energy that was utterly evil.

And so, Hell was born, a place of the damned.

"Become silent, Sorcerer," Mordred muttered.

"For a brief time only," Haeglin added. "After we take counsel together, then we can renew this endless and wearisome pursuit of our enemies." In this region of Otherwhen, a dense, glistening kingdom of ice ruled, though no hint of frost touched the two Dark Lords as they slid away from Houma, leaving the Sorcerer to stand alone in the icy wasteland, as a wicked, chilled wind whipped at his cloak. In the distance, a pale sun radiated red and gold streams over the whiteness, with a halo of flickering light gathering around the distant orb.

Houma stared at the departing Dark Lords with narrow eyes. *What is happening at this moment? I feel a shift in power, as though we are at the edge of some momentous event, while matters are unfolding that I cannot begin to understand, so —*

At that moment, a remote, hidden voice spoke into his ear: Alcman's. "Absent yourself from your dark masters. We must talk."

"They have already distanced themselves. Their mandible-like mouths are not moving, but I will guess that they converse from one distant region of Otherwhen to another distant realm — where Un-Maurag journeys. Is this so?"

"Indeed," Alcman murmured. "Un-Maurag stands alone in the distance, as he has done before, I believe, when conversing with his fellow Dark Lords. Some momentous event transpires: the Demon Princes have long labored on some secret device, and the same miracle work that once brought forth the Marids is now building to a climax.

"Listen closely, Houma of the Withered Hand. These Demon Princes, who would rule the entire known universe, are not above boasting, and so if this new act of creation were no more than some new device that would enhance our cause, we would be learning of it from Demonic mouths that smoked and flamed in triumph. That we know nothing of this mighty event is a cause for great concern. Guard yourself."

"I am warned," Houma said quietly, and he focused on the two Dark Lords who stood silent in the distance. They were completely still, as though they had become gnarled dark columns frozen onto a white, glistening landscape. Yet Houma could feel their turmoil, for an aura of dark sorcery shimmered from their grotesque, towering forms.

No words were spoken aloud between the two Dark Lords, though from a distance they conversed with the most powerful of their brethren: Un-Maurag.

The Demon Princes have long struggled to control alternate dimensions, Un-Maurag sent words into their minds. *Now they have brought forth an enormous receptacle for dying and dead magic, a place they have named Hell.*

Once, Mordred's thoughts raced across the void. *Once we considered that we might over time learn the devices of the Demon Princes and then unseat them. Is this still possible?*

The thoughts of Un-Maurag were tinged with bitter irony. *Though we ourselves may be stronger than many of these so-called Gods, the Demon Princes represent roughly twice our combined strength, and they grow stronger, while we have been unable to gain new power. Our original plans are reduced to dust. Now is the time for us to consider a strategic withdrawal.*

What?!?! Haeglin thought.

How? Mordred countered, having himself entertained thoughts of escape.

Otherwhen beckons, Un-Maurag thought to them. *Not today, not tomorrow, but sometime when the Demon Princes grow so powerful that they no longer need us, or even in the unlikely event that they become challenged by events, and falter. I will draw the Crystal from Alcman the Worm, while you two gather its sister device from Houma the Maggot.*

Since this is a time for truth, Mordred's mind whispered, *we must acknowledge that each of us has held the Sorcerer's Crystal, yet neither of us could force its magic to perform.*

Only seize the Crystal, Un-Maurag raged at them, *then I will break the Maggot's hold over it!*

· ☽ ·

Alcman watched closely as the distant form of Un-Maurag stared intently into the mists, his tall, gnarled form tight with tension. *Un-Maurag is angry, Alcman thought, though his mouth is grim and motionless, his mind is raging at Haeglin and Mordred. Now he is done, and instead of returning the Dark Lord surges deeper into the mists. Still filled with menace, Un-Maurag splashes his way through rain pools and banks of mist, leaving me alone to contemplate the endless dampness and drizzle of this forsaken world. Power and anger surge from the Dark Lord's form, yet not even a hint of dampness touches his long, greyish, dark cloak. Why has he not returned to me and attempted again to wrest the Crystal of Otherwhen from me? Perhaps he is trying to calm himself first, and so some deception will be planned. A child would not be deceived by this monster.*

Alcman shook his head grimly and continued with his dark thoughts. *Rainworld, I am trapped in Rainworld, left staring into overcast skies. I reach for the edge of the overhead cloud cover, yet in this portion of Otherwhen, the clouds and rain have no end. What happens to all the water of this world if no sun shines? Does its water slide off its oceans into some other portion of Otherwhen? Into some Desert World? And why did Un-Maurag require me to bring him to this forever, forsaken place? Did he seek to distance himself from the Demon Princes as they fashioned their great miracle work?*

As Alcman watched Un-Maurag from a distance, a hint of red fur flashed in the corner of the Sorcerer's left eye. Alcman wheeled and blasted Julian's small fox-servant with dark fire. In one split second nothing was left but a tuft of darkened red fur. *Rafir, Alcman thought, the creature was called Rafir. Now it is gone forever.*

Alcman knelt beside a rain pool and turned the blackened red tuft through his fingers. Something remarkably close to sorrow flooded through his mind. *Why did I destroy it? I no longer believe in the Demon Princes and their cause, so why would I so quickly blast a small emissary without even asking its purpose? And why do I now feel such sorrow? In our madness, Houma and I destroyed Tel-Alantir with all the mindless ferocity of the insane. Now I falter at this small death. What is happening to me?*

As Alcman knelt and entertained strange thoughts, a clear, soft voice whispered into his ear:

"You're supposed to be glad that I'm dead, but you're not. The Great Guardian will be surprised. Anyway, I'm alive. What you killed was only a ghost, a ghost with a message. The Great Guardian uses me as an emissary, and I'm supposed to tell you that Hell has been created. I don't know what that means, but I can feel the Great One's fear. He says you must guard your Crystal of Otherwhen carefully because the Dark Lords will wish to escape from the Lake of Fire. Do you understand?" Alcman nodded imperceptibly, and suddenly the voice and the presence of the fox vanished.

The Sorcerer stood. Finally, Un-Maurag had turned and was moving toward him, slowly and cautiously, passing untouched through banks of mist and drizzle, but the Dark Lord was unable to disguise the menace of his approach.

Alcman let the tuft of red fur slip from his fingers. *What has just happened in these last seconds? If our roles were reversed, I would encourage our opponents to quarrel and fight among themselves, and even destroy each other. The fox has been sent to warn me, and this must be the strangest event to take place upon this completely and utterly perverse Isle of the Demons.*

When the Godlings wished to speak privately, their nearly lightless bodies rode the offshore winds. As sunset passed into dusk, the Godlings rose over the Isle's shore, gleaming into the oncoming night: Phaedra, with the red hues of the Demons, and the silver of the Spirit Lords; Turin with the gold of the Seraphs, mixed with the green of Dragons; and Magog radiating the blue and dark grey colors of the Mid-World of the Truce. All three floated in midair as the soft winds of nightfall held them aloft, though the gentle airstreams could no longer calm their thoughts.

"We cannot win this war," Phaedra murmured into the oncoming night.

"Has our alliance not grown stronger over time?" Magog asked. "Thus far we have freed three Guardians, and now we are linked with the greatest of the Guardians. Have not events turned in our favor?"

"Our own strength increases, hour by hour," Turin added. "Already I can foresee a time when we three alone might match the power of the Dark Lords."

"Ha!" Phaedra muttered, then she subsided. "No, you may be correct; I do know that not one of us, alone, could prevail against Un-Maurag. Yet one day, we three, as a combined force, might equal the three Dark Lords. Yet at the core of this unequal struggle lies the enormous power of the Demon Princes. Nothing in Alantéa, or upon this Isle, or in the Far Lands, is their equal."

"Then why," asked Turin, "have they not moved more openly against us?"

Phaedra stared silently into the oncoming night for a moment before speaking. "You know that I have little affection for the Wizards, but Merlin's perception is powerful. As he stared into the Forge of the Demons, he saw that some great demonic miracle work had begun. A new dimension has been created, a deadly, evil underworld universe that will power the cause of the Demon Princes. Hell has been born, a place of the damned that draws all dead and dying magic into its dark substances."

Turin stared at Phaedra, his own gold and green radiances gleaming in the last light of dusk. "So, the Demon Princes have sent images to you, accompanied by words. Do I understand this matter correctly?"

Phaedra nodded slowly. "Not only has Hell been born, but the Demon Princes are now released to come against us in the fullness of their own, matchless strength. We cannot win this war. And so, when Zikar, Prince of Demons, reached out to me, I listened only, refusing to respond. Thus, I have not betrayed you, my brethren."

Turin continued to study Phaedra. "Still, you are conflicted, as all three of us are. If we examine our true natures, the Mid-World of the Truce — with all its confusion and malice — created us to be at war with ourselves. What did Zikar, Prince of Demons, and great architect of the Demons' war against the Mid-World, suggest to you?"

Phaedra stared for a moment into a distant star-scape, then spoke in a low voice. "Zikar noted that since we have now grown to full power, that we should be entitled to the lone Crystal of Otherwhen supporting our cause, and to the ordering of those Guardians that have been freed by virtue of our power."

"Malice," muttered Magog. "Pure malice. I have not the subtlety of thought shown by you two, my brethren, but I can recognize the pure malice of Demon Princes when it shows itself so transparently."

Turin nodded thoughtfully. "I do not see us waylaying the Apprentice and seizing his Crystal. Aside from our sworn allegiances, we should note that the newly freed Guardians are never far from Julian. But it does seem reasonable to ask of the Great Guardian and of Merlin what is to come in the next phase of this war."

Phaedra still would not meet Turin's eyes, but Magog murmured, "Let us have that discussion. We will learn much not only from their words, but from how much fear radiates from their faces, and how their bodies twitch when they lie to us." The three Godlings began drifting downward, while above them the Cloudshelf sustained by the Emissaries of the Gods, gleamed brilliantly in the night sky.

· Ж ·

As Dark Lords approached crystal-bearing Sorcerers, and as Alcman readied for flight from his Rainworld, and as Houma schemed one last coup of malice in his Iceworld — suddenly, an image of Zikar projected itself into both of these dismal portions of Otherwhen. In its projection, the figure of Zikar was gigantic, dwarfing even the enormously tall figures of the Dark Lords. And Zikar's image radiated a power that could not be withstood.

"You must return to the Isle of the Demons." Zikar's image loomed high over desolate landscapes. "Much has been asked of you, while even greater efforts are now required. The Mid-World of the Truce has launched two incursions upon our heartland, yet the so-called 'Gods' have never understood that the Isle of the Demons will be the capital of an empire that will one day encompass so many galaxies. These intruders are about to be destroyed. Leave your small discords aside and come before us. You must return — *now!*"

Nor did the image of Zikar dissolve until skulking Dark Lords had gathered to the sides of Sorcerers and all the servants of the Demon Princes had returned from Otherwhen back to the Isle of the Demons. Then Rainworld and Iceworld were left again to their silent, desolate half-lives.

· Ж ·

As the Godlings descended from the upper skies, dusk finally passed into darkness. Down at the edge of a coiled, sandy beach, Merlin was waiting for them, together with his emissary, the eagle. Overhead, the last glow of dusk had yielded to starlight, joined by the pale yellow of a haunted Sickle of the Maker Moon. The Cloudshelf to the north seemed to gleam with an unusual intensity as though the Gods had been stirred by the birth of the Hell Dimension, and more of their greatest Emissaries were being drawn to the Mid-World's Cloudshelf stronghold.

Merlin and the eagle stood near the shore's edge, while a few hundred paces inland, Julian and Eléna watched from a distance, with Kalanin to their right and Galad to their left. Behind the humans loomed a force of three Guardians. Phaedra and Magog glanced at Turin and nodded, a sign that Turin's understanding had been correct: Guardians lingered near Julian, becoming both allies and bodyguards of the Apprentice.

Phaedra led the Godlings as they approached Merlin: three tall gleaming figures towered over the Wizard and his emissary, the eagle. Dusk had calmed the ocean so that only faint rippling noises could be heard from the shoreline behind the Godlings.

"It is time, Wizard," Phaedra said, "time for a council of war."

"Time for a council," Merlin said softly, glancing into each of the Godlings' faces, "and so we stand before you."

"In this matter," the eagle croaked, "I speak not for my master, Merlin, but as an emissary of the Great Guardian. Behold! The Great Guardian tells us that Hell has been born, a dimension that converts dead and dying magic into powerful energies that flow into the dark devices of the Demon Princes. We must all stand ready, for the next assault will come with unparalleled ferocity."

"We know of Hell, and have been warned," Phaedra said, eyes narrowing as she stared down at Merlin. The Wizard said nothing, only regarding the Godlings evenly, while behind the three, a fringe of white surf spread itself quietly over the moonlit shoreline of the Isle of the Demons.

Magog stared into the nighttime pattern of stars, glancing briefly at the Cloudshelf housing the Emissaries. "I am unsubtle, and so I will ask you directly: what is our plan for the coming battle?"

"We must arm ourselves mightily," Merlin replied, "and while preparing to flee, we might look for an opening, a knife thrust in the dark that might wound our foes — but we can deliver only light wounds, for we lack weapons capable of dealing a death blow to a Demon Prince."

"Ha!" Phaedra snarled. "This is a plan?!?"

But then Turin interrupted, waving her to silence. Glancing into the distance, he asked, "Why does the Apprentice not stand at your side? We have watched his progression from follower to forerunner. Surely, he was fated to become one of the great principals of this war. Why does he not stand before us to speak of his visions, to add his own insight?"

·))(·

From a distance, Julian murmured these same words, for the Seer's Sight within him, had now grown so powerful that no spell-work was required for the Apprentice to overhear distant conversations.

"Turin is speaking. He asks, 'Why does the Apprentice not stand at your side? We have watched his progression from follower to forerunner. Surely, he was fated to become one of the great principals of this war. Why does he not stand before us to speak of his visions, to add his own insight?' Kalanin and Galad watched Julian closely, for these thoughts had also arisen in their own minds.

"Now comes Merlin's response," Julian whispered under his breath. "He must speak the truth, and his reply may be most embarrassing. Let us leave this alone."

"We need to know," Kalanin said softly; Julian nodded slowly, then continued.

"Merlin speaks: 'Julian the Apprentice has been the savior, not only of the Wizards' League but also of the Mid World of the Truce. Yet it is unwise to consider him as a Power; instead, think of him as a catalyst capable of transforming events. Where Julian moves, Destiny and Fate are challenged, but do not think of him as a Power....'"

Julian trailed off, then added, "I am content to be nothing more than a catalyst. Who would truly wish to be a Power contending with Demon Princes?"

"Their mouths are still moving," Eléna prompted.

"The Godlings have grown angry," Julian said. "They raise their voices against Merlin and the Eye, while Wizard and Familiar provide even-tempered responses, prompting the Godlings to bicker among themselves."

Galad stifled a yawn. "It feels like time for a nap. Our own roles as lower-level, dimwitted guards have become noticeably unchallenging. If only fate would send us some minor threats like a few fire-breathing gnats that could easily be swatted by our mighty, sorcerous blades."

Then, Galad yawned openly. "So, Captain Hangnail, what do you think of our chances in the next battles? Warfare between Powers looms; we leap around bravely, waving our swords in defiance until some casual blast of magic ends our portion of this tale. Do I have that right?"

Kalanin nodded grimly, but Eléna lowered her voice until it was almost a whisper. "Julian is strongly protected, and the Wizards cannot be touched by stray magic. Noting our vulnerabilities, the Great Guardian is forging amulets and talismans to protect the three of us. Battle looms, yet we will be shielded before our next collision with Fate. As for your boredom, Galad, you may soon long for a return of these days."

"Protection, that's to the good," Julian added, "and also, one less worry for this Apprentice." His eyes had been following the glow of the Cloudshelf refuge. "Yet now the bickering between Godlings and the Wizard fades, and a real dialogue is renewed. Do you wish to hear these words? The three humans nodded, while behind them, the orb-eyed Guardians leaned forward intently."

· Ж ·

"Enough," Phaedra said, struggling to control herself. "I now understand that the Demon Princes have deliberately disengaged themselves from this struggle so that they might enhance their already enormous power. Now they are mightier, and free to come against us. That is why I told my Godling brethren that we could not win this war. I challenge you, Merlin, and you, the spokes-creature of the Great Guardian to refute my understanding of these matters. Let me say again, in clear words, untouched by twisted thoughts: we cannot win this war!"

"As 'spokes-creature' of the Great Guardian," the eagle croaked, wings flaring, "I see matters through his eyes. His vision is far broader than yours, encompassing the heights, and the breadths, and the depths of this tormented Isle. He beholds a massive wall of black clouds advancing toward us, a fate that is filled with a fury of destruction, determined to crush us forever. Yet off to either side of this darkness, brilliant bright lights dance in the haze, and beams of hope flicker, trembling with new possibilities. And so, we are *not* doomed."

"That is *not* an answer," Turin said, and even his normally clear and calm voice shook with anger.

"May I be permitted to restate your original question?" Merlin asked evenly. "Do we see a clear path to victory in this war? And the answer is, of course, that we cannot perceive any such path. Are we doomed to be defeated and destroyed? And the answer to that question is also negative — we are not doomed.

"But let us suppose for a moment that we were doomed," Merlin continued. "Death is not the end for any of us. Behold: all things will be remade in brilliant hues by the Maker at the End of Time. I live with the certainty of our revival, and through Gates of Dreams I walk through vales more wondrous than any of Earth's gardens."

Merlin sighed. "Yet the creation of Hell has made of death the greatest of nightmares. If the Maker gave me the strength, I would hurl the Hell Dimension into the depths of space, into the void, to drift forever chilled and frozen until the end of time.

"Hell is the most evil creation ever conceived by the Demon Princes, evil beyond any of our worst fears; though at present the nightmare exists only for immortals, but not for humans. Mortals cannot be drawn into the Abyss — not at this moment, anyway. Hear me: if our enterprise were truly doomed — which it is not — the Wizards would send the immortal Godlings and Guardians through side passages of Otherwhen back to Alantéa, to aid the Powers of the Mid-World in forging new defenses against the Demon Princes. With them would go our four young human allies and their servants, as seedlings to spread hope among mortal peoples of Alantéa the Forerunner.

"As for the Wizards, Thorian, and Balardi and I have agreed to form a sacrificial rearguard. We would raise the standard of the Maker upon this tortured Isle — and we would be quickly overwhelmed and destroyed. Yet at the last, we would perish having fulfilled our core purpose. Perhaps even the Maker, who sits at the heart of the universe, at the center of all understanding, would take note of our deaths, and activate yet another of his deeply hidden, multiplex devices. Now, are you answered?"

The Godlings could only stare down in wonder at the slight form of the Wizard, and the even smaller winged emissary who stood on the beach beside Merlin, an eagle who stared at the Godlings with bright, defiant eyes.

· 𝕏 ·

Julian walked slowly through the moonlight toward the beach where Merlin conversed with the Godlings. As Kalanin followed, he felt a chill of cold metal touching his skin: around his neck, three loose bands of metal ringlets settled, while bracelets of slender steel covered each wrist. Kalanin turned to Galad and Eléna to confirm that both had been given similar amulets and talismans, forged, as promised, by the Great Guardian.

And so, battle loomed; but which battle, which struggle came first — the intruders on the Isle, or the Emissaries of the Gods on their Cloudshelf? Kalanin looked to Julian, while behind them, the huge grey Guardians cast broad moonlit shadows over the beach, and their feet sank ankle deep into soft sands as they followed behind the four humans.

"I believe that the Cloudshelf will be first," Julian said softly, as though reading Kalanin's mind. "The Demon Princes see almost nothing of us, while each day an Island in the Sky offends the vision of the Demon Princes and tells them that the Powers of the Mid-World remain undefeated." Julian fell silent as they neared Merlin and the Godlings. As they drew closer to one another, Thorian and Balardi emerged from around a slight curl of the beach, walking toward their allies.

Behold my father, Eléna thought. *How strong and determined he seems! At his side is Balardi, Julian's mentor and benefactor. I have spoken perhaps ten words with my father's Wizard ally, and so I know little about him. I should, I will speak with Balardi, during an interval between battles — if we are granted an interval.*

"Now, you have all come together," the eagle croaked. "The Great Guardian has long studied the ways of Demon Princes, and he believes they will seek first to clear the Cloudshelf, the Island in the Sky. Apprentice with a Seer's Sight, what is happening overhead?"

Julian stared up into the night sky. Words, halting words, slipped hesitantly from his lips. "Portals are flashing as the Emissaries of the Gods prepare for battle...many hundreds of the Gods' chief Emissaries have now gathered, some bearing sorcerous machineries of war, and so, the Powers are also preparing for this moment..." Julian trailed off, then took a deep breath before continuing. "I can perceive matters only from a distance, and from what I can see the Emissaries move with strength and purpose — yet I can also feel their fear."

"Even I feel fear," the eagle murmured. "The Cloudshelf will be the first focus of the Demon Princes. The intruders upon their Isle will be next. Be prepared to flee." As the eagle spoke these last words, the Eye of Merlin vanished.

Dark thoughts flashed through Galad's mind. *A vanishing act, a device we never dreamed of mastering. But now I must bring a halt to these wayward thoughts, for the Eye of Merlin has always been the most stalwart, even headstrong of our allies. In spite of his words, the eagle has truly never shown the slightest fear, but I can feel dread all around me — from Godlings, and Guardians, and Wizards, together with their mortal followers — including the fears of this clumsy warrior, known as Galad of the Tarnished Sword.*

· ☿ ·

Fear also troubled Alcman's thoughts as he stood under a broad, cloudless moonlit sky, surrounded by the forces serving the Demon Princes. *From a distance, I studied the Powers of the Mid-World in all their willful majesty and might. Envy grew within me until I wished for enormous, God-like strength, and life everlasting, and step by step I have lowered myself down into an abyss of horror.*

To the north, the Island in the Sky radiated increasing might, gleaming as the Gods sent waves of Emissaries to reinforce their Cloudshelf stronghold. But below, to the south of the Cloudshelf, the Sorcerer's allies were arrayed in arcs of unmatched force: at the forefront stood the three Demon Princes, Satanis to the right, Iblis to the left, while Zikar stood centermost. Alcman understood that Zikar could not claim to be the greatest of the Demon Princes; instead, Zikar was the guiding force and architect of their war against the Gods.

Behind the Demon Princes loomed three tall, gnarled Dark Lords: Un-Maurag at the center, Mordred to his right, and Haeglin to his left. Beside Haeglin stood the tiny figure of Houma, hunched and leaning forward, staring into the moonlit Cloudshelf on the horizon with all the Sorcerer's customary malice and intensity. Alcman stood to Mordred's right, his demeanor carefully shielded by a deep chill so that none could read from his body the tumult of emotions that surged through his mind.

Houma and I have become no more than the tiniest of creatures, Alcman thought, *ranged as servants the size of insects beside enormously powerful Gods. We stand together on the killing fields of the Demon Princes; I can still smell the scent of death rising from those fields. We are aphids frozen in the moonlight, trapped in a graveyard that's filled with ghosts. How did our quest for power come to this?*

Behind Dark Lords and Sorcerers stood an arc of six Guardians, orb eyes gleaming, ready to beam transforming energies into the skies. Silently, Alcman counted the Guardians. *Six of ten Guardians have been drawn into this moment, leaving only four to guard the Isle of the Demons and maintain its internal sorceries. Somehow, I do not think we need to fear a counterstrike.*

The last arc was composed of Marids, a total of less than forty God-destroyers remaining. Alcman used the power within him to count the Marids, without overtly turning to glance behind him. *What were there in total at the beginning, seventy-two Marids? And now only thirty-nine remain. Let us see...the greatest of them was lost in some struggle orchestrated by the Wizards. I could communicate with the first among the Marids if only a little. That Marid wished for power beyond that granted to him by the Demon Princes, and each of us understood that we might be able to use the other, but then the most powerful of the Marids vanished forever.*

The Sorcerer continued with his count of Marids alive and destroyed: *And after the fall of the greatest Marid, in the Vale of Whispers, two fell to the war-party led by the Apprentice, while twenty-seven were destroyed in battle with the Gods, together with Cronar and Eudox...strange that I no longer think about our sworn Sorcerer confederates, while Houma might even struggle to recall their names. Since those battles we have passed through many great expanses of Otherwhen, then joined battle upon the Isle of the Demons. On this day, that great struggle with the Wizards and their League seems no more than a distant dream.*

One more Marid was destroyed in the hold of the warship Alantéa, Alcman continued. *Finally, two more were lost in battle beside the underground lake, killed by the slender but deadly sorcerous arrows of our foes. Thirty-three have been destroyed of seventy-two Marids birthed by Demon Princes, and that leaves the thirty-nine behind me.*

So much for the Marids. Greater events await us, for now begins the destruction of the last outpost of the Mid-World. A whisper within his mind distracted him. *One of my warning devices is telling me to stop up my ears, yet all is silent except for the deep and heavy breathing of the Marids behind me. Yet I constructed these whispers for just such a purpose and so I will add to the chilling of my troubled body, a great lessening of my hearing...there, I can no longer even hear the deep breathing of the Marids behind me.*

But Alcman could feel the stress rise, the tension all around him building. In unison, the three Demon Princes took one great step forward, eyes fixed on the Cloudshelf. Magic, unbidden, was being drawn from Alcman's body. Over the years, his human form had become a storehouse of sorcerous energies and now those forces were leaving him. Alcman struggled to stop the flow, but he could not. *I have become a **thing**, a small cog in a great machine when once I dreamed of being a viceroy, even the true ruler of Earth behind three Demon Princes who were only figureheads.*

Then the Demon Princes hurled a great surge of dark energy at the Cloudshelf, a blackness that absorbed light and blasted all forms of magic from its path. Great clusters of cloud-matter were sent hurtling away, reeling into the night skies. Moonlight was hidden for a moment by scattered cloud matter. A hint of a smile creased Alcman's mouth. *That was simple, and it was almost silent, so that only the rushing sounds of distant machineries could be sensed. Perhaps I should have stopped up my nostrils, for the stench of the Demon Princes when they wield such power is nearly overwhelming.*

Suddenly Alcman was blinded by great sheets of lightning. Damaged, but not destroyed, the Shelf had responded: lightning surged down from above, smashing at the Demons' fortress; waves of flame surged over the headlands so that its upper forests burned; great ocean waves were sent spilling over the shoreline, lashing at the Isle's interior; and earthquakes shook the ground so that the granite and limestone plates beneath the Isle trembled, and hundreds of cavern-systems collapsed, crushing thousands of the monstrosities that lay concealed within the Isle's hidden places.

Alcman's sight cleared, and he steadied himself so that he would not be thrown from his feet. Blasts of thunder were breaching his hearing barriers, so he reinforced those devices, though even minor magic was becoming a struggle. *Weak, I am growing weaker, and though I struggle to regain control of the magic within me, my own body will not respond to my mind. I have become no more than an ancient, diseased Goblin, controlled by forces I cannot hope to counter.*

Now, the Demon Princes stepped a second pace forward. Mouths open, torrents of fire were followed by a **Shout,** focused rage followed by destruction. Alcman sank to his knees as his body weakened, while behind him Marids boomed and hooted in agony, their sense of hearing overwhelmed by pain, huge feet stomping the ground in desperation. Dark Lords and Guardians wobbled, struggling to maintain themselves while Houma fell to the ground, writhing and shrieking with pain as he struggled to stop up his hearing with both hands.

That **Shout**, sonic rage powered by an enormous, focused blast of magic, tore the Cloudshelf from its moorings and blasted its substance into scores of lesser cloud masses. All the Shelf's inner structures were destroyed. As Emissaries floated free from the Shelf, Portals flared, then the Emissaries of the Gods fled in terror. *It is over,* Alcman thought, *and I will survive to restore myself...unless the Gods...have become foolhardy. Hear me, Powers of the Mid-World! Know that I have no love for you, but do not come here! Hell will be invoked, and you will be swallowed up and burn eternally in its depths! Flee to your own domains and reinforce them!*

Yet the Gods in their pride and their blindness would not be so easily turned aside. Enormous Portals flared and the Greater Gods who supported the age-old Mid-World of the Truce used their power to reach down into scattered Cloudshelf so that all its matter gathered again in the skies to the North of the Isle of the Demons.

Alcman's hands trembled with fear. *The Gods are not content to simply counter the Demon Princes. I can feel the **trembling** in the skies above me! My hands twitch, struggling to reach the Crystal of Otherwhen, but I no longer can control my own body!* Alcman, still on his knees, stared helplessly upward as an accumulation of Skyfall began toppling toward the Isle of the Demons.

From overhead, scores of huge sky-stones were being gathered by the Portal-magic of the Gods. Some hovered overhead, while others raced toward the Isle, and now meteors of molten stone, and comets flaring trails of vapor began surging toward the Isle.

Guardians turned skyward, orb eyes flaring as they launched transforming energies at the huge masses of metal and molten stone, and frozen cones of vapor cast down at them. Comets and flaming meteors were transformed into ashes, or great billows of air, or sheets of rainwater — though not all the debris was transformed. Explosions rocked the Isle as Skyfall struck both the earth and the ocean surrounding the Isle.

Concussions, waves of destruction radiated from impact craters, while from the surrounding ocean, tsunamis — gigantic walls of water — raced toward the Isle of the Demons, ready to wash it clear of all its dark, Demonic magic. Alcman struggled to his feet and stood, staring overhead, transfixed by doom, as did Marids and Guardians and Dark Lords. Only Houma remained stricken on the ground, though the Sorcerer's arms and legs thrashed, while his mouth gibbered and shrieked insane defiance at the skies and the universe beyond.

At the farthest edges of the Isle, Julian invoked his Crystal and led his masters and their allies and followers deep into one of the most remote kingdoms of Otherwhen.

While upon the Isle, with destruction raging everywhere around them, the Demon Princes smashed their fists together and called upon their most powerful magic, drawing sorcerous energies from all those around them. Marids sank to the earth, groaning and pounding the earth with their huge fists. Alcman collapsed, joining a senseless Houma on the ground. Guardians sank to their knees, orb-eyes slowly closing as they lost focus. Haeglin and

Mordred would have sagged down, yet they were not permitted to do so, for Un-Maurag held each of them upright, though his tall, gnarled shape shuddered with the strain.

A sky shield formed above the Isle of the Demons. Comets and meteors were deflected, surging off to the horizon's edges, ready to spread ruin to the Far Lands. Explosions within the Isle were dampened, muted, turned back upon themselves so that all their radiating waves of violence boiled down through the trembling foundations of the Isle, or surged upward, passing with shuddering sounds through the sky shield overhead.

Alcman lay senseless upon the ground. He shook with pain, and his eyes blinked open: face skyward, he watched as a few hundred feet overhead, mountains of dark ocean water passed over the Demon's sky shield, speeding on their way to the Far Lands, preparing to spread ruin to all the other continents of Earth. Alcman sobbed, struggling to breathe. He was spent, for all the sorcerous energies within him had been squeezed from his enchanted body by the Demon Princes. Water still surged overhead. Comets were still rebuffed by the Demons' sky shield.

Alcman groaned, gasping. Air finally filled his lungs, and he rolled onto his side. Clutching his Crystal with both hands, he tried to activate it — but he was drained, and nothing came of his efforts. *Doom...but wait, wait.* He reached *through* the Crystal for sources of magic — and power began flowing from Otherwhen back into his body.

Now he was at least partially restored. In a few moments, he could flee into Otherwhen — though that would leave Houma and his Crystal behind. That Crystal would likely be used by Houma and other allies of the Demon Princes to follow him into Otherwhen. Perhaps now was not the best time to flee. Did his Sorcerer ally still live?

Still on his side, pretending to gulp air, Alcman's mind reached out to Houma's.

Houma, listen! You are a dead thing unless you reach through your Crystal and draw energy from Otherwhen. Houma, draw magic to your body, or be drained and die!

Hell is coming, Houma's mind gibbered. *Hell is coming — for us! HaHaHa.*

Houma, arise now, or die!

Houma has become completely insane, Alcman thought. *Once there were four Sorcerers, and now I am alone — although now, Houma is quieting, and I can feel a strength of magic building within him. So, part of his mind was able to hear me, and now he draws upon Otherwhen. Houma will survive, at least for a while — is that good, is that really, really a good thing?*

Alcman stared skyward: overhead, meteors had become distant streaks of light and the walls of ocean water assailing the Isle had passed, though storms still lashed at the Isle's shoreline, and fires continued to rage in its forested highlands. He struggled to his feet. Bewildered Marids still lay gaping at the skies, but now a few were crawling, struggling to stand. All but one of the Guardians also stood, orb-eyes fixed on Demon Princes...and finally the last of the exhausted Guardians was standing.

The huge heads of Demon Princes rested upon equally enormous necks, so when Zikar wished to regard the mass of drained and bedraggled followers behind him, his whole body was forced to turn toward them. Dark Lords, Guardians, Marids and Sorcerers were all now standing, and Zikar nodded. Yet when Zikar glanced at the Sorcerers, Alcman sensed a hint of surprise.

Alcman stared back at the Demon Prince impassively. *You did not expect us to survive, did you, Zikar? Houma and I were to become convenient casualties, were we not? How astonished you would have been that the Crystals you wished to inherit have become attuned only to your two mortal allies and are now almost worthless in your hands, and worth even less in the scaly, claw-like hands of Un-Maurag and his hideous brethren.*

Demon Princes and their allies stood, arrayed as before in arcs of power. Energies flooded back into each rank. Alcman renewed the chill within his body but let his hearing return to normal. Drawing a deep breath, he glanced first at the Cloudshelf, then stared intently at the Demon Princes.

For a third time, the Demon Princes stepped forward, raising their hands as though invoking a distant force of magic. Slender lines of sorcerous fire began to reach skyward. A remote portion of Alcman's mind told him that the lines of fire were truly no more threatening than a lightly burning grape arbor, with grape leaves being slowly consumed from the ground up; but all the senses of sorcery built up over the long decades understood that he had come into the presence of Hell, and his chilled body shook.

Hell is coming for me, Alcman thought, *and I must flee — but Houma, supported by powerful allies, would track me down into the most remote crevices of Otherwhen. When I sought my future among thousands of alternate futures, none of those possibilities included my tortured soul burning in endless agony, trapped in a Lake of Fire....*

The grasp of Hell seemed slight, but spider web networks of Hellfire were reaching skyward. Heavy rains slashed down from above; Hell feasted on their waters and on the sorcery supporting them so that the strands of Hellfire sped higher.

Fools! Alcman's mind shouted at the Emissaries powering the Cloudshelf. *Your magic only feeds the fires of Hell!*

Now, billows of dust gathered overhead; descending dust storms strove to choke the always climbing network of flames. Wild winds lashed dust and rain at coils of Hellfire. The flames of Hell only burned brighter, reaching always higher into the night skies.

Great Gods of the Mid-World are you insane, or merely stupid?!? Alcman's mind shrieked at them. *You seek to counter Fire with Earth and Air and Water, but you deal not with Fire alone, but with Hellfire! Pull your Cloudshelf far from here, before Hell feasts upon it!*

The Cloudshelf seemed to tug itself skyward, as though the Gods had finally understood the reach of Hell. Yet now it was too late. The first strands of Hellfire reached into the Shelf's lower banks, and a dull ruby glow began spreading upward from its base.

Just beyond his hearing, outside of his senses, Alcman felt the sky weep, and for the first time since his childhood, he prayed, no longer as he once had, to the many Powers of the Mid-World, but now to the Maker, a God in whom he had never believed.

Lord of the Universe, I cannot begin to comprehend your true nature, nor the reach of your power, nor will I ever understand your unwillingness to intrude upon the affairs of Earth. I do know that you will not intervene to save your servants or punish your adversaries. But surely here, at this moment, when the greatest evil in Earth's long history reaches from a pit of horror, seeking to consume the sky, you should put this malignancy down. Maker, I beg only this of you: rid Hell from Earth.

The terror in Alcman's mind passed beyond words. Face stiff with horror, he stared skyward as Hell's coils swept upward like a tide of enormous spider webs. The Cloudshelf, a mass that now seethed with dusky hues of ruby-red, was gathered down to the lower depths of the Isle of the Demons so that Hell could gorge itself upon the Cloudshelf's power until the last strands of its magic were consumed.

Chapter Sixteen

Into the Farthest Reaches
of Otherwhen

JULIAN STOOD, BODY MOTIONLESS, staring into the gloom of a dying portion of Otherwhen. Even from this remote region of Otherwhen, Julian could sense the birth of Hell, and he bowed his head and prayed: *Maker, I know you wish the Powers of Earth to resolve all these matters themselves, but I must beg this of you: do not permit Hell to be born. Hell is the end product of all our bad choices, our final nightmare. Please stop it, Lord of the Infinite Universe.*

Julian looked up. Eléna reached out and held his hand. They had hidden cautiously in the most remote regions of Otherwhen, where an overcast, dreary sky left only vague shadows on the ground.

A short distance away, Godlings and Wizards had called up an enormous Vision Portal, and stood with Guardians and mortal allies, watching as Gods and Demons fought over the sorcerous Isle of the Demons. With the gloom around them, Hellfire's radiance, blazing from their Vision Portal, cast a red glow over their faces.

Julian turned away, unwilling to watch any longer. Eléna clutched his hand, eyes watching transfixed, as Hell began to grasp the Cloudshelf of the Gods.

Phaedra finally turned to Merlin. "What are we doing here, Wizard?" she snarled. "Death and Hellfire are coming for us, while your so-called Gods have scurried away, gone to hide in their Mid-World bolt holes. How did we, the Godlings, ever let ourselves become linked with this feeble alliance with mortals?"

Merlin pulled himself away from the nightmare of Hellfire. "The Demon Princes will focus on the destruction of the Cloudshelf," he murmured. "Do we now flee forever into the depths of Otherwhen, or is there time for a brief counterstrike?"

"We have a chance to free another Guardian," Julian said, turning to the Wizard. "But first — Eléna, does the Great Guardian need our aid against this new force of Hellfire?"

Merlin studied the two younglings carefully, while Phaedra's face flared with hostility. How had their decision making been passed to these two feeble mortals?

"I do not believe the Demons can discover the Great One's hidden places," Eléna said softly, then her mind reached out into Julian's: *Dream empires lie within dream empires. As he has done before, the Great Guardian will retreat into the inner reaches of his own enchantments. I, too, was shielded there for a time, until I was permitted to walk beside you along the shore.*

"The Mid-World's Cloudshelf is doomed, Wizard," Turin said, "and Hellfire burns more brightly with each second that passes. It is time now to withdraw into the depths of Otherwhen."

One Guardian stepped forward; orb-eye gleaming intently. "Do we understand this matter correctly?" the Guardian asked, voice soft, almost unused, and hollow. "You are discussing whether to free a fourth of our imprisoned brethren to join our ranks?"

"A foray back to the Isle," Julian said, speaking swiftly. "You, who were first freed, and a second Guardian will join us, together with Phaedra, and Eléna, armed with her enchanted weapons." He turned toward Phaedra and Merlin. "Godling and Wizard, our moment of opportunity closes. Do we return to the Isle now — or never again?" The Wizard nodded slowly, then watched warily as Phaedra turned her face toward dark skies, muttering in frustration before finally bowing her head in resignation.

Julian activated his Crystal, leading his strange, mixed war party seven paces over stone fragments. Then with a *shudder,* they passed from a lost, dying portion of Otherwhen back to the Isle of the Demons, cloaked and disguised by the transforming energies of two Guardians.

As they vanished, Galad glanced around him and took a deep breath. As always, at the fringes of these fading portions of Otherwhen, the air was stale, though still breathable. They stood on a rubble of broken grey stones. In the distance, a seam of light — a dampened sunrise or sunset — was beginning to glimmer over a pale, chilled, lifeless sea.

Galad caught Kalanin's eyes, and his lips parted, ready to speak dark sardonic words — but Kalanin shook his head. Glancing to the sea, Kalanin again shook his head, then grasped the hilt of his sword.

Galad straightened then took another deep breath; Kalanin was telling him that battle was coming, not here in this fading portion of Otherwhen, but somewhere else — and soon.

·)(·

Julian's war party slipped hidden back to the Isle, passing into its underground depths, just as the Isle's cavern systems shuddered, pounded by meteors smashing into the Isle's surface. Slabs of stone groaned and grated all around them, sending clouds of dust swirling upward as torrents of broken rock vanished down dark chasms.

Somewhere off to their left, Kul-Ghouls were crying aloud, high pitched hyena voices echoing through the caverns — trapped in some remote underground stronghold, they were being crushed by tons of rockfall. Shrieking sounds gradually died down, leaving only the low moans of dying Ghouls. As those moans diminished, their war party could hear thrashing and slithering sounds echoing from beneath them: Dusk Snakes were seeking refuge in the deep chasms below.

Julian glanced cautiously in each direction. Their only illumination came from Phaedra's shimmering form and the pale gleam of the two Guardians' orb-eyes. Danger lurked all around them because they had returned to the Isle of the Demons while great magic raged overhead.

"Rockfall should open a path for us in the next few moments," Julian whispered. "That path will lead us to a hidden burial chamber, where a Guardian lies sleeping. Make ready."

"Apprentice," Phaedra asked softly, though her voice was filled with hostility, "why precisely am I here?"

"You now have more pure sorcerous strength than any Wizard," Julian said evenly. "Also, you and the Guardians all have great physical strength — we will need your power to remove any rockfall barriers."

"No, no, and no," Phaedra muttered. "I have had enough of this nonsense. Either you will now pass to me your Crystal of Otherwhen, or I will kill you this moment, whether you be a sworn ally or not." The two Guardians edged forward, orb-eyes gleaming, while Eléna with one swift motion drew an enchanted arrow to her bow and shifted forward to stand beside Julian.

"Wait," Julian whispered, and he stepped forward, pressing his Crystal into Phaedra's hand. "Behold the third reason you were asked to join this war party — so you might slake your thirst for this Talisman. Focus upon it, master it if you are able, though quietly, softly, gently...."

As Phaedra struggled with the Crystal, crumbling slabs of rock grated and crashed in the distance, shuddering down to the chasms below, while billows of dust mushroomed upwards. Julian studied Phaedra's face for a time, then looked away, for the intensity of her frustration was painful to watch.

After a time, Julian explained softly, "All three Crystals remain linked, and learn from one another. The Sorcerers' Crystals have become so completely joined to their holders that even Powers with the strength of Dark Lords cannot bend these devices to their will. This Crystal, passed to me by Thorian, has become bonded to my thoughts, so that —" Julian halted suddenly, for a remote, soft voice was whispering into his mind.

Child, little one, although the Sight has grown powerful within you, you have strayed into a trap.

Julian glanced around, *reaching*. Neither ghost nor wraith being could be seen or sensed. And the voice seemed strangely familiar — was that the voice of his grandmother, who had died so many years ago? Was she calling to him from beyond the grave? No...it was somehow similar, but it was not the voice he recalled clearly from his childhood, so many years ago.

And now images were flooding through his mind, sent by the same source — another hidden Guardian lay concealed just beyond the shores of the Isle, a Guardian that might yet be freed! He turned back to his war party.

"Touch my hands," he whispered and reached out to them. Eléna met his hand, then the huge grey flesh of the Guardians' fingers also reached down to him. After a moment's hesitation, Phaedra reached out to touch them with her gleaming left hand, right hand still clutching Julian's Crystal.

Guardians, Julian's mind whispered, *reach out to the underground realms surrounding us. Have your brethren prepared an ambush? Or have the Sorcerers laid a trap for us?*

A Guardian's voice spoke into their minds: *Transforming dream-snares lie all around this place. Our brethren have been lying in wait for us. How did we fail to foresee this intersection?*

This moment was planned a short time ago, and also, it has the smell of Sorcerer about it, thought the second Guardian. *Yet have we not grown powerful enough to smash these corrupted waylayers and betrayers?*

We might survive this encounter, Julian's mind whispered, *but we would also fail to free a fourth Guardian — except that far from here lies another, also hidden Guardian, one that may equally serve our cause. Let us transform our failed expedition from a disaster into a triumph. Phaedra, future Goddess and Power of the Mid-World, know that I am a lesser player in these great events, but Sight has been granted to me. If you pass to me the Crystal, I will return it to you after we secure a fourth Guardian.*

Phaedra stared grimly at the Apprentice, then her hand moved out slowly and handed the Crystal back to Julian. With all her ambitions exposed and opportunities wasted, she withdrew her emotions from the moment, focusing instead on the forces of magic all around her until she, too, could sense the trap set by corrupted Guardians and one of the Sorcerers — Houma, this ambush had the smell of that wolfling Houma at its core.

I have become a Power, Phaedra thought, *though I behave as a plaything of Powers. I must **take** control, and no longer **be** controlled.*

The shape of the surrounding stone was changing, and lights shifted all around them as transforming dream energies of their adversaries sought the intruder's war party. Julian invoked his Crystal, then took three steps towards what seemed to be a solid rock wall, one that faded into a misty curtain as he touched it. Others followed behind him, and their war party passed again into Otherwhen.

Behind them, all the transforming energies that groped for Julian's war party exploded in frustration, sending more slabs of stone crashing against one another, and another torrent of rubble sliding down into dark caverns below, destroying more underground monstrosities.

· X ·

They entered a region of Otherwhen ruled by brilliant, hot sunlight. Nothing flew overhead. Only fringes of clouds lingered on the horizon. An expanse of desert surrounded them, and over those burning sands nothing grew, and not even insects moved. As they stood, the humans began perspiring heavily, partially blinded by bright light while Julian reordered his Crystal. After a few moments, he looked up at them and nodded.

"We have escaped back into Otherwhen," Julian murmured. "I can feel the fury of our foes from a distance. Now we will surprise them again, and they will be doubly angry. At the far southernmost edge of the Isle lies a deep cavern that can only be accessed by an underwater passage beneath the ocean's surface. Who among you can accomplish this?"

Both Guardians glanced at Phaedra, one commenting, "If we transform water to air, our brethren who serve the Demons will surely become aware of us."

"So, you require," Phaedra muttered, "that a chamber of air be formed below the ocean's surface, to allow you to pass back to the Isle? This I can do."

As she spoke, her mind was whispering, *And perhaps during that passage, this war party will drown, except for one Goddess who will, fortunately, escape with the Crystal...but no, a multiplex battle would ensue, and I might not even emerge as the victor. Did the Apprentice bring Eléna with him for just this purpose — that her enchanted weapons might tip the scales of power against me? Have I been outwitted, not even by a Wizard, but by this stripling Apprentice?*

Julian watched Phaedra closely, as though reading her thoughts. "Come," he murmured, "a fourth Guardian remains to be freed." He held his Crystal up, leading them over burning sands that blazed hot against their feet until they passed with a *shudder* back to the Isle's chilled, underwater shoreline, where storms still lashed at the Isle's beaches.

·)(·

Suddenly it was dark, cold, and damp. They were deep underwater, but moisture fled from them as Phaedra extended an envelope of air to encircle their war party. On all sides, stormy water, dark with debris and menace, lashed at their undersea pocket of air.

Their eyes adjusted to the darkness, and they could glimpse light on the shore's surface, as the ocean above them rose and crashed in its tumult. Then bright light flared suddenly overhead, and they stared, frozen. Above them, to the North, a ruby-red fire was spreading upwards as Hell consumed the magic substance of the Gods' Cloudshelf.

Red, sickeningly red evil, Phaedra thought, *though a portion of my own being greatly desires to wield its power.*

"We have only moments," Julian whispered, and he began to push forward, Eléna at his side. The Guardians, too, moved with speed, though they were forced to hunch down as they neared the shore. Phaedra followed belatedly but swiftly, extending her membrane of air around their war party and they advanced.

At less than a hundred paces from the shoreline, the Guardians were forced to crawl on their hands and knees. Yet now just before them loomed a huge culvert, a drain with slabs of stone blocking its underwater entrance. Phaedra and the Guardians tore the slabs from the entrance, while Julian and Eléna slipped swiftly inside. The passage within remained low, and the Guardians continued to crawl. Phaedra was the last to enter, and as she passed from the ocean, she hesitated, taking one last glance at the ruby red Cloudshelf, while thinking dark thoughts: *has the Mid-World of the Truce placed me completely on the wrong side of this struggle?*

Still underwater, Julian and Eléna pushed forward, with Julian's staff flashing light. Their feet slid over a bed of stone and seaweed and sharp barnacles. As their passage rose from the seabed, Phaedra maintained a pocket of air around them, though now they could almost reach the water's surface overhead. The tunnel passage also grew higher, so the Guardians were able to rise to their feet, though they were kept hunched down, still wary of the tunnel's jagged roof.

They broke the sea level surface of the tunnel and Phaedra released her spell-work. Julian and Eléna were waist deep in water, with a chilled cross current tugging them seaward into the night ocean. Guardians stood ready to brace them, but Julian and Eléna pulled free from the current and began to splash uphill until the water around them was less than knee deep.

They curled left, entering a high-ceilinged chamber, where remote, shadowy stalactites dripped limestone moisture down upon them. With the upheavals shaking the Isle, many of these huge stone daggers had already collapsed and lay smashed in jagged fragments on the tidal floor of the cavern.

Phaedra put forth her power, and light, silverish red, radiated through the chamber. Crabs fled from her radiance. Green seaweed flapped back and forth with tidal motions of the chamber's seawater, while purple starfish began their incredibly slow escapes from the intruders who entered their chamber.

There, in the cavern's center, lay a great boulder, covered with barnacles, mollusks, and seaweed. *We have discovered a fourth hidden Guardian,* thought Phaedra. *Only the slightest portion of my being shares in this triumph.*

"Torment," murmured one Guardian.

"Behold our brother," added the second Guardian, staring at the boulder, "one who fought most bitterly against the Demons and against our corrupted brethren. So, they have added torture to his transformation — see that they have made sure that he feels the deep chill of the ocean and the pain of many small intruders gnawing at his surfaces."

"That torment has come to an end," Julian murmured, and he stepped forward, touching the boulder, speaking only one, clear word: "Arise!"

And the boulder began to transform, but with shuddering, staggered motions, as though it struggled to restore itself. Only when its brethren touched its shifting mass was the Guardian within able to emerge. This fourth Guardian was leaner, more haggard, though its orb-eye flared with defiance.

"Well met," Julian said to the newly awakened Guardian. "Yet now our foes are aware of us, and we cannot wage battle in this place. We will fight them with all our strength — but elsewhere, and at another time."

"Once again," Phaedra said, grimly, "it is time to flee." Julian led them over stones covered with barnacles and seaweed as they *shuddered* with the change and fled back into Otherwhen.

· ☽ ·

Following the deliverance of a fourth Guardian, the Demon Princes exploded in wrath. Otherwhen had become a sanctuary for their foes, a honeycomb of secret passageways — not the miraculous multi-dimensional tool promised by the Sorcerers. Alcman and Houma had failed to destroy or trap the intruders, and so their servants the Sorcerers had to be punished — perhaps even destroyed.

The Demon Princes sat in their place of power. Torrents of flame poured from their mouths as they raged against their mortal servants. Alcman and Houma had yielded their Crystals of Otherwhen, abasing themselves, groveling, while murmuring prayers, explanations, and promises of future victory. After a time, Houma's shrill explanations gradually made less and less sense, while Alcman's soft words subsided into groans and finally, silence.

A deep chill froze Alcman's body, though his mind twisted and turned. *At the End of Time, if the Maker calls me to judgment, what might I possibly say? I could not even bring myself to beg for mercy.*

Lacking opponents of stature, or slaves capable of enduring substantial torment, the Demon Princes turned against one another.

"Put them to the torture test!" Satanis raged, with torrents of fire surging at Zikar, "then we will truly learn the devices of these maggots!"

"Dead things tell no twisted tales," Iblis roared, flames also aimed at Zikar. "Simply feed them into the Lake of Fire!"

"Fools! Both of You!" Zikar blazed. "You two have always sought destruction instead of any deeper understanding!" Then Zikar astonished his brethren, for he stepped down from his podium, striding to the chamber's center until he stood engulfed in torrents of the enchanted flames hurled from the mouths of Satanis and Iblis.

Such was the power of Zikar that as his skin boiled and charred, it healed immediately, so when the fires surrounding him faltered and died down, Zikar stood unscathed.

"Do you not recall," Zikar said in his deepest, darkest tones, "how we once invoked simulacra of the Maker and sought to compel answers from these constructs? We failed then and will fail again with these Sorcerers. Consider that these frail mortals are the flimsiest of tools. Once they are ruined or destroyed, they can never be used again."

"Then seal them away in stone chambers," Satanis said, traces of fire still seeping from his mouth.

"Or transform them into the stuff of the unliving," Iblis muttered. "Then we can deal with them after the interlopers are destroyed."

"I have already summoned Guardians," Zikar said evenly. "Let the Sorcerers remain trapped in the dream empires of our Guardians for a time until they can be put to use again." As Zikar spoke, strands of transforming dream magic reached out from granite slabs, enveloping the two Sorcerers in the gleaming white magic of the corrupted Guardians, and then they were gone.

The three Demon Princes regarded one another with menace for a moment, then stepped down from their thrones to view the Crystals left behind by Houma and Alcman. Each of them knelt on one knee, studying the two Crystals intently, watching light patterns change while probing the energies within.

After a time, Iblis looked up from the Crystals and said quietly, "These Talismans are organic constructs. In their travels through many dimensions, their organic substances have grown more powerful. Yet now they are linked closely to the thoughts of two specific organic beings: the Sorcerers Alcman and Houma."

"Before us lie intricate keys to the front doors of Otherwhen," Zikar said, "keys for doors we cannot find, keys that would not turn for us even if we found those doors."

Satanis stood and laughed, rumbling the stone of the chamber. "Yet if the front doors of Otherwhen remain barred to us, gates to these enchanted kingdoms can be torn from their hinges, walls smashed asunder, towers ripped from their foundations. Before creating Hell, we investigated the structures of many strange dimensions, and so Otherwhen will also be open to us."

·)(·

A fourth Guardian, Galad thought, *that's to the good. These four Guardians seem to gather strength from one another, while the Wizards mumble among themselves just to the Guardians' left. Beyond the Wizards, somewhat in the distance, the Godlings are arguing, and I have no idea what they might be quarreling about.*

In their fading Otherwhen redoubt, Kalanin and Galad, Julian and Eléna were speaking softly together, and while part of Galad's mind watched their allies, he was listening carefully to the words spoken by Julian:

"I have mentioned this only to Merlin, but some other force involved itself in our struggle to warn me of danger. It was not the Great Guardian. The Sight within me has grown more powerful, yet I became careless and had to be guided by some being with even greater Sight than my own."

"Then perhaps what I encountered a few days ago," Kalanin added, "was something more than a dream. For a time, all my night visions of Géla and Serena were tangled with confusion, and their images were obscured by dark shadows. I think now that they were in great danger. And yet in my last dream, they stood safely in the sunlight, radiating joy and love at me across the great gulf of distance and magic that separates us. This last night vision was so clear and strong that it seemed like a gift. Could that vision have been sent by some outside force? We can certainly use a few more powerful allies."

Julian stared for a moment into the distance. "When the Sight within me looked to Khiva some time ago, I felt strife and danger, and now I sense peace and strength and purpose."

Galad tapped the Tarnished Sword in its scabbard, and he sighed. "So invisible beings have communicated with the two of you, though not to me. What of you, Eléna?" When she shook her head, Galad continued: "So I suppose that we have at least one new ally, something like a discreet, invisible ghost. I may sound churlish, but I would have preferred assistance of a somewhat higher order — perhaps an incredibly powerful OverGod, standing a thousand feet in height, an angry being, capable of hurling Demon Princes and Dark Lords into the depths of space."

Eléna laughed, then turned to Julian. "Do our two knights know about Phaedra?"

"They understand that she is conflicted," he said. "Merlin must speak with her. Of the Godlings, Phaedra is most at risk — she was formed partially from the essences of Demons, and now the Demon Princes are reaching out to her. Turin and Magog, though still challenged, grow more strongly allied to us, so they seem considerably less likely to betray us."

As they spoke, Otherwhen shuddered, its fading sun blinking as though it were no more than a candle, fluttering under the force of a strong wind.

"Is this sub-world dying?" Kalanin asked.

"Left to its own devices," Julian said, "it would linger for a thousand or more years. But it feels as though all Otherwhen is under siege. Come." Godlings sought Wizards. Others joined them, huge Guardians leaning down to hear the Wizards' soft words as they spoke to Godlings.

"It does not matter that we have provoked the Demon Princes," Thorian replied evenly. "They would have moved to destroy us whether we attempted a foray or not."

"All future choices must be made in a Council of War," Phaedra murmured in an angry voice. "If I am three times more powerful than I was at birth, I have now ten times the wisdom. I cannot belie —" She faltered, for Otherwhen was shuddering again. Its sun flickered, and this time the sun blew out, and all light vanished. They stood still and silent in the darkness; their only illumination came from the glowing orb-eyes of the Guardians and the radiance of the Godlings' forms. Then came the rushing sounds of air sweeping away from a suddenly dead sub-world, its atmosphere passing into the void.

As Balardi and Thorian spoke spell-words to retain air for their people, Magog murmured, "And so another branch of Otherwhen dies around us. Where do we turn next?"

"We have no real choices," Turin replied in a flat, distant voice, "except to flee, and flee again until we are finally trapped and destroyed."

Instead of challenging Turin's forecast, Merlin turned to Julian. "Lights are vanishing all around us, while sentient beings perish in fear in the middle of collapsing sub-worlds, and everywhere the air is pouring into a void that never fills. What is happening?"

Julian shook his head slowly. "It would seem that the Demon Princes are crushing all regions of Otherwhen close to our hiding place. Unable to use the Crystals that are aligned with the Sorcerers, they are simply blasting a passage toward us, destroying any portion of Otherwhen that lies in their path."

"Can we escape?" Merlin asked. "Seek nearby places of concealment?"

"None of the nearby regions of Otherwhen will last for long," Julian replied. Then a second concussion boomed over their portion of Otherwhen, and the ground beneath them trembled. Thorian's staff flashed, and a cone of light surrounded them. With the light, they could see that beneath their feet, the sub-world's substance was fading. The heavier forms of the Guardians were beginning to sink downward.

"Flee to other brief havens anyway," Turin muttered. "It feels like an ugly End-game to this Godling." Voices murmured all around them, but Julian lifted his hand, palm out, requesting silence.

"Duskland," the Apprentice said softly. "Powerful sub-worlds exist within Otherwhen, places that have anchored themselves to very different energies." Turin and Magog shrugged, while Phaedra stared into the darkness. Merlin only nodded.

As Julian invoked his Crystal, a pathway of gleaming paving stones began to form, leading from their fading cone of light into a portion of Otherwhen that was lit by volcanic plumes, and surges of molten lava. They passed from a dying portion of Otherwhen with a *shudder*, into a far more vibrant sub-world.

· X ·

Duskland surged with energy and power, though it glowed from internal fires, without a hint of radiant light above them; only reddish, dark clouds loomed overhead. Its barely breathable air was choked with ash.

"The sun," Phaedra murmured, voice subdued, "what has happened to the sun?"

"The sun's mass still turns the planet," Turin said, staring upward, "but its fires are dead."

"That same force" Julian added quickly, "that destroyed the sun, first stoked the fires of the planet. Watch yourselves, for Duskland is perilous — it will defend itself!"

Turin stared above him, where plumes of smoke surged into a starless night sky, and lava glowed as it poured down a hillside to their left, boiling moisture from the air around it. One volcanic cone dominated the land surrounding them, though in the distance other cones were belching smoke and ash. Below them lay a slope leading to a broad plain where husks of stone were partly obscured by shadows.

The magic within Turin's mind reached out: *Things that are partly alive surround me but why should I be troubled? The ghosts of Otherwhen will never challenge the growing strength of a Godling.*

But then Magog caught his arm and pointed below. "Those great boulders are stirring," Magog said. "They were not alive when we first stepped out upon this hillside, yet now our presence seems to have roused them." Across the plain below them, huge forms were moving, motions partly obscured by dark red shadows. On the farthest reaches of the plain, fissures in the ground were opening, and from these gaps, smaller, more agile beings were scrambling to the surface, then shambling toward the interlopers from the Isle.

"Behold a range of larger and lesser monstrosities," Julian murmured, "vampiric ghoul creatures. Each of them seeks our magic, our sentience — and our flesh."

"Then those of you bound by flesh should tremble," Phaedra muttered, and she rose from the ground. Extending one hand, she sent jagged dark lightning surging toward the foremost monstrosity. As the lightning struck, the creature staggered, shuddered, and toppled to the plain. But then, still smoking, it stood and continued its upward progress.

As Phaedra rose higher, huge bat-winged creatures began rising from the field below them. Turin and Magog lifted from the ground in support of Phaedra. Warfare flared in the skies.

On the field below them, the pace of the ghoulish creatures began to quicken. Their shapes became more distinct: heads of huge ghouls were attached to bulky bodies that raced forward on a dozen tentacle-like arms and two rear stump legs. Volcanic vapors drifted overhead, while from the volcano's cone, a plume of ash shot into the air with a muffled concussion.

Galad shook his head and reached for the Tarnished Sword. *Very, very nice. Of course, now our invisible allies have grown silent.* But then laughter reached from deep within his substance, an emotion that belonged to another being.

What's happening? Galad's mind called out. *After a parade of monstrosities across the years, I'm supposed to grow crazed with fear? To break down now when I'm surrounded by Wizards, Guardians, and Godlings?*

"We must stand together," Merlin called up to the Godlings. "As a first test, these creatures may be vulnerable to the transforming energies of the Guardians."

As Duskland creatures pressed toward them, Julian felt a wave of hunger radiate from them, and he recoiled.

Guardians gathered together, their grey shapes ranged against an arc of predators gathering from the shadowy fields below. Orb-eyes radiated transforming energies and the vampiric ghoul shapes began to be transformed: the first rank became thousands of reptile birds that took wing and fluttered blindly and helplessly into the tumults of vapor that ruled the skies overhead.

But though the second rank of Duskland monstrosities shook and shuddered, their forms could not be transformed. With a hunger that increased with every step, they pressed up the slope.

"Duskland is strong," Kalanin murmured. Biting words came to Galad's lips, but he clamped his mouth shut — though he was having increasing difficulty controlling his own body. He hunched over, beginning to twitch and tremble as though with the plague.

Warfare flared overhead. Bat-winged monstrosities were battered by the Godlings' power but could not be turned aside. As the Godlings drifted closer to their allies, Wizards and Godlings fought as one force, using a wide array of sorcery: battle magic shook Duskland; transforming energies attacked their foes; all the material energies of earth, air, fire, and water assailed Duskland. A great frost held the stricken monstrosities for a moment. Chasms opened, swallowing ghoul creatures, though the fissures could not keep them down. Duskland monstrosities were too strong — and their hunger was too great. Tentacles were reaching from below ground, hauling ghoul shapes back to the surface.

Duskland creatures struggled upward, and the intruders from the Isle gave way, shifting upslope into an intersection where streams of lava would consume them.

"We are running short of time," Merlin said softly to Julian.

"Demon Princes batter at the gates of Duskland," Julian murmured. "Find a way to hold these things a short time longer, then they will turn on the Demons and their allies."

"Time," came a deep voice from behind Wizard and Apprentice. "We will give you a gift of time." Julian turned in surprise. The voice came from Galad's mouth, but it belonged to another being, and the voice did not even belong to a human being.

Then Galad raced downslope, moving at incredible speed. Smoking and flashing with all its grim energies, the Tarnished Sword swept through stump legs and grotesque tentacles. Duskland creatures began toppling, falling toward Galad, but with incredible swiftness, he was gone. The Tarnished Sword moaned and smoked, then slashed again as toppling monstrosities collapsed downward, blundering into other forms in jumbles of severed limbs and thrashing torsos. Ghoul voices groaned and gasped with horror.

From Galad's mouth came an incredible, inhuman cry of triumph. Then his body was moving, slashing, darting, with a speed no purely human form could have mustered.

What are you doing to me!?! Galad's mind cried out to the being that had taken control of his body, and then a voice spoke into his mind:

I need only to borrow your form for a brief time, youngling. And after I will heal your strained and stricken body. Ah, but it feels like the Maker's Will to rise once again against our foes!

Then Galad's form was racing, slashing again and again at monstrosities that were too slow to counter him. Within his body, tendons stretched and tore, while his lungs gasped and strained, and his mind flashed with pain. Then would come a millisecond's pause, and Galad could feel a healing strength race through his body. His body was being stretched to its outermost limit — but it would not be broken.

Lord, Galad's mind whispered, after a time. *Why, as Binder of Creatures Indomitable, are you not merely restraining these beings?*

Using Galad's body, Nablus leaped to the top of one gigantic ghoulish creature, stabbed down, spun in midair to slash at a bat-winged flyer, then sprang to the back of a second ghoul.

For the task and hand, I must use the tools at hand, came the thoughts of Nablus.

Lord, I greatly regret all my words concerning invisible ghosts and my preference for a thousand-foot OverGod.

Always be careful what you wish for, came the thought, followed swiftly by another. *We are done here, youngling. Maker's Peace to you and your allies.*

Exhaustion overcame Galad. He sagged to one knee and bowed his head. The Tarnished Sword, smoking and shimmering with its own fatigue, slipped from his grasp. Julian and Eléna came swiftly downhill and knelt beside him, while Kalanin, a step behind, pulled Galad to his feet and pressed a skin of water into his hands. The exhausted warrior sheathed his enchanted blade, then stared down to the fields below: ghoulish creatures were reassembling. Yet now they had turned toward a different slope many paces to the right of the topmost volcano.

There, the fabric of Duskland was being torn asunder. The Demon Princes were breaking through, leading a tide of Dark Lords, and Marids, and corrupted Guardians into battle with Duskland's ghoul-creatures.

Galad drank a bit more water, then he drew a deep breath and began trudging up the slope to join Wizards, and Godlings, and Guardians. Midway up the slope, he turned and called out,

"Lovely beings of Duskland, it seems that humans are off the menu for the moment! I suggest instead a brace of tangy Marid tendons and gnarled arm of Dark Lord for tonight's feast! Duskland, farewell!"

· ⋊ ·

The inn was chilled and dark. Every evening the inn's wine became thinner, while its ale cloudier, flavor tainted by the ash floating from the tavern's smoking, sputtering fireplaces. Its interior lights seemed to be fading; even the shadows on the floor were becoming darker, more tangled, less distinct.

The old Shaman turned from the interior of the tavern to glance into the alleyway, staring through grimy windowpanes that had been lined with dark, grey lead. He sipped the last of his cloudy ale and shivered. Outside, nightfall was coming, and the evening rain was growing colder, with traces of sleet spattering against the glass. Inside the Inn, people sat glumly, or moved from table to table, mumbling only a little, and smiling never.

Fewer and fewer of the townsfolk were seeking advice from the old Shaman, for his visions were clouding over, and the tongue in his nearly toothless mouth stumbled over even simple words. He bowed his head, though he did not let himself weep. *Babbling, I can do no more than babble. What has become of the wisdom of old?*

Age or illness was ruining his body and his mind. Soon he would be ejected from the inn, as others had before him, and forced to "pass into the village" that lay beyond the alleyway outside. He had trouble imagining anything beyond the alley, for just a few paces from the alleyway, the substance of matter grew hazy and insubstantial, then seemed to fade into nothingness.

Leaving the Inn was a death sentence, and the end was coming for him, all too soon.

The Shaman's time at the Inn had not always been so cold and dark and grim. He remembered leaning forward, speaking to questioners with blazing insight, while bright fires crackled behind him. He had been drinking a wine that sparkled on his tongue, and words had flowed brilliantly from his mouth.

What had they been discussing at that time? They had asked him about some sorcerous device, a "Crystal of Otherwhen," a mysterious Talisman; the Shaman could no longer picture the device. But the Crystal had been multifaceted, utterly magical, and he had known so much about it. After those discussions had come a time of slow failure, with each day darkening toward winter, his table being moved farther from the warmth of the hearth, with fewer people asking for his services and everything becoming more difficult — and it was colder, always colder.

A flurry of motion made him look up. People were always passing in and out of the Inn from the alleyway beyond its doors, yet they seemed no more than shadows, slipping back and forth with only whispers of wind sliding past the Inn's door. Now, the door opened wide, bringing a wintry gust of wind, while ice crystals spilled over the grimy sawdust on the Inn's floor. A solid being of a substance far greater than the usual shadowy figures entered the Inn. Some sort of shielding surrounded him, as though he was armored with gleaming enchantments. With slow, deliberate motions, the newcomer drew a chair toward the Shaman's table, then sat down opposite him and stared directly into his face.

A patron? Someone who would pay for his services? The newcomer's eyes were as grey as an overcast sea, but they were penetrating. He was dressed like a seasoned wayfarer, while at the same time he had the bearing of a great lord. The Shaman leaned forward, beaming, his smile revealing that only a few blackened tooth-stumps remained.

"Your worship," he murmured, "it is my pleasure to serve you. How may I help you on this fine evening?"

"In truth," said the newcomer, "you have been calling to me, and this event is so strange that I felt compelled to speak with you." The stranger's palms flashed, and two pewter goblets emerged from the dim shadows that hung over the farthest reaches of their table. He pushed one forward, murmuring, "Sip slowly, and be in part restored."

The Shaman sipped, then sipped again. As dream-weaving controls over the Shaman's mind faltered, the cunning, even brilliant mind of Alcman began to emerge.

"Are you then a Wizard?" Alcman whispered in the smallest voice possible, afraid that he might be overheard.

Hestaur — or the slowly evolving ghost of Hestaur, a being of power who had once sat in the Hall of the Dreamers — shook his head. "You do not know me. You may one day learn my name, yet it is unlikely that you will ever truly *know* me."

Alcman closed his eyes and *reached*. After a moment, he murmured, "I am ensnared in a dream empire created by those Guardians who serve the Demon Princes. Forces filled with malice have me under their control. An unknown force perhaps as powerful as a Wizard or Master Sorcerer arouses me from my enchanted prison. This Power has love neither for me nor for the Demon Princes whom I serve. How has this intersection come to pass?"

Hestaur studied Alcman for a moment. "When Hell was born," he finally asked, "what made you pray to the Maker?"

Alcman sipped, staring into the depths of an Inn that was populated only by dreamworld shadows. "I was lost. I was desperate. Yet why would the Maker, who never seems to respond to any of his mighty, untainted servants, bother to heed my prayers?"

"The Maker," Hestaur said evenly, "has not sought to govern all matters across this enormous universe, and so his people must wait for justice until the End of Time when all things will be made perfect in the Maker's Mind. At times, however, strange intersections occur: when counterforces arise to defend the Maker's Will, those forces sometimes feel an obligation to respond to invocations. Yet I, too, am astonished that I sit here before you, Alcman of the Tormented Soul."

"Counterforce," Alcman muttered, nodding to himself. "So, there *will* be a confrontation."

Hestaur smiled grimly. "Did they teach you little sayings when you were a child? Recall: 'Good will overcome evil and bright sunlight will shine down upon the just.' It does not always end that way, Alcman. I must tell you that there are portions of the universe where such interventions have failed, and so dark energies rule. Those portions of the universe must wait until the End of Time to have their fates transformed.

"Yet here, upon the Isle of the Demons, there *will* be a confrontation. There *will* come a time when your Crystal of Otherwhen is returned to you. There *will* be a time when you will be permitted to flee into Otherwhen. The challenge before you is this: when you are free, will you then attempt to save Houma of the Withered Hand? And how would that Sorcerer respond?"

"He would only betray me again," Alcman said, shaking his head slowly. He stared around the Inn. Now, with some of his vision restored, all the Inn's other inhabitants were revealed as artificial constructs, half-heartedly built, beings without even the faint voices of ghosts, or the hazy substance of wraiths.

Alcman had always known that the corrupted Guardians resented the Sorcerers and the Marids, perhaps even hated them. After all, the corrupted Guardians were the first allies of the Demon Princes in their quest to overthrow the Truce. When the Sorcerers and the Marids rose to battle,

Guardians felt shunted aside. Now the dream-weaving Guardians thought so little of their former Sorcerer ally, that their efforts to ensnare him with enchanted visions around him were half-hearted. Why, indeed, should they bother? The Sorcerers and the Marids were a spent force.

Alcman raised his head and stared into Hestaur's powerful, determined, and judgmental face. A haze of ash-filled smoke lay between them, and also a great gulf of understanding and wisdom. Finally, Alcman drew a deep breath and looked away. "I do not know what to say to you. If you entrust me with the rescue of Houma, I would fail you. And if I came before the Maker at the End of Time, I could not even bring myself to beg for mercy."

"No being can be charged with the rescue of Houma," Hestaur said grimly. "In the long history of Alantéa the Forerunner, there are very few forces that might be willing to *attempt* the rescue of Houma of the Withered Hand, even from himself. You must flee when the great confrontation comes, and after, find something useful to do; you might even carry out some act of mercy in Otherwhen. If you could preserve yet a single blade of grass from a gust of cold wind, that would be a new beginning, and a vast improvement over your life to date, Alcman of the Tormented Soul."

· X ·

Once more they were hidden in the farthest reaches of Otherwhen, where all substances had been reduced to shadows and all the intruders moved like ghosts and spoke in whispers. Julian stood beside Merlin and the two spoke together in soft whispers, unwilling to be overheard.

"So, we believe," Merlin said softly, "that the ghost of at least one Dreamer has traveled to this Isle."

"When Galad spoke, that was not Galad's voice," Julian whispered, "and Galad was moving with speed never shown by any mortal warrior. I have heard that voice before in the Hall of the Dreamers, and it belonged to Nablus, or the spirit of Nablus, the binder of Creatures Indomitable. As for his speed of motion, that swiftness and the cunning of Nablus must have enabled him to deal with much more powerful beings."

"And the voice that warned you that a trap had been set for you," Merlin continued, "belonged to yet another being."

"I search back in my mind," Julian said, "and that voice seems strangely similar to that of Orissa, the Seeress, also a Dreamer, though I cannot be certain."

Merlin stared into the shadows. "When we speak of ghosts in a land of ghosts, nothing is certain. Still, the Eye brings word from the Great Guardian of yet another meeting. For strange, unknown reasons, Alcman lies enchanted in the Dreamworld of the Corrupted Guardians. He was roused from his enchantments by another being that the Great Guardian did not recognize, though his powers seemed remarkably similar to those of a Wizard or a Sorcerer."

"That would, or might be Hestaur," Julian said. "Is it possible that the ghosts of the Dreamers drift through the Isle of the Demons? But how could the Dreamers have been released from the Temple of Waiting?"

"Please say nothing of this to the others, not yet," Merlin said. His eyes met those of Julian's, and they nodded together, each of them understanding that any words they spoke to Phaedra were likely to become known, through strange pathways, to the Demon Princes.

"If we are right," Julian said, "three of six Dreamers have made their presence felt, while the three most powerful — Voritar, Prince of Demons, Llara, great among the Spirit Lords, and Voll, Elf-Lord and powerful Elf-Mage — still pass unmarked through the Isle. What would they possibly be doing?"

·)(·

Zikar, Prince of Demons, sat alone on his throne, contemplating their struggle against the Mid-World of the Truce. He was mentally alone, though not physically, for Satanis and Iblis sat on their thrones equidistant from Zikar. But their minds were far, far away, viewing their great Sending as it hurtled through the cosmos, blasting its way through every obstruction, as other forces in the universe struggled to block its passage. Flashes of fire, and smoke and dark laughter slipped from their mouths as they viewed the destruction created by the Sending's passage.

But Zikar was troubled. Some remote portion of his mind was whispering to him, and he could not understand its message, though it felt as though he was being warned. He stood down from his throne and left the hall and its two remaining Demon Princes to their dreams.

Nothing seemed amiss; fires still burned in their dwelling place, and smoke still gathered like distant fog in their high ceilings. He sent a blast of pain into the minds of the Guardians serving him, and they became suddenly alert.

Wincing, they reported that no forces stirred on the Isle, that the intruders were hidden in the deep crevices of Otherwhen, and that Hell still seethed with growing power. Given their history of losing focus, Zikar was only partially reassured.

He paced through their dwelling, unable to locate the source of his anxiety. Finally, Zikar spoke openly into his own mind: *Come now, whatever force calls within me. I yield my body to your concerns. Take me to the source of your distress and show me what is troubling you.*

Zikar's feet led him down through three barely used levels of their Citadel where dust and ash covered the ground, and the air seemed moldy even to a Demon Prince. As they neared the Citadel's granite foundations, and the Forge of the Demons, Zikar allowed his mind to speculate: *Has one of our long dead, hidden failures stirred? Which of our failed monstrosities could possibly have roused itself?*

But no, his feet stopped one level short of the Forge, in a place once intended for dungeons, but only used now to keep sealed the three Simulacra of the Maker, a separate set of failures.

Is one of these Simulacra of the Maker calling to me, and is it now prepared to collaborate with the Demon Princes? If so, which of the three might have changed its mind?

It was then that Zikar sniffed the presence of intruders and his body stiffened. He approached the cell holding his own Simulacrum, one that revealed itself as a panel of radiant light. He opened the door; all its radiance had been stilled, and the Simulacrum lay flat and dead — but surrounded by flowers: gold Lantanas and blue Lilies.

Moving swiftly, Zikar tore open the doors to the other two chambers that housed Simulacra: both were lifeless, surrounded by blue and gold flowers, and on their faces were looks of unusual peace. In none of the three could Zikar sense the torment and pain visited upon them by the Demon Princes.

Zikar spoke dark *words*, and the air trembled. He peered through the corridors and alleys of several different dimensions but not even the slightest of shadows could be seen. None of Zikar's powers allowed him to sense what had transpired down here in the lowest dungeons of the Demon Princes. He snarled in frustration with fire and ash spilling from his mouth.

Finally, he sent a summons to his brethren: *Rouse yourselves. Intruders have roamed our fortress and destroyed our Simulacra of the Maker. My powers may be enormous, but none of the energies available to me can tell me anything about this intrusion, and so I have summoned the two Sorcerers from their Dreamworld prisons. Perhaps their wretched and devious little minds can tell us more about what has transpired.*

Chapter Seventeen

"Call Back to Earth
the Great Sending"

"WHAT IN ALL OF the thousand dimensions of this wide universe is the matter with him?" Satanis asked, and the Demon Prince could not control the ash and sparks of fire that flowed from his mouth. They stood outside the dungeon chambers that had once held three simulacra of the Maker.

Alcman stood just to their left, a hunched, tiny figure beside the Demon Princes, while the four stared down at the figure of Houma, who lay twitching and giggling on the floor. At times Houma's mouth would speak words, though Alcman and his masters could make no sense of them. And whenever Houma's eyes blinked open, they seemed to see nothing of the real world around him.

"He was close to madness before," Alcman murmured, his eyes still fixed on Houma. "Some aspect of the dreamworlds created by your Guardians seems to have driven him completely insane."

Iblis stared down at the twitching human, and with difficulty restrained his huge left foot from crushing Houma, ridding himself of this troublesome, wounded maggot forever.

As Zikar caught some of the thoughts of Iblis, he glared at the Demon Prince, then turned to look down at the hunched and haggard figure of Alcman. "What should be done to restore him, Sorcerer?"

"If I speak my thoughts," Alcman said in a remote, detached voice, "you will simply wish to destroy both of us, and you may not be able to restrain yourselves."

"SPEAK, MAGGOT!" Satanis roared, and flames surged toward Alcman. Only the Sorcerer's complex, reinforced sorcerous shields saved his life. Strangely, Alcman did not cringe or grovel. Instead, he stared directly and without reverence at Satanis as though seeing the Demon Prince clearly for the first time.

"Stand back," Zikar snarled. "Both of you, stand back. I must restrain myself, and I will restrain you also, my overly rash brethren. Sorcerer, what is to be done?"

"All of creation dreams," Alcman spoke in a remote voice. "An earthworm dreams of tunneling forever through rich earth, without fear of age or the predation of moles, or the pecking of gulls when the fields flood. In Houma's case, he dreams of the victory of Demon Princes, and how they will rule the universe around them. But in Houma's dreams, he is the subtle counselor, the power behind all three of your thrones, secretly controlling and guiding events. If he is allowed that dream, within the dream empires controlled by your Guardian servants, he might regain his sanity, healing over time. That is how I would deal with him, had I your powers."

Satanis and Iblis could barely restrain themselves, while Zikar glared at them, then turned back to Alcman, noting that the Sorcerer no longer used cautious, deferential words when speaking to Demon Princes. "How did your mind survive while Houma's did not?" Zikar asked.

"Lord, my expectations were much lower than Houma's," Alcman said, sending a chill into his frame to disguise his lie. The Demon Princes did not need to know that the ghost of one of their adversaries had aided him.

"You may be speaking the truth," Zikar murmured, "though I suspect it is not the complete truth. Now, Sorcerer, I have called upon Guardians to shield this crippled Sorcerer, Houma, in an empire of dreams where his own role is much greater. Later, you can advise the Guardians directly yourself, so that this Sorcerer's mind can be repaired."

Zikar watched for a moment as dream strands of gleaming white wrapped themselves around a twitching, giggling Houma, then the Sorcerer vanished, leaving only a smear of saliva in the dust where his body had lain.

"Now," Zikar continued, "we have been caught unawares, for, in great secrecy, intruders have invaded our hidden places, and destroyed the three constructs that we used to simulate the mind of the Maker. We are able to follow each of the beings opposing us on this Isle — even those blockheaded, Giftless warriors — and yet none of the intruders has left a trace here in the depths of our Citadel. What can you tell us about these events?"

Alcman's mouth sagged open, but then he shut it swiftly, and he struggled to control the thoughts that surged through his mind. *They created "constructs?" Did they wish to mimic the mind of the Maker? All the Powers of the Mid-World had learned to avoid even discussing the Maker, for when they probed the Maker and his devices, events turned against them, as though they had invoked a stubborn force of doom. No wonder the Demon Princes have operated under a curse! No wonder they have been stumbling into traps!*

"Lord," Alcman forced his mouth to speak, "Let me take a brief time to investigate this matter. A wide range of Divinations lie at my disposal. As well, if you will return to me my Crystal of Otherwhen, I can use it to probe adjacent realities, and so learn more about this intrusion."

· ☿ ·

*Phaedra stared at Julian as the Apprentice spoke secrets to Merlin. Some significant event had taken place, and she had no idea what had happened. The Mid-World of the Truce had created her and sent her so casually into a struggle that she barely understood. At some level, she was a Power, but she had been treated as a **thing**. The Elves had taught her about The Game of the Masters and had even created a lesser game for their own amusement. What was the lowest ranked piece of this lesser game? A "pawn" — she had become no more than a pawn.*

Phaedra stared up into the dark skies of this fading portion of Otherwhen. Not even clouds were visible. Only the faintest glow of night penetrated the haze overhead. If she were back upon the Isle, she could lift into the skies and capture a stream of winds that would take her back to Alantéa the Forerunner and have done with this misadventure. Would Turin seek to stop her? Probably.

But she could not even escape from this sub-world without the aid of the Apprentice and his Crystal. How had she come to this?

As the anger rose within her, a *flicker* of movement flashed across the corners of her enchanted vision. Were ghosts moving in this lost land? Was she the only being aware of them? But no, the Wizards and their Apprentice were standing frozen, suddenly alert — and then they deliberately relaxed, trying to ignore the motions of ghosts, trying not to alert the Godlings that other beings were now present.

Phaedra raised her frozen face into the dark emptiness above her while her mind raged: *By all the Nine Billion Gods I must free myself from this fate, this death trap!*

Then she forced herself to glance back to the mortals: Merlin was stepping forward, both his arms partially raised, ready to speak — as though the Wizard himself had been reduced to a spokesperson for the Apprentice and a servant of ghosts!

"Events are building toward a climax," the Wizard said, barely raising his voice. "Separate visions of the future are preparing to collide. Before that moment comes, we will have a chance to rouse two more Guardians. If we are fierce and swift enough, we can become more than a little stronger."

· 𝄞 ·

Alcman was studying the third of his Divination Screens when the Demon Princes began roaring in frustration. Many levels down from their throne room, the stonework of their fortress was trembling as their feet smashed down in rage. The Sorcerer looked up, his hand drifting to his Crystal. *Is this the time for me to escape, to leave this mess forever and vanish into Otherwhen?*

He was still clutching his Crystal when Zikar suddenly flashed into view. The face of the Demon Prince reflected both suspicion and malice.

"What do you have for us, Sorcerer?" Zikar's words were soft, but ash and sparks were spilling from his mouth.

"I can show you much that is interesting," Alcman said, "though it is most unlikely to give you pleasure. What has happened to rouse your brethren to such rage?"

"Two more Guardians have been freed. What do you know about these matters, Sorcerer?"

"Nothing," Alcman said, shaking his head. "Houma and I only wondered why your three great majesties would leave powerful creatures such as Guardians transformed and concealed like hidden treasures waiting to be discovered by your foes."

Zikar's face twisted as he struggled to control his rage. "It may be that six Guardians have been freed," Zikar said. "Yet now the remaining six will be sealed away in the heart of this fortress so that our foes must come at us with a pure power that they will never possess, instead of their treacherous cunning. That phase of this struggle is over. What have you to show us, Sorcerer?"

Alcman turned away from Zikar, back to the dungeons that had once housed three simulacra of the Maker. "Lord, you have been invaded by ghosts, three separate ghosts, who were almost completely concealed. It was only when I coated their recreated images with entirely different, though fading sorceries of Otherwhen that I could discover the outlines of the forms they once held before they became ghostly entities."

As the Sorcerer spoke, he was aware that Iblis first, then Satanis stood behind him. The other two Demon Princes had joined Zikar, and they were watching Alcman with barely concealed menace.

"In this chamber," Alcman continued, "was the shape you seemed most likely to recognize." He entered the chamber where the simulacrum of the Maker held the image of an aging Demon. Flowers covered the dead being and its face was at peace. Looming over the simulacra, outlines glistening with gleaming dust was a huge form, remarkably similar in its outline to the forms of the three Demon Princes.

"Voritar the traitor," Satanis breathed out.

"The ghost of Voritar," Iblis murmured, "a figure we saw drifting through the Temple of Waiting, as dead as any immortal could ever be truly dead."

"I suspect then," Alcman continued, leading the three into the next chamber where the simulacra with the form of a Seraph also lay at peace, "that you may also recognize this form." Looming tall, gleaming in the darkness with a silver light, was a lean figure, showing the outlines of long hair.

"Llara," Zikar muttered, "one of the mightiest of the Spirit Lords, second in power only to Voritar in the Hall of the Dreamers."

"I can perhaps help identify the third form," Alcman said, as he led them into the last of the dungeons, where the simulacra showing the form of radiant energy lay stilled. Hovering above it, gleaming like the other ghosts, was a form no taller than Alcman's, though it was leaner, and lighter, seeming almost to float in midair.

"The Kindreds," Alcman continued quietly, "were often present in the halls of the Mid-World Powers, and so I have met a goodly number of Tanu and Sidhe and Elves. This form seemed remarkably similar to that of several Elf-Mages I encountered in those palaces."

"Voll, Elf-Lord," Satanis said, voice flat.

"So very, very dead only a few circles of the moon ago," Iblis murmured.

"Three ghosts of six Dreamers attended to these simulacra of the Maker," Zikar said softly, "dealing with them as though they were holy relics that had to be allowed to sleep in peace."

"While the other three of these ghostly Dreamers," Satanis continued, "helped the intruders survive our traps and then free two more Guardians."

"When they interfered with us," Zikar said, "we watched these Dreamers from afar before we destroyed them. Two were Ancient Powers: a Prince of Demons and a Greater Spirit Lord. Two came from the Mid-World: an extremely powerful Elf-Lord, and Nablus, whose origins we were never able to discover, but who was known as binder of the so-called Creatures of the Darkness. For strange, unknowable reasons, these four were joined by lesser beings, two humans: a Seeress named Orissa, and a Greater Mage named Hestaur. Why these six were chosen we could never learn."

Alcman sent a chill through his body to prevent the Demons from reading his thoughts. *Hestaur must have been the forerunner of Wizards whom I met in my sub-world prison. Hestaur, or his ghost, gave me aid and yet I am still serving the Demon Princes. That service must very soon be ended.*

Silence filled the dark dungeons for a time, while the Demon Princes sent thoughts into each other's minds.

"The Maker," Iblis finally muttered.

"So peaceful and seemingly soft," Satanis said, "yet deeply devious and crafty to the point of duplicity."

Zikar shook his head. "We should have known — were we not warned when we saw how the Seraphs, even in death, were able to torment their destroyers? And so, even victorious in battle, we were forced afterward to confront the Death Sting of the Seraphs. The Maker searched deeply within each of us and understood far more than we recognized. He knew that we would seek to overthrow all his designs and rule his creation."

"So now we have discovered the Maker's Death-Sting," Satanis muttered. "When Powers seek to supplant the Maker or even to investigate his devices, they are confounded by his cunning, treacherous traps."

Zikar stared upward, peering through layers of stonework into distant skies. "There is still time for us to transform this struggle and destroy our foes."

Iblis also stared upward. "It is too far away, so long gone."

Satanis shook his huge, grim head. "It can return far more quickly than it has traveled into the depths of space. First, it now understands how to fashion a passage through the stars. And secondly, there will be no further resistance to its voyage."

Alcman stood silently, his mind racing. He had no idea what the Demon Princes were proposing.

Finally, Zikar spoke these words: "We will deal with the Maker after all of his servants and secret allies and hidden devices have been destroyed. Our need is greatest now. We must call back to Earth the Great Sending."

Chapter Eighteen

Under Pressure,
Alliances Fragment

JULIAN SAT BESIDE HIS two Familiars in yet another dark, chilled, and lost realm of Otherwhen. Sebastian and Rafir shared Julian's cloak, though they were still shivering from the cold. The three sat some distance from the rest of their war party, except that a force of six Guardians loomed tall less than fifty paces from them, orb-eyes watching for any threats to Julian the Apprentice.

Julian was speaking to them in a low voice, almost a whisper: "I've been seeing things that are truly staggering. The Seer's Sight inside me grows stronger each day, and I'm learning things that I never understood before. We look up at our moon and it looks like a dead world that will last forever, but with some planets, the moons gradually work their way free, or are battered free and then they wander through the void. Suns don't always decline, either. We think they will just gradually fade like a dying fire, but some burst into a fire of red energies and destroy all their nearby planets. And that's just the beginning of my learning, with so much more to come."

Rafir shivered, head on Julian's lap, while Sebastian held Julian's hand and nodded as Julian spoke.

"The Great Guardian also sees much," Sebastian said, "and he shares some of these visions with us. But something has changed with the Demon Princes and their Sending, their Dagger to the Maker's Heart. The Great Guardian asks: can you tell us about that change?"

"The Sending," Julian murmured. "I can see it as it was in the beginning, a creation of pure, unmatched force, filled with all the hatred and malice of the Demon Princes, hurtling through space, passing beyond light speed, always growing faster, more powerful. Then the Dagger was challenged by Powers and Intelligences from other star systems, and so it began to change.

"Now, the Sending is no longer pure energy — in its struggles, it has gathered mass. Dust clouds from shattered asteroids swirl around it. Fragments of broken ships of space lie scattered over its surface. Many different kinds of beings roam the Sending's surface, seeking some way to disable it. Lights flare over the Sending's surface as supernatural entities clash with sentient machine creatures whenever they encounter one another. Over the Sending's surface wild growths are spreading, as star systems seek to infect it with malignant organisms — a kind of warfare attempted only by Great Dark Gods here on Earth.

"But still the Sending surges through star systems, undaunted and unchecked — until now. Now, the Sending is sweeping through galaxies in a long, arcing turn, preparing to return to Earth and defend its masters, the Demon Princes. Tell the Great Guardian that the Sending is returning, and it will increase their power enormously. Also, it is traveling at a far greater speed than when it first started — and so it will be here in a very short time."

Rafir shivered again, shook his furry fox's head. "We didn't need to have this thing get any more complicated."

"Not many days from this moment," Julian said, "everything will become much less complicated. One of two future visions will prevail, while the other will vanish forever."

"But still," Sebastian said, smiling up into Julian's face, "we sometimes watch you from a distance, and then we have to laugh when the Wizards keep coming to you for advice. Do you remember just a few years ago when you had trouble getting Merlin's attention?"

"Even the Godlings seem to come and ask you questions," Rafir added.

"Except Phaedra," Julian said, lowering his voice. "Everything that Phaedra sees and hears eventually becomes known to the Demon Princes. Does the Great Guardian understand that?"

"That's one of the messages we brought," Sebastian said.

"What the Guardian said was a bit less clear," Rafir added, "something like 'Turin will seek to counter Phaedra.'"

"Turin watches Phaedra," Julian said, "like the Eye of Merlin stalking an intruder who has slipped over the border onto League soil."

Sebastian glanced at the faces of the six Guardians. Portions of their minds were watching for threats to Julian, but mostly they were lost in dreams of their own design. "The Great Guardian wanted to ask you another question. For some strange reason, Alcman and Houma were held prisoners in the dreamworlds created by corrupted Guardians. Alcman has been freed, while Houma is still lost in those dreams, as we were once lost, and Houma isn't even aware that he's trapped. What can you see? What can you tell us?"

Julian drew a deep breath. "Under pressure, complex alliances are likely to fragment and fail. From a distance, I can see the Dark Lords struggling to escape from their pact with the Demon Princes. Like the Marids, they are trapped. Alcman and Houma are mistrusted by their powerful masters, the Demon Princes, for if they decided to escape together, they could vanish into Otherwhen where the Demon Princes would have difficulty following them, and so both Sorcerers were held captive for a time in the dreamworlds of corrupted Guardians.

"Alcman is now free, and he wavers. His lust for power and his fear of death once made him both evil and insane, but at last, his mind is clearing. In one of the strangest moments of this conflict, his tormented mind cried out for help when Hell was born. And that call was answered by the ghost of Hestaur, who made his way into Alcman's dreamworld prison. In one of my dark night visions perhaps I will be allowed to listen to the conversation between the two of them.

"As for Houma, his mind has finally broken under the pressure of this long conflict, and the creation of Hell and his own imprisonment. It seems that the corrupted Guardians both resented and hated the Sorcerers. Now those Guardians have been ordered to heal Houma's mind, so they have created a fantasy world for Houma — the Demon Princes wish the Sorcerer to recover so that he can add his knowledge and cunning to their war. In the coming conflict, it is possible that both Sorcerers may be arrayed against us — or it may be only one Sorcerer or even none."

Julian shook his head, then rubbed his hand over Rafir's soft fox fur before adding, "As for our side, we will be fortunate if even one Godling fights on our behalf."

"When Alcman thought he had destroyed me," Rafir said, "suddenly his face was filled with sorrow. That was very, very stran—"

"Wait, now wait," Julian interrupted. He stood and stared into the murky distance. "Something equally strange is about to happen. Alcman is at the gates of Houma's dreamworld prison — and those gates are being grudgingly opened by corrupted Guardians. Is Alcman bringing Houma a message from the Demon Princes, or is he going to set his fellow Sorcerer free?"

·))(·

Alcman shivered as he entered Houma's dreamworld prison, for he remembered his time in the ghostly inn of his own dreams. Trapped at the inn, the corrupted Guardians had slowly forced him farther from any source of heat, and his world had grown chillier and darker each day, while his intellect diminished like the heat in that shadowy inn, where it grew colder hour by hour.

But Houma's dream prison was so much warmer and brighter than that imaginary inn. Alcman passed through a courtyard where green ivies wrapped themselves around tall white pillars. Slabs of white marble formed curved paths through lush inner gardens. Fountains sprinkled drops of water onto lily pads and the ponds surrounding them, then the ponds sent their excess waters gurgling softly down hidden pipes into clogged drains. Scribes scurried over garden paths carrying parchments with plans, maps, and diagrams to their great master, Houma, the hidden power behind all three Demon Princes. Stringed instruments played delicate, soft music in the background, while the huge green leaves of surrounding foliage beaded with moisture.

A strange, dark humor swept over Alcman, and the Sorcerer laughed. *Once we were the Sorcerers and the Marids, a mighty challenge to the Mid-World of the Truce; and now we've been reduced to lunatic lapdogs, the insane servants of Demon Princes.*

His pathway ended in a small courtyard. Before him, six huge sentries faced outward, backs against a great wall, faces sneering down on Alcman the intruder. These dream sentries were three heads taller than Alcman and twice as wide. Their bodies were mostly shaped as humans, though their faces were grey-hued, thick-lipped, with large, hooked noses and twisted features — more like giant Gargoyles than humans.

Behind the sentries, tall doors stood sealed, and behind those doors, Alcman sensed the presence of Houma. As Alcman shook his head with dark humor, the doors slid open, and a slender human-seeming servant dressed only in a grey smock slipped past the line of sentries.

Glancing nervously at the sentries, the servant murmured, "The Great Councilor will see you now, though he is most preoccupied with plans for the coming battle, so your discussions must be very, *very* brief." Alcman followed the slender servant until they stood before Houma. Then the servant — after all, only a minor dream-construct created by Guardians who had little use for the Sorcerers — scurried around a corner and vanished forever.

Houma did not even look up but continued to scribble instructions on a parchment. Alcman studied his fellow Sorcerer carefully: in his dreamworld, Houma's arm was no longer dark and withered, though it still pulsed with power. After a time, Houma finished his notes, then pushed himself back from his broad, polished platform desk and finally glanced up at Alcman.

"I only agreed to see you," Houma said, "because their Great Majesties, the Demon Princes, insisted. But I am building a master plan, one that will reorder this portion of the — by the by, have I dealt with you at another time? Your face seems strangely familiar to me."

Alcman looked around: no place had been set for him to sit, so he was forced to remain standing.

"Once, you and I were part of a shared dream," the Sorcerer said, "a dream in which you were called Houma and I was named Alcman. We served their Great Majesties, the Demon Princes —"

"Wait!" Houma stood in alarm, glancing around to make certain that no one else could hear them. "You speak their old names, titles that must never be used again!"

Alcman shook his head, then continued. "We served their Great Majesties in a dream. I come before you to tell you that we will be recalled to that dream, a place where we must destroy Wizards and Godlings and Guardians and all other beings who serve them. After, you can return to this reality if you choose, but you must come when called."

Houma allowed himself a slight grin, his face filled with his old cunning. "Their Great Majesties are most wondrous, but I have developed my own devices, my own ways. It may not be necessary that I return to some strange, ancient dream."

"Let me show you a vision, Houma of the Withered Hand. Here is what is happening out in the enormous universe of that old dream." Alcman waved his hand, and an image flared to the left of Houma's platform desk. This image was large, twice Houma's height, flashing bright lights across the chamber, showing the Sending as it turned back toward earth. All the Sending's power was revealed as it hurtled through space. Also clear were all the details of the Sending's smoldering wounds, and they could also see flashes of warfare as supernatural entities, and well-armed alien warriors, and powerful machine constructs roamed the surface of the Sending, clashing with each other as they struggled in vain to halt the Sending's passage and then destroy its dark designs.

As Houma's mouth slipped open in astonishment, Alcman continued, "I am showing you some of the details of this most powerful dream. You ignore this night-vision at your peril, Houma of the Withered Hand, for if you do not return to that vision, it will invade your own reality and destroy both your dream world — and yourself."

Alcman stared for a moment at the open-mouthed Houma, then he turned and left. Now, with the Sight within him focused more strongly, he could sense, almost see the malice of the corrupted Guardians: Houma's dream world seemed to be bright and shimmering with life, but in its darkest shadows, the tiny eyes of rodents gleamed, and serpent tongues flickered out of nothingness, tasting the air, waiting for Houma to fall back into madness, and be imprisoned again in that dark, chilled nightmare universe.

Was there any way Houma could be warned of the malice of the corrupted Guardians? Houma must have realized that their alliance had never been some quaint "merry band of outlaws." Dark Lords hated Demon Princes; Sorcerers conspired to gain power, and Guardians resented all those coming after their early alliance with Demon Princes. Nothing could be done now to warn Houma, but perhaps a quick word could be spoken, when they met again, about an escape to Otherwhen.

As Alcman passed back through the Guardians' dream world, it became gradually hazy and indistinct. Just before slipping back to the Isle of the Demons, Alcman sent a single thought into the minds of the corrupted Guardians and to their masters the Demon Princes: *Houma is healing, but he has not yet sufficiently recovered, and so he needs more time.*

Alcman felt a *shudder* pass through him as all the hatred and unhappiness of Demon Princes and their Guardians sent pain surging through his body.

Grimly, Alcman shook free from the pain and shielded his mind with layers of cold so that none of his thoughts could be revealed. *There, I have done what I could for Houma, gaining him a few more days of dreaming glory so that he can pretend to rule star systems as a power behind the thrones of Omnipotent Demon Princes. As for the Marids, we, the Sorcerers, had little ability to communicate directly with the Marids; and now we have none. So, as the offspring of Demon Princes, their creators would have to look after their remaining Marids. All my Sorcerer "blood brothers" are either dead or insane. It is over, it is done; and so ends that alliance, one that was once known as The Sorcerers and the Marids.*

· ☓ ·

After a more than a month of peace, Serena had begun crying again, and nursing Serena gained Géla no more than a few minutes of peace. Finally, Géla sat with her daughter on their broad but simple bed, hugged her, and spoke with her as though she dealt with a child of six years, rather than six months.

"Little One, what is the matter? Where is the pain?"

Then Serena grew completely quiet, and after, crawled so that she faced to the north and raised her chubby right hand, aiming it upward. As she pointed, dark curls on Serena's forehead lifted slightly with a breeze from their northeastern windows.

"So, there is no pain," Géla said softly, "but we need to do something to the north of us, moving higher up the hillside. Is it about Rostov? Do we need to visit Rostov?"

Serena nodded her head gravely while Géla stared at her in disbelief. *What do we have here? We knew she was born with the Gift, but to display such understanding at this age has never been known before. Maker's Touch!*

Now, with all the agents, assassins and double-dealing merchants cleared from Tuvan, the journey to the city's heights had become much easier. Still, a score of guards accompanied their simple carriage as Géla and Serena rode uphill, seeking Rostov.

Up in his hillside hospice, Rostov was finally growing stronger and healing.

"Even if I have to leave a little trail of blood wherever I go," he said to Géla, "I should be down from this hillside sometime this week." When he saw the look of worry on Géla's face he added, "But I can see that you have come not just to comfort the sick. What is happening?"

"I think that Serena is seeing something none of the rest of us can see," Géla said. "She wanted to come to see you. Even if you have only a portion of the Sight, still you may be the only person in Khiva able to share her visions, or at least guess at their meaning." She sat her child on the bed so that Serena and Rostov could study each other's faces.

Rostov smiled down at her. "So, little princess, what do you see?" Serena's right hand pointed upward uncertainly and finally settled above a window that faced east.

"Eastern skies? What could —" Suddenly, images flashed across Rostov's mind, of a brilliant light growing steadily brighter as it surged toward them out of the east.

"Some great disaster is coming for us," Rostov muttered, and he stumbled awkwardly to his feet, wincing in pain. "I cannot even guess at its nature, but the first question is when? And the second question, what should we do?"

Serena frowned, then lay on her side as though asleep. She repeated this process three more times, then sat up, with a look of frustration on her small face.

"Serena is trying to tell us the number of sleeps before disaster comes," Géla murmured, "but she cannot yet form words, nor can she count well enough yet to give us the number of days. I would guess that less than a week, let's say four days remain to us."

"So, what do we say to our people?" Rostov asked.

"We cannot sound the alarm based on the visions of a child," Géla said, "no matter how powerful the Gift within her. I must seek council through Gates of Dreams. Perhaps one of the Great Powers will take pity on us."

Later that evening Géla stared out of her windows that faced west, watching as a red sun sank beyond the surface of the ocean. Bowing her head, she whispered an entreaty to Pallas Athena:

"Holy Mother, my service to the Maker prevents me from praying to you, but if you still look down upon us with some favor, I beg you to guide us at this moment. Disaster is upon us, and our only warnings come from an infant who cannot yet form words, nor can she even count the days left to us."

And that night in dreams, Géla found herself standing before the great throne of Pallas Athena. All the calm, peaceful power had left the Goddess, so that Pallas Athena stood, agitated, staring into the distance as she spoke.

"What your child sees is the Sending's return — for the Demon Princes hurled a Dagger at the Maker's Heart, and now they have called this mighty weapon back so that they will regain its old power. I fear that Serena foresees the end of Alantéa. The Gods have also seen fearsome visions, though nothing is certain. You have less than eight days to prepare. Warn all your people to flee from the shorelines and to seek the heights. Even if by some miracle they heed these warnings, you will surely not be able to save all of them."

The next morning, swift riders were sent out to all the coastal regions of the League bearing messages that disaster was coming in less than a week and that they needed to flee to higher ground. Without the guidance of the Wizards, however, the peoples of the League engaged in a widespread debate about what actions needed to be taken, so that many simply went about their daily tasks, believing that they could always scramble to safety at the edge of disaster.

Under the pressure of what seemed an endless war, even the Wizards' League was beginning to fragment.

· X ·

Phaedra smiled down at Thorian's daughter and drifted away. She had been speaking soft words with Eléna, though the young human seemed only mildly interested in Phaedra's opinions. As always, Turin was watching her with interest, so she stared into murky, dark skies as though dreaming of faraway places.

With part of Phaedra's powerful mind, she continued to study the Dreamers who were beginning to transform themselves from ghosts back into their original forms. No longer invisible, the Dreamers had become smoky beings, showing hazy outlines of their original shapes when they had sat as powerful beings in the Hall of the Dreamers.

Phaedra kept a soft, dreamy look on her face, while inside, her mind boiled with dark thoughts.

*I have been sent as a **construct** to the wrong side! The losing side! Each day I have less in common with Turin and Magog. These "Dreamers" are taking so long to restore themselves that they will not even be made half whole before the Sending returns to destroy them for yet a second time. There will be no Temple of Waiting for them, for Hell will consume them in its fires! They will wish they had been left to drift endlessly, mindlessly through their Cathedral of Sorrows.*

What am I to do? Can I simply change sides, or should I escape back to Alantéa the Forerunner and then go into hiding? The Demon Princes invite me to join their alliance. They pretend to have hierarchies, places of intermediate power for their favored allies, but what I see are two levels: Demon Princes, and their servants. At present, their servants are sometimes indulged, but later their servants will become no more than slaves.

So, I must escape. I must look for a time when Turin is distracted. When the Sending arrives, so many more chances will be opened for me. The Mid-World is large; I will build my power far, far from the Isle of the Demons and all its nightmares.

The Demon Princes had sent Phaedra images of their Dagger. Their Sending was no longer speeding at the Maker's Heart; now it was returning to destroy the enemies of the Demon Princes. All the images shown to her had been carefully detailed: the Sending was converting much of its matter into additional energy, and its speed was building. Ships of space disintegrated as they fed the Sending's inner fires. Machine entities and supernatural beings on the Sending's surface were seeking desperately to escape, but less powerful beings were being caught and converted into powerful energies to increase the Dagger's speed.

Phaedra had seen moments of terror on the Sending's surface, and she shuddered. How could completely inorganic machine-beings show such fear? It would be a matter of days not months before the Sending returned, and then soon, too soon, it would be her turn to feel horror — unless she could escape.

Chapter Nineteen

The Mid-World of the Truce

IT WAS NIGHT AND overcast in the Vale of Whispers, a place where The Mid-World of the Truce had been created, so many ages ago. Two tall columns of smoke circled one other warily, gradually closing the ten thousand paces distance that separated them. Around them, ghosts increased their wailing and weeping, crying out their ancient tales of woe, though neither of the two columns paid them the slightest attention. One column of smoke was bluish grey with glints of gold, while the other was pitch black, though sparks could be seen flickering within its smoky column, as though the column was unable to contain the energy inside it.

As they drew closer, gradually all the ghosts in the Vale of Whispers grew silent and began watching intently. Two of the greatest Powers of the Mid-World were about to change the destiny of the Mid-World of the Truce.

It was Set, from within his column of dark smoke, who spoke first: "End-game."

Wotan sighed from his bluish grey column and was silent for a moment before speaking. "The Dagger, the Great Sending, returns to Earth. What will happen when it returns?"

"In stark, brutal visions, I have seen it take shape as a scimitar, slightly curved, glittering with power, slashing at the foundations of Alantéa the Forerunner, and then the Land of Enchantments, the source of all our power is fatally wounded and we are doomed."

"And why," Wotan asked, "why would this weapon strike at Alantéa? It was sent out to destroy the Maker. Why would it return and doom the Forerunner?"

"I understand the Demon Princes all too well," Set replied, "having once been among the most powerful of the Adversaries. Filled with hatred and confusion, this Sending was launched at the Maker. Yet the Demon Princes abhorred the Mid-World of the Truce with an almost equal force. The Sending has inherited that hatred, and it will not be able to restrain itself as it curves back down to the Earth. It will slash at the foundations of Alantéa, and the Forerunner will be destroyed."

"I only seek to understand these events," Wotan murmured, "not to deny them. For I have seen destruction, horror, and death every time I gaze into the future. Although, after the ruin of Alantéa, our own doom comes slowly, a gradual weakening over the years as our powers lessen. Toward the end, we become invisible ghosts, with voices that only a few mortals can hear, and finally, none can hear, though it no longer matters, for our minds have withered and we can only babble the nonsense of demented wraiths."

The two were silent for a moment, then Wotan said, "Several circles of the moon ago, four of the Mid-World Powers were present in this place, creating the so-called Godlings. Were you among them?"

"I think that you understand that I was not, and I do not believe that if either or both of us had been present that we could have changed that outcome. The Godlings were given neither the wisdom nor the power to confront the Demon Princes. In addition, they were filled with all the malice and confusion of the Mid-World."

Set looked away for a moment before continuing. "Now, since we are at this End-game, and since it was our destiny to speak together once, and once only, I will say the words that no other being has heard or will ever hear again: for so many thousands of the circles of the sun I learned nothing, only entertaining myself with my own self-absorbed malevolent intrigues and sinister devices. And yet in more recent years, I have allowed myself to dream. Painfully, drop by bitter drop, wisdom has been slipping into my sleeping mind through gates of dreams. I am like a chained Creature Indomitable with thin streams of burning acid pouring down upon me. That is the pain, that is the price, though when I wake, I am finally able to glimpse the limitless wisdom and enormous majesty of the Maker's Mind."

Wotan nodded slowly, grimly. "I have also paid a price, though mine has not been nearly as bitter as yours. I gaze into starlight sometimes from a great distance, following the passage of our fellow beings through the void of space. Seraphs and Spirit Lords and Dragons and Demons have long since passed beyond light speed, and in their passage, they continue to grow in strength and purpose. With their journeys, beings with only a fraction of my original power and intellect have become greater than I ever was or might possibly have become. I do not regret my own choices. I do not begrudge other Ancient Powers their transformations. But I must acknowledge that I have paid a price."

Set nodded; each had spoken the truth. "Before we call down the Mid-World of the Truce, what do you believe will transpire?"

"We must create a great Shield," Wotan replied, "capable of smashing this Dagger far from Earth."

"First a Shield and then a Sword," Set said, "a Shield to deflect, a Sword to destroy."

A curious peace descended over each of them, and they were silent for a moment, staring into the Vale of Whispers, where silent ghosts twisted and turned in anticipation. Then speaking simultaneously Set and Wotan spoke the words that called down the Mid-World of the Truce.

Guardians stood transfixed, orb-eyes staring into the gloom: the Great Guardian was sending them images, showing a congress of Mid-World Powers — the Gods — and all their greatest servants as they gathered in the Vale of Whispers. Godlings, themselves creations of the Mid-World of the Truce, also stared into the distance, able to see at least a portion of what transpired in the Vale of Whispers. Magog's face was grim, while Phaedra's mouth curled with malice, and Turin glanced back and forth between the other two Godlings, his mind churning with troubled thoughts.

Galad usually kept his impatience under control, but now his right foot tap-tap-tapped as he waited for Julian and the Wizards to sort matters out and then explain them to their ragged followers, the "Giftless warriors." Eléna held her father's arm while studying Julian's face and listening to Merlin's words. Kalanin stood, head slightly bowed, listening, and waiting, though he looked up with interest as the shades of the Dreamers drifted toward them.

"Each of us," Merlin said patiently, "can see glimpses of events in the Vale of Whispers, and we hope that the Mid-World of the Truce will, at last, come in force against their true foes, the Demon Princes. Yet we stand only a few paces from Orissa, the great Seeress, who has always seen most deeply into the depths of space, and into the past, and the future. Perhaps we should simply ask her this: Orissa, what is happening, what is to come?"

As the Dreamers drifted toward Julian, Orissa spoke: "Wizards, I have only a portion of my ancient strength. Yet images are surging into the mind of your Apprentice. Sentauris was my descendent, and Julian is the great grandchild of Sentauris. So Julian, my descendant, so many times removed from me, set aside all your quiet reserve, and tell everyone what you see."

"A great Shield will form," Julian began in a low, soft voice, then as others clustered closer to hear his words, he raised his voice. "A great Shield will form, with all the power of the Mid-World behind its creation. Beyond the Shield is a Sword, intended to clash with the Dagger after the Shield blocks its passage. I can only see that there will be warfare in the upper reaches of the skies, for the outcome is not clear to me."

Behind the shade of Orissa, the ghostly figure of Llara loomed more than twice the height of the mortal Seeress. "I have no visions to speak of, though I have some grave insights to add: had the Shield and the Sword clashed with the Dagger when the Dagger was created so many months ago, the outcome would not have been in doubt, and the Sending of the Demon Princes would have been destroyed.

"Yet in the Hall of the Dreamers we have watched powers, dominions, intelligences become so much greater as they journeyed through space, seeking the Maker. This strengthening is a gift to all those seeking the Maker — even though they might wish to destroy him rather than learn wisdom from him. The Sending has grown many times stronger as it surged through space. The Demon Princes may not yet realize what they have done, but their Sending is filled with hatred of Alantéa, and it may not be able to restrain itself. I fear for Alantéa and the Mid-World of the Truce."

Phaedra kept her face frozen, though her mind was shrieking: *Alantéa will be destroyed! Now I cannot even flee into the Mid-World of the Truce! I must either die in battle and writhe in Hell or become a plaything of Demon Princes! But yet — there is still Otherwhen. It is still better to be a fading creature of Otherwhen, living perhaps only a few thousand years. I would rather wither slowly than be destroyed or enslaved in the next few days. How can I gain access to Otherwhen? Julian holds one Crystal, but he is protected, always more carefully by these ungainly constructs known as Guardians. The Sorcerers hold the other two Crystals — what of the Sorcerers? If I cannot reach the Apprentice, I need to snare one of the Sorcerers and rip the Crystal from his feeble, mortal hands.*

· ⚹ ·

This time, as Alcman stormed into Houma's dream kingdom, he abandoned all his earlier pretenses. One of the Sorcerer's hands waved aside gardens and glistening streams. Another hand dispensed with all the imaginary messengers who carried meaningless messages. White pillars and green plants faded into nothingness. Alcman snarled, and the armed sentries before Houma's inner gates vanished like mists blown away by a great wind.

With both hands clenched, Alcman smashed at the huge wooden doors, and they splintered into kindling. Houma was seated at his broad pedestal desk, and now he looked up, astonished, at his fellow Sorcerer. Alcman clapped both hands together and Houma's desk and chair vanished, spilling the Sorcerer to the ground.

"Wait, no, wait," Houma sputtered. "I am almost at the edge of —" Alcman reached down and with one strong arm ripped Houma from the ground and pulled him to his feet.

"Houma, you must come now," Alcman snarled, "or be a dead thing forever."

"You do not...." Houma trailed off, for all the remaining portions of his dream world were fading as he struggled to speak. Alcman drew a deep breath and with a *shout*, blew all the remaining, fading images into nothingness.

The two Sorcerers found themselves again upon the Isle of the Demons. They stood looking out over the ramparts of the Demons' black basalt fortress. Overhead, the sky glinted with a strange light. Houma's mouth opened, but he was unable even to form a question.

"What you see," Alcman muttered, "is a Shield created by the Gods — to defend the Mid-World. That Shield hopes to defend the earth. Behind that Shield lurks a Sword. What approaches like a swiftly growing point of light, is the Scimitar, the extraordinarily powerful *Sending* of the Demon Princes. Houma of the Withered Hand, two realities are about to collide and only one of them will prevail. Prepare yourself. Gather all your old cunning and whatever remnants of sorcerous power you can still muster."

Beyond the gleaming Shield, Houma could now for the first time see the *Sending* and hear distant howling noises as it hurtled toward the Earth. As Houma's mouth sagged open, Alcman touched Houma's cloak and spoke directly into the Sorcerer's mind:

In victory or defeat, our time upon this Isle may well be over. If we are indeed finished with the Demon Princes, they will never find us in the hidden places of Otherwhen.

Cunning and malice flashed through Houma's eyes, and Alcman laughed darkly to himself. *There, I have warned Houma, but he will only find some way to betray me, in order to gain favor with his masters, the Demon Princes. It would be wise to flee now, and yet I **will** see, I **must** see, the outcome when these two realities collide.*

Chapter Twenty

A Clash of Weapons

KALANIN GLANCED UP INTO skies that had no stars, where clouds produced only thin strands of mist, but not a single raindrop. At least this fading portion of Otherwhen had air that could be breathed without a struggle. Kalanin sighed as his eyes drifted downward. Not thirty paces away, Julian and Merlin were whispering softly together. Like all the other ghosts, magical constructs, and other beings in their strange alliance, Kalanin's eyes kept returning to the discussion between Apprentice and Wizard.

Galad was standing at Kalanin's side, and when Galad's foot started its impatient tap-tap-tapping, Kalanin laughed softly.

"Yes, I know," Galad muttered, "but I think we're heading into a battle where all the 'hack and chop' lads, like the two of us, will be pushed off to one side...hold on. Enter the Familiars —out of nowhere." Rafir and Sebastian had popped suddenly into view, one to each side of the Apprentice.

Kalanin nodded. He and Galad stepped forward to join with the Apprentice, his two Familiars, and their Wizard master.

Merlin's mouth closed slowly as Kalanin and Galad approached, but then the Wizard nodded. "Yes, you four have been linked since the beginning of our struggles, and it is only right that you come to stand with Julian the Apprentice at the end."

"I have been saying to Merlin," Julian said in a voice that was no longer a whisper, "that the Sending of the Demon Princes has almost completed its journey back to Earth, and so we must return to the Isle."

Merlin shook his head. "And I have replied that I do not believe that we are strong enough to counter the Demon Princes." Now, as the voices of Wizard and Apprentice were raised, all their allies halted their own conversations and stood listening.

"First comes a Clash of Weapons," Julian said quietly, "then a Battle of OverGods."

Merlin bowed his head. "I cannot foresee these things, and yet now I must trust the Sight that has become so powerful within you, Julian. So be it."

"Galad believes," Kalanin added, "and I agree, that we have moved beyond swordplay, that we will be no more than bystanders in the coming struggle. Are we right?"

Julian shook his head: no. "Hatred consumes both Demon Princes and their corrupted Guardian allies. We should never underestimate the malice of our foes. Eléna will join the four of you, and you must guard one another, for they will attempt to destroy you. Be wary, and very, very careful."

Merlin turned to their allies. "The great Sending of the Demon Princes has nearly completed its journey back to Earth, and so our time in Otherwhen has ended. We must return to the Isle of the Demons. Prepare yourselves for battle."

Kalanin glanced up one last time into starless skies, then turned to watch the Apprentice as he clutched his Talisman.

Julian invoked his Crystal, and now a great-arched Portal opened. On the other side of the Portal, just a few thousand paces away stood the

Citadel of the Demon Princes, with wreaths of dark smoke lifting from its slabs of black basalt. Nothing grew on the plains surrounding the Citadel. Boulders had been clustered in mounds, though no huts or ancient walls of stone remained on the plains. The Demon Princes had created a vast killing field should the Powers of the Mid-World or lesser intruders approach their fortress.

Standing before the Portal, Julian took a deep breath, drawing in the air that drifted toward him over dark plains. The scent of death lingered over these lands: here was yet another place where Demon Princes had buried dead things. Whether these were ancient sea-monsters that had died when the Isle was raised, or other failed experiments, was impossible to tell. But many, many crypts and graveyards lay beneath the plains surrounding the Citadel.

Phaedra was also able to smell dead things, but she ignored their scent. As others gathered toward the Portal, Phaedra edged forward. *Once we emerge from this gateway, I must seize Julian's Crystal then flee. I **will** find a way to call upon the Crystal's power and then I **will** become Queen of Otherwhen!*

When a protective phalanx of Guardians gathered around Julian, Phaedra struggled with the shrieking voice inside her and only muted, choking sounds came from her throat, noises that were drowned out by all the heavy shuffling footsteps of the Guardians as they passed back to the Isle of the Demons.

· ✕ ·

Alcman stood beside Houma on the upper ramparts of the Demons' fortress, staring up into a sky that glinted with the Shield's protective light, though storm clouds were gathering to the west. Lights grew brighter as the

Sending surged toward them like some gigantic comet. When the Portal opened on the plain below, both Sorcerers were drawn to that gateway, watching intently as their adversaries spilled onto the plain that surrounded the Demons' Citadel.

The slight figures of Julian and Merlin emerged first, and Houma laughed, but then the Sorcerer began muttering darkly as he counted a total of six Guardians following behind the Apprentice.

"Yes," Alcman murmured, "take note that not all events have favored the Demon Princes." Houma's eyes glanced at Alcman with a mixture of malice and calculation, then he turned back to the comet-like Sending that was speeding toward the Earth; for now, it was upon them.

Smash!!!

A great concussion shook the Earth, and the two Sorcerers were hurled from their feet. The sky overhead shimmered in agony. Vibrations from the clash shook the two Sorcerers as they lay slumped on the basalt of the Demons' fortress.

As the shaking subsided, Alcman groaned and forced himself to stand. "The Shield created by the Mid-World has withstood the Sending's first blow," he murmured in hushed tones. "I did not think the Mid-World's Shield would last, not even for a half-second. Behold the Sending, Houma, for you will never see events such as these ever again."

They stared upward, watching as the Sending recoiled, then began shedding mass: all the remaining otherworld invaders and intruders carried by the Sending were being cast down to the Far Lands, some fleeing, some toppling in midair, desperately seeking enough power to counter Earth's gravity. Supernatural entities and machine intellects and alien biologies were being cast to the Far Lands, where they would spread endless mysteries and deadly, dark dreams, forever haunting the humans waking in those lands.

"Defending only Alantéa, the Shield has let them pass like meaningless debris to the Far Lands," Alcman murmured, shaking his head. "As if Gods and Demons were not enough. Now, these alien constructs and alien entities will double, even treble the endless nightmares of Mankind."

Light flashed overhead. A second shuddering sound made the two Sorcerers hunch down in pain.

"The Sword fashioned by the Mid-World lashes at the Sending," Alcman murmured. "However, I do not believe that the Sword will prevail."

"In the end, nothing will ever stand for long against three Demon Princes," Houma said, but then he pointed downward "but what is happening now on the plains beneath their fortress? Some sort of struggle is taking place in the lower skies."

Alcman's eyes shifted from the upper skies and stared downward. Words came to his mind, and he spoke thoughts that had been formed by others — yet somehow Alcman was now able to voice them: "Under pressure, complex alliances falter and fail. The Godlings are at war with each other."

· ✕ ·

Phaedra hurled another blast of lightning at her fellow Godling, Turin. "I have changed sides! It is as simple as that," she cried. "Why would I wish to die beside weakened, feeble mortals, ghosts with little substance, and strange, orb-eyed constructs who were defeated so many years ago? Just leave me to my own destiny!"

Like Phaedra, Turin had risen in the air, but he sought to restrain Phaedra, not destroy her. "The Godlings *must* stand together," he called out. "We *will* stand together!" A third blast of lightning forced a great cry of pain from Turin. He dropped a hundred feet down, farther from Phaedra, but Turin would not be driven from the skies.

When the sky again shook, both Godlings glanced upward: the Sword of the Mid-World and the Sending of the Demon Princes were clashing high above Earth.

"That was the Sword of the Mid-World," Phaedra cried aloud, "and like so many of the Mid-World's devices, it is part of a confused, lost cause. Behold! In the most powerful of visions, I have seen the Sword shattered into a thousand fragments!"

"Visions crafted by Demon Princes!" Turin called back, and this time he brushed aside Phaedra's lightning strike and closed with his sister Godling. Below them, an uncertain Magog also began lifting into the skies.

Alcman stared down at the Godlings' struggle, and he drew a deep breath. Carefully and cautiously, he attuned his farsight to the skies below so that he was able both to see the Godlings and listen to Phaedra as she fought to free herself from Turin. As he heard the words that the Godlings shouted at each other, another portion of his powerful, enchanted mind reached back and replayed the words the ghost of Hestaur had spoken to him at the inn: *"You must flee when the great confrontation comes, and after, find something useful to do; you might even carry out some act of mercy in Otherwhen. If you could preserve yet a single blade of grass from a gust of cold wind, that would be a new beginning, and a vast improvement over your life to date, Alcman of the Tormented Soul."*

Suddenly Alcman's mind cleared, and his hunched shoulders straightened — he would do much more than save a "blade of grass." He glanced over to Houma, who was watching his fellow Sorcerer with a mixture of amazement and cunning. Alcman smiled mildly at his former ally, sensing that Houma could read a portion of his mind. Now was a wonderful time for Houma to gain favor with his Demon masters by betraying Alcman, but Houma understood so very little about the clash of forces in the skies far above Earth.

Smash!!!

The Great Sending shattered the Mid-World's Sword into a thousand fragments, sending shards of light hurtling through the skies in all directions.

As Houma recoiled in shock, staring up at the shattered Sword, Alcman invoked his Crystal and vanished. A half-second later, the Sorcerer was dropping through the skies into the struggle between the two warring Godlings. Bolts of lightning lashed at the Sorcerer, but Alcman's complex spell-shields held. Strands of sorcery grasped Phaedra and Turin. Suddenly, Turin, Phaedra, and Alcman were drawn into Otherwhen, taking the conflict between the two Godlings far from the Isle of the Demons.

An astonished Houma forced his mouth to close. Then the Sorcerer called aloud, "My Demon Masters, they will not get far! I will find and destroy all three of them!" Corrupted Guardians stirred, filled with all their old distrust and hatred of the Sorcerers. When they heard Houma's words, they reached for the Sorcerer with dream-strands. As Houma searched his Crystal for Alcman and the two Godlings, tendrils of dreamworld power reached up through slabs of black basalt, grasping Houma with powerful white strands.

Before Houma could shift into Otherwhen, the Sorcerer underwent his last and final transformation: under the pressure of complex, conflicting magics, Houma's body took the form of an enormous crab, with one, dark sorcerous claw and a second pale claw that sagged as though wounded. Only the head of Houma remained human, and yet his eyes had become the shining, red, demented eyes of a Kul-Ghoul. Then the being that had once been Houma passed into unknown regions of Otherwhen, still bearing one of three Crystals.

· X ·

Shards of light from the broken Sword shimmered through the skies overhead. On the dark, stony plain before the fortress of the Demons, Julian whispered, "Alantéa the Forerunner."

"Is the Forerunner doomed?" Merlin asked quietly.

Julian, in shock, nodded his head. "The Shield will not hold, and the Sending will not be able to restrain itself for it was filled with enormous hatred and malice."

Smash!!!

As before, the concussion cast Julian to the ground, and as before, Kalanin and Galad pulled the Apprentice to his feet. When Julian stood, he turned to his right where a tall seam in the air was opening, and the Great Guardian stepped through, joining them on the plain.

"Doom is one thing," the Great Guardian said, "and yet I do not believe that the Maker would wish us to surrender Alantéa without a struggle. Come, join with me and see if we cannot strengthen this Mid-World Shield as it struggles to defend the Earth."

Guardians gathered to the Great Guardian's side; each of the six stood only two-thirds as tall as their leader. Shades of the Dreamers drifted to the Great Guardian as did the Wizards and Magog, the lone remaining Godling. Power surged upward, an erratic, confused mixture of magics. Then, as the Great Guardian began to understand all the varied energies at his command, the surge of power grew more focused; and the Shield began to glisten with new force.

Smash!!!

Now the Sending was hurled from Earth's upper atmosphere back into space. From the Demons' fortress came cries of rage, with his farsight, Julian could sense three torrents of fire as flames spewed from the mouths of Demon Princes.

Light overhead grew brighter as the Sending gathered itself to strike again at Earth's Shield. In the distance, Marids were pulling slabs of basalt from the base of the Demon's citadel, forming an exit from the fortress. Then they began gathering on the plain, preparing to assail their foes. Behind the Marids, the three tall and twisted forms of the Dark Lords emerged, as did the ten corrupted Guardians, five on each wing of the Dark Lords. From three thousand paces away, they began advancing on the foes of their masters.

"The Demon Princes do not understand what is at stake," Julian murmured, "and so comes the doom of Alantéa the Forerunner."

"An uncontrolled malice," Kalanin added softly, "will always breed stupidity. It has always been so, and it will always be that way, forever."

"Maker," Galad whispered, bowing his head "have mercy upon Alantéa the Forerunner."

From the corrupted Guardians came pale, translucent arcs of dreamworld energies surging toward their foes; from each arc, white tendrils, like ghostly snakes, slithered through the air.

The Great Guardian and his brethren began trembling and gasping under the pressure of dreamworld magic. They shook and twisted and called aloud, but finally, they were forced to abandon the Shield. Grimly, they turned from the skies toward their foes and began to counter the powerful energies of their adversaries.

A great surge of Seer's Sight blazed within Julian. *Do you not understand?* his mind shouted at the Demon Princes. *If we do not protect Earth, then Alantéa the Forerunner will be destroyed!*

Surrender and abase yourselves, or you will die and be delivered to the fires of Hell! came the response.

"They offer nothing but rage," Julian murmured, "so, no hope comes from demented Demon Princes."

Julian bowed his head in prayer. *"Now, my Maker, great Creator of the Universe, at this final moment, will you not come forward? For you are our last hope."*

Smash!!!

And now fissures formed in the sky as the Shield fashioned by the Truce began to fragment. One last blow shattered the sorcerous barrier. Unlike its companion Sword, the fragments of the Shield broke into huge segments that slid slowly across the upper skies like tectonic plates. Light reflected on the plains below became mottled and strange, as though it came from many different suns.

From the Citadel of the Demon Princes came shouts of triumph, accompanied by columns of fire.

Merlin came to stand beside Julian, the being who had once been his Apprentice. With a faltering, shaking hand, he touched Julian, murmuring, "Urge the Demon Princes to recall their Sending, Let them draw it back to the Isle of the Demons. And after, we must, we *will* find some way to deal with it."

"My Wizard Master," Julian said softly, "you must prepare to defend yourself, for after the Doom of Alantéa, there comes a Battle of OverGods."

Chapter Twenty-One
A Battle of OverGods

In the Demons' place of Power, shouts of triumph were replaced by dark muttering sounds, then a louder command.

"Return to us, now!" Satanis called out in a voice of doom. "Sending fashioned from our own powers, you must come back to the Isle, and become one with us again!"

As the Sending arced higher over Earth, Iblis muttered, "Where is it going? Why was it not drawn back to the Isle as ordered?"

"There is a lust for destruction within it," Zikar said softly, "and so it will not heed us. See how it rises in triumph high above this planet." Glittering with power, the Sending circled Earth three times, then it surged down toward Alantéa.

"No! No! No!" Iblis called out, torrents of fire spilling from his mouth as the Sending hewed at Alantéa's the Forerunner's foundations.

Satanis turned on Zikar. "Make it return! "You must *force* it to return!"

"*You* must force it to return!" Zikar snarled in reply. "It is your own malice, and the lust for destruction within Iblis, that have become the greatest forces within the Sending, and now the darkness within you two has brought destruction upon Alantéa the Forerunner!"

Helpless to stop the Sending, the Demon Princes watched in horror from a distance as their own construction hewed a second then a third time at Alantéa, leaving its foundations in ruins.

· ☿ ·

Géla sat beside Rostov on the upper hillside overlooking Khiva's "Goblin Market". Serena was being held on Géla's lap, staring wide-eyed into the glittering skies overhead, cringing as the sounds of warfare radiated downward from the clash overhead. Below the Market, Khiva was mostly deserted, though as always, some had hidden rather than heeding the call to seek the heights. Above the city, more than a few people were sampling goods at Khiva's wine stores, and Géla could hear their mindless babble as Khiva's "Goblin Market" hosted its final party.

"It's what you expected," Géla murmured to Rostov. Despite her soft words, her hands were clenching and unclenching as she watched doom dance in the skies overhead.

"I've learned a great deal in the last few years," Rostov said. "Predicting the behavior of Khiva's citizens has become a routine matter. Anyway, I've doubled the guard in case the revelers become rowdy. That is the least of our worries. I'm afraid that we are watching the last of Khiva, and probably, the end of the League."

Then they were silent, staring overhead as the Clash of Weapons sent shock waves over Alantéa, and most of the revelers were hurled from their feet. Géla hunched over, shielding Serena, as the child turned toward her mother, closed her eyes, and began crying softly.

When the Sending struck at the foundations of Alantéa for a third time, huge chunks of Khiva's hillside, with all its many stone houses and luxurious gardens and tree-lined streets slid down into the deep harbor. Much of the "Goblin Market" was lost, including most of the revelers.

Khiva's beautiful natural harbor was destroyed as was the greater part of the city.

Géla and Serena could do no more than weep; yet they still lived, as did Rostov, and all those who had sought safety on the upper heights of Khiva.

· ⅄ ·

All of Alantéa was shaken. The skies darkened as millions of birds across the Land of Enchantments lifted from the ground, calling out in panic. Beasts raced mindlessly through forests and fields. Buildings collapsed, burying the dwellers within. In the great forests of Alantéa, enormous thousand-year-old trees shattered, crushing those below. Creatures of the Darkness were battered by rockslides in hidden caves of stone and bellowed in pain and fear.

At Nemesis, all the temples dedicated to the Great Dark Gods slid into the ocean. The Halls of Merlin were swallowed by the shoreline. Hestari vanished beneath the waves, while huge sections of Mount Evergrey slid from the mountain's peak, destroying many of the plateaus beneath those peaks and the valley settlements they sheltered.

Tsunamis raced from Alantéa, spreading death to the Far Lands. All the coastal cities and harbors within the Isles of the Sorcerers were drowned by towering waves.

Shaken, the Great Gods again called down The Truce, and all the combined power of the Mid-World struggled to stabilize Alantéa the Forerunner. The land trembled then steadied, but still, the shoreline lapped at the Forerunner's shores, slowly drawing the Land of Enchantments downward into the ocean's dark depths.

· 𝕏 ·

"Can Alantéa yet be saved?" Satanis asked, in the softest words ever spoken by a Demon Prince.

"We can bring enormous power to that task," Iblis murmured, equally subdued.

"That power may still not be sufficient," Zikar said, "and before we turn to Alantéa, we must first prevail against our foes. Come. Battle awaits us."

"Our opponents seem so feeble," Iblis said, "perhaps this struggle is simply a matter for our servants and slaves."

"It has been among our greatest flaws," Zikar said evenly, "that we have always underestimated our foes, and failed to understand the complex assortment of forces arrayed against us. We must endure the pain once again, and become one being, absorbing all the slaves and our so-called 'allies' in our alliance. Then we will triumph, and in the process perhaps come to understand all things, including some method of preserving at least a portion of Alantéa."

The three Demon Princes stepped slowly, almost hesitantly, from their thrones of power, as though they feared the pain they first encountered when the three had fused to become one, far mightier being. They strode through the gates formed so many centuries ago. Guardians, Dark Lords, and Marids stood aside until the Demon Princes passed to the forefront, facing only an empty plain.

Satanis stood in the center with Iblis on his right, and Zikar on his left.

"I will ask this again," Iblis murmured, "and this one time only: is this joining together absolutely necessary?"

"In the distance, our foes are gathering and will be forced to become one being — a lesser OverGod," Zikar said, "yet they will have only a fraction of the power that we shall have. A greater OverGod will face only a lesser, cringing thing."

"So now it comes to this — again," Satanis said.

"No other choices remain," Iblis muttered, "except pain."

And then all three Demon Princes groaned as they began to fuse into one being.

Suddenly, standing tall on the plain, more than a hundred feet high was a Greater Demon Prince, staring into the distant edge of the plain, where their foes sought to gather their own, tiny, ineffectual strength. Then it turned to regard its allies with a far different expression.

The Greater Demon reached first for Un-Maurag as though a Storm Giant groped for a fawn.

"This was never a part of our pact!" Un-Maurag shouted. "I am done with you!" A Portal with a huge arch sprang up before the Dark Lord, but before Un-Maurag could escape, he was gathered to the Greater Demon, and bellowing in pain, the Dark Lord was absorbed.

Before Un-Maurag even finished shrieking, two enormous hands reached down and grasped the stunned forms of Haeglin and Mordred. The Greater Demon surged even higher, towering over the plain, and now it looked down at its Marid and Guardian allies with something that had nothing resembling a hint of gratitude — only hunger.

· ⋊ ·

Their adversaries were gathering some distance away, at the far edge of the plain. Galad and Kalanin were shifting slowly away from those beings who wielded powerful magic. Uncertainly, Eléna, Sebastian and Rafir followed behind them.

"Isn't this what you wished for?" Kalanin muttered to Galad. "What did you call it, 'a thousand-foot OverGod'?"

Galad laughed a short, bitter laugh. "First of all, it's not quite that high, at least not yet," he muttered, "and secondly, I spoke only in jest. But what I really wished for was something that would crush our foes forever, not this overly huge Demon."

"The Great Guardian is very powerful," Eléna said, catching up to the two warriors, "but how could he ever be able to respond to this?" Two by two, the Greater Demon was absorbing Marids and Guardians as it surged higher.

"Watch as this Demonic thing twitches in pain," Galad said, beginning to jog further from the Great Demon. "I knew there would be a struggle between powerful beings, and that we would be forced to one side, and yet I never thought it would come to such an ugly ending."

"Recall Julian's warning," Kalanin said, running beside Galad, "about the malice of our foes. They will seek to destroy their lesser foes — us, while a greater battle takes place. We need space, we need a high place. We cannot let ourselves be casually trampled underfoot. Now, Sebastian, Rafir, can you aid us as sentries? I think that Julian left you with us for just such a purpose. Will you help us?"

"That's better than watching a five-hundred-foot Demon get bigger and bigger," Rafir muttered.

"We are your watchers," Sebastian added, "but look, there's a third watcher!" Overhead, the Eye of Merlin was circling downward beneath the sliding sky-plates formed by the shattered Shield, and the eagle seemed to be searching for them.

"There's nothing like a hill on this plain," Kalanin muttered, "only mounds of stone. We'll choose the largest of them as a wall that shields us. These mounds probably mark the graves of misshapen monsters, but we have no other choices." They began jogging farther from the Demons'

Citadel, heading westward, where storm clouds were gathering beneath the strange light patterns cast by the shattered Shield.

As they ran, Eléna called out, "Look behind us, the Great Guardian is responding!"

"Sentries, watch for foes!" Kalanin called to Sebastian and Rafir. Then they stopped and turned toward the Great Guardian. From a few hundred paces away, they could hear groaning sounds as six smaller Guardians struggled to join with their leader. The Great Guardian's form lurched upward, shaking with his effort to grow, moaning in pain.

As they watched, the Eye of Merlin descended and landed on the ground just in front of the five.

"Without Julian," the eagle croaked, "you are blind and headed in the wrong direction. To your right, north of you, lies a lesser mound of stones, but around it and beneath it are catacombs where dead things fester — I can smell them even from here. Follow closely behind me."

The three humans nodded and drew deep breaths. Then they jogged north, as the eagle flapped its way in front of them. Behind them came powerful groaning noises, and again they turned. The Great Guardian stood tall, a colossus — but even now, it was only a fraction of the height of the Greater Demon — and now the Great Guardian was shaking and shuddering and gasping with the effort to maintain its form.

With a last cry of agony, the Guardians became again seven smaller figures, all of them sprawling or kneeling on the plain beside three frail seeming Wizards, the ghostly shades of the Dreamers, and one lone Godling.

"Hurry now!" the Eye called down from overhead. "Your own dooms and the fate of Earth are gathering to this moment, and to this place! Go! And quickly!"

They raced north, glancing back every twenty paces, and now, the first traces of dust could be seen speeding from the Demons' Citadel. A huge, even greater menacing version of the Snake God had been sent to destroy them and bounding along beside it was a large band of Kul-Ghouls, hyena voices crying aloud with dark laughter.

Galad forced himself to keep silent, though his wayward tongue wanted to call out to the corrupted Guardians, to tell them that no matter how powerful they had become, they were also dim-witted, lacking creativity — at least a new variety of monstrosities should have been created for this last, ultimate battle.

With a final burst of speed, they reached the northern stony mound just a few moments before their foes. Others turned to watch events on the plains, while Kalanin, still panting, edged around the mound trying to see how it might aid in their defense.

The Eye landed on the peak of the mound and called down, "This will *never* serve as a back-shield! They have come at you with pure power, and your only hope is to defend yourselves in the narrow passages below! Do not seek to prevail! Try only to stay alive!" The eagle fluttered to the ground some twenty paces from Kalanin, croaking, "Over here is an opening. Ignore the stench of death — and seek to live!"

Kalanin stared back to the Citadel where so many things were taking place:

The Snake God was speeding for them with Kul-Ghouls bounding behind it, and the Eye was right — it was too large to be fought on open ground; they would be dead in seconds and Kul-Ghouls would feast first on their flesh, and then break open their bones and feed on the marrow within.

Far from the Snake God, Voritar, or the Shade of Voritar was trying to absorb their force into a second OverGod; and the form, though larger than the colossus formed by the Great Guardian, was filled with smoky portions of ghostly Dreamers, and shuddering with the strain.

And now the Sending of the Demon Princes had been drawn down to the plains. It stood, taking form as a curved scimitar, gleaming with power, taller even than the Greater Demon before it. Yet the Sending seemed to be struggling with the Greater Demon as though it wished to rule the Demon Princes and not simply be absorbed. Energies flowed back and forth between the two enormous figures as Sending and Greater Demon fought for control. Great, deep gasping sounds echoed across the plains, following by the vibrations and thudding sounds as great forces of magic collided.

Kalanin turned away. To believe that the Demon Princes and their own Sending might destroy each other was too much to hope for, and so it simply would not happen.

"Below," Kalanin said, "we can only fight them in the deepest, most narrow of passages."

The Eye of Merlin flapped his wings, seeking the upper skies. Eléna edged forward into the tunnel, light gleaming from her open palms. A stench of dead sea monsters rose to greet them as they scrambled down.

As they passed deeper into the catacombs, light diminished, though sounds still reached them. The first came from their allies — sounds of pain, while the second came from the clash of battle, with more distant concussions echoing from the struggle between Greater Demon and its Sending.

Light flashed more brightly from Elena's hands. "Voritar has failed," she whispered. "What will they do now? And yet the Demon Princes still struggle with their Sending, and that contest has turned into open warfare. My father, you have fought so valiantly, and yet now you are only one of many struggling forces! Julian, you are the catalyst, the pathfinder, but can you find a way to win this one-sided conflict?"

Galad tried to quiet his cough, and then he asked softly. "While these wonderful events unfold, can something be done about the air?"

In spite of their situation, Eléna laughed. "Even my limited powers are good for a bit of wind. Here is some wind —" Her words were interrupted by a great *thumping* noise as the Snake God began pounding down into their hidden refuge.

"Wind, and fresh air," Eléna finished with a whisper, and suddenly, the stench lessened so they could at least breathe freely.

"Hear me for a moment," Kalanin said in a low voice. "We are greatly overmatched, and yet the corrupted Guardians serving the Demons have repeatedly been careless, and so there may be some way we can prevail. Rafir, find for us the deepest narrowest of passages so that the Ghouls are forced to come at us one by one. Galad, as they push down against us, you must take point for we have both noted the hesitations of my blade."

Kalanin's enchanted blade let out a keening sound.

"It is just another, bitter truth," Galad muttered, "that can no longer be denied. Your sword brings to battle all the incredible confusion of the Mid-World."

"Julian," Sebastian whispered, "what are you trying to do?"

Kalanin and Galad's eyes flashed together. "It's what we feared," Kalanin said softly. "But let me finish first. Rafir, seek deep passages. Eléna, you have powerfully enchanted arrows. Do not waste them on the Kul-Ghouls. Save them for the bulging eyes of the Snake God."

"Yes," Eléna said nodding, "I also thought those things, but you have some understanding about Julian that I don't yet grasp. What is happening?"

Grating noises and the sounds of heavy breathing interrupted them and they stared into the upper passages, watching as the red, gleaming eyes of the lead Kul-Ghoul grew brighter.

"Find the narrow passages, Rafir," Kalanin muttered. "We feared that Julian as a force of destiny would be forced to stand against this OverGod, mustering whatever power the Apprentice was able to wield."

"And no 'destiny' would ever be enough for that task," Galad said. "Now, get behind me. Kalanin, try to distract these creatures. Guide me and look for an opening yourself. Ignore the hesitations of your own weapon, for it has destroyed Kul-Ghouls before."

As the Kul-Ghoul's red eyes grew brighter, they could hear sounds of pain out on the battlefield, and those sounds came from Julian the Apprentice, though his voice had grown much louder and deeper — the voice of a giant.

· ✕ ·

Julian's body was wracked by pain as it surged upward. His bones shuddered and fragmented and fused as it struggled to grow larger and absorb all the powers inside him. All the many voices inside his form were crying out in torment. His body surged upward; now he was three times Kalanin's height and he cried aloud as every part of his body was torn apart and restructured. Surging higher, Julian's body thrashed in agony.

As he moaned and surged upward, he forced himself to glance at the Greater Demon and its wayward Sending. The two beings were fighting for control, and yet it was impossible to believe that the Greater Demon would not succeed in controlling its own offspring.

Groaning, Julian glanced down at his own distended body, and he staggered backward in shock: he was becoming a misshapen monster. The shape of his legs and his torso no longer looked anything like the young Apprentice of only a few minutes before. He touched his forehead; he had begun with two eyes, and now there was only a single, huge orb eye. Down at his right elbow, a second head was forming, and it held the features of the lone Godling, Magog. The Godling's mouth was open, and it was crying aloud in pain.

He surged up another two human lengths. Lightning flashed. A concussion of thunder rolled over the plains as Greater Demon and Sending fought for control. Julian stared again down at his lower body: his left leg was stumpy and grey, like that of a Guardian, while his right leg was ghostlike, strands of cloud matter like the Wraiths of a Dreamer. And his left arm was formed of thin smoke, almost shapeless.

Still struggling to grow, Julian's mangled body collapsed onto the surface of the plain, and great cries of agony escaped from his mouth.

"Maker who made us, or let us be made," Julian whispered. His mouth could barely form words, for now, it held twice its normal number of teeth, and many of them felt crumbling and decrepit, as though they belonged to the mouths of ancient Wizards. Yet now, as he spoke those words, all the moaning voices within him gradually stilled, even Magog's, though the Godling had never voiced allegiance to the Maker.

"Those were the words," Julian whispered to the voices within him, "that Kalanin spoke after the Sorcerers and the Marids first destroyed the League. This moment is far more desperate, for we, all of us in this confused form, have now become the Maker's Last Stand, at least on this one planet. Come, help me, and find ways to assist each other. We must rise as one being, even if we become no more than a frail, lesser OverGod. We must, we *will* make a stand."

Grimly, Julian stood. All the voices inside him had grown silent, and now he could feel them working together, struggling to manage Julian's growth. Magog's face slowly faded from his arm. Julian's own mouth lost its choking number of ancient teeth. Moans still escaped from his mouth; his body was still wracked by pain, though now as he surged higher, his form began to regain more of the shape of Julian the Apprentice, even if portions of his body were formed by the cloudy smoke of Wraiths.

· X ·

As the Kul-Ghoul toppled backward against the bones of a sea monster that had been dead for ages, the glow from its red eyes slowly faded and it, too, was a dead thing.

"That's the third of them," Kalanin muttered.

"I only accounted for one," Galad said, and the Tarnished Sword moaned in complaint.

Kalanin nodded. "I will rename my blade 'Ghoul Stabber'."

"And thus far," Eléna added, "I haven't loosed a single one of eight arrows that were constructed for me as destroyers of Marids. Are you sure you want me to hold back?"

"More so than ever," Kalanin replied. "As I said, I'm rethinking the Eagle's advice that we simply try to stay alive."

Galad laughed. "And so, Captain Hangnail, the warlord, emerges from the shadows. Do you truly believe that we can do more than prevail underground?"

"We might," Kalanin said, "and Julian will need all the help we can give him."

Galad's laugh was now briefer and more bitter. "So, we disable or destroy both the Snake God and the Kul-Ghouls, and we emerge onto the plains. Then we wave our feeble weapons at a thousand-foot Greater Demon, and when it turns to crush us with its enormous feet, perhaps it trips over a mound of stones and hurts its poor little self. Is that the plan?"

"A distraction," Kalanin said, "launched into its huge feet. Recall the distance when Eléna's bow was used against the Marids. We have a total of eight enchanted arrows. Three arrows may well destroy the Snake God — one for each eye, and one down its throat. The remaining five arrows could be launched into the lower body of the OverGod. Recall that much of its substance will have been drawn from the bodies of Marids, and Eléna's shafts were created as Marid banes."

"A distraction," Galad muttered. "I —" The catacombs shook, and clumps of overhead earth collapsed down on them as the Snake God's huge head began pounding at their mound, groping its way down toward them.

"I wondered when it would change tactics," Kalanin said, almost to himself. "It will tear open a passage for the Ghouls. Rafir, can you get us farther down, even deeper?" As he turned to the fox, his eyes caught a glint of red. A Kul-Ghoul had been forcing its way quietly toward them, squinting to mask the red radiance from its eyes. Swords flashed, and after Galad's blade caught its throat, the Ghoul could not even manage a death cry.

"Down deeper," Kalanin said, then they turned to follow Rafir.

· X ·

On the plains surrounding the fortress of the Demon Princes, two OverGods faced one another. One was a gigantic being, a Greater Demon whose body shimmered with bronze and red radiances, while the second was simply enormous, a much smaller and frailer being that backed away from its remaining opponent.

Only two Powers still stood, as the Greater Demon had reduced the Sending into Broken fragments that still twisted and thrashed on the plain, while Death slid over its sorcerous components.

"Now comes the time," the Greater Demon boomed out, "when the two of us are to trade promises of doom. Yet how can you possibly threaten *me*?"

Julian backed, testing, reaching. He said nothing to the Greater Demon, only whispering to the other Powers who shared his form *Be ready. First comes a test of Dreamworld Guardian energies. Yet we are too weak by far! There must be other energies we can tap!*

Julian slipped back, sideways, then to his left, while the Great Demon advanced, arms raised, palms extended. From those palms, thousands of White Wraiths surged at Julian.

From Julian's palms, an almost equal number of Blue Wraiths flew out to meet their white brethren. The Great Demon slowed, watching the conflict with something like detached amusement, as neither White nor Blue Wraiths could prevail.

"Have you ever," the Great Demon boomed out, "been deceived by an ally? Our Guardian allies swore that their ten beings could easily defeat the seven Guardians within your feeble form. And once again they have failed us. Has this ever happened to you?" Although the Great Demon spoke in reasonable tones, it continued to edge closer to Julian, its twisted, groping hand betraying its true purpose.

Julian said nothing, only backing, testing his own strength, and reaching for sources of power that were still hidden to him. *Maker, my Great God, there is more power, more strength. I can sense it! But where?*

"A contest of dream energies was only a curiosity," the Great Demon continued, "yet now we come to open warfare — a test of Battle Magic."

Storms burst over the two OverGods as they fought with lightning and blasts of fire, alternating with arctic chills. Transforming magics were hurled back and forth, and both forms shook and shimmered with efforts to maintain themselves. Gradually, Julian was forced back, driven toward the edge of the great plateau, almost into the stony foothills beyond. He began to take wounds, and pain again radiated through his body.

"I fear," Julian whispered to the forces sharing his form, "that there is only one true OverGod on this battlefield."

"Hold on!" Llara called to him. "Voritar is reading portions of their inner thoughts! They have secrets! Do not lose hope!"

Julian staggered back, took another blast of power, and recoiled. Then, using the great strength within his own form, he reached up and tore a huge section of the broken Sky Shield, and then smashed it down on the Great Demon. As the Great Demon responded with other sections of Shielding, both OverGods were smashed from their feet. The Earth shook all around them so that even the great slabs of basalt forming the Citadel of the Demons began to topple.

· ⚭ ·

With the ground shaking all around them, Julian's allies struggled to avoid burial by an earthquake. Only the strength of Galad and Kalanin allowed them time to use the bones of dead Sea Serpents to reinforce portions of the catacombs' tunnel systems. Fearing burial, Kul-Ghouls and the Snake God had escaped upward, and now they were caught in the battle on the plains, hurled back and forth, tumbling across the plains surrounding the fortress, unable to find shelter.

Then came a moment of silence as the battle subsided, and only a few aftershocks rolled back and forth across the plain.

"Julian!" Sebastian called out, then his voice lowered to a whisper. "Julian, I can no longer touch your mind, and so you are lost to me, lost."

"That's what we feared," Galad said. "The Apprentice was never intended to be a match for an OverGod or even a Greater Demon."

"That's beyond our control," Kalanin murmured. "For now, we need larger pockets of air — Rafir, can you guide us with your fox's tunnel sense? I think that the Snake God will return for us, with Kul-Ghouls coming first. We need air before we can deal with the Ghouls and their master. After, we can fight our way up toward Julian."

Sebastian was weeping quietly. "There's no Julian left to save. Whatever is left of him is no longer Julian."

·))(·

Jarl woke slowly into an unimaginable nightmare. He was lying dead or dying on some dry, dusty plain. Pain filled a gigantic thing that was nothing like his own body. Small but harsh croaking sounds were calling into his ear.

Jarl's lone orb-eye flashed open. Some creature was raging at him in a croaking voice — it looked like an eagle, but it was as tiny as an insect. He glanced down at his own body: he was lying on blackish grey, dusty sands that were becoming red with his own blood. His orb-eye stared down at a shattered left leg that had lost its foot. At his side, his elbow had somehow grown its own face, a completely inhuman face that was filled with the same pain that wracked his own body. Explosions and the noise of battle were shaking his broken form.

And inside his broken, pain-filled body, voices were beginning to shout back and forth. Jarl recognized none of the voices shouting at him.

Spasms of pain shook his body again, but Jarl forced his orb-eye open and glanced up. A gigantic Demonic monster was lurching over those same dark sands, struggling with some invisible adversaries, batting at them like a human struggling with a swarm of wasps.

Jarl! A voice was shouting inside of him, a woman's voice he could not recognize. *Jarl, we have lost a battle, but we have not lost the war! We have pulled Ghost Hauntings from Otherwhen, to lash at the Great Demon, though they will not last forever! As we peered into the Great Demon's mind, we suffered a great blast of transforming energy, and so we were changed. Yet within the mind of the Great Demon, we discovered that it had found a line of Maker Force. Watch!*

Jarl's mind filled with images: gleaming blue and gold strands were reaching through a land he could not recognize; lines of unknown force and power were passing through nameless lakes and hillsides up through mountains that had no name.

The same voice called out again, *Jarl, these are healing strands of Maker Force. You must reach for them with your mind. And yet, in the Maker's Name, I must warn you that after you touch them, much will change, including yourself.*

With battle magic pounding all around him, Jarl's eye closed, and his head slumped back onto greyish black, gritty soil. His last memories were of being dragged into the Temple and approaching the ebony, dark Idol. They had been forced to drag him because Jarl had known he would be transformed forever. But what was happening to him here was worse than he might ever have imagined.

Jarl's mind began groping gleaming strands, while his mouth muttered, "I am reaching for your unknown strands, strands that lead me to a completely strange destiny. Nothing could be worse than dying in this nightmare of confusion!"

· X ·

Down in the underground burial chamber, Rafir was racing back and forth along a narrow tunnel corridor.

"I smell Ghouls," the fox whispered. "And now they are coming for us from both directions — two Ghouls from each direction. We are trapped."

"We'll need to fight back-to-back," Galad said, "and yet here, the hesitation of your sword might prove fatal."

Kalanin laughed a dark laugh. "The time for the old, pure heroes is over. Eléna, can you use light to blind the Ghouls that come towards me?

Gain me a few seconds so that the strange weapon in my hands can decide whether to kill Ghouls or not?"

"I still have arrows," Eléna said quietly, "but you must be thinking not only of this battle, but of the one to come, and so I'll provide one surge of light for you and a second surge for Galad."

Sebastian had been quiet, letting soft tears slide down his face. Now he looked up in wonder and murmured, "Julian was completely gone, and yet somehow now he's returning. Maybe there's still something we can do to help him."

"One battle at a time," Kalanin murmured, watching as a wall of their tunnel was pushed down and flashes of red from the eyes of Kul-Ghouls could be seen not twenty-five paces away.

· X ·

Julian's broken body thrashed and moaned in pain. Some sort of healing force was struggling to rebuild his body, but it was doing nothing for the pain. And there were voices inside him shouting at him:

Apprentice, ignore the pain and stand! See, your leg is healed!

Julian struggled to his feet and took two, awkward, hobbled steps. His broken body had been smashed and left down near the plain's edge. The chasm below was deeper even than his recovering giant's form. As he edged away from the abyss, he drew another deep breath, reaching....

Lines of blue and gold powers were flowing into him. Was that the same force that had guided them as they slept in the Gangean Range and dreamt of victory over Demon Princes. *Yes! There was a line of force, not supremely powerful, but still. It was Maker Force! At least, a residue of Maker Force.*

He looked back to the Great Demon, watching as it waved aside swarms of distracting Ghost Hauntings, and turned again toward Julian.

Two gigantic beings faced each other but only one of them was showing any fear. Julian edged away from the Great Demon, and away from the chasm at the edge of the plains.

As Julian backed, the Great Demon laughed. "So, you cannot even manage to promise me doom at the Maker's hands. Yet here at the last, it occurs to me that I might have a role for you. Might we perhaps, together, rebuild the foundations of Alantéa the Forerunner? Or do you wish only to feed the fires of Hell?"

As Julian slid sideways and away from the plains' edge, he murmured, "You have no real alliances. In the end, you have only slaves and the servants of slaves. Anyway, no matter what you offered, I would never serve you." And as Julian shifted away from the Great Demon, his mind whispered to the beings within him: *I am linked to an ancient line of Maker-touched power. O Dreamers, heal yourselves, but do not lose your disguises as Wraiths!*

Apprentice! came the response. *Now comes Hellfire! As we search for power within this form, we are touching the lone remaining Crystal of Otherwhen.*

Use the strands of Maker Force to heal, Julian's mind whispered, *then reach for Otherwhen.*

The Great Demon groped for him, but Julian dodged down and away. As a healing strength poured into Julian, he became taller and somewhat greater in breadth.

"And so," the Great Demon snarled, "welcome to Hell."

A torrent of Hellfire raced toward Julian. Shields, silver, and white radiances met Hellfire — but as they burned away, layer by bitter layer, his shields grew thinner by the second, and now his face began to blister, and a great fear of everlasting torment swept over Julian.

Now, came whispering Wizard voices within Julian, *we are linked to Otherwhen. Use those energies! Tap those powers!*

Julian *reached*, and strange mixtures of energy flowed into his body. All those alternate realities that still retained power were tapped. Pure power came from Duskland where the sun had died. Warmth flowed from the land where the Demon Princes and Guardians had made peace with the Mid-World and both Dragons and butterflies soared through the same skies. A grim strength surged from the tower in the land where some metaspell had fused Demon Princes and Guardians together. Now came a chill from the alternate world where the offspring of Demons rather than humans ruled, and its seas were cluttered with glaciers.

As the silver and white radiances defending Julian grew stronger, Hellfire died down fitfully, slowly, as though confused by its inability to prevail. Then the flames before Julian vanished.

"So," the Great Demon murmured, "this Maker of yours has set up so many little devices, intending to prevent domination of the Earth by Demon Princes. Yet now, all these stratagems will come to nothing, for our conflict comes down to pure physical force — and so, you are doomed."

This time, as the Great Demon groped for him, Julian was forced to leap backward and away from the open plains, back toward the open chasm that separated the surrounding plains from a series of stony hills.

· ☿ ·

As they pushed their way past the dying Kul-Ghouls, one red eye flashed open and a hand groped for Eléna. This time, Kalanin's sword lost its hesitation, and the hand was severed instantly. Overhead, the Snake God smashed downward repeatedly as it opened a wider passage so that it could follow its Kul-Ghoul allies deep into the catacombs.

"Down, down, and deeper," Kalanin muttered.

"There's nowhere left to go," Rafir called back to them. "I mean, there's space for me and Sebastian, but none for you three!"

"Go through those narrow passages," Kalanin said, "then wait for us. We are not done — not yet." Kalanin and Galad turned, hunching down, with earth falling over them as the catacombs shook under the Snake God's power. Eléna stood less than a step behind them, with a partly notched arrow in her hands, and a scattering of soil on her soft hair and her shoulders.

And now through the wider passage forged by the Snake God, the Kul-Ghouls were able to advance three abreast.

"I will take the middle one!" Eléna called out. "Just give me the word and there will be one less Ghoul!"

"Not yet," Kalanin muttered, and he and Galad leaped forward, smoking swords slashing and hewing. As Kul-Ghouls died, the red fire in their eyes faded slowly out. When they slumped to the floor of the catacomb, behind them emerged the fierce green eyes of the Snake God.

"Now!" Kalanin called out, and Eléna buried her first arrow, then a second, in each of the gleaming eyes of the Snake God — and buried those arrows so deeply that only the feathered portions of the two arrows were still visible.

The Snake God recoiled with such pain and terrifying power, that the roof of the catacomb began to collapse down upon them, so that they again struggled to avoid burial beneath a tombstone formed from boulders and clumps of soil.

· ✕ ·

As Julian alternately backed and evaded the Great Demon, voices were now whispering openly to him:

"Power flows into you, Julian," Nablus whispered. "Will you choose strength — or speed? You will understand my own preference."

"Speed, certainly," Merlin added in a whisper. "But for the strength of your right arm and your right shoulder, you should gather the physical power of the Great Guardian and that of Magog. You may have time for one, and only one, killing thrust."

And so, power gathered to Julian, and he began to change. As Julian scrambled away, he was able to conceal his greater speed, but he could not disguise the change in his right shoulder and arm.

The Great Demon laughed. "Look at you, Enemy Mine. With a portion of my mind, I watched you transform yourself while I struggled with the Sending — you were ungainly, with a second head forming at your elbow. And now you become again a shambling, gawky thing, with one bestial arm and other limbs made of smoke. How did you ever dream that you could defeat me? Behold! I will show you the greatest of mysteries — a prolonged death with everlasting agony — in Hell."

Movement drew the Great Demon's eyes down to the plains. The Snake God was coiling and thrashing in agony, destroying its Kul-Ghoul allies with its blinded power so that only a few could escape, and those Ghouls raced away toward the chasm surrounding the plain and toppled, shrieking, to their deaths.

"Stupid! Stupid! Stupid!" the Great Demon cried. "Why must I be served by clumsy, idiot constructs with no brains!" Stepping swiftly toward the Snake God the Great Demon crushed it like a tiny garter snake with one gigantic foot.

But now Julian advanced, whispering, "Behold."

The Great Demon turned and laughed. Not a great distance away, tiny forms no larger than insects had emerged from broken catacombs and were racing toward Demon and Giant while the Eye of Merlin circled overhead.

"Behold, what?" the Great Demon said, shaking his head, as he turned from the tiny forms. "What shall I look for?" The Great Demon laughed then stiffened in pain. He halted and peered down. Searching, he finally found three tiny shafts sticking out from each leg. Not far away, a gaggle of insignificant humans and their even smaller allies were racing away, while the Eye of Merlin circled downward, trying to provide another distraction.

"Behold, more vermin," the Great Demon muttered.

"Behold," Julian said, almost in a whisper, "you must know that at the end of time, only the Maker's Will shall remain." And Julian leaped at the Great Demon. With one powerful blow, Julian smote the Great Demon's chest. As the Great Demon gasped in pain and groped for him, Julian's right hand brushed the Great Demons hands away and smashed again.

Now the Great Demon stared down at the huge fissure that was opening through its chest. All the beings inside its form were writhing in agony.

Julian reached within, drawing Satanis back to the Isle of the Demons. Satanis was held so tightly that the Demon Prince could not even breathe fire. Whirling and spinning, Julian hurled him through western storm clouds into deep space.

Iblis was next, only able to breathe a single plume of flame, calling out "We shall still —!" Then Iblis was sent tumbling through the upper atmosphere, passing into the chill of outer space.

Only Zikar could complete the threat: "— return and destroy Earth!" Then, Zikar, too, was gone. So astonished were the Dark Lords that they could not even conceive of threats, much less speak them, but they were hurled one by one after their masters, the Demon Princes.

Broken, shattered in ruin, all that was left of the Great Demon was a thin crust of bronze. Now it toppled to the ground. From within this broken crust, ten Guardians and the remaining thirty-nine Marids emerged, stumbling onto the killing grounds of the Demon Princes. In the end, they stood staring up at Julian with the frightened eyes of children confronted by their worst nightmare.

Chapter Twenty-Two
An Outcome; An Ending

"**M**Y FATHER," ELÉNA MURMURED, staring up at Julian the OverGod as he towered over Guardians and Marids, "my wonderful, long suffering, weary father. I can feel that you somehow still live within the gigantic construct that looms so high above us. But can you emerge from that being and be again the father that I love?"

"Hold back, just for a moment," Kalanin said to Sebastian and Rafir. "This moment feels like an unexpected sunrise in the middle of a long, dark night, but it is always wise to be cautious. In the aftermath of battle, I've seen adversaries who seem more dead than alive rise from the ground and stab rejoicing victors in their backs. Watch these Marids carefully. Be very cautious near those corrupted Guardians."

Galad laughed softly. "Those are wise words, but somehow, it feels as though all the death and dying are behind us." He held up the Tarnished Sword. "What do you think, Sword? Are bands of skulking traitors going to murder us in the last moments of this conflict?" The Tarnished Sword could only let out a keening, confused sound, as though filled with sorrow because all the violence of battle had finally ended.

"I didn't think so," Galad said. He sheathed the Sword and spoke one word to the Familiars: "Go." Sebastian and Rafir raced away, while the three humans walked much more slowly across the dark, dusty plains toward Julian the OverGod, who towered over the broken shell of the Great Demon and its remaining components.

Far away, the storm that had lingered over western skies finally broke, and they could hear distant, tiny sounds of thunder, as swirling columns of water poured down into the ocean. The sun still struggled to shine overhead, while the eagle, the Eye of Merlin, was circling slowly down through dusty skies, as though still searching the battlefield for hidden foes.

"You know," Galad said quietly to Kalanin, "you keep referring to my desire for a thousand-foot OverGod, but from this perspective, our OverGod, Julian, seems less than a thousand feet, perhaps only nine-hundred feet tall." Then Galad laughed.

·)(·

Julian had always looked up in fear at Marids, and trapped in the dream empires of corrupted Guardians, he had learned the depth of their malice. Now as he stared down at the small figures of Guardians and Marids, *they* seemed both tiny and fearful.

"Rest for a moment," Julian called down to them, "and dream if you wish, though some of you may wish to study the skies with the fresh eyes of those who have been released from bondage." And Julian breathed a healing peace down upon them so that their fears subsided. All ten of the corrupted Guardians slumped to the ground and retreated into dreams, while many of the Marids stood uncertainly, staring into the distance, while a few boomed questions softly to each other, wondering what was to become of them.

"Now," Julian said aloud, "My greatest wish is to yield this form, and yet much remains to be done. Come, there is a congress of powers within me, fused in form, but each of our component minds is free to speak. What is to be done?"

"First," said the Great Guardian through the lips of Julian, "we should free the remainder of my brethren." Julian stared back to the great citadel of the Demon Princes, with its partially collapsed slabs of basalt, and he spoke *words*.

Moments passed in silence as the afternoon sun struggled to pierce through the dusty haze created by the battle of OverGods, and through the smoke that continued to rise from the ruins of the Demon's black basalt fortress.

While Julian waited, Sebastian and Rafir came to rest, staring up at their now enormous master. A few minutes later Kalanin, Galad, and Eléna finished their trek across dusty plains. From overhead, the eagle finished his long glide downward and finally joined them. When they had gathered together, Julian smiled down at them.

"I heard the Eye urge you to simply stay alive," Julian murmured down to them, "and you accomplished much, so much more than that. Maker's Grace to you and to all of us, because that's what saved us on this day."

Julian looked up, turning to the Citadel, where the six transformed and imprisoned Guardians were emerging, each of them streaked by the black dust of the broken Citadel. With limbs stiff from long imprisonment, they shuffled slowly across the plain, coming to stand before Julian, and then they knelt.

"Come," the Great Guardian spoke from Julian's mouth, "you are kneeling not before the Maker, but before what is only a temporary construct. Rise and join us in our discussions. This construct must sit in judgment and help to decide the fate of our brethren. Can any of our

Guardian brethren outside of this OverGod construct speak for our corrupted brothers?"

One by one, the six newly resurrected Guardians stared with little affection at their ten corrupted brethren, then slowly shook their heads.

"Can any of our brethren within this form speak for them?" the Great Guardian asked, "or any other beings in this congress of powers offer a defense for them? Or can the allies of the Apprentice speak for them?"

Only the fox had anything to say, and Rafir simply muttered in a faint voice, "We're supposed to defend these things after they released the Demon Princes, then imprisoned us and tried to destroy us? That's more than a little hard to do."

"In the end," Thorian said, after a moment of silence, "beyond all belief, Alcman turned away from his evil ways, and yet your brethren had so many more centuries to choose different paths, that it is hard to believe they might ever truly change their ways."

"I can offer no guidance," Merlin added. "Guardians must judge Guardians."

"Only the Maker can judge them," said the Great Guardian. "We must let them rest in the Temple of Waiting until the Maker's Return." Julian's hand hesitated, then finally reached down, touching each of the ten corrupted Guardians, and they vanished.

"Now, we must deal with the Marids," Voritar spoke through Julian's mouth. "This is a much more difficult test of our collective wisdom. The Demon Princes forged Marids as weapons to destroy the Powers of the Mid-World. There may well be a strength within this construct to simply change their natures, to make of them new and different beings, but is there justice in that choice?"

"Justice for the Marids comes hard," Julian said, "and that justice is complicated by the destinies of other beings. Can we deal first with other matters? Can we agree to unmake some of the evil of the Sorcerers and the Marids and of the Demon Princes? A curse lays over Thorian, whereby he agreed to forsake his own life for that of his daughter, Eléna. Also, Balardi's long lifespan was sacrificed so that he might heal in time to aid the Wizards in their struggle with the Demon Princes. Can those two dooms be lifted? Let the Powers of the Mid-World note that I seek no additional advantage from the power within me. By this act, we will simply reverse some of the damage of our long conflict with the Demon Princes."

"It is only justice," the Great Guardian spoke. Within Julian's form, Thorian and Balardi felt something like a weight lift from their bodies and from their minds, and they sighed.

"Far from here," Julian said, "Harlond, a great Captain of the League, lies dying in a vat of bubbling, enchanted fluids created by Thoth, waiting for a miracle to cure him. If you agree, we will become that miracle."

"Once again, that is only simple justice," Magog said. "If our roles were reversed, I would demand much more from the Mid-World of the Truce." Julian nodded.

· ❌ ·

And thousands of leagues from them, Harlond woke, groaning. Finding himself underwater, he pushed his way to the top of his tank. He gasped, taking his first breath of real air in more than a month. Then he recoiled, for the air was filled with the strange smells of many other wounded creatures sheltered by Thoth.

Still panting for air, Harlond stared in wonder into the gloomy nighttime darkness of Thoth's chambers of healing. Fully healed, he lifted his body to the tank's top and dropped lightly to the ground. In the darkness and stillness, he began searching for weapons and an exit, tracking enchanted puddles of water onto the tiles beneath his feet, as he left the chamber.

· ☿ ·

"Since we deal with justice," Merlin said, "what now of your own parents, Julian? For far too long has some Mid-World Power imprisoned them in his own kingdom and kept them distant from you. Power within this form might easily free them. Should that be done?"

"I am greatly tempted," Julian said quietly, "and yet we are undoing the evil of this war, and the fate of my parents has nothing to do with this struggle. Let the Mid-World of the Truce, which speaks so often of its own desire for justice, let the Great Gods find some way to obtain the release of my parents."

"Since we are going to unmake the destruction of the Demon Princes," Voritar said, "what of those who perished defending the Truce?"

"I will name them," Llara added. "Tor-El-Baldur was utterly heroic, while Yuai Quin Yin sacrificed herself in defense of the Maker."

Julian raised both his arms aloft, and power surged from his form. "There, it is done," he said. "The Temple of Waiting yields both these former Gods and returns them to the Mid-World of the Truce. They must live for a time as Wraiths, rebuilding their strength, as did the Dreamers. After, they will become as they were before the destruction of this war. They have been released, and they shall be redeemed."

Julian seemed to ponder events for a moment. "We cannot yield the power of this construct, at least not yet," he said. "What will happen after we are done? I can sense that the Dreamers will be restored, for there is power within us to remake the Hall of the Dreamers, as it was before the

Sending destroyed it. But after we are done, Guardians of the World, what would you wish for?"

"To be again, as Guardians," said the Great Guardian softly, "and though we have seen that some of the perils of this world have been reduced, many other dangers remain. Otherwhen remains a great hazard, for enormous powers gathered in the Alternates might some day be turned back upon the Mid-World of the Truce."

"When we are done, I will yield our Crystal of Otherwhen to the Guardians," Julian said. "Yet you should add to your guardianship of the Alternates, two other great perils. First, the Timeways have been traveled by my two Familiars, but not mastered. Those passage must be watched closely — can you imagine the great Dark Gods going back in time to reverse matters so that they triumph? That must not be allowed to happen.

"Second, nightmares have been unleashed to the Far Lands in the form of powerful machine intellects and warlike supernatural entities from other star systems. Let the Guardians of the World restrain those beings or at least restrict their impact on this Earth."

As these great discussions continued overhead, the three tiny human allies had seated themselves some distance from Julian, leaning back against a fragment of the reddish bronze husk of the Great Demon.

While the future of the Guardians was being discussed overhead, Kalanin yawned and leaning over, he whispered to Galad. "Even if it's only nine-hundred feet tall, here's the OverGod you wished for. Why not ask Julian to find you a wife?"

Galad shook his head, only moderately amused.

"This is the first I've heard about that particular 'quest'," Eléna whispered back.

"It was the wine," Galad said quietly. "After several goblets, I told Kalanin and Julian that I was tired of merchant princes trying to become barons or earls or margraves of the League by attaching me to their daughters."

Eléna thought for a moment then she laughed. "Don't worry," she whispered. "Surely Géla and I can manage to find someone for you." Galad nodded and smiled halfheartedly.

A few paces away, the Eye of Merlin croaked out a harsh laugh. "You joke among yourselves because you have no idea of the challenge that is to come, do you?" Three humans and two Familiars shook their heads, then stared back up at Julian.

Far above them, Julian was speaking with Magog: "What do you wish, last of the Godlings? Power lies within this form to make you one of the Great Gods of Alantéa. Is that your heart's desire?"

"What of yourself, Julian?" Magog asked. "When we are done, will you confer Godhood upon yourself, to become the first mortal to be transformed into a deity?"

Julian shook his enormous head. "When we are done, I will become again Julian, an Apprentice with an Adept's power and a powerful Seer's sight."

"So, I might have guessed," Magog murmured. "Here, then, is my desire: before you pass your remaining Crystal to the Great Guardian, would you draw my two Godling brethren back from Otherwhen? After, if we three Godlings are given some strength to become wiser, to outgrow the confusion laid upon us by the Mid-World of the Truce, that would be my heart's desire."

"It is done," Julian said. "I have placed a dreaming sleep over Phaedra and Turin, and in a fortnight they will gather to you. Hopefully, you three will grow in wisdom and strength together."

In his form as OverGod, Julian took a huge breath before continuing. "And so now we come to harder tasks. What should be done with the Marids?

Here are the reasons for my previous hesitation," Julian said. "The Marids are not the only beings born into a universe without choices. First came the Creatures of the Darkness, born powerful and twisted and demented and unexpected from the fiery loins of Dragons. In my own brief time upon this Earth, several Creatures Indomitable have whispered among themselves of a 'Destroyer,' while other Creatures dreamt of a 'Redeemer.' At times, both whisperers and dreamers have suggested me as that person, and yet I would choose neither to be a 'destroyer,' nor a 'redeemer.'

"Instead, I would wish to become an 'Opener of the Ways,' returning to both Marids and Creatures Indomitable some of the choices that they were never given at the time of their creation. Now, speak openly. Is this too large a task for the construct that stands before you? Should the fate of Marids and Creatures Indomitable be left to the Maker?"

Voritar rumbled a deep answer through Julian's mouth: "So often have I looked down upon the Creatures Indomitable with both horror and pity. These, along with the Marids, are the nightmare offspring of Demons and Dragons, and if something can be done to aid them — even if only a few choose to be helped — then we should let each of them make that decision."

"And I speak from the right hand path of the Seraphs and Spirit Lords," Llara added. "Redemption of Marids and Creatures Indomitable may seem too great a task for any collection of Powers, and yet it feels like justice, it feels like the Maker's Will."

Julian raised both hands, palms extended outward. "Then let the Creatures Indomitable come before us." Scores of Portals boomed into existence, and then the silence of the aftermath of battle was broken by howling, growling, and baying sounds as first scores, then many hundreds of the Creatures of the Darkness spilled from tunnel mouths into a land that was completely strange to them.

Marids rose, and banded together in an arc, beginning their own hooting and booming noises. Kalanin and Galad drew enchanted weapons, while Eléna stared around, searching helplessly for spent arrows — or any other weapons.

"Rest for a moment," Julian said, and he breathed a healing peace down over them — over Marids and over hundreds of distended, misshapen Creatures Indomitable. Confused and bewildered, the Creatures stared around at one another, wondering what force had brought them to the Isle of the Demons. Finally, Marids and Creatures Indomitable fell silent, and all turned to stare up at Julian.

"You stand before me," Julian murmured down to them, "like children who have never known love, and yet I cannot remake your lives, giving back to you the care that most beings receive at birth. Nor can I offer you instant redemption, for a great task lies before all of us. Of what use would it be for you to become Godlike and choose your own destinies, then to live only a brief time before Alantéa sinks beneath the waves and you all perish?

"Here are images of what will come unless we change that destiny." And Julian sent them images of Alantéa sliding seaward until even Mount Evergrey sank beneath the waves. More sounds emerged from the mouths of the Creatures Indomitable — groaning noises of horror and anger.

"Even if we cannot completely avert this doom," Julian added. "Perhaps we can gain time for Alantéa by renewing its foundations. Can we gain another five hundred years for Alantéa or even a thousand years? I cannot say.

"I will yield power to you to change, to become something other while you labor at the foundations of Alantéa the Forerunner. You will not suffer pain. Your hardships will not break you. There will be time for you to rest and time to dream. As you labor, you will learn and grow and choose, and if you wish, become something completely different from what you are today.

"Or, you may choose *not* to join in this heroic effort to renew Alantéa. None of the Powers within this construct will punish you should you choose not to rebuild the Forerunner's foundations. Here is an exit back to Alantéa should you choose to reject this new destiny."

With a faint *booming* sound, a Portal with a huge arch loomed open behind the assembly of Creatures Indomitable and Marids. Slowly, uncertainly, less than a score of Creatures Indomitable and four Marids shuffled toward the Portal. As the last of them passed through the Portal, the opening vanished with a muffled clap of thunder.

Julian turned to the remaining Marids and Creatures Indomitable. "Behold, you are now the rebuilders of the foundations, even saviors of Alantéa the Forerunner. As you build, you will become stronger and wiser. Let mercy and truth, and justice and wisdom become powerful within your increasingly subtle minds. Farewell."

And suddenly, Marids and Creatures Indomitable vanished.

"Now comes our most challenging task," Llara said through the mouth of Julian.

"I do not believe," Voritar said, through those same lips, "that we are strong enough."

"That remains to be seen," Magog murmured. "We are ready and so we must begin."

As the ground began to tremble, the Eye of Merlin's wings flared in alarm.

"I thought this war was over," Galad muttered, and he stood, hand reaching for the Tarnished Sword.

Kalanin stood beside Galad, hand drifting to his own sword's hilt. "Eagle, what is happening?"

"They are struggling with the Hell that lies beyond the hills in an underground Lake of Fire," the Eagle croaked. "Hell is too powerful to be overcome by sorcery, and so they will try to cast it far from Earth — and yet, they are not nearly strong enough."

As the ground settled, Julian turned toward a distant, shaken, crumbling Alantéa, and he spoke calm words in a voice of doom.

"We must call upon you, Powers of the Mid-World, yet you should know that your destinies are threatened by Hellfire, while we are removed from that fate. Mortals cannot now be touched by the Fires of Hell, nor will it reach the Dreamers in their great Hall. We have strength to remove the Guardians and Godlings from this doom, leaving only beings of Alantéa to be drawn into the Firepits of Hell.

"So, when we call upon you, we do not seek to burden you with our own troubles, but to release Alantéa and the Mid-World and the Earth from a terrible doom."

Then from his huge OverGod mouth, Julian boomed out the words that called down the Mid-World of the Truce.

There came a split second of hesitation, then suddenly, two beings stepped from seams in the air to stand before Julian: Set and Wotan. These two Gods, each of them tall and radiating power, did not even reach as high as Julian the OverGod's enormous thighs.

They did not bow to the OverGod, but Wotan gathered to Julian's right and Set to his left. Then Set and Wotan called out in unison — again speaking the words that called upon the Mid-World of the Truce.

And suddenly the plain around them was crowded with Portals, and the air was filled with a concussion of shattering sounds so that the humans on the plain had to stop up their ears. Heralds and Emissaries of the Gods emerged, bearing the banners of mighty Zôs, and Quarezokziil, and Marduk, and Thoth, and Moloch, and Set, and Ptah, the Opener of the Ways, Poseidon of the sea, Vishnu the Sustainer, and scores upon scores of others.

The Powers of the Mid-World followed behind their servants. None of them bowed before Julian; instead, they turned north, away from the Citadel of the Demons and the hills that ringed it. They focused on the vast underground lake that had become a Lake of Fire, hidden beneath earth's crust.

Murmuring sounds became the chanting of many spells, as Powers were joined by their Emissaries and most powerful servants.

As Julian the OverGod raised his arms, the ground began trembling. Eléna was shaken from her feet, but Kalanin caught her before she fell. In the distance, more of the Citadel's basalt slabs tumbled to the ground.

Beyond the hills ringing the Citadel a great Lake of Fire was rising into the air. Heat surged at the three humans on the plain and they raised their hands to ward it off. From all the assembled Powers came walls of cool air, pushing the Lake of Fire further from them, but still, it hovered, trembling, in midair, spilling sheets of flame to the land below, so that every living thing beneath it was incinerated.

"It will not rise," the Eye croaked softly, almost in a whisper. "We are not yet strong enough to cast Hell from Earth."

"We have come to the last moment," Julian's voice boomed over the battlefield, and the Lake of Fire began sagging back to Earth. "There are forces that lie outside our control, and now we must call upon them to save Earth and to save themselves."

Now, as Hell sagged downward to the Earth, chants and invocations rose from scores of Mid-World Powers.

Elf-Lords and Elf-Mages were first to appear, as though long prepared for this moment.

Seconds later came the Creatures Indomitable and Marids that Julian had released back to Alantéa.

As these stumbled about in confusion, Julian called to them: "You have been released, but first you must join us to save Earth, and also to save yourselves from Hellfire." And he pointed to the hovering Lake of Fire.

A torrent of hidden Sorcerers and Mages of all species followed, and as they understood that they were fighting for their own lives and their afterlives, they all raised their arms to join with in the powerful, complex invocation.

Shamans and Hag-Witches were drawn from the Far Lands, and they shuffled and stumbled in confusion, having woken to the most incomprehensible of nightmares.

Last came two of the powerful, hidden Creatures Indomitable. First, the Dark Emissary, freed from imprisonment by his own people, and now he stood fearless, armed again with a metal staff, staring around the battlefield so that Kalanin and Galad drew swords. And finally came the hulking Spellweaver, drawn against its will from some hidden dimension.

As all these disparate, confused forces began pushing against it, the Lake of Fire began rising slowly into the skies, still dripping poisoned flames to the Earth below.

"Come!" Julian called out, in a voice that trembled with power. "We have no need of confusion. This Lake of Fire can never be used as a source of power by any being on this planet! Now push! Push with all the strength within each of you!"

As Hell finally surged skyward and vanished, an exhausted OverGod construct collapsed, broken, to the ground.

Set and Wotan stood guard over this construct, while only a few of the assembled Powers remained on the battlefield, waiting until they could see that those beings from within the OverGod's shell were able to emerge onto the plain, stumbling in exhaustion. Then, as the last of the watchers vanished, Set and Wotan passed forever from the Isle of the Demons.

·)(·

It was night when they made their passage back from the Isle of the Demons to Alantéa the Forerunner. Layers of heavy cloud cover blocked much of the light from faraway stars and a Sickle of the Maker Moon. Only pale lights shone from the Wizards' staffs. A lone Portal passage took them back to Gravengate, the last of the Wizards' remaining fortresses.

When Balardi stood again before the great gates, he tapped them gently with his staff, calling upon them to open; the enchanted gates obeyed the Wizard and groaned slowly aside. Guards sprang into action, not able to believe that their old Wizard-masters were returning — all their recent history was filled with cunningly disguised adversaries and grim surprises. Bonfires were lit. Weapons were raised. Streams of arrows were launched. The Wizards waved all these aside and entered Gravengate, slowly and carefully explaining in low voices that they had won the most bitter victory. Now they needed rest, and in the morning, they would begin to rebuild what was left of the League.

Julian, Galad, Kalanin, and Eléna followed the Wizards, so filled with fatigue that they stumbled as they passed into Gravengate. After a night's sleep, they would gather a force of arms and ride west to rescue Géla and Kalanin's daughter Serena, and finally, Rostov, who had been standing guard over mother and daughter. Once gathered, they would then return to Gravengate.

It was over.

Their story was finished.

Their great struggle with the Demon Princes had finally come to an end.

Chapter Twenty-Three

A Gathering at Gravengate

S THEIR LEAGUE SLOWLY rebuilt itself, the Wizards felt a consensus gathering among their peoples: they needed an interval, a breathing space, a time of recognition for all of their efforts over so many weeks and months. And so, the Wizards declared a time of modest celebration at the two-year mark after surviving all their many conflicts.

Unwilling to halt their own use of sorcerous power to rebuild, the Wizards turned to their captains and leaders to organize a discreet, low-key event that would avoid offending the Powers of the Mid-World, the proud and overly sensitive Gods of Mankind. However, a week before the coming observance, the Wizards found themselves interrupted when each of them discovered at daybreak a note that flashed before their eyes in their three separate fortresses. This note, scrawled on parchment, read:

Wizards:
You three should gather,
each in your own place of power,
to consider my farewell message.

Alcman

Astonished, each Wizard retreated to his own stronghold. After they linked, Alcman's message unfolded, with the parchment script rolling down to reveal the following script:

Death is coming to me. I am seeking it, and it is rightly my reward.
Before I pass, I will share with you, things you may already know.
Your Maker is ten thousand times wiser than any of us.
When Balardi stumbled upon the Crystals of Otherwhen,
it was as though an old, bewildered miner, who sought only
stones with thin strands of gold, found his hands suddenly
holding a sack filled with diamonds and emeralds.
However, the three Crystals he discovered were greater
than any treasures to be found on Earth.
When Houma and I intercepted Balardi,
and captured two of those three Crystals,
it felt as though we had given the Demon Princes
a great gift. Instead, that "gift" provided nothing
but confusion and division for our ranks, and
huge opportunities for your own. And so,
from a distance, it feels like your Maker,
seemingly so wise and remote and benevolent, also
put in place many hidden devices to guide events.
And now, farewell forever, for I do not believe that
we will meet in the same afterlife, if there is one.

Alcman

"A strange message," Balardi murmured.

"From the strangest of our adversaries," Thorian said quietly. "Was this some scheme to shield his presence in Otherwhen, so that he might emerge and confront us at some future time?"

Merlin sighed. "A short time ago, when I sought for Alcman, he had removed himself to Otherwhen, to a time and a place where a great sky stone would destroy the peninsula of land where Alcman, the last of the Sorcerers, had chosen to live out his last days. And now, he is dead."

"So, all we need to worry about in the near future," Balardi said, "isn't Alcman, but something greater."

"That 'greater' problem is offending our mighty, though touchy Gods," Thorian added, "during our forthcoming 'Celebration.'"

·)(·

For most of the history of the League, the Wizards had been very cautious about their use of Portal magic to travel from place to place. In the early years of the League, the Powers of the Mid-World had often sought to block their passages and otherwise wished that the Wizards were far less strong than they had become. In the aftermath of the unlikely and unforeseen victory of the League in its struggle with the Demon Princes, however, the Powers had finally decided to ignore Portal usage by the Wizards.

Still, the Wizards remained careful, anxious to avoid challenging the Gods of Alantéa, and so the Wizards traveled by Portal only when cloaked by shadows. So, it was dusk when the Portal Passages took the leaders of the League back to Gravengate for a reunion, two years to the day after their return from the Isle of the Demons.

Thorian was first, leading Eléna, Julian, Sebastian, and Rafir from Stone Mountain, passing from an overcast dusk at Thorian's stronghold to Gravengate, where starlight was just beginning to shimmer. Thorian's place of power was still known as Stone Mountain, though it was no longer a fortress on a pinnacle. Stone Mountain was now being rebuilt as a strengthened fortress set back from the ocean on firmer ground so that the tremors that shook Alantéa almost daily would never again reduce Thorian's stronghold to rubble.

Seconds later, another Portal flashed open in the shadows, one leading from Sea's Edge to Gravengate. Merlin emerged, leading Kalanin, Géla, and their daughter, Serena. Sea's Edge had been almost completely rebuilt, though it was also set some distance from the shores of the Atlantic. The ocean, as though greatly tempted by Alantéa's weakness, was now lashing at the small continent's shoreline with increasing hunger.

Gravengate's ornate gates had been opened wide, with men-at-arms bearing torches lined on both sides. No horns sounded, no bugles blew, and only the quiet sounds of humans speaking in low tones could be heard as Balardi led Galad, Rostov, and Harlond out to greet their guests. Each of them reached down to pat Serena on her shoulder as the two-and-a-half-year-old clapped and laughed, delighted to be still awake far beyond her bedtime.

Inside, they were seated in a great hall, on broad-backed chairs before tables place-set with polished silver on white cloths. Wines and ales were poured for the guests, with a sparkling fruit drink provided for Serena. Invisible beings played soft stringed instruments in the hall's background. Captains and warriors of the League sat with half-amused smiles on their faces, while the three Wizards gathered at a lone table set on a slightly higher dais and began speaking together in subdued voices. As their host, Balardi sat centermost, with Thorian on his right, and Merlin on his left.

Three Familiars were also present at the banquet, though no places had been set for them. Those with wings, the Eye of Merlin and Sebastian, gathered on the upper balconies of the great hall, so they could watch the proceedings from a distance. Rafir stayed below, amusing himself by remaining invisible and attempting to hunt the also-invisible providers of music. Whenever Rafir brushed past them with his soft fox fur, their music grew dimmer before rising softly.

As they sat, Eléna leaned over to speak with Julian. "Serena is most astonishing," she whispered. "She knew each of us by name and spoke about meeting us this time last year when she was less than two. Do you know of any two-year-old with a command of language that she has?"

"When we gathered together last year," Julian whispered back, "Rostov told me how much she was able to communicate without speech at less than a year old. She is remarkable."

Eléna touched Julian's hand so she could speak directly into his mind: *Do you think that our own children will have this kind of ability?*

They will be wonderful, each of them extraordinary in very different ways.

Ten seats away, sitting on her highchair, Serena leaned over and smiled at them, face gleaming in the candlelight. Aware of both the glances and the non-verbal exchanges, Kalanin and Géla nodded to each other, smiling softly.

Galad sat quietly, a glass of wine in his hand, listening to Harlond and Rostov as they spoke of their efforts to rebuild the League. After a time Galad straightened and glanced around the table as though counting. "We're missing someone from last year," he said. "Where's Harmadast?"

"That's right," Harlond said, "Balardi's old Captain-General, who later served Thorian. He was here last year and now he's retired."

"Thank goodness he's retired, not dead," Rostov replied. "I'm hoping that will be the fate for the rest of us too."

Galad nodded, glancing at Kalanin, his mind murmuring, *not yet, no retirement for that great Captain, not for a while, anyway.*

Food was set before them, much of it brought inland from the sea, for the livestock and farms of Alantéa had suffered enormous damage from the attack on its foundations, and its continuing tremors, and earthquakes, and flash floods, and fires from dying forests made cultivation of the soil much more difficult. From the corner of his eyes, Julian watched Serena poke and push seafood around on her plate, while casually consuming slices of fruit and pieces of soft rolls.

When Serena glanced up again at Julian, she flashed a quick, conspiratorial smile; she was eating only foods that she liked, and no one was bothering to correct her.

While cupbearers brought more wine and ales with other small courses, the three Wizards smiled gently and spoke together in low tones.

"I can feel a sense of peace settling over the people of the League," Balardi said. "As it was last year at Sea's Edge, we now have another quiet moment, the Council of the League, with no challenges from the Powers of the Mid-World. Last year we were at Sea's Edge, this year here at Gravengate, and if we agree, next year we will all gather again — continuing with our limited celebrations — at Stone Mountain. What are your thoughts?"

Merlin nodded, while Thorian hesitated before speaking. "I agree that we must restrain ourselves. Our rebuilding work is too important to risk creating enemies among the Great Gods. But we are not alone in our efforts, and so perhaps we should begin to include others who are important to the League, say our foremost wise men, builders, and shift captains from each of our three strongholds. In short, I suggest a larger gathering."

Merlin stared into the candlelit depths of Gravengate's long hall before nodding slowly. "A larger, though still restrained gathering of the League should present few problems for the Great Gods. You have other considerations, however. What else do you suggest?"

Thorian leaned forward, growing more intent. "I did have more to say. As I study the Mid-world of the Truce more closely, I see that a great deal of quiet diplomacy takes place in the courts of the Powers. And so perhaps beings from the Mid-World, like the Tanu, or the Sidhe, or the Elf-Mages, or others present in the courts of the Powers should be invited to join us."

"Let us take small steps," Merlin said quietly, "as a child does while learning to walk. Next year, we will include our allies within the League. The following year they will be joined by the Kindreds, and others made welcome in the courts of the Powers. Do we all agree?"

After Thorian and Balardi nodded, Merlin continued, "You have a third suggestion, Thorian, have you not?"

Thorian's face flashed a brief smile. "We cannot quite read one another's minds, though we can sense some of each other's thoughts. Yes, here is a final suggestion: should any of the Emissaries of the Gods wish to speak with us collectively, in a diplomatic capacity, then perhaps we should make those beings welcome at our annual gatherings."

Merlin drew a deep breath. "Small steps. Next year a larger gathering, and the following, invitations to Elves, Tanu and Sidhe. Then in year three —" Merlin broke off, for tremors were rattling through the stonework of Gravengate, and traces of dust were floating down from the upper reaches of the fortress.

Above them, Sebastian cringed, and the Eye of Merlin's wings flared with tension. Both Familiars glanced upward to see if Gravengate's reinforced stonework would hold — and it did.

"In year three," Merlin continued, "if contrary voices from the Powers are not too numerous or too filled with anger, we will invite Emissaries to speak with us, prior to our own discussions. Yet now, as Gravengate shudders, we should remind ourselves that our future depends on efforts to repair the Forerunner. Among us, Julian is most involved with those efforts. Last year, when we questioned him, he said, 'Alantéa is doomed.' Yet when pressed, the Apprentice expressed a hope that work upon the foundations might gain us another five-hundred years. I wonder where we stand today."

·)(·

Seated at the lower tables, Julian could hear those words, and he shook his head, then shrugged. The Wizards were prompting him to speak, and Julian had no wish to say anything.

Serena whispered something into her father's ear, and Kalanin turned to Julian.

"So, Apprentice," Kalanin said in an undertone, "the stonework of Gravengate trembles, and three Wizards stare down at their former 'Apprentice,' wondering if the efforts to rebuild the foundations of Alantéa will gain a century or so for our peoples. How are we doing?"

At upper and lower tables, all leaned forward.

Julian sighed. "Our work continues," he said quietly. "Creatures of the Darkness and Marids grow stronger as they struggle not only to rebuild Alantéa's foundations but also to slowly transform themselves into wiser, even kinder, beings. At any rate, predictions and promises are useless, yet I will say that we greatly desire to gain another thousand years for Alantéa the Forerunner. But that is only our hope, and the reality may be far different."

Eléna reached over and squeezed Julian's hand with both of her own, murmuring, "We know that you are trying to guide both the rebuilding of the Forerunner's foundations and the transformation of our former foes. We are going to trust in your hopes and not share in your fears."

· 💥 ·

Not much later, when the gathering broke up, Kalanin and Géla sought out Julian and Eléna. "Our little one is still awake," Kalanin said, smiling, "She wanted to say goodnight to you, though she also wished to say goodbye to Sebastian and Rafir."

So, four humans and two Familiars walked together to an upper wing of the fortress where guests were housed. Serena was lying in a side chamber, propped up in bed, surrounded by only dim, muted lights. The curtains to her windows were closed, but moonlight glowed through them, and gentle breezes passed soft air into the chamber.

When Serena saw Sebastian and Rafir, she insisted on hugging each of them, though she was gentle with them, and the two Familiars smiled.

"I see so little of these two," Serena said to Julian, "and I enjoy the stories of their adventures so much. Can you visit us at Sea's Edge more often? Sometimes I'm a little lonely, and these two make wonderful companions."

"We will try," Julian said. "We should ask Merlin first. But you won't always be alone — you will have a brother some time in the future, will you not?"

"Years, and years from now," Serena said, and she yawned, beginning to feel the lateness of the evening. "Sometimes I speak with Corey in dreams, and he can't wait to be born. Often, he talks about his sword — he knows that one day father's sword will become his own, and then the sword will no longer be confused."

Julian nodded. *She sees parts of the future even more clearly than I do. I wonder what else she sees.*

"And before Corey comes," Julian added softly, "I can see that you will have other playmates and that they will be cousins."

Serena's eyes blinked wide open. "I'm not supposed to talk about that."

"It's all right," Julian said, glancing at Kalanin and Géla. "I raised the matter first because I'm able to see far enough into the future to know that you will have cousins to play with."

"Cousins," Serena said with considerable satisfaction. "Many, many cousins and I will be the eldest."

Julian took a deep breath. There was a question he wished to ask, but now was not the right time or place to ask her.

Serena studied the Apprentice. "You were going to ask about Galad, weren't you?"

When Julian nodded slowly, Serena continued. "Yes, some of the cousins will be the children of Galad, and yes, very soon Galad will be much happier than he has ever been."

Julian leaned down, embracing Serena again, then he turned to go. *She will become the leader of our League one day, and I will become her Grey Counselor.*

The muted lights surrounding Serena became even darker, and her eyes were closing, but Julian could hear the last words she whispered to him as he left her small chamber:

"One last thing, Julian the Redeemer," her tiny voice whispered. "Alantéa will survive for many more than a thousand years. It might even be two thousand."

Chapter Twenty-Four
Merlin in the Hall
of the Dreamers

NCE EVERY CENTURY, THE three Dreamers who had once been humans gathered together in a side alcove of the Hall of the Dreamers. They called these moments "Times of Remembrance," for with the accelerating pace of change on Earth and the surging civilizations of so many distant star systems, they wished to recall Alantéa the Forerunner as it once had been, and the history of humans in the Far Lands, in its aftermath.

It was night in their great Hall, with starshine pouring through glass walls and overhead panels of glass. In their side alcove, muted candlelight barely offset the gleaming starlight. As was their custom, the three had called up cups of tisane that steamed gently before their faces, and they spoke of previous "Times of Remembrance."

"I can sense," Hestaur said to Merlin, "that you will again return to the League, to the time of its strength and struggles. After, will you again revisit the time of Excalibur and the Grail?"

"Nothing more can be learned from returning to those later moments," Merlin replied. "It was painful to become again a child and grow up among people that I loved, whose dreams I shared, only gradually realizing that my goals were contrary to their own desires. Yet after I extracted Excalibur and the Grail, it was so much easier for humans to turn away from the dead paths of dying magic. Anyway, I am done with that time. Instead, in the next few moments, I will walk through the streets of Tuvan as it was in the early days of the League, and then of Khiva as it was when the great warship *Alantéa* was under construction."

"A fitting 'Time of Remembrance,'" Hestaur commented, nodding gently. "As for my own journey, my mind will return to Nemesis where I once stalked evil beings, slipping through the shadows cast by the temples of the Great Dark Gods. What, if anything, do those Powers remember today? After, I will search again for hints of Alantéa the Fallen. In the past, I have found only a few shards in dusty, forgotten museums of the Far Lands, so instead on this night, I will search in the ocean's dark depths. Do any temples remain? Do any monuments still stand? We shall see."

Orissa nodded and smiled. "I will seek again for the bloodline of Sentauris, first in Alantéa after the early struggles of the League. Then I will search for that same bloodline in this day's world, for mortals in the Time of Machines are greatly in need of true heroes. Do the Children of Sentauris sleep or are they dead forever? I will see if there is even a glimmer of hope for the future of the Far Lands."

The three Dreamers caused the lights surrounding them to dim. Then they leaned back, closing their eyes, and they dreamed.

· ✕ ·

Once again, Hestaur's dreaming mind took him first to Nemesis, where the many Temples of the Great Dark Gods gleamed with incandescent evil, and their greyish black stonework sent puffs of black smoke into an overcast night.

He watched closely as his former great adversary, the most powerful of the Carag-Mages, slid through the shadows. Passing through a pool of darkness, the Carag-Mage finally took the form of a Priest of Ahriman.

Though the Carag-Mage was ancient, his steps were light as he climbed the three hundred steps leading to Ahriman's place of power. The face of the Mage gleamed with satisfaction: all his plans had gone well and in a short time, tens of thousands, perhaps hundreds of thousands of mortal humans would perish and be replaced by Carags.

Seated in the Hall of the Dreamers, Hestaur watched the Mage, and he shook his head slowly. The Carag-Mage had failed because Hestaur had brought ruin to his plots. Though now, those events were separated by such an enormous distance of time that it was difficult for Hestaur to take any satisfaction from his victory. Hestaur let shadows and darkness fill his vision so that his dreaming mind passed from Nemesis.

Unwilling to view again the fall of Alantéa, Hestaur took himself to a time hundreds of years after the Fall, to the Aftermath, a time when the fading forces of magic within the Far Lands of Earth still held power. To sustain themselves, the Gods had gathered into Pantheons: Set, Osiris, Thoth, and Ra, and Isis into one; Wotan, Thor, Tor-El-Baldur, and Lokus into another; Poseidon, Zôs, and Hades into yet another; and so many other Pantheonic Alliances had been formed. Had not humans joked quietly among themselves about the many deities, referring to them as the "Nine Billion Gods?"

For their own use, the Gods had drawn to themselves all the greatest amulets and stones of power they could find from the broken Forerunner. They even allowed some of their followers to wield the small magics of lesser talismans, enabling mortals to search for sources of power to sustain the fading Gods. Mortals were completely unaware of their situation, for so much of early human history had been driven by the Gods' desperate quest for power sources to prevent their much feared but inevitable declines.

As before, Hestaur found no hidden sources of power in the Aftermath of the Fall, so he let his dreaming mind drift into the Temple of Waiting. After all, he and the other Dreamers had been stirred from that same place, and might it be possible that some of the Great Gods could also be roused? But no, they were only ghosts, shadows that shuffled endlessly, drifting, sliding without a hint of awareness, waiting for the Maker's Return.

Finally, Hestaur turned to the graveyard of the Forerunner, watching as the Atlantic rose and fell, wracked this time of year by storms. As always, he looked to see if undercurrents had shifted the seabed, to reveal stonework that marked the passing of Sentauris, or Julian, but nothing remained. The ocean shifted, tumbling, and twisting fragments of Alantéa's stone pillars in the lightless depths; and those shards were all that remained of the Forerunner. Alantéa was gone, and the forces of magic on Earth had dwindled into nothingness.

· ⅄ ·

As Orissa searched for the bloodline of Sentauris, she looked for men and women who moved with great speed and force in time of need. After guiding those around them to shelter and safety, the bloodline of Sentauris always returned, unchanged, to their own lives. After each crisis, they never sought glory or power or great wealth for themselves.

Orissa found millions of heroic people, sacrificing themselves while dying with quiet strength and resignation. She found hundreds of thousands of humans with great speed and strength of mind, though many seemed unable to lead others. She found great leaders and wise counselors, but as always, their own needs for personal wealth and glory often offset their own sacrifices.

Orissa sighed, and her dreaming mind rose high over the Earth, looking down on it as the planet rotated swiftly below her. She had finished her last search; her quest for the bloodline of Sentauris was over. The line of heroes was gone, vanished like Alantéa and the forces of magic that flourished in the Forerunner.

Suddenly, as though finally understanding Orissa and her quest, tiny lights began flickering beneath her, so many of them, spread across the seven continents of Earth, and its many island chains.

Understanding flashed through the mind of Orissa, and the Seeress drew a deep breath. A great crisis was coming. In Earth's first encounter with beings from far, distant planets, they would meet a completely unbenign species, exceedingly selfish, predatory beings. To meet that challenge, the bloodline of Sentauris, many scores of them, a new line of heroes was waiting to be born. Instead of magic, they would learn to use the complex systems of humanity and its powerful machineries, for the sum of all those devices was beginning to mimic the most powerful sorceries of the Mid-World of the Truce.

Having been granted a great vision, Orissa found herself seated beside her fellow Dreamers, staring up into starlit skies, yet now a sense of peace gathered over her dreaming mind.

·) (·

Merlin drifted as a Wraith through the streets of Tuvan in the early days of the League, watching as Orantes the Adept meandered his way through the night, retracing his own steps from a time three years earlier. Tuvan was under siege, and so it was silent on this night; even its guards moved with stealth. Outside Tuvan's walls, the watchfires of the besieging Vorrs and Carags and human legions serving the Enchanters glowed dimly in the night sky. Only the infrequent growling noises from Creatures of the Darkness broke the stillness.

Why was Orantes shuffling through the night, prowling in the darkness? Was he seeking some hidden weapon that would help him break the siege of

Tuvan? Finally, the Adept halted before the door of a dark, shuttered inn. Magic surged from Orantes, and lines of force gleamed from the doorway's frame.

Merlin's shook his shadowy Wraith's head: Orantes was attempting to return to a time three years ago at this same inn, so that he could secure a small cask of red wine from the Gangean range, then pound some miscreant who had deceived Orantes and otherwise been less than faithful to the League. The Adept was powerful enough to make time's gateways quiver but fortunately for the League, he could not force an entry back in time, and weight his agile mind down, again, with an overload of wine.

What a strange hero of the League! Yet Orantes was a hero, nevertheless.

Merlin's wraithlike mouth whispered, and he passed from Tuvan the Besieged.

Now Merlin slipped through the night darkness of Khiva, to a time when the warship Alantéa the Forerunner was under construction.

This night in Khiva was much louder than Tuvan's, with sounds of conflict coming from the waterfront. Motion flashed through the darkness as Kalanin, and two night guards, sought shelter in an alley. Unsuspecting, one of the night revelers slipped briefly into the entrance of the alley. Merlin watched as Kalanin's hands clenched, wishing to close over the throat of the drunken intruder and throttle him. But the warleader had sense enough to restrain himself and let others deal with the brawls of fools.

Had the League ever been blessed with a warrior-captain as gifted as Kalanin? Only Sentauris equaled Kalanin as Captain-General of the League.

Merlin's wraith-mouth whispered, and he returned to the Hall of the Dreamers. His 'Time of Remembrance' was over and now he sat as one of seven Dreamers staring out into the night sky.

· ӂ ·

Such was the nature of the Dreamers' visions that all their revelations became known to one other. From Hestaur's dreams, Merlin confirmed again that all Alantéa's force of magic was gone forever, and that nothing would ever again stir in the Temple of Waiting. Visions from Orissa's mind, however, had surprised Merlin: a great crisis was coming, and the distant offspring of Sentauris were being gathered to deal with those moments.

And so, the touch of the Maker still lay over Earth.

Sitting in the Hall of the Dreamers, Merlin nodded his head slowly. Yet the fate of Earth was also bound to its sun and its own sister planets, and so Merlin's dreaming mind turned toward the sun's brilliant second planet. Long ago, the Demon Princes and their allies, the Dark Lords, had been hurled — not into the sun — but to the planet humans now called Venus. There, on the planet's surface, those six Powers battled among themselves and struggled also against the thickness of the air, the planet's sulfuric rains, and its plumes of volcanic ash. Underground empires had been constructed and destroyed as the six fought constantly, wearing down the lesser residues of magic left to the second planet. As energies around them ebbed, the six grew exhausted, and finally sought refuge in the shifting mantle of the planet's surface.

Merlin shook his head. Demon Princes and Dark Lords slept a forever sleep, waiting for the Maker and the End of Time. How would the Maker judge them? Was it even possible that tasks could be assigned to them so that they might counterbalance their creation of Hell and all the other destruction they visited upon Earth?

Hell still haunted the dreams of mankind, yet all its power to harm any being had passed long ago. Merlin turned from Earth's nearby second planet, and stared into the depths of space, toward the sun's fifth planet, a colossus. Around the planet that humans now called Jupiter, like a gigantic, boiling red eye, was a never-ending storm. Hurled into the depths of space, Hell had gathered around the sun's most massive planet, where it seethed and swirled endlessly, although all of Hell's malice and power to do evil was gone forever.

Merlin turned from the systems of the sun, back to Earth and all the many dimensions surrounding the planet; Otherwhen's fading power had reduced the Alternates to corridors of shadowy ghosts, but as always, Merlin searched for Houma. It had been many thousands of years since Merlin had last seen Houma — then, a gigantic crab with a human head and blazing red eyes, shambling down a beach formed of black sand. Might the Sorcerer still live, its dark pincer-claw throbbing with malice? Stranger things had happened in the wide universe, but it seemed almost certain that Houma now slept the Long Sleep.

Merlin took a deep breath and stared beyond the circles of the sun, watching the motions of comets, and stars, and clusters of stars. Flashes of the Maker's guiding forces continued to flare and gleam throughout the cosmos.

Over the many ages, a steady stream of Powers, Dominions, and Intelligences had joined the Quest for the Maker in the starry universe. Millions of beings were leaping from star to star, heading backward toward the Beginning: galaxies, star systems, stars, and their planets had all been speeding out from one central core.

So their quest for the Maker was taking those searching Powers back to that center, toward the event that created all the matter in the known universe.

When the Creatures Indomitable were born, five great Lords of Dragons left Earth to seek the Maker. These five formed the First Wave. Five Lords of Dragons had long ago reached the Maker at the Heart of the Universe. Grown mighty as they leaped from star to star, the five great Lords of Dragons now learned wisdom from the Maker — and the Maker, who had chosen not to know all things, not to guide each fragment of his creation — was learning from them.

After the Truce was formed, a Second Wave of Ancient Powers left Earth. In the Hall of the Dreamers, Merlin followed their progress, for the Second Wave had moved well beyond light speed, surging beyond distant star systems in seconds. All the Seraphs, Spirit Lords, Demons and Dragons in this throng had grown mighty in wisdom and power. Even the lone Creature Indomitable had become so much greater than at its beginning; during its journey, the Creature had molted and transformed several times, leaving only husks of what it once was. At times, the Creature studied these old forms, noting how different each being was, wondering what might become of it when it finally reached the Maker. And yet within its new form, the Creature Indomitable was beginning to feel a stirring of something like joy as its quest neared its end.

From afar, Merlin felt that joy, and then with a sigh, he turned his dreaming mind back to events on Earth. Staring down on his birth planet, Merlin again felt the old surge of fear — a fear laced with traces of wonder. A time of great challenge was coming. Would the children of Sentauris be able to provide the people of Earth with sufficient guidance?

For humans had gained great power to do both good and evil. With their mastery of the physical universe, they were beginning to rival the Ancient Gods in power. Yet air and water and soil were being corrupted, and quarrels based on ancient myths endured, and new struggles among emerging forces were flaring up each day. So many humans — those with the intellects of an Alcman or a Hestaur — were seeking overlordship and great wealth, or status as demigods, power over those around them, instead of pursuing a quest for deeper understanding and the well-being of others.

Now, as Merlin stared upon Earth from the Hall of the Dreamers, he wished with all the power of his dreaming mind that humanity would put its own house in order, deal with its next great challenge, and then join the Quest for the Maker in the starry universe, using their intricate machineries to travel to the Heart of the Universe, into the Center of All Understanding.

The Isle of the Demons is the fifth and final book in
The Mid-World of the Truce series

Manufactured by Amazon.ca
Bolton, ON